Praise for Mark Helprin's
The Pacific and Other Stories

"Long before J.K. Rowling or Susanna Clarke wrote their big books of magic, readers were being awed by Mark Helprin's unique brand of enchantment and exotic atmospheres. He established his reputation in the early 1980s and 1990s with *Winter's Tale* and *A Soldier of the Great War*, huge novels of vibrant décor and imagination. *The Pacific and Other Stories* is a worthy descendant of these, for there is plenty of magic here, though it isn't produced from the tip of a wand. Helprin's magic is earthly, human."   —*Los Angeles Times*

"It's been a great run so far this autumn for lovers of the short story . . . but none of it would matter much if Helprin's prose weren't so exquisite . . . 'a brave and wonderful thing.' "   —NPR's *All Things Considered*

"As ambitious and imaginative as any of Helprin's past works (*Memoir from Antproof Case; Winter's Tale;* etc.), the sixteen stories collected in the author's first book in nearly a decade are gloriously rich and varied . . . each demonstrating immense faith in the power of love. These are sturdy, rewarding stories from a master of the form."   —*Publishers Weekly* (starred review)

"God is in Helprin's details. . . . He is a master at precise and lucid explanations; in his hands a manual for a toaster oven might read like a prose poem. [His] descriptions . . . are small masterpieces, testaments to the perfectibility of explaining the minutiae of life, if not life itself."   —*San Francisco Chronicle*

"Writers like Mark Helprin are a vanishing breed on the American literary scene. . . . He writes without irony, without the wink of postmodernist qualification about age-old themes of beauty, truth and honor. These are the great qualities he has championed in such majestic novels as *Winter's Tale* and *A Soldier of the Great War*. . . . These stories sail across the page on a tide of precise observation and deft lyricism."   —*Newsday*

"At times heart-wrenching and at times humorous, Helprin's stories are about living lives of integrity and the rewards of doing so. . . . Helprin is a master of the genre, and he writes of people, places, and ideals with a superb simplicity that is at the same time realistically complex."   —*The Miami Herald*

"Contemporary fiction is awash in self-serving characters happy to parade their weaknesses as badges of honor. So it's especially satisfying to read this collection from Helprin (*A Soldier of the Great War*). . . . [His] characters act with almost old-fashioned moral rectitude, and Helprin is gifted enough to make them seem real . . . Highly recommended."

—*Library Journal* (Fall Editor's Pick)

"Helprin is a gorgeous writer, at once lush and disciplined. . . . His eye for small moments is the stuff poems are made of. . . . This collection glows with an ethereal beauty that I found bewitching." —*Elle* (Reader's Pick)

"Helprin's short stories should not be consumed in one sitting. . . . That these characters' losses hit us in our gut is a testament to Helprin's special genius— his ability to evoke a time and place so authentically, it is hard to imagine that he didn't live through the Second World War or visit a newly liberated Paris." —*Esquire* (Big Important Book)

"Few contemporary writers display Helprin's knack for creating mesmerizing and memorable characters. His stories about people's ability to adapt reflect a certain wisdom and grace, and I was totally immersed in each character and the drama of their lives. This is a fantastic collection of short stories." —Book Sense (2004 Highlights)

"In *The Pacific*, Helprin reaffirms his place as our most elegant moralist. . . . [His] range is staggering, but no more so than the convincing, unsentimental case he makes for the importance of honor. Even in this day and age." —*Entertainment Weekly* (Editor's Choice)

"Sixteen tales of war, love, the achingly beautiful and the fallen present. It's been about a decade since his last novel . . . so Helprin tosses out a story collection, as if that will be enough. And it almost is. . . . Even in these short bursts, he often accomplishes what others take hundreds of pages to achieve." —*Kirkus Reviews*

"Mark Helprin . . . returns with a collection every bit as strong as his first. *The Pacific and Other Stories* opens with pieces in an almost classical mode and then cycles from fabulist yarn spinning to roman á clef style intimacies. . . . As in [Hemingway's] best works, the characters here do not so much quest after grace as encounter opportunities to achieve it." —*The Seattle Times*

"Incomparable prose . . . the work of a master . . . rhythmic and magisterial and ornate . . . a remarkable, stunning, overwhelming collection." —Bookreporter.com

PENGUIN BOOKS

THE PACIFIC AND OTHER STORIES

Born in 1947 and educated at Harvard, Princeton, and Oxford, Mark Helprin served in the Israeli army, Israeli Air Force, and British Merchant Navy. He is the author of, among other titles, *A Dove of the East and Other Stories*, *Refiner's Fire*, *Ellis Island and Other Stories*, *Winter's Tale*, *A Soldier of the Great War*, and *Memoir from Antproof Case*.

THE
PACIFIC
and Other Stories

MARK HELPRIN

PENGUIN BOOKS

PENGUIN BOOKS
Published by the Penguin Group
Penguin Group (USA) Inc., 375 Hudson Street, New York, New York 10014, U.S.A.
Penguin Group (Canada), 10 Alcorn Avenue, Toronto,
Ontario, Canada M4V 3B2 (a division of Pearson Penguin Canada Inc.)
Penguin Books Ltd, 80 Strand, London WC2R 0RL, England
Penguin Ireland, 25 St Stephen's Green, Dublin 2, Ireland (a division of Penguin Books Ltd)
Penguin Group (Australia), 250 Camberwell Road, Camberwell, Victoria 3124,
Australia (a division of Pearson Australia Group Pty Ltd)
Penguin Books India Pvt Ltd, 11 Community Centre, Panchsheel Park, New Delhi–110 017, India
Penguin Group (NZ), cnr Airborne and Rosedale Roads, Albany, Auckland 1310,
New Zealand (a division of Pearson New Zealand Ltd)
Penguin Books (South Africa) (Pty) Ltd, 24 Sturdee Avenue, Rosebank,
Johannesburg 2196, South Africa

Penguin Books Ltd, Registered Offices:
80 Strand, London WC2R 0RL, England

First published in the United States of America by The Penguin Press,
a member of Penguin Group (USA) Inc. 2004
Published in Penguin Books 2005

1 3 5 7 9 10 8 6 4 2

"Passchendaele" and "Mar Nueva" first appeared in *The New Yorker*; "The Pacific" in *The Atlantic*;
"Last Tea with the Armorers" in *Esquire;* "Jacob Bayer and the Telephone" and "Vandevere's House"
in *Forbes ASAP;* "Reconstruction" in *The Wall Street Journal;* and "Perfection" in *Commentary*.

PUBLISHER'S NOTE
These selections are works of fiction. Names, characters, places, and incidents either are the product
of the author's imagination or are used fictitiously, and any resemblance to actual persons,
living or dead, business establishments, events, or locales is entirely coincidental.

THE LIBRARY OF CONGRESS HAS CATALOGED THE HARDCOVER EDITION AS FOLLOWS:
Helprin, Mark.
The Pacific and other stories / Mark Helprin.
p. cm.
Contents: Il colore ritrovato—Reconstruction—Monday—A brilliant idea and his own—
Vandevere's house—Prelude—Perfection—Sidney Balbion—Mar nueva—Rain—Passchendaele—
Jacob Bayer and the telephone—Sail shining in white—Charlotte of the Utrechtseweg—
Last tea with the armorers—The Pacific.
ISBN 1-59420-036-X (hc.)
ISBN 0 14 30.3576 2 (pbk.)
I. Title.
PS3558.E4775P33 2004
813'.54—dc22   2004050505

Printed in the United States of America
Designed by Stephanie Huntwork

FOR PETER JOVANOVICH

Intelligence, Compassion, Integrity, Courage

Contents

The Pacific and Other Stories

Il Colore Ritrovato

I DIDN'T GO TO VENICE of my own accord. I was sent there, forced to go, by that . . . that woman, she who has worshippers throughout the world, she who, despite a corrupt and failing body, limitless greed, and the personality of a broom, has—still, after all these years—the voice of an angel. It isn't surprising that she has power over me. Why shouldn't she? Even after a big meal, and I mean a big meal, she can walk onto a floodlit stage, stare into darkness and blinding glare, and then, with inimitable self-possession, make thousands weep. That all her gifts have been so concentrated is a miracle, and though she has no talent or virtue but this, it's more than enough.

I've represented her since 1962, when neither of us was known and we both were unrecognizably young. She was almost beautiful then, and almost innocent. Everyone assumes that I had an office, and, one day, she, a professional singer, walked into it. I have an office now, but I didn't then. I was a bookkeeper in a dark little factory that made gears for motor scooters. Everything there had oil on it, even my ledgers, which were so splotched that sometimes you couldn't read the numbers. And when it rained, the floor was covered with ankle-deep water.

Naturally, I didn't want to stay in such a place for the rest of my life, and I believed that unless I did something impulsive and courageous, and unless

I had a great deal of luck, I would. So I waited for my luck, and it came one day as I was walking home, not five minutes from the factory, in front of an industrial laundry. The doors were open, and, inside, one of the laundresses was lifting heavy wet sheets onto a cable that took them into a dryer. As she clipped them to the line, she sang. Working with arms raised is so difficult that most people would not have been able even to talk. But she was singing, and the singing, as she has proved many times since, was worthy of La Scala.

"Who the hell is that?" I asked one of her colleagues, a woman who looked distressingly not so much like a Picasso as like Picasso himself. It was a question that was to shape not only my life, but that of a substantial part of the world if art is to be accounted, even if these days art hardly is.

"Oh, she's always singing. Everyone says how good she is."

"Does she sing professionally?" I asked.

"No, she's a laundress."

"I see that, but, perhaps, on the side?"

"Her boyfriend won't let her."

"Why not?"

"He's jealous."

"Is he a soprano, too?"

"He's in the army."

"The army."

Not wanting to be killed, I was going to leave right then, but then she said, "Yes, he's in New Zealand, at the embassy, for two years. It has something to do with ostriches, I think. When he gets back, they'll be married."

"Oh," I said. "Well, please tell your friend. . . ." I reached into my pocket and pretended to be surprised. "I seem to have left my cards in the office. Tell your friend that I'm an impresario, and that I'll come tomorrow after work—which is?"

"Which is what?"

"What time does she finish work?"

"Six. We all do," she said, looking at me as if I were an idiot.

"At six, then," I said. "She should sing at La Scala, the Metropolitan Opera, Covent Garden."

"Why don't you tell her? We can stop the line, it's just sheets, or you could wait ten minutes. People fall in love with her because of her voice." Suspicion crossed her face like a cloud. "You don't look like an impresario."

I laughed artificially. "I have an appointment," I said, "for a contract signing with Lucida Lamorella. I'll be here tomorrow. Tell her." All the while she was singing so beautifully that I could see why people fell in love with her even if I did not, because I could tell from a distance and despite a voice that one could love forever that she was—how shall I say it—spiritually blank. I don't know how I was able to tell. Certain things are more or less self-evident.

That night I pressed my shirt and thought of a plan, and the next day I put on my suit, quit my job, and made a reservation at a restaurant. I paid the headwaiter to say, "Signor Cassati, how are things at La Scala?" I bought contract papers and stamps, and an impresario's hat, a Borsalino. By the time I went to the laundry, I had become an impresario, for, after all, what is an impresario but someone who in less than a day can transform himself from a bookkeeper in a motor-scooter-gear factory into an impresario? Having convinced myself of my transformation, it was easy to convince her.

She was really something. She ate like a hippopotamus. God intended for one to be able to see the beauty and soul of nearly all women. And there I was, twenty-seven years of age, in a restaurant with a girl of twenty-one, who was really quite pretty, and, if not slim, possibly svelte. She could not have helped but have some of the charm of youth, and her voice must have meant something in respect to her soul, but I felt no attraction to her whatsoever. She ate olives so fast that many of them fell from her mouth and rolled across the tablecloth and onto the floor. She kept a wad of bread in each cheek pouch—just in case—while she shoveled food in through the main mouth part. It's always good to have a reserve: her smock had pockets and she used them. She never stopped eating. I was worried that I wouldn't have enough money left from my small savings to get us to Pflanzenberg, where solely by the balls of my feet I had tentatively booked her to sing the part of Norma with the opera club of one of the Volkswagen subcontractors that made windshield wipers. I could do this because I knew them through the gear factory, and had gotten their president tickets for La Scala.

"Do you know *Norma*?" I asked.

A black olive fell from her mouth. "Norma who?"

"Bellini's *Norma*?"

"Of course. Mama made me memorize it. She made me memorize everything—before she died." She went back to eating.

"What do you mean, 'everything'?"

"Operas."

"How many operas?"

"Oh, I don't know. Sixty or seventy."

My eyebrows went up and my face jerked forward. "Sixty or seventy?"

"Yes, what's so strange about that?"

"What's so strange about that?" I repeated in astonishment.

"Nothing," she said, as if I had really asked her. "Do they have any nuts?"

"Who?" I asked.

Before I could even think, she said, in her very powerful soprano, "Waiter, do you have nuts?"

Soon she was cracking nuts as she ate, as she spoke, and as she drank. "I know them perfectly." She closed her eyes and stuck out her tongue, which, in those days, was how she emphasized a point.

"Perfectly?"

"The whole thing, all the parts. It just comes to me after I've seen it once, and then I don't forget. It all makes sense, and flows naturally from one thing to another, so it's no big fuckin' deal."

"That's good," I said, "because, with your permission, I've booked you to sing Norma in the opera house at Pflanzenberg."

"Me?"

"Yes. You know you're good."

"But Quagliagliarello won't let me."

"Who's Quagliagliarello?"

"My boyfriend."

"Where is he?" Of course, I already knew, but I made myself look curious.

"In New Zealand."

I said nothing, letting it dawn on her. It took a while, but then she asked, "Where's Pflanzenberg?"

"In Germany, nowhere near New Zealand."

"Germany! What would Quagliagliarello think?"

"He would fly back and kill me, that's what he would think."

"He would."

"So don't tell him. Why does he have to know? By the time he gets back, you'll be singing in La Scala, and it will be a fait accompli. In fact, it will be a fait accompli when, in New Zealand, he sees your picture on the cover of an LP. You know, in a gown, getting out of a carriage and alighting onto a red carpet, fountain in the background, nice shoes, glowing complexion, happiness. He won't even place you, because he won't expect to see you on the jacket of a Deutsche Grammophon Gesellschaft recording, but then he'll see your name, but it won't matter, because he'll be so shocked he won't be able to kill me. What *is* your name? Here we are having dinner, and I don't even know."

"Rosanna Scungili," she answered, as if she knew that this was soon to change, as indeed it would. Imagine an American or English opera singer whose name was *Jane Octopus-Slice*. She might be the greatest singer in the world, but much would stand in her way.

"How about Rosanna Cadorna?" I suggested after my eyes had swept the restaurant and stopped at a painting of the famous general.

"Who's she?"

"She would be you." Rosanna's expression was blank. "You would be she."

"How?"

"You'd change your name."

"I see," she said. "All right." She was the quickest to decide absolutely anything of anyone I've ever known. She still is. She has no hesitation. It's as if nothing matters to her. I think she may be psychotic. When her father died, the first thing she said was, "What time is the European Song Fest?" Back then, in the restaurant, just after she had so quickly agreed to a different name, she said, "Let's go to Germany. I already know the part. When do we leave?"

For someone who didn't like German food, Rosanna ate a lot of it. In addition to the meals we had at the *Scheibenwischeroper,* the windshield-wiper opera, I had to buy her several kilos of bread, sausage, and cake every day. I have heard—I have seen—that really crazy people can eat ten kilos of food a day and not gain weight. That was Rosanna until she was forty. Then something changed, and she began to gain weight as inexorably as a tank into which water is dripping. Now she cracks marble floors as she passes over them, and stalls elevators as she gets into them, but back then the Germans thought she was just a typical starving Italian girl. Indifferent to her appearance and her manner, they remained unimpressed until at the first rehearsal she opened her mouth to sing.

The Germans, after all, produced Bach, Mozart, Beethoven, and Brahms: it's not as if they're insensitive to music. And at the end of her first aria all those stolid Germans were so moved they were in tears. They were astounded that she was there with them, and they had the touched, trembling, holy air of those present at the creation, for it was easy to see that she was going straight to the great stages of the world.

It wasn't exactly straight. After her flawless performances in Pflanzenberg, we went on to one flawless performance after another in—if memory serves, and it should, for these were glorious days of rising and success—Wachenrauss, Hofheim, Würzburg, Karlsruhe, and Heilbronn. The engagements in these cities were all in opera clubs. She had to sing near machine tools, gymnastic equipment, and walls of boxes. Once, she brought down the house—that is, the people on blankets on the grass—while a Turkish soccer game raged off to her left. She was as unconcerned as if she were playing in the hushed spaces of the greatest opera house. There she stood, despite the most despicable noise and distraction, a monstrous woman, really, floating in a sea of ineffable beauty and transforming the world about her without either self-consciousness or delicate temperament.

You know how great singers and musicians are always supposed to be prisoners of temperament? It's the opposite of what's true. In fact, what so distinguishes them in this regard is that they have no temperament: they are absolute. It is we, who are not great, who are prisoners of mood. It is we who vary and change, and when we who spend our lives trimming and ducking encounter those who make no adjustments we imagine that it is they who are in a frenzy, such are the laws of relative motion.

I have never seen Rosanna sing with adjustment for anything. She could be in a dirty garage in Saarbrücken or at a command performance for the queen of England, and it would be—indeed, it was—exactly the same. Indeed, she is a miracle of temperament, or lack of it. She is seized each time by the divinity of the music and she neither varies nor falters. Well, she does sometimes falter, but only when her body has failed her and she is sick. Even then, though she may not sing well, she sings better than most, and when you see her struggling against her affliction—she is not anymore a healthy woman—you know that to finish her aria she would sing even unto death.

But when not singing, she's intolerable. She has always been intolerable. In our almost forty years of association I have seen several hundred of the scores of thousands of young men who have fallen in love with her voice. These are the ones who, like the hardier sperm that can swim close to the egg, come to her entranced and obsessed. And then, unlike sperm, they turn away in horrified disillusion. Most women would have been suicidal after two or three such rejections, but (though it doesn't happen anymore, because she is too fat) it did not affect Rosanna. "They're idiots," she used to say. "They're in love with something Mozart or Bellini plucked from the ether, not with me. That's why they could never sing themselves. They try to make their lives something other than pedestrian, because they have nowhere else to go. When I come back from where I go, I want just to be a laundress. And when I come back from where I go, I have no strength left to be anyone else. Besides, I never loved anyone but Quagliagliarello, until you took him away from me."

"I didn't take him from you, he was jealous of your career."

"Can you blame him? He got back from New Zealand and what did he see? Did he see Rosanna Scungili, laundress, who hangs wet sheets and sings like a nightingale?"

"And eats like a hippo."

"I had a high metabolism. No, he sees Rosanna Cadorna, just become world famous, who rides around in long cars and talks to the Pope, who makes in one night by opening herself to others like a whore, more than he has made in his life, who lives in the most expensive suites of the best hotels, and who, in two years, has become old. What was he supposed to do?"

"Anything but what he did."

"He was a soldier, he had a gun."

"He should have killed me, not himself. That's what I would have done."

"No. I was gone, and could never come back. It was too late."

"Do you think, Rosanna, that had you stayed a laundress and married Quagliagliarello when he got back from New Zealand, you would have been happy?"

"I don't know. I loved him. We could have had children."

"You would have given everything up for your singing. You wouldn't have been able to help it. If I hadn't found you, someone else would have. You could have waited for Quagliagliarello, but remember how quick you were to go to Pflanzenberg?"

"Yes," she said. "I know. I hardly hesitated an instant."

AFTER HEILBRONN, where we were in a real theater with lights, we went on to Nürnberg, Stuttgart, Munich, and Vienna. Her mastery of the repertoire was so flawless that, like a diva who has been on the circuit for decades, she could without preparation take any part anytime. This was noticed as much as the inimitable quality of her singing, and it was why, a year and a half after her debut at the windshield-wiper opera in a warehouse, she went on stage at La Scala when Adriana Rossi could not sing on account of a high fever, to take the part of Amenaide in *Tancredi*.

The moment she started to sing, the breathing of the audience was altered. And you could see them rise effortlessly in their seats. The light was suddenly clear and perfect, and there was not a cough or a shuffle as the whole world was put on notice that Rosanna had arrived. The magnificence and joy of her singing did to this refined—you might even say jaded—audience what it did to me when first I heard her at the laundry. She went from strength to strength, and that night it was as if the music had not come long before from Rossini, but was issuing suddenly from Rosanna.

When the performance ended, the other singers, who, as you may imagine, were not a humble group, melted back from her in a crescent, and, half in envy and half in awe, applauded from the semidarkness of noncenter stage as if they, too, were the audience. Shouts of *"Brava! Bravissima!"* came

for twenty minutes, until Rosanna pulled and set the hook forever by storm-
ing off the stage, as only a true diva could, and shouting in dismissive anger,
"Basta! Basta!"

They loved it more than I can convey, and from that moment our fortunes were assured in terms of opportunities offered, monies earned, praise
lavished, oceans crossed in quiet airplanes, and distant respect tendered by
millions.

Rosanna's success was so astonishingly quick partly because she was already in the semimonstrous state of disconnection for which most people require years of constant flattery, ready limousines, and obsequious retainers.
She skipped her education in the cruelties of status, having had them from
the beginning even in her laundress bones. Which is not to say that she had
no regrets, but only that she would do whatever was needed to be done, instantly and in spite of them, as if they did not exist.

Were it not for her beautiful voice, I never would willingly have come,
once I had known what she was like, within a hundred kilometers of her.
And I was never interested in her other than professionally. Although she
must have a soul, someplace, loving Rosanna would be like—how shall I put
it?—smoking an unlit cigar, walking a dead dog, swimming in an empty
pool, or listening to the radio when it is off. One thing that has made her tolerable is that in return for my plucking her from her wet sheets, she has
shared her considerable fortunes with me. One might even say generously,
were it not for the original contract of representation and the half-dozen
times she has tried to break, evade, or alter it. It was, however, very carefully
worded. Don't forget, I was a bookkeeper, whose eye was trained in har-
rowingly close textual analysis.

She even proposed to me. Granted, it was because of a quirk in the law
that would have dissolved the agreement upon our marriage, a marriage that
quite apart from its nearly-impossible-to-express repulsive attributes, would
have been quickly followed by divorce so as to render Rosanna a free agent.

"Naturally I won't marry you, Rosanna, and you know it."

"Why not?"

"Because, as you know, our representation agreement would cease to
govern upon our marriage."

"It would?"

"What a surprise!" I said. "Last week you spoke to the lawyer, who. . . ."

"What lawyer?"

"DeMarco."

"Oh, him."

"Who told me that he had given you, at your request, a disquisition on this very subject. I was expecting you to ask me to marry you. But, Rosanna, even were all things equal, I couldn't marry you, because of Lucia."

"What is she to you!?" Rosanna asked indignantly.

"My wife."

Rosanna stormed off, laundress-style. I'm thoroughly used to it. I bear it. To this day, she's responsible for half my income, and although she's a lot of work, the work consists of choosing offers rather than begging for them, and there is a difference. Even were she struck dead by more cholesterol, the revenue from CDs and broadcasts would continue, though it would be reduced. Maybe I would find another great diva. Maybe not. What's the difference? My children are grown. Neither Lucia nor I are anymore interested in living grandly. I like to fish, shoot, and read. She is content running the house and helping to take care of the grandchildren. In short, for me the age of Rosanna Cadorna could come to an end and I would not be unhappy.

Still, because we are not quite ready to retire—perhaps in three or four years—and from long ingrained habit, I continue to serve Rosanna above and beyond my essential obligations. This is not because I want to, but as a reflexive defense learned after her three nonperformance suits. I am not required to find the tentlike clothing that fits her, arrange for special water filtration at her villa, or sit with her while she eats, but I do, solely to build immunity. Thus, when she came to me last summer (the summer of 2001), and more or less ordered me to Venice, I went.

That I would go was not a certainty, not these days, when I am more and more able to take or leave her, and at first I resisted.

"Cassati," she said, putting a book in my hands, "look at this." On its dark cover was a detail from a painting, a beautiful young girl who reminded me painfully of my daughters when they were young, before they had left home—*Il Colore Ritrovato: Bellini a Venezia.* "Color refound," or, better, "rediscovered," or, even better, "Color Restored: Bellini in Venice."

They had washed Bellini's paintings until they glowed like jewels, and now these were exhibited in the Accademia in Venice, with this book the record of both his effortless genius and their ingenious efforts.

"Beautiful," I said.

"And amazing," she added.

"Yes."

"To think! He was a great painter!"

"He was."

"Too."

"'Too'?"

"As well as composer."

It took a moment for me to understand. "Bellini?" I asked.

"What a genius!"

"It was a different Bellini," I told her. "There were two, you know. One was a painter. He came before. The other was a composer. He came after."

"Two?" She was skeptical.

I nodded.

"Are you sure?"

"Positive."

"I didn't know that, Cassati, but I still want you to go to Venice and check it out."

"Check what out?" I didn't want to go to Venice. I had other plans.

"Bellini."

"I told you, it's a different one."

"Okay, check him out anyway."

"What do you want me to check?"

"See how things are."

She saw the way I was looking at her. I had no idea what she was talking about. "What do you mean, 'How things are'?"

"See if you can buy some of the paintings. I like them, especially the one of Father Christmas taking the mummy."

"I assure you, Bellini painted no such scene."

"Yes, he did, it's on page a hundred and six."

I turned to the page. "That's not Father Christmas, Rosanna, it's a priest of the temple, and that's not a mummy, it's the Baby Jesus in swaddling cloths."

"So much the better."

"You can't buy these paintings, they're the property of the state."

"Maybe for me they would make an exception. I'll ask the president."

"He won't do it."

"I'll ask the Pope."

"Neither will he."

"Go, anyway."

"To Venice?"

"Yes."

"Why don't you go to Venice? Why do I have to go to Venice?"

"Too many people would recognize me. Besides, I leave tomorrow, as you know, for Buenos Aires."

"What exactly do you want me to do?" (I had lost.)

"Check out the paintings, in person, look around, report to me, and get a copy of this book."

"But you have a copy of the book."

"You can keep this one. Get me a fresh one."

That was why, last summer, I went to Venice.

To THE QUESTION what is the difference between Venice and Milan other than a difference in tone, in the sunlight, and in the air, the answer is that Milan is where you busy yourself with the world as if what you did really mattered, and there time seems not to exist. But in Venice time seems to stop, you are busy only if you are a fool, and you see the truth of your life. And, whereas in Milan beauty is overcome by futility, in Venice futility is overcome by beauty.

It isn't because of the architecture or the art, the things that people go to look at and strain to preserve. The quality of Venice that accomplishes what religion so often cannot is that Venice has made peace with the waters. It is not merely pleasant that the sea flows through, grasping the city like the tendrils of a vine, and, depending upon the light, making alleys and avenues of emerald or sapphire, it is a brave acceptance of dissolution and an unflinching settlement with death. Though in Venice you may sit in courtyards of stone, and your heels may click up marble stairs, you cannot move without riding upon or crossing the waters that someday will carry you in dissolution to the sea. To have made peace with their presence is the great achievement of Venice, and not what tourists come to see.

What Rosanna can do with her voice—the sublime elevation that is the province of artists, anyone can do in Venice if he knows what to look for and what to ignore. Should you concentrate there on the exquisite, or should you study too closely the monuments and museums, you will miss it, for it comes gently and without effort, and moves as slowly as the tide.

Despite the fact that you are more likely to feel this quality if you are not distracted by luxury, I registered at the Celestia. The streets near San Marco are far too crowded and not as interesting as those quieter areas on other islands and in other districts, and they have a deficit of greenery and sunlight. And the Celestia, with its 2,600-count linen and stage-lit suites, is the kind of luxury that removes one from the spirit of life, but I went there anyway almost as a way of spiting Rosanna, who was paying for it, and because that is where we always stayed in Venice, and I wanted to accumulate more hotel-stay points. In that I am compulsive. Once I start laying-in a store of a certain commodity, like money, I get very enthusiastic about building it up.

Also, I'm somewhat known in Venice, and were I to stay in a less than perfect hotel word might get out that either Rosanna or I were not doing as well as was expected, and in the public eye position is not half as important as direction of travel. People are clever, and just as they find comets and shooting stars more of interest than simple pinpoints of light, they wisely ignore the fixed points of a career in favor of its trajectory.

I arrived in the evening, swam for a kilometer in the indoor pool, bumping on occasion into an old lady who was shaped like a frog and kept wandering blindly into my lane, and then I had dinner in my suite. Because I'm unused to sleeping with the sound of air-conditioning and in curtain-drawn darkness—at home the light of the moon and stars filters through the trees as they rustle unevenly in the wind—I slept as if anesthetized, and the next morning, parted from my current life, I woke up as if the world was new to me, as it used to be every morning when I awoke when I was young.

Still, I look my age, which is right and proper, so when I walked to the Accademia to "check out" the Bellini I stopped feeling like a youth, because I was brought back by the registering glances of passersby, the deference, the treatment one receives instantly and with neither word nor touch from strangers on the street. Young people look at you only quickly, as they would a post or a gate, saving their more intense concentration for one another. This, for someone of my age, constitutes the kind of dismissal for which, not inexplicably, one can actually be grateful. And for someone of my age it is a pleasure when older people look at you knowingly—for what you have seen, what you have done, for the wars you have lived through, the pains you feel, the energy you lack, and your bittersweet knowledge that you are not young anymore.

So by the time I paid admission to the Accademia I was in a state of perfect balance, my youth fresh in feeling and memory, my age clearly in mind, my reconciliation of the years that had passed with the years that were to come much like the reconciliation in Venice of land and sea.

The first thing you do in the Accademia is go upstairs, and this I did, rising into the same kind of rarefied world into which Rosanna provides entrance with her voice, and into which she had sent me to see what had happened when the paintings had been made young again, how it had been done, and how their colors, liberated from the sadness and fatigue of centuries, shone through.

I AM NOT A WELL EDUCATED MAN except that I have educated myself, and, because I have educated myself, what I say will not stand up, for lack of recognized authority. This in turn leaves me free to say what I will, in the hope that, like those small forces that do not threaten empires and are thus not fully pursued, the things in which I believe can survive in some high and forgotten place until the power of empire subsides.

And although I know that few will listen to or credit this, I think we are in a lost age, in which holiness and charity have been traded for the victory and penetration of knowledge, though all the knowledge in the world has not brought us any further than where we can go without it even in the outermost halls of grace. I believe that more is to be known and apprehended from the beauty of a face than in delving, no matter how deep, simply into how things work, no matter how marvelous that may be. The greatest substance of the world is immaterial, the province of the heart, and its study cannot be forced or reasoned. Merely to touch upon the edge of things in parsing their mechanics is to forswear their fullness, for the entry to this fullness lies not in science but in art. I cannot prove this, for it cannot be proven, but I claim, assert, and have seen it.

There in the Accademia, among so many magnificent paintings that their import was almost lost, was the girl who reminded me of my daughters when they were young. She was one of the two saints in Bellini's *Madonna with Child Between Two Saints,* the one to the Madonna's left. Sometimes in a simple sequence of notes a shaft is opened into precincts of pure and perfect light. Rosanna has this wonderful gift, but music is by nature sequential, and moves in time. In the painting, where I saw, among other things, the souls of my daughters in the face of a saint, the revelatory sequences coexisted: in the way the light fell; how their eyes were directed, focused, and drawn; in the position of their hands; the rendering of expression; the tint of flesh; depth of darkness; softness of air; and composition of the ineffable. More was to be found in that one painting, in the construction of faces and the action of light, than in all the ponderings of the world.

Only when I had been there for God knows how long, and people had come and gone in untold numbers, silently pulling up and gliding away like fish in an aquarium, did I fall back almost in exhaustion, and come to my senses. That was when I realized that I had been hearing music, and that it was not imagined. Music is my business. I can remember it and hear it almost as vividly in recollection—and, just before sleep and in dreams, *more* vividly—than when it is real. So I thought at first that I was simply remembering a great singer singing a great song.

But, no, a soprano, accompanied only by a guitar, was singing somewhere, and the song floated across the air and through the open windows of the Accademia. As I looked up at these windows and at the warm and motion-filled light that bathed them, the song grew stronger. Singers on the streets are often students with neither experience nor promise. This was different. She was different. She was obviously young, not entirely polished, and not entirely sure, but the quality and power of her voice were of the first rank. I had not heard an unrecognized voice of this quality since the moment forty years before when first I heard Rosanna.

I ran through the Accademia like a merchant in pursuit of a thief. I wasn't quite sure of where the song came from and did not want, in searching the side streets, to lose it. People don't run in the Accademia. Well, perhaps American children, but not Italians of my age. Someone like me is rarely seen at a run in any circumstance, anyway, so I attracted the attention of the guards, who insisted that I submit to a search. They took me aside, patted me with their hands, and made sweeping motions with their electronic wands. "Forgive me, signore," one of them told me, "but you have the air of someone who has stolen a painting—not to sell it, but out of love."

"Obviously I don't have a painting," I said, breathing hard. It was hot and I was lightly dressed, with neither coat nor cape. The guard knowingly shook his head from side to side. "In this field of maneuver, they cut with a knife, and roll the canvas. It fits neatly down the thigh or inside the front of the jacket. Sometimes, but not always, they leave the knife behind."

"Oh."

"But you're all right. Why were you running? Late for an appointment? You must be a lawyer."

"No, I'm not a lawyer. The singer outside—I don't want to miss her. I have to find what street she's on. She might go away. It's very important. Let me go." I started off.

"Don't worry," the guard said, "she's been here every day for a month. They're on Foscarini, right in front of the Bancomat."

"The Bancomat."

"Yes."

"Thank you," I said, and gave him ten thousand lire. Then I rushed off.

"She stays there all day," he called out after me, "no need to run."

Only a great voice could sing, all day, as beautifully as that, only a great voice.

ON THE WHITE STONES of the Rio Terrà Foscarini just before the Calle Nuova Sant'Agnese, in front of the glass windows of a bank, in which the huge, rough walls of the Accademia were reflected, was a young woman of about twenty-five, who was singing. To her right, on an expensive folding chair, was a man of approximately the same age accompanying her on guitar. The guitar case on the sidewalk in front of them—of heavy grade, to protect an instrument worth perhaps seven or eight million lire—was held open to receive donations that appeared to be about twenty-five thousand lire for the morning. I calculated almost automatically that for singing that long Rosanna would earn no less than two hundred million lire and, depending upon the arrangements, possibly a billion lire, not to mention expenses that might easily be a hundred million or more.

And there I was, in a position perfectly illustrative of the essence of arbitrage, able to reconcile two rashly conflicting valuations. For her voice, though not as polished and confident as Rosanna's after decades of performance, was a touch more beautiful, and would ripen with experience and time. I could bridge the irrational discrepancy in valuation, and take my share for doing so. As I have said, my reaction was almost automatic, and had been since I had started to run in the Accademia, but I was not comfortable. A counterweight to my obvious desire was pulling me back. I was in considerable distress, and had no idea why. I tried to ignore it. I tried to calm myself and, by listening intently and looking closely, take control of the many contradictory currents that had been set in motion within me.

Though a dozen people who had paused to listen formed a semicircle about the two performers, many more passed indifferently in both directions, as if they were busy with things of paramount importance, or were deaf, or viewed the soprano and guitarist as beggars. It was hard to tell the nationalities of those who had gathered. There are so many foreigners in Venice, especially around the Accademia at this time of day, and these days clothing is so universal that Eskimo children (in summer) dress like the youth of Palermo. It was women, mainly, who were watching, and, except for me, not one man unaccompanied by a woman. Only a few people of the twelve or so had cameras, and only one, an Englishman in a blue blazer, with blond hair and that masterful English bearing that Italians find entertaining even though they consider the same quality in Germans insufferable, was in the process of taking a photograph. He was next to his wife and daughters, who were truly beautiful and as tall as giraffes. Otherwise, the cameras remained sheathed.

The guitarist had a weak chin but strong eyes. His hair was pulled back, and rested at the base of his neck. It was so evenly dark that I thought it was either wet or dyed. If he had been there all morning it couldn't have been wet—it didn't look wet—but why would so young a man color his hair, unless he were not as young as I thought, and was perhaps considerably older than she, who surpassed him in promise and in youth. He wore black pants and a white shirt open at the collar, with the sleeves rolled up just beyond his elbows. A superb musician, he was playing from music set before him on a chrome stand. Deeply intent, he appeared to be suffering immensely, and never looked at the crowd, although he graciously acknowledged the few contributions tossed into the guitar case.

As a longtime impresario, I could see at a glance that he was a fine fellow who would treat me like a snake. I knew beforehand the full spectrum of his suspicion, anger, contempt, rage, helplessness, resignation, and grief. If things went the way all forces pushed them, he would come against me and fight hard until he realized that I was the representative of both inevitability and his own desires. For, after all, what were they hoping for on that street corner if not to be discovered by an impresario of La Scala? They were not singing just for bread and wine. In that regard, I noticed that they had no bottled water, and though they were in the shade, it was very hot. Everyone in Venice that day was drinking water from plastic bottles, and they had none. It made me wonder what people did in the previous ages of man. Not so long ago, it was possible to exist in the summer without carrying around a plastic bottle full of water, but perhaps people were unhappier then, though I know that I myself was not. (We used to drink from fountains and taps, and we didn't get typhoid. Well, some of us did.)

If she had not been beautiful, she would have been beautiful nonetheless. I don't know how she would be judged by common standards. For me it was impossible not to be enthralled as she sang an aria from *La Clemenza di Tito,* the first performance of which occurred in September of 1791, three months before Mozart died, and which was undoubtedly one of the many songs that carried him aloft. I am constructed so that when I heard her singing this, I reacted very strongly, which was unfortunate for me and for my fortunes, but fortunate in a far greater sense. It did, however, complicate things. A lifetime has taught me not to fall in love with a woman just because transcendent music is flowing from her breast. The men who fall in love with Rosanna this way are such idiots, and I've always been in a position to see this clearly. Perhaps I'm an idiot, too, for to add to the many difficulties I was experiencing in regard to this singer, I now was in love with her in the way that old men can briefly be in love with youth, which is like standing on the platform as an express train that doesn't stop at your station goes by at full speed. It's exciting, the wind comes up, your clothes whistle in the air, you awaken, and then it's gone, without even having seen you.

Let me describe her, for in my infatuation I burned into memory every detail, and for a woman I have never touched (she made sure, for his sake, not even to shake my hand), it is as if I have slept next to her for decades. First, she was, for a singer, very slight. I could easily have lifted her into my arms. Doing that with Rosanna would be as inconceivable as tossing a hippo across the English Channel. But this beautiful singer was, at the same time, full, so that, though I might easily have lifted her, I could not have held her effortlessly or for long. She was not a delicate, weightless creature, all bone; she was, although trim and strong, a woman. The strength of her singing had to be more than just spiritual. Her body, though not overbearing, was alluring. Physically, she was dense and substantial, quick, self-possessed, and sexually willing. I knew that. How I knew, I don't know.

I never remember what anyone is wearing, even I myself. My wife will sometimes command me to close my eyes. "What am I wearing?" she asks. I cannot say. "What are *you* wearing?" I cannot say that, either. But, strangely, I am able to remember what everyone there was wearing, not least the soprano. She stood in black sandals, and her toenails were painted. This shocked me, for I think it is barbaric and makes women look like the rhinoceroses in the Babar books. Why would such an angelic and unparalleled person stoop to such vulgarity? I immediately thought of Rosanna, who hires experts to buff and paint the nails on her feet, and suspected that this rhinocerine practice might somehow correlate with divine song, though why would it?

She wore pants that, though tight enough to show her perfect figure, were loose enough and black enough so that as she stood with her legs together it seemed as if she were in a sheath skirt. Her sleeveless top with narrow shoulder straps was black as well. It embraced her tightly, accentuating her firm and attractive bosom. Because the shoulder straps were so narrow, her brassiere straps, also black, had escaped their bounds and were visible on both sides. She was slightly sunburned, and on her left wrist she wore a cheap Japanese watch with a silver band. The face of the watch was rectangular and its diminutive blue dial against the black of her clothes was ravishing.

Her chestnut hair, though not colored, was pulled back and had the same quality as his. That is, it seemed wet, though it was not. And then I realized that—in Venice, in peak season—they could not afford a hotel room. They were probably living on the street. A woman who, with a season of apprenticeship to learn techniques of the stage and how to live richly, would, or, rather, could be one of the two or three highest-paid sopranos of the world, whose talent was equal to, if not finer than, that of Rosanna Cadorna, the highest-paid singer in existence, was, for all her beauty and majesty, living on the street.

I have mentioned that she was beautiful, and she was. Her face was as sharp as a hawk's, and as strong. And her eyes were the strangest eyes I have ever seen. Unless she looked directly at you—and as she sang she looked either at her feet or up at the high walls of the Accademia—you could not see them. It was as if she were blind or they were hooded like a hawk's, neither of which was the case. Much as he would not engage his audience, neither would she, but whereas he was obliged to look at the music, she could not, and here the highly unusual eyes served to protect her privacy. Perhaps she was ashamed of singing and living on the street. But when she sang, the shame vanished. Perhaps it was this that gave her the ability to sing for so long, that her singing was the only thing that kept them in the light and warmth of the world.

When she finished with the aria, some people tossed a few thousand lire into the guitar case. It appeared that she would rest a few minutes, so I took my time in removing from my wallet my card and some money. I wanted to put them up immediately in the finest suite of the Celestia. It would have been perfectly appropriate, and though it might have made them slightly grandiose in negotiation, it would have made them feel indebted to me and thrown them off balance. But something told me this was not right. You give a starving soprano soup, not roast oxen and cake. And, although I didn't know why, I didn't want them to feel indebted to me, even though I knew that no matter how little I helped them, they would.

My card announces me as an impresario of La Scala and the sole representative and manager of Rosanna Cadorna, Philippe Juneaux, and Lèandra Busoni. I gave it to them, to him—the proper etiquette—rather than putting it in the guitar case, with ten one-hundred-thousand lire notes, all freshly printed. He read the card, felt the money, and almost had a cardiac arrest. Seeing this, she came over to look, and followed suit. They couldn't talk. They looked at me, as I knew they would, as if I had risen from the dead.

"I would be very happy," I said, "if you would join me for dinner tonight at the Celestia. Please meet me in the lobby, at eight."

They didn't understand Italian very well, so I said it in English, which they did understand. All they could say was "Thank you, thank you . . . ," which I interrupted by asking how long they had been in Venice.

"We arrived last night on the train," he offered as precisely as if talking to a magistrate.

"But the guard at the Accademia told me you've been here for a month," I said.

He looked puzzled. Then he moved his hand in a kind of backward, hitchhiking motion, thumb pointing to the bank. "The people in the bank gave us coffee," he said, "and thanked us. They said that African drummers were here for ten days. They liked it, at first." He smiled.

Duplicating his gesture but with my thumb pointing to the Accademia, I said, "In there, they're not musical, but visual." This put them at ease.

"You represent Rosanna Cadorna and Lèandra Busoni?" she asked, as if it could not be true.

"Yes."

"We just got here," she said. What she meant was what my late friend Federico, a cellist, meant when he told me that, on his first trip to England,

in the nineteen thirties, half an hour after exiting the station he found himself standing on a Whitehall street corner next to Winston Churchill. It was
true: Federico was an absolute literalist and could not lie.

"Will you join me for dinner, then?" I asked.

They nodded.

"Good." I turned and made quickly for the Accademia Bridge. I had no
reason to hurry except that I knew they would be looking after me, and, as I
walk self-consciously when I know I am being watched, I wanted to get out
of there. And I wanted to give the impression that I had something to do,
even though I didn't have anything to do at all.

With the million lire they could find a room, bathe, and spend the rest of
the afternoon speculating. I had made what was perhaps the second great
discovery of my career, and yet I was profoundly unsettled. I looked forward
to taking them to dinner, but I did not look forward to the rest. By the time
I reached a point almost at the center of the bridge and walked over to the
rail to look back, they were gone.

AT THE CELESTIA I stayed on my terrace fronting the Grand Canal and the
Isola di San Giorgio. Although I could see out, behind a balustrade and a
dense hedge of miniature orange trees I was visible to no one. In bright sun
and a breeze, I read the papers, drank several liters of water, and looked long
at the view.

Unsure of what lay ahead and fearful that they might not make the right
choices, they would be in a state of excited agitation. Knowing what lay
ahead for them on whatever road they might take, I felt sadness and regret.
What, exactly, would I have to offer? No one in his right mind would think
it anything but glorious, but perhaps I was not in my right mind. I thought
of Rosanna, glorious only when she sang, and even then glorious only from
afar, like a plain woman made up to be strikingly beautiful in the unnatural
light of the stage.

Exhausted by the glare of the sun, I slept until ten of eight. I awoke in
confusion and rushed to dress. Rather than wear the suit I had planned to
wear—the quality of which bespoke great wealth—I threw on a blazer and

went without a tie. As long as a handkerchief was in the breast pocket, the blazer was elegant enough for the restaurant.

Sunburnt, of advancing age, and attired in a way that made me look like the magnate I am not except in the little world of managing singers, I ran once again, this time through the narrow carpeted corridors of the hotel and down increasingly widening staircases until I reached the lobby, where I stopped disappointedly because they were not there. I looked at my watch, which said 8:12. Surely they would have waited for twelve minutes. It was possible that they hadn't arrived yet. I glanced at the clock in the lobby, one of those bulging glittery things that looks like it was once possessed by Marie Antoinette. It said twenty-seven past the hour. A gift from Rosanna, my watch was so rare, expensive, and delicate that it was never, ever, accurate. I truly regretted having been seduced by its prestige.

At first I was upset, but, then, thinking that perhaps they had come and, when I did not show up, decided that the whole thing was a hoax and left, I was relieved. It was as if I had discovered that a furious and incendiary telegram I had sent and would regret for the rest of my life had not been delivered, because the lines were down, or a dog had eaten it, or a telegraph messenger had pedaled his bicycle into a canal. Though I felt the missed opportunity, I was pleased that nothing had happened. Walking toward the restaurant, my relief was confirmed in an after-reaction of happiness that seemed to spring from nowhere.

But when I entered the restaurant, they were sitting in the vestibule like nervous mice, without even a drink. "Ah," I said, in a nearly dread-filled voice that probably threw them into despair, "there you are."

"We're sorry for being early," she said.

"No," I contradicted. "I'm late. I'm the one who should be sorry."

"Please," he said, "you needn't be sorry. We're sorry."

Had I wanted to I could have signed them right then and there and for a tenth of what they deserved, but in this negotiation I could not be their opponent, I had to be their advocate, something I realized in amazement as we were shown to our table.

I made hand signals to the waiters without even looking at them, the way really rich people do. I don't know what the signals mean or if I am actually saying anything when I use them, but the waiters know that when someone is so confident of being served properly without even looking at those who are serving him, they will receive a spectacular tip, and therefore they always do the right thing. In this case, instead of allowing us time to settle in before bringing the menus, they brought them immediately (which is what I wanted), and did not stay to talk about the special dishes for that evening, something I never like.

"The menu has no prices," she announced in alarm.

"Mine has the prices," I told them, "and as the host I cannot reveal them. That's not the paramount rule, however. The paramount rule is that you must eat extravagantly. If you don't, I'll be insulted."

They ordered, trying their best to be extravagant, but they didn't know how. They both wanted soup and the seafood "bouquet," and to know if the soup came with bread. The "bouquet" would stun them, as it consisted of a whole American lobster, chilled and shelled, half a dozen immense shrimp, cold scallops, smoked salmon, a great amount of Alaskan king crab, smoked oysters, smoked trout, and caviar. I ordered the same, and, in addition, for the table, a different type of caviar, Champagne, scotch, grilled boned quail, and truffled wild rice. Dessert would be another production.

Almost before we spoke, the half a glass of Champagne she drank transformed her, as it does some women, into a creature of angelic grace and happiness. A shot of scotch made him a touch belligerent—just a touch—and yet relaxed and ready for whatever might happen. For my part, I like caviar and I had a double Glenlivet, which made me reckless and determined, which, I believe, is what the heart most requires even if it brings trouble, for recklessness and determination make life come alive.

"You're not Italian," I began, "and you're not English, I can tell. What are you?"

"Most people, hearing our accents," he said, "say, 'What the *hell* are you?' Guess."

"German?"

"Of course not," she said, and laughed. She was charming. Her speaking voice was as intensely beautiful as might have been expected.

"Russian?" I asked.

Now they both laughed, at ease. She shook her head back and forth. They liked the game.

"Vietnamese," I said.

Their eyes widened.

"Congolese?"

"Consider northern Europe," he suggested.

"You're not Finns," I said, as if I had evidence. They looked at one another, it appeared to me, knowingly. "Are you Finns?"

"No, but close," she said.

"Estonians."

"Yes." She was pleased. "No one speaks our language except other Estonians, and even in Europe many people have actually never even heard of Estonia."

"Are you from Tallinn?"

"Rapla."

"Rapla."

"There are probably more people in this hotel than in Rapla," he said, with a trace of bitterness. "We both studied in Tallinn."

"With whom?"

He looked at me almost painfully. "No one you would know."

"Not necessarily. I've been there."

"You have?"

"Rosanna Cadorna sang there . . ." I looked at them, and said, with some embarrassment, "before you were born."

They gawked at me. That I had known Rosanna before they were even born put me, evidently, beyond the realm of their understanding. "It's amazing that you really represent Rosanna Cadorna," she said as the food was laid down in great profusion.

"Yes, it is amazing," I answered with irony that flew by them, "and it's been amazing since nineteen sixty-two, when I discovered her. It's not a secret, and has been in many magazines and books. I heard her singing as she was hanging wet sheets on a line in a laundry in Milan."

"No one had heard her before you?"

"No one who believed that she should sing in La Scala."

"What was an impresario doing at a laundry?"

"Look, even impresarios need clean clothes, but this wasn't that kind of laundry, it was an industrial laundry, and I wasn't an impresario at the time, I was a bookkeeper."

They didn't know the term *bookkeeper,* and they looked mildly amused. "Honey?" she asked.

At first, I didn't know what she meant: I thought she was beginning to ask me a question in a manner that was both flirtatious and insane, but then I understood, and I said, "Accountant."

"Oh."

He got right to it, maybe because of the scotch. I was sorry. I wanted not to get to it. I wanted to know them more. But someone had to get to it eventually, someone always does, and it's usually me. He was apparently nervous to be taking the initiative, but it is a gift of young men that despite their fears they so often do. "We are grateful for what you gave us," he said, trying not to be formal, though it came out like the speech of the many university presidents who have given Rosanna—who reads romance comic books and thinks that electricity is a liquid—her many honorary doctorates. ("Rosanna Cadorna," they say in a universally stilted manner, "you have brought to the peoples of the world the ineffable beauties of song. In your work of many decades . . . blah, blah, blah.")

"We are grateful for what you gave us," he said, "not only because it was more than what we have earned in all our time in Prague and Vienna. . . ."

I was hardly listening. Instead, I studied them to see what difference, if any, the money had made. He had shaved. They had washed their hair, and hers, at least, had the quality of easy perfection that young people's hair has when they are healthy. He wore a kind of Eastern European safari jacket, which was probably the most formal item of clothing he had with him, and had the handkerchief been in his pocket instead of mine he would have looked more like a tycoon than me. That's because tycoons these days are very casual. His long hair did not count against him. It might even have counted for him. Except for the fact that he was not relaxed, he might have been taken for an industrialist's son who has just returned from racing sports cars in Africa.

She was wearing the same shoes, the same top, and the same black brassiere the straps of which were still seductively out of control, but instead of the black pants she had worn during the day she was in a silklike, probably rayon, sheath skirt of very dark blue and black in a tight and subtle print. She had made up lightly, and my eyes jumped from feature to feature, noting the changes. In some ways she looked less austere than she had, and in some ways more so. Her lips were now redder with a light application of lipstick; her face was paler and smoother; and her eyes were even more striking than they had been, for now their hiddenness—only occasionally did they flash in the light, for she modestly averted her gaze most of the time—was abetted by mascara and eye shadow that had touches of chestnut and deep green. When I looked at her eyes I thought of a seraglio and of dark vines in a Persian garden, so hooded and hidden and mysterious were they, and then, on those rare occasions when she would look at me directly, their intense blue would flash both wet and bright. Her peculiar beauty was so strong that it was almost frightening. As if I could see into the future and long past my own death, when the world was still busy, worried, and moving, I saw the rarity and severity of her beauty as it had settled. I saw her isolated and apart, having risen almost without limit, frightening those who were neither as pure nor as sharp of feature. In my spark of clairvoyance she was no longer a young woman, nor even entirely human, but almost birdlike, mythical, a vision her forbears had had as they crossed the sea-ice. Whatever had taken possession of her voice had shaped her face and was obviously resident within her. She was only in her early twenties, with a power unlike any I had ever seen, and yet she was also shy and uncertain, soft, slight, in many ways still possessed of the charm of girlhood.

"So, we thank you," he said, finishing.

"Please, don't even consider it," I told him with the same bizarre formality. Then the quail came, interruptively, sizzling on iron salvers.

The world has changed beyond measure. When I was young you could find musicians everywhere, and because all around the world there were so many, there were many great ones. Now that music is faithfully reproducible, musicians are not needed as once they were. And music itself has changed. Though small cadres of classicists keep the sacred and ineffable alive, they are under siege by coarse generations whose music is hardly as musical as a bus engine or a chain saw. Something must have occurred during their mothers' pregnancies. How else is it possible to explain that playing Bach keeps them away from public spaces the way iron spikes drive pigeons from cathedral ledges?

Which is to say that, not long ago, Segovia, Manitas de Plata, and Liona Boyd could tour internationally and fill great halls. What chance would they have today? What chance would this young Estonian have? I didn't know if they were married or engaged, but I knew from the way they sat that they were in love. I knew as well that even were I to help them take the very first step—the thing that at this meal was, as the English say, I think, "the insect in the room"—I would have to spend half my energy making work for him. He would appear at libraries and in schools. A few times, until it was sadly driven home to him that only twenty or thirty people would show up, I would rent halls for several hundred. He was a fine guitarist, but the world was never liable to honor guitarists, and surely not now, whereas a soprano or two can still rise as high as royalty.

"Do you know what it would be like to eat this way every night?" I asked.

They didn't understand what I was working toward, and smiled pleasantly, knowing that they didn't get the point and hoping, perhaps, that I would not test them.

"No, truly. Think what it would be like to eat like this every night."

"It would be wonderful," she said out of politeness.

"No it wouldn't. If you eat simply, and struggle for a living, it's wonderful to have an exception now and then, but, when it's the rule. . . . Have you seen Rosanna Cadorna?"

"Wasn't she always that way?" he asked, a fork speared into quail poised in his left hand, and a crystal tumbler of scotch in his right, airborne.

"You mean that, when she was nineteen, she had to sit in the center of the backseat of a car or it would go around in circles because it would lean so much that the metal would scrape the ground? No. She was always a big eater, but she was once as thin as either of you."

"What happened?"

"What happened? She got what she wanted, and to get it she gave up what she needed."

They looked at me as if they didn't understand what I was saying, because they didn't. At their age and in their position it would have been impossible for them to understand.

"You think she's happy?" I asked. "Do you think that with her villa, her apartments in Rome, Paris, and London, her Bentley, her special African-mud-wasp facial stuff, or whatever it is, with deference and solicitude everywhere, she's happy?"

"She isn't, then?"

I shook my head. "No, she's not happy. She's just a commodity, hardly a human being anymore. Everyone feels obliged to tell her how wonderful she is. She believes none of it. She had a few great moments, but now she suffers from every decline in the gate, from every fall in CD sales, from every bad review, and although they still cannot justifiably fault her singing, they attack her anyway. They attack her for failing to do what they arbitrarily feel that she should do but what she never intended to do, for her politics or the lack of them, for her missing personal life, for her appearance.

"I'm the manager, so I take some of the blows, but even when we do make a good contract it's like buying and selling a slave. What makes it worse is how the people who are buying profess to love her singing. All I can say, and you may never understand this, is that if you are in the business of buying and selling singers, you cannot credibly say that you love singing."

"What about you?" he asked.

I briefly closed my eyes. "I never, ever, tell anyone that I love her singing, or his singing. Because I am an impresario, it would not, to a singer, be credible. Only God knows what I feel."

"What about me, then?" she asked. "I sang for you. It's not easy to put oneself out like that, for strangers on the street. . . ."

"Which is why he is rightly so protective," I interrupted.

"Which is why he is, yes. You won't tell me what you think?"

"I will tell you what I think you can do, where you can sing, what your life might be like."

"Then tell me."

They braced themselves. Here it was. We were finally getting down to it.

"I'm relatively certain that after a year or two, perhaps more (depending upon what you know of the repertoire and how fast you learn), you would be a rising star, and that, not long after, with luck, you could be one of the two or three leading sopranos of the world. Perhaps, if your beauty and severity of appearance took the right turns, and others fell back, as they tend to do, you could be, as they say, *facile princeps,* the leading soprano of the world."

They were stunned. They believed me, but they could not believe me.

"You would be wealthy beyond what you can imagine. You would have villas and obscenely expensive automobiles. You would stay in presidential suites. Everyone you meet would treat you with deference—even royalty and prime ministers, even the Pope."

I paused, and then I said, with great difficulty, "You, not he," pointing at him almost accusingly. "Not he. He would be the afterthought. He would fade away. If he had been a pianist or another singer, he would have had his own chance, even if impossibly small. But not guitar. He'll drop back, and then he'll drop away. I saw it even this afternoon, on the street."

"How did you see it?" she asked, determined to defend him.

"In his expression, his position, his eyes."

"Why are you telling us this?" he said with justifiable indignation. "Why are we here?"

"I'll sign both of you," I said. "I would love to. She can rise . . . there is no limit to how high. But I refuse, I refuse, to do any further damage."

"What damage?" she asked. She did not actually know.

"Immense damage."

"We would be fine," he insisted. "As long as I can play, I'll be happy."

"What are you suggesting?" she insisted. Now that the picture of triumph had been complicated, she was greatly disturbed.

"I'm suggesting, although I know you would never be able to believe this, that what you have now, as you struggle, is something you may regret to lose."

"What's the difference if we sing on the street or in an opera house?" she asked.

"What's the difference if *you* sing on the street or in an opera house?" I repeated. "All the difference in the world. The difference between hope and success, youth and age, and, in some ways, life and death."

I knew what was coming, and was ready for a minute or two of storm. As I expected, he leaned forward in his chair, made a fist with the index finger extended, and lectured me passionately on their deprivations, beginning with "You don't know. . . ." They came, with great power, one after another. "You don't know . . . this," and "You don't know . . . that," and so on.

When he was finished, and somewhat exhausted, after relating to me what it was like to sleep under bridges and go without meals and washing, I nodded, and said quietly, "But I do know. I grew up in the war, so I know very well."

"Who would choose not to have what you have said we could have," she asked quite sensibly, "in favor of what we have now?"

"No one," I answered.

"Then, you tell us," she went on, "what should we do? What makes sense?"

"First of all," I said, "I'm not the only impresario in the world. You can always appeal to someone else—and then," I said, almost as an aside, "I'll have even more regrets to live with."

"We don't know how to appeal to impresarios except by accident," he said. "It's not that easy."

He was right. I nodded. "Could you teach in Rapla?"

"Far too small."

"Tallinn?"

"Yes, but it would be nothing like what you have held before us."

"And you never thought of it before?"

"Of course we did," she said, "but now you've made it seem real."

"Because it is real. And it will remain real. This is what I suggest. First, stay for dessert, and don't be angry with me." I looked up at them. They agreed, and, to my surprise, happily. "I want only the best for you." This was true more than they could know.

"You should understand, first of all, that if you do sign with me I'll ask only ten percent."

They looked at one another as if perhaps ten percent was a lot and they were about to be cheated. This made me laugh. "Anyone else, as you will see if you care to look, will take much much more than that. And anyone else would try to sign you immediately—my own first impulse. When I heard you, I ran down the stairs at the Accademia. And anyone else would never urge you to do what I am going to ask you to do now."

They looked both expectant and disappointed.

"First, I'm going to give you ten million lire."

"For what?" he asked.

"For nothing. You don't have to pay it back. It will cover your expenses for the rest of the summer, and you can concentrate on what you do, without desperation. Then, go home. Think about what may happen, what life could be like. Think carefully, and keep working. It's the work that in the end is worth something, and when you exchange it for something else, it leaves you in more ways than you know. Because of your perspective and your position, you won't be able to believe me when I say this, but what you have now is more than you will ever have.

"Perhaps next year you'll want to come to Milan. If you lose my card, just remember *Cassati*. You can find me. Even if you forget my name, you'll never forget Rosanna's, and you can reach me through her."

"Next year," she said, "our chances may not be as good."

"No. Next year, your chances, once you have considered them in tranquillity, will be better. And if that is what you decide, next year, they will not seize you, you will seize them. Something that people are often afraid to know or say is that life is more splendid than career."

"How do you know?" she asked.

"From regret."

The waiter was sweeping crumbs from the table before bringing dessert. He was my age, his hair was slicked back, and he must have wondered who we were.

THE NEXT MORNING, when I left Venice, I felt older than I am. The hotel provided a gondola that took me, via the Grand Canal, to the station. I had time to make the trip this way rather than on the vaporetto, because the fast train left at eleven. You cannot help but feel either very old or very young, like a child, when you are helplessly borne along in a gondola, and see young people making their way on the streets and crossing the bridges, knapsacks on their backs, sandals on their feet, their strength and youth a blessedness that they only half know.

I suppose they may have envied me, riding easily in the gondola, my luggage stacked, my hat, my suit, its cream-colored linen suggesting someone of influence and consequence, which I know is not true. They may have envied me, but I envied them—sunburnt, straight of leg, firm of arm, awake as I can never be awake again. It is in the nature of things, however, that my envy be quick and benevolent, for I have had my turn, and now it is rightfully theirs. And for all my dignity and wealth, I am an impresario, and an impresario, you know, is nothing more than a glorified parasite.

I have had this discussion too many times not to know where it leads. I explain the truth of my condition, and the people I am with—usually in a restaurant—protest. How can I say that? I brought Rosanna to the world, enriching it immeasurably. That is when I shock them, because I say that I should have left her in the laundry. And when they get their breath they pronounce with annoying certainty, no, for if I had, the world would be immeasurably poorer.

"Listen," I say, "let me tell you this. I'm an impresario. I know the job. I know what to do. I work in the service of art, the art that you love, and I love. But if in my lifetime in service to art, surrounded by it, moved by its beauty again and again, I have learned one thing, it is that in its every expression and in its every utterance it is adoring of the human soul and the human heart. If I had left Rosanna in the laundry, her life itself may have been a work of art greater than the sum of all the songs she has ever sung."

They don't understand. They never understand. Why would they? They have not intervened, as I have. They have not interrupted the course of things. They have not broken apart lines. Or, at least, if they have, they seem not to care. I am now old enough to choose where I stand at the last, and though my friends and acquaintances in the world of music may not understand or approve, I stand on this. I see clearly. I know what I have done. And I know, finally, what is right.

In the gondola, on the Grand Canal, I felt that I was borne back toward where I had started, not by the power of the gondoliere and not merely with the gentle flow of the tide, but as if on a river that, though running into darkness and oblivion, was running swift and bright.

Soon after pushing off from the dock at the Celestia, we passed under the Accademia bridge. I strained toward the Rio Terrà Foscarini, but heard nothing, only the water and the noise of the crowd. It felt like sitting in a dark room, and I looked ahead as if I had lost every chance in the world.

But then, as if the lights of a room had come up, or the great and powerful lights of the stage were pushed to the full so that the rouge on the singers' faces looked like roses in the summer sun, I heard her as she began to sing.

Her voice, not even a full day later, was more powerful, more masterful. She had ascended from her very high position at least a step or two, and her song was the most beautiful thing I had ever heard, far more beautiful in its promise, despite a younger and less accomplished voice, than any song Rosanna has ever sung, for, you see, Rosanna was not allowed to bloom.

And as I passed over the waters and heard this song that she sang on a side street, it said to me that no matter where you lead or you are led, no matter how the waves may break upon you, and what sins you may unknowingly commit, it is true that by the grace of God you can sometimes make amends.

Reconstruction

THE MOST DIFFICULT of the dinner parties I ruin are usually around Christmas, and always those of the younger members of the firm, who, no matter how well they have done, have yet to find their place because they have yet to fall from grace and restore themselves. They know I have built and rebuilt, that, quite apart from my military history, I have, in corporate terms, come back from the dead. That very thing, though I did not ask for it, is what they fear the most to get and fear the most in me.

It is why, while I sit still and merely smile, they hold forth in a volume of words that would blow up a tire. You would think that because they talk as enthusiastically as talking dogs, they would win. While they say everything, I say nothing. I am shown the second-tier paintings, and harried children who can play Mendelssohn, and from the corner of my eye I see the ineluctable Range Rovers, the Viking stoves, and the flower boxes perfectly tended by silent Peruvians with broken hearts.

Still, I win, they lose, and I couldn't throw the game if I tried. They just don't know. They're younger than my sons and daughter. I find their claims embarrassing: I don't care where they went to college; I don't even care where I went to college. I want only to spy the youthful graces they cannot see in themselves, and encourage them to do well and spend more time with their children than I spent with mine. They won't. I didn't. They can't. I couldn't.

"We've just come back from Venice," said the lady of the house, the wife of one of our foremost earners. He is less than thirty years old, and she is stunningly beautiful and looks eighteen.

"He knows," her husband said, "he sent me."

Her answer to this cruelty was, "Oh." But that was not the end of it. Thinking that something was sure to follow, I sat there like the Sphinx. Unlike the Sphinx, however, I acknowledged with my eyes that she was alive.

"Do you know Venice?" she asked. I saw that I was now a strategical point in her troubled marriage. "What with the dollar so high, it's like Disneyland. There are more Americans than in New Jersey."

"Americans don't live in New Jersey anymore," her husband added, "and they actually wear mouse ears. I saw them."

"Sometimes," she qualified. "Sometimes they wear mouse ears, some of them. Have you been there?" she pressed, turning toward me as slowly as the aft turret of the *Missouri*.

"Yes, I have."

"When?" she inquired, as insistently as the Bronx district attorney.

Thinking of the bayonet that had once been at the end of my rifle, I picked up my butter knife, and then returned it to the damasked tablecloth. "Right after the war."

"The Gulf War?" she asked.

I must have looked incredulous that she would not understand which war "the war" was.

"Vietnam?"

"I don't think so."

"What war?"

"Alicia," her husband said severely, because she had had three glasses of champagne, and because, of the long list of names by which the world knows our firm, mine is the only one that belongs to someone living.

"I want to know, Jared." When she pronounced his name she did so as if she didn't care for it, and then she looked up at me like a woman with whom you have been arguing and whom you are about to kiss, and she said, "Which one, babycakes?"

"The Second World War," I answered. "World War *Two*." I did want to kiss her.

"Well, you can't possibly remember the Second World War," she said. "How old are you?"

"I was born in nineteen forty-two," I told her. Here I was, talking, I who am famous for sitting through social engagements like a ghost. "I was in Venice in 'forty-six, when I was four, and I remember everything. I remember the weave of the towels in the bathroom of the hotel. I remember the color of the paint on the iron chair on which I sat one day in the Piazza San Marco—it was green—and the shape of the dish in which I had yogurt and sugar. I remember the pigeon that lit upon the balcony, the slate gray and iridescent purple of his neck feathers. His eyes jumped when an ocean liner just outside the Grand Canal blew its whistle and scattered every bird in Venice but him. He stayed put, strutting like a pigeon. I wore a compass on a lanyard, and carried a rubber hunting knife in a cardboard sheath, in case there were any wild animals."

Just as I realized that I was really building up to something—and I really was—my wife broke in with her accustomed diplomatic skill and turned the conversation to the reconstruction of Venice, to the floods in Florence, and to the restoration of wetted works of art in general. To make the break invisible she informed them of my ability to pull from the past the most extraordinary details of memory, saying with no apparent bitterness, "That's the part of his life that is most vivid. If you lose him in your conferences, look for him there." Now these people had become strategical points in our marriage, and though I cared, I drifted. I lost them, they lost me, voices faded, and the room became pale.

IN ITS STEAD, reconstituted before my eyes as if it actually existed, was a glass of amber-colored scotch, what I now know to be a double, on a white tablecloth next to my father's dinner plate. We were in Venice, in a restaurant where everyone had to shout. In October 1946, my chin just cleared the table. I looked up like a cat at the glasses and plates, at the dishes and bowls and bottles that arrived or were taken away with surprising speed and a musical clinking. The room was bright, hot, and full of smoke, and women at other tables wore shoulderless gowns of what seemed to be a cloth of gold.

I can put the scene in order now from what my father told me long after and from what I have come to know myself. Although he was relatively young and worked for someone else, he and his friends were bankers and moneymen, American, English, and French, not long separated from their wartime units, investing in broken enterprises that they chanced would revive. My father put everything we had, which wasn't a lot, and much more of other people's money that, were it lost, would have dragged him down for the rest of his life, into businesses that had suffered the destruction of their plant, the death and dislocation of their workers, and the disappearance of their markets. "They have no factory," he would say. "The railroad was destroyed. The roads were bombed. And the canals are full of explosives. But what is important is their habit of mind. What is important is the high probability that civilization, having come undone, will repair itself." Though at the time it hardly seemed possible, he believed that Europe must be restored.

We had driven to Venice through Germany, Austria, and the Veneto. Because of that drive I thought that Paris, where we lived, was an island in a world of rubble. Whole cities were represented merely by blackened chimneys standing like fired trees on a savannah of brick and broken stone. And the few buildings that remained were like wounded animals, pockmarked and cracked, their balconies hanging by what seemed like threads. Refugees choked the roads, and military convoys passed with precedence.

My father and I were alone and had left my mother at home, the object of this being that I would by knowing my father gravitate less toward protecting my mother from him after, having invaded Europe, he had invaded our household. I met him only when I was three and had grown quite comfortable with the idea that he was a symbolic figure. This was our first time alone, and though I liked him I was convinced neither of his value nor his legitimacy. When he kissed me his beard was like sharkskin and his mustache like thorns. Although my mother may have been, I was not impressed that he looked like Ronald Colman. That my parents had had their difficulties was not surprising: they had not been able to touch or speak from February of 1942 to December of 1945, just short of four years. Without knowing it, I was the reason for the continuance of their marriage, and had become its strategical point. Evidently, a marriage without a strategical point is like a rhinoceros without a horn.

Late for me, perhaps at ten or so, the dinner ended with a torrent of words about business and politics that I could not fathom even though they were English, and my father and I broke out into the night air. The sky in Venice is too often the color of the *Financial Times,* but that night it was laden with stars. A wind blew steadily over the Adriatic, lifting it, swelling the cloudy melon-green waters until they lapped at the doorsteps. In the Piazza San Marco hundreds of people were walking about or had gathered around a little orchestra of the kind that plays concert waltzes on the terraces of expensive hotels. Sheltered beneath a canopy while the water rose in the piazza, the musicians were playing as if they were the orchestra of the *Titanic.* I was amazed by the river that was upwelling on the north side, with starlight broken in reflection on its streaming wind-blown waves. I wanted to go to an island, between ranks of abandoned café chairs, that it had not yet covered, but I did not think that possible. My father asked why.

"Because of the water," I said.

"Why would that stop us."

"Our feet would get wet." Children are mystically upset by water out of place.

The island seemed ideal, and I yearned for it. God knows what I would have given to stand on its dry surface, surrounded by the rough and rising sea. This must have shown in my face, so, just as the orchestra had finished a song, he picked me up and, holding me in the crook of his left arm with his right hand pressing lightly against me to keep me in balance, he began to walk toward the ribbon of water.

I bent my head upward, blinking in the wind. More exciting than the island itself was the casual, unhesitating way my father walked into the water. Soon it covered his English shoes. The pants of his pin-striped suit disappeared almost to the knees. Although it was October and the water must have been cold, he seemed to enjoy it. He had crossed many rivers and streams in the four years that had just passed, in conditions that made this a blessing. He waded through without wincing or betraying concern. He wanted to show me who he was, and what I could be.

And by this action, he did. When he put me down on the island and I ran and jumped about near the waves we had just crossed, I was shaken by new thoughts I could not put into words. I did not have to, for the music began again. They had begun to play a song that, like *"La Vie en Rose"*—a beautiful phrase, not quite translatable—was an anthem of the liberation. Though I never knew the name of this song, it was sung on the streets, I knew it well, and I was not surprised to hear it. Perhaps because I had lived in France for almost a quarter of my existence, in an ordinary neighborhood in Paris with people who had lived through the occupation, even at four I was deeply moved by it. Or perhaps this was due just to the nature of the song, which, in minors and majors, perfectly expresses both the great joy and unspeakable sadness of having come through the war. No song I have ever heard has its depth and complexity. No song I have ever heard unites strength so great with beauty so shy. And this is what I knew, when I was four, having come to Paris more than two years after it was redeemed. By necessity my father knew much more.

STEPPING FROM A C-47 into a void over Normandy, with rifle, pack, and a heavy load of ammunition strapped to his leg, he felt the rush of breath and blood subside as his parachute opened in magic air, as white as a cotton ball. A major and pathfinder of the 101st, he floated down to what could very well have been his death, and prayed as if his last, thanking God for his full life to that moment, for the blue morning, for his near-silent flight, and for the seconds as they passed.

He landed in a quiet and empty field, completely alone, and lived to become part of the greatest conquering army the world has ever seen, an army that, as it pressed toward Germany, was bent by the massive gravity of Paris, and, contrary to plan, rushed toward this city of light. Because he was French-speaking, he was put in the front of the Fifth Corps, and entered Paris with the French Second Armored Division.

"Until that day," he told me when he was old, "I had not really seen gratitude or joy. If God, in remembering His work, had decided to replicate the glory of the Creation, He might have done so in the liberation of Paris. That's what it was like. That's why I took you and your mother there. Because it was as if the whole world was born on that day. And I thought, we can do the same."

Quite so. History had never been nor would it be so buoyant as in a single day to rise from such darkness to such light. Most of the people who, at the end of August, surged across the Place de l'Étoile, running to follow flags, were in white. When seen from above, they were like the foam of a rising tide, their mass unlike the normal mass of crowds, being as quick as driven cloud. That they could move on that day almost as airborne as angels was because the idea that France would be free was more beautiful even than the idea of France itself.

Just to hear the song of the streets, the anthem of liberation, as we stood amid the windblown water, was enough to make my father cry. Seeing this, I embraced his leg, perhaps not so tightly as the bag of ammunition once strapped to it, and when he picked me up I put my arms around his neck. I did not know what he had seen or what he had come through, but my father was moved by the resurrection of a shattered world, and this I understood well enough.

Then came our own rush, a breathtaking run through the darkened streets of Venice, that I will remember for the rest of my life. I don't know why he ran. He was astonishingly strong, but he could have walked. The passages through which we coursed at great speed were in renovation, and half the time scaffolding blocked the sky in alternating segments. We would run through terrific darkness, and then the boarding above us would disappear and we would emerge again to see the stars. I cannot forget that alternation of darkness and light, which is the way it has been ever since.

AT THE DINNER PARTY, because of my silence, they thought I was thinking about them. And so I did begin to think about them, which broke the spell and brought me back. Also, my wife kicked me.

I nodded, as I do when I'm brought back. I said something, I don't know what. You see, they imagine that I have everything I want—cars and pools and appliances and Picassos—only because I have what they want. But what I want I cannot have. I cannot have so much time ahead of me that it is seemingly without limit. I cannot any longer be quite so deeply in love with the world now that I know that my love for it is unrequited. I cannot ride in my father's arms. I cannot know any of the great store of his memories that he did not tell me. And I cannot change the fact, as I am the last one who re-members him, that all he saw, and learned, and loved, will have a second death when they die with me.

That is why, for me, reconstruction is so urgent and its appeal so strong. Floating down, in the last quiet seconds, it is indeed possible, with precise and joyous recollection, to return to life the roseate glow that once it brought to you. This I have tried to do, even at risk of smashing up a dinner party, or two. And when we left that night, I kissed Alicia, and we embraced for a second or two longer than anyone expected.

Monday

FITCH FLEW DOWN the few steps that descended from his front door, as he had done thousands and thousands of times. Landing on the pavement and pivoting lightly a hundred and eighty degrees left, he walked east, with many things on his mind.

Toward the end of January and early in the morning, the cold was dry, the air was still, and the light was not yet as white and full of glare as it would be later on, when the wind would rise to freeze the cross streets and whistle down the long avenues. For several months now he had left earlier than necessary, so early, in fact, that he would arrive at jobs before his crews and have to walk many times around the block or duck in to buy coffee that he did not want to drink.

By leaving early, he made it much less likely that he would encounter the mortuary convoys, which, just as he did, used Twenty-third Street to cross town. He told himself that this was a matter of convenience, because of the time he lost when they passed, when he would stop, turn to the street, put his hand on his heart, and bow his head. But those convoys raced by quickly, sirens blaring, always escorted by flag-bedecked fire trucks and many police cars, and for Fitch it was not a matter of convenience at all. Even by January, when the convoys were running with just body parts, he could not get used to them, and would never fail to bow his head in respect, though by January he was just about the only one who still did.

He had fifteen men flexibly apportioned among four crews doing five jobs. His rule was always to have at least one man on any job on any day, unless floors were drying or other contractors needed to work unimpeded. Despite trying to keep roughly the same men on the same job, the shuffling was prodigious. Although clients didn't appreciate it, it was necessary for meeting his payroll. His men often had large families. They were immigrants for the most part, but also actors, writers, and painters who painted walls by day and then returned to unheated lofts to paint their canvases by night. One of these, a hair-thin Scotsman named Starr, whose paintings had greatly increased in size after he had begun to paint walls, lived on a diet mainly of hard-boiled eggs and beer. Because he was feather-light and driven, he could feed himself on twenty dollars a week, and did, so he could pay for his share of a loft in Dumbo and spend the rest of his earnings on colors, which he needed in prodigious amounts.

Fitch had two cell phones, and by the time he reached Eighth Avenue had already taken two calls, one in English and one in Spanish. His three best men, his foremen, were Colombians who in their country had managed large enterprises—a furniture manufacturing company, a group of restaurants, and a trucking line. They each would direct a job and sometimes two, running them with what might have been characterized as Swiss precision were it not as easygoing as they were.

Fitch was faultlessly honest, his lieutenants were skilled and efficient, and he and they were well spoken and civilized. Because of this, the Fitch Company was backed up for two years and could have been backed up for ten. They gave reasonable estimates, did the highest-quality work, finished on time, and had the bearing of hidalgos: that is except for Fitch, who had the bearing of Fitch.

Everything ran at a wheeled pace, and what had to be done was done with energy and rapidity. They were tired neither at the beginning nor at the end of a job, because for them it was all an even tapestry. After punch list and payment, Fitch would go right to the next site, where his crew would already have been at work. They rolled through each day at the same fast, sustainable pace, renovating and finishing interiors in every borough of the city. As Fitch sped along, his phone rang again and a dozen people looked at their purses or felt their pockets. "Ya," he said unceremoniously, thinking that it was Gustavo, who had told him that he would call right back with a materials list for the space they were doing in the Thread Building. Clients never called before seven, and people who wanted an estimate would always call after dinner. Static on the phone as Fitch walked and changed position briefly cut out the other party, so he said, "Gustavo? Gustavo?" and then the connection was reestablished.

"Mr. Fitch?" asked a woman's voice.

"I'm sorry. I thought you were someone else."

"I apologize for calling so early. Is this a bad time? If you like, I can call later."

He stopped, to make sure the connection was pure and stayed that way. "No, this is a good time. Are you happy with the kitchen?"

"You recognized my voice."

"I did."

"After two years? That's amazing."

"I do that," he said.

"The kitchen's worked out very well. We had a problem with the microwave oven, but that had nothing to do with the renovation."

Fitch nodded. "What can I do for you?" he asked, as the subway rushed by, pushing warm air up through the grates, and then pulling frigid air in after it as it disappeared, its noise growing fainter.

"We redid the kitchen so we could sell the apartment, and last summer we finally did. The closing was yesterday."

"I hope you did well," Fitch said.

"Yes, and this morning I'm going to close on a duplex in Brooklyn Heights." She told him the address.

Because there was silence on the line, he moved around to pick up a better signal, saying, "Hello? Hello?"

"It needs some work," she said. "It's unoccupied, which I suppose would make it easier than the last job."

Fitch was totally backed up with work, but rather than simply turning her down—if he did not turn her down he would lose half a dozen other jobs—he was indirect. "The question is," he said, "how long can you stay where you're staying? Because we're so backed up. I've got jobs scheduled one after another for. . . ."

"I'm staying with my parents," she interrupted, "in Westchester. It's not a problem. When would you be free?"

"Two years," he said. Usually, he enjoyed saying that, because of what it meant about his work, his business, and himself. But, this time, he didn't enjoy it.

"Two years?"

"Look," said Fitch, for no reason that he could discern save something in her voice, "if it's small, if it's a small job. . . ."

"It isn't," she told him, expecting that the conversation would soon end. "A kitchen, two bathrooms, moving some walls, painting, floors, windows, everything."

"Let me look at it," Fitch said. This made no sense, because he could not afford to take on anything new. It was one of those decisions that contractors make, in memory and fear of lean times, that subsequently they cannot honor. "I'm going to be in Brooklyn in the afternoon. If you like, I can meet you there. What time would be convenient?"

"Can we make it later, in case of problems at the closing? How about five o'clock? I should be able to get there by then."

"See you then," Fitch said. "If you're not there, don't worry. I'll wait for you, Lilly."

She was pleased that he had remembered her name. "How long?" she asked, which seemed strange, even to her.

"Until you arrive," he replied.

"There's no lobby."

"That's all right, they don't let me wait in lobbies anyway."

"Thank you."

A bus went by, and in its ugly brown roar the connection vanished.

As HE WAS WALKING in the cold wind and blinding sun, he recalled this woman and her husband. They were almost young enough to be his chil-

dren. The husband, who worked on Wall Street, wore dark horn-rims and
had the face of a rabbinical student. A genius of sorts in the abstract, he had
delicate hands and seemed actually to fear the resistant power of the apartment's walls and woodwork that had to be pulled apart and put together
again. Fitch knew that this was because of the precision of his nature, that
what he feared was the breaking of more than had to be broken, the pulling
out of more than had to be pulled out, and the damage to parts that were to
remain, creating in irreparable shattering not only more work than was necessary, but chaos as well.

A contractor, however, learns early on to deal with chaos, and the technique is simple: if you can build, you need not fear the terrors of demolition.
For example, if you know how to build a window-opening into a wall, how
to set a window in it, how even to build a window itself, and how to do the
trim and painting around it, you need not fear any of the process of taking
the window out, for you can go down clear to the bone and come back
cleanly, rebuilding, better than in a partial repair.

Like her husband, she was delicate and dark. Graceful and beautiful, she
had treated Fitch and his men neither patronizingly nor with false sympa-
thy, as was often the case when clients dealt with the Fitch Company. An
academic, she taught classics and was working for tenure at Columbia.
"That's my country," Gustavo had said dryly.

As Fitch walked, he thought about her closing and then his own, when
he had sold his apartment on the Upper West Side before moving to Chelsea.
He had owned the apartment in the clear, and was sitting calmly at a table
with half a dozen lawyers, waiting out the hours of paper shuffling, when a
man burst into the room and, with evident pleasure, held up his right index
finger and declared, "I'm from the Hapsburg Fund, and nothing closes here
until we say so!"

He had the wrong room. Nevertheless, everyone froze, even Fitch,
though only momentarily, for, having no mortgage, he had nothing to fear.
"Please sit down," he asked the officious interrupter. The man from the
Hapsburg Fund sat down. Fitch cleared his throat. "We're going to close
without you," he said.

"You can't close without me."

Fitch nodded to the lawyers, who laughed.

"You think it's funny? I'm going to shut this whole thing down. It's within my discretion entirely."

"It's not," said Fitch.

"You can't close."

"Yes we can."

The man from the Hapsburg Fund said, "Guess what? It won't go through unless I sign off."

"Ah," said Fitch, "that's where you're wrong. You see, we're from an-other planet, and your law doesn't apply to us. Isn't that right, lawyers?" he asked the lawyers, who nodded with certainty.

"You're insane," said the interloper.

"Sign where there are arrows," said one of the lawyers, pushing a tide of papers toward Fitch, who signed on page after page.

As HE WENT FROM ONE SITE to another, hauled materials, made deliveries, and took measurements, Fitch thought about how she had referred to *her* closing, not *his,* her husband's, or *ours.* Perhaps this was in the self-centered way many women refer to shared bedrooms as "my bedroom," something every contractor has observed. But she was not that kind of woman. Nonethe-less, while he waited for her on Columbia Heights he was saddened to think that her husband had left her, or that she had left him. Half his renovations, it seemed, were associated with recent or impending divorces, but when he had dealt with this couple he had thought that they were destined for a long life together. It was none of his business, but when they did a job he and his men would discover in many conversations far more than they needed to know about their clients' lives.

The building was a brick double-wide with limestone sills and lintels on the street side. Hers were the top two floors and, he assumed, a roof terrace. It had a separate entrance, which was excellent from his point of view—no paying off superintendents, and work at any hour as long as it was quiet. And though it was set back from the Promenade enough to keep it from the roar of the BQE, the building had a magnificent view of the harbor and lower Manhattan. He and his men loved to work with a view. Still, whatever its attractions, he dared not take this job, because he simply couldn't work it in without the risk of badly disrupting his business. She would be disappointed, but he would give her invaluable advice that would protect her in dealing with whoever would bid for and do the job. He would keep them there until eight, until she and her husband—who, if they were not divorced, would probably show up, since he worked just across the river—were giddy from hunger. And if they remembered every detail, or took notes, it would save them two months' time, a hundred thousand dollars, and much heartache. Though he couldn't do the job, Fitch would in this way make up for it, because they had been kind to him. And he hoped that when he saw someone walking with the tense and expectant gait of a person who is rushing to a meeting, whoever was moving toward him on Columbia Heights as the sun was setting would not be moving toward him alone.

IN THE DUSK the street was briefly empty—with not a single person or car moving along it. Though the wind was blowing and it was twelve degrees, still the lull was otherworldly, because at a quarter of five people should have been returning from work. And though the wind was terribly cold it was clean, having come from the south over the ocean, from the empty parts of the world.

Three people suddenly appeared near Pierrepont Street and the playground. Given the way they walked, he knew they were coming to meet him, especially when, still two minutes away, a hand went up tentatively from the one in the middle—Lilly—like a semaphore. From the unmoving attitude of their heads he could tell even several blocks distant that their eyes were on him. It was impossible to discern except indirectly, by noting that the upper parts of their bodies seemed immobile in comparison to the far greater fluidity of the rest. When people walk, everything moves, except when they are anxiously fixed upon a destination.

They had probably brought the architect. Fitch hated architects the way anyone might hate someone who demeans him for not being able to realize perfectly a bunch of vague instructions in service of foolish and unnecessary theories. Not a week before and in the presence of the client, Fitch had answered an architect's hectoring and accusative question with the words, "Because, if I hadn't put it there, the upper floors would have collapsed, that's why. You forgot to support them properly. It was correct on the early drawings, but you left it out of the finals. Perhaps your hand slipped when you were clutching your automatic pencil."

"I don't use an automatic pencil," the architect had said, his face the color of a cherry.

"You should," Fitch said as the architect stormed out, "it would do a better job." And, then, to the distressed client, "Don't worry. He's not building this, he just thinks he is."

Neither an architect nor Lilly's husband was flanking her, but two older people who walked as stiffly as cranes. Divorce, thought Fitch, and a bad one. He left *her*. Screwed her. Her parents are paying for the apartment and holding her up between them. As badly as the woman might take it, for the parents to see their child wounded was far worse. These people were in their seventies and probably their most fervent prayer was that she would be happy again before they died. Fearing that she would not be, they would be so protective that they would treat Fitch like a plunderer.

They were suspicious, as Fitch knew quite well anyone has the right to be upon meeting a contractor, and they seemed so reserved and so intent upon protection that it was as if they had said, "If you do anything to harm our daughter or exploit her in any way, we will eviscerate and burn you."

The father was tall and thin, with an old-fashioned brush mustache, very neat. He too had dark horn-rims and an intelligent face. He wore a gray greatcoat, a plaid scarf, and no hat. He looked like Robert Trout. To Fitch's relief, the mother was not in a fur. Every winter day in New York Fitch passed a hundred thousand old ladies doddering along in furs. Though they could afford them, they could not carry them. Someone of fragile build in a fur coat always seemed to Fitch to have been devoured by a wolf or a bear. If underneath a heavy fur there was not a gorgeous fertile body, it was just the preface to a funeral.

Fitch himself, at fifty-three, might have been taken for a bear. His massive face appeared to be bigger than the faces of the three people he was about to meet even had their faces been fused into one. His immense hands were strong from wielding hammers. His body was like a barrel. And yet he had the same quality of expression, the same kind of glasses, the same careful and thoughtful look, as they did. Were the parents academics, like their daughter, they would have their higher degrees, as she did, and as he did, too, although he had never done anything with his except, in the sixties, earn them.

It was his nature to read rather than to write, to listen rather than to speak. Erudite and learned, he had been overcome at an early age, upon the death of his father, with a reticence that would never leave him. As if guarding what he knew and saving it for heaven, he confined his output to the production of beautiful rooms with plaster moldings as white as wedding cakes, with deep and glistening floors, magnificent cabinetry, walls like smooth prairies, and tranquil effects of light and shadow. That was his output, and all the rest, all his knowledge and contemplation, which was so immense that it seemed to require his very large body to hold it, stayed and developed within as he read, pondered, and learned, and as the work of his intellect perfected neither article nor book but only his soul. That is not to say that he was comfortable with this, but that he had no choice in the matter.

"You're Fitch?" asked Lilly's father.

"I'm Fitch," said Fitch, with no choice in the matter. The way he said it was a signal to Lilly's father that he, Fitch, was never going to take advantage of her.

AFTER THE HEAVY DOOR had been pulled shut by its spring, they stood for a moment, listening to a faulty radiator valve. Someone once had tried to close it and broken it further, and as it rattled and hissed it made the pipes knock with the lonely sound that haunts the winters in New York and echoes from floor to floor of apartment buildings and tenements like the complaints of a dying man. The air was hot and dry, as it will be in most empty apartments in winter, but Fitch refrained from opening a window, for he was a guest, even if, just having taken possession, Lilly, too, moved as carefully as a stranger.

Had the place had a soul it might have been offended that its owners had abandoned it and left it dirty. Dust lines on walls and floors betrayed where

furniture had been and currents of air had run along its edges. The wall behind the stove was almost blackened, the exhaust fan covered by dust and
grease with the texture of velvet. Porcelain had yellowed and chipped, light
fixtures in bathrooms and in the kitchen were the mass graves of hundreds
of desiccated flies, and the windows were anything but clear.

They took creaky stairs to the upper floor. In each bedroom and in one of
the bathrooms the previous occupants had left telephone books, hangers,
and dead lightbulbs. In one bedroom window, one of the panes had been replaced with cardboard from a frozen-dinner box. The only illumination on
the second floor was the mysterious glow, as if from an astronomical photograph of distant galaxies, of the office buildings across the river in Manhattan. It was wind-whistling and bleak, but beautiful nonetheless—white,
tranquil, and deep.

Aided by her hands moving like those of a policeman directing traffic,
Lilly explained to what extent she wanted to enlarge one bedroom at the expense of the other, and that she wanted to change the hall so that one entered
the bathroom from the enlarged bedroom.

"Do you want to keep the skylights?" Fitch asked with professional detachment, almost brusquely, looking up.

"Yes," Lilly answered, bewildered. "The roof garden is mine alone." The
skylights were of opaque glass, and privacy would have been assured even
had she not been in sole possession of the roof garden.

Fitch had asked about them not in view of privacy but because the roof
garden was accessible from the roofs of adjacent buildings, and skylights
were a common means of forcible entry. Had she seemed less vulnerable, he
might have gone on to reinforcement and alarms, but he was silent, unhappy
that she might be thinking less of him because it seemed that he was unable
to appreciate the even and filtered light that opened up the rooms beneath
the roof to something more than simply day.

On the roof itself the wind forced its way through their coats and chilled
them as much as they had been overheated moments before. The office towers of lower Manhattan, cold and brilliant, loomed up like an immense cliff.
Red lights at their tops blinked arrhythmically. One could see even the flow
of the river marked by the movement of its speeding and broken ice, and the

traffic on the bridges looked like sequins on an evening dress. Snow was left on the roof, and the wind would pick it up capriciously and move it from place to place, sometimes blowing a sparkling veil of it over the parapet and into the night. The roof was three quarters covered by a deck, and Fitch had noticed that the ceilings of the floor below were stained. The deck would have to be replaced and the roof redone.

"Let's go down," said Lilly's mother, the coldest, and they gladly descended to the first of Lilly's floors, the building's fourth, where they gathered to talk, in a room lit by the dim light that came from across the river, as the radiator hissed and the pipes knocked.

"Do you have an architect?" Fitch asked.

"Do I need one?" Lilly asked back.

"An architect would think so, but it depends on what you want to do and how much you trust me. An architect will tell you that without him I'll pad the job, use inferior materials, and run with the money. And many contractors would do exactly that."

"You won't," she said. "When we redid the kitchen it was the architect who cheated us, not you, and you easily could have, couldn't you."

"Yes," said Fitch. "I wouldn't have done a good job of cheating, but I've been cheated enough to know the rudiments."

"I heard you say something then," Lilly told him, "that you didn't know I heard."

Fitch waited.

"You didn't know I had come in, because one of your men was on his way out and the door opened and closed just once as we passed each other. I was taking off my coat, and you were talking to . . . the foreman. Gustavo?"

"Gustavo."

"And you said, 'I *hate* liars.' You were angry. You were very angry. You see, I trust you. And I'm not going to give you a huge amount of money to start."

"What I can do depends on what you want to do. What do you want to do?"

She told him: the kitchen, baths, changing the bedroom dimensions, painting, repairing the little things that were broken, bookshelves everywhere. "My husband and I have many more books now than even what you saw in the apartment two years ago. We moved them from our parents' houses, and they just keep coming in."

Fitch was pleased to discover that it seemed there had been no divorce. "I'll work up an estimate," he said, taking out a little notebook. "Give me a fax number."

She did. It had a 914 area code.

"In a few days, you'll get a rough picture of what I can do and for what price." He had completely forgotten the impact upon his schedule that this job would have. "Then you can add, subtract, replace, modify, and we'll go back and forth until I can show you some plans, and cut sheets for materials, fixtures, and appliances. Is that okay?"

"Yes, that's fine," she said. The parents said nothing.

Fitch was hungry. He wanted to get home and eat. He needed to talk to Gustavo and Georgy. He needed a hot bath. But he wanted to leave with less abruptness than the sudden silence suggested, so he took a step toward the windows of the living room, his face lit by the skyscraper light, and said, "On September eleventh, we were working on Joralemon Street. When we heard that the first plane had hit, we went up on the roof. Everyone kept on saying, 'Jesus, Jesus,' and we stayed up there, and watched the towers come down. The dust on the windows is from the Trade Center. It will have to be washed down very carefully, or the mineral grit will scratch and fog the glass. And it will have to be done respectfully, because the clouds of dust that floated against these windows were more than merely inanimate."

When he turned back to them, only the father was there. He could hear Lilly on the stairs, and her mother following. Fitch thought this was somewhat ungracious. Then her father moved a step toward him and took him lightly by the elbow, the way men of that generation do. His tweed coat reminded Fitch of old New York; that is, of the twenties and thirties, when the buildings were faced in stone the color of tweed, when the light was warmer and dimmer, and when in much of the city, for much of the time, there was silence.

"Her husband was in the south tower," the father said quietly. "He didn't get out." Then he turned and went after his daughter, walking stiffly down the stairs, like a crane.

By SEVEN O'CLOCK, Fitch had returned home, with fresh fish and vegetables, to a Chelsea apartment that overlooked a large garden and was as quiet as the New York of his childhood. He made a fire in the woodstove, quickly did the mail, and prepared his dinner. When he was forty-eight and the first Mrs. Fitch had left him for a new life and a new job with an investment bank in London, he had decided that he would refuse to become, like so many divorced men, a habitué of restaurants, and instead had learned to cook.

He had one immense room with a tiny bedroom off it, and a luxurious bathroom that he had copied from a luxurious hotel. As his dinner cooked slowly over the fire in a Japanese wrought-iron pot, he sat close by on a rush chair, staring into the flame. The only light other than firelight was a warm fluorescent beneath the cabinets suspended over the kitchen counters, blocked except where it glowed within a pass-through.

Normally as he made dinner he would read, or listen to the news, but now he just sat still and watched the broth lightly boiling in the pot. For almost an hour he stared into the fire. Then he replenished it, ate, cleaned up, and returned to position. For a man with no living family and very few friends this could have been quite lonely, but wasn't. He was counting with his fingers, shuffling numbers in his head, calculating square footage, weeks and days, hours, costs, taxes, fees, and rates of interest. He was calculating them neither desperately nor greedily, but, rather, casually, as if he were watching a tennis match. And yet, underlying his ease and relaxation was an inflexible resolution. At nine-thirty he picked up the phone and pressed 1. "Gustavo, are you busy?"

"No."

There was a pause while Fitch thought. Gustavo knew that when Fitch called and ten seconds were held in suspension, changes were due. "We've got five jobs at the moment."

"Yes."

"They'll finish in the order Smilksteen, Yorkville, Liechtenstein, the chicken restaurant, and Requa, is that correct?"

"I don't think so," said Gustavo. "Put the chicken restaurant at the end.

We still don't know the dimensions of the rotisseries, and we won't until they come in. I asked them a million times, but they say it's hard to call up a factory someplace in Korea and get a number you can rely on."

"Okay, the chicken place at the end."

"Why?"

"How far are we in Yorkville?"

"You saw. Twenty-five percent, maybe thirty."

"They haven't paid us," Fitch told Gustavo. "They're six weeks late. They think they can get away with it, but we're almost even, because their first payment covered most of our overhead until now and we can cancel the materials that haven't been delivered yet."

"We've already put ten thousand dollars in lumber, electrical, and the start of the plumbing rough-in."

"We'll eat that," Fitch said. "Shut down the job."

"When do you think they'll pay?" Gustavo asked.

"No, close it down. I'm not going to play games. They think we won't walk away from ten thousand dollars. I'll bet they've done the calculation to the penny. Shut it down and take the tools."

"Okay, tomorrow morning."

"Now we've got four jobs. How fast," Fitch asked, "can we finish Liechtenstein?"

"With the Yorkville crew, now," Gustavo answered, "ten days."

"And Requa?"

"That's two months, anyway."

Fitch thought. "What I want you to do," he said, "is to pull people off the other jobs to finish up with Liechtenstein and Requa, those two."

"So we slow down chicken and Smilksteen?"

"Yeah, no more than two men on either, until they're done."

"They won't like that. You're talking about a month late for both, at least. That'll kill us with penalty, not to mention reputation."

"That's all right."

"Just because you want to go to U.N. Plaza?" Gustavo spoke as elegantly as an ambassador, and could have been one. In the beginning, Fitch had had to convince him not to bow and kiss women's hands, explaining that Americans would think either that he was mocking them or that he was insane.

"I didn't say anything about U.N. Plaza."

Now Gustavo paused. "Wait a minute, Fitch," he said. "At the cost of twenty or thirty thousand dollars and three angry clients, in two weeks we're going to have most of our people free. How could we go anyplace but U.N. Plaza?"

"We're going to be two or three weeks late there, maybe."

"If they let us in late," Gustavo added.

"I'll talk to them."

"If we're late there, the whole job line will be pushed back. It'll be a disaster. What did you get, Fitch, Gracie Mansion? The White House? The New York residence of Mr. Bill Gates? It must be very important, and very lucrative."

"It's not lucrative, but it'll be the best job we've ever done, and we're going to do it faster than hell."

"What job?" asked Gustavo. "What?"

"You know," asked Fitch, "how knights would die for the Virgin, would yearn to die? And how everything in the world seemed unimportant next to their peculiar, settled, certain devotion?"

"Yes, I know," Gustavo said, "because that is still very much in the heart of my country."

"Well, then you know. Sometimes you find something that's truly important, and even though it throws everything into disorder you know you have to do it . . . and it gives you new life."

"Let me guess," said Gustavo. "This new job is for a woman."

"Yes."

"And you're in love with her."

"No, I'm not. I don't know her, and she's almost young enough to be my daughter. I suddenly came to love her, but I'm not in love with her."

"That's even more dangerous."

"Right," said Fitch. "It is. I'll see you tomorrow."

IN THE FIRST TWO WEEKS of February, Fitch met Lilly five times at the site and sent her thirty faxes—some quite short and composed of just a single question, but others of many pages, with sketches and lists of costs and materials. He had to have this job, so he priced it honestly but as low as he could, certain that he would get it, and he did. For the high quality that he would provide, he would charge three hundred thousand dollars, a sum that was slightly under her expectations and her father's.

Because he was closing down projects in Manhattan, and because she came into and left the city at Grand Central, they agreed to meet for lunch on Friday, the fifteenth of February, at the Oyster Bar. He never met clients for lunch, but he had a great deal to say to her about the contract he would be bringing for her to sign. He knew that she would be surprised that he would have it ready for signing, and surprised as well by its terms.

"It's so noisy in here," she commented as they entered. "How will we be able to hear?"

"It's the vaulted ceilings," Fitch said, leading her forward, "but if you sit at the far end of the oyster bar itself, the effect almost vanishes."

"Oh," she said, stopping short. "I can't eat shellfish; I have to sit at a table."

"No no, I know, I thought that might be the case," Fitch told her as they moved toward the quieter place. "You can order anything here that you can have at a table, and I won't have any shellfish."

"Please do," she said. "Have whatever you want. It's not a problem. I have, in my time, eaten every kind of shellfish. I love it. But my husband came from an Orthodox family, and we just never. . . . I stopped eating shellfish."

It was remarkably quiet at the end of the bar. They sat and opened their menus. Fitch, who knew what he was going to have, put his menu down almost immediately. "Take your time," he told her. "I already know. I've come here—in fact, to this seat—a lot."

She studied the menu with the triple difficulty of someone avoiding shellfish at the Oyster Bar, trying to hurry, and not being clear about who would pay. Because of these multiple confusions, it took her some time, and as time passed she felt embarrassed, and she, Lilly, turned the color of a rose.

He was obliged to look at her at intervals to see if she had finished and was ready, and he spent as much time looking at her as he spent looking away. He had known that her eyes were blue, but he had not known how blue. Behind her polished lenses they were exquisitely beautiful, he thought, not merely because of their extraordinary Prussian-blue color but because of the intelligence and spirit they betrayed in their quick and alert motion. Even when immobile, they seemed ready to move, to judge, compare, and take in fact and sensation from the center and from the periphery.

He could not possibly love her the way her beauties invited him to love her, because he was too old, and because she had just lost her husband, whom she loved, and she would not, she could not, be ready until Fitch was not merely too old, but far too old. Still, when he looked at the several tiny crescents at the corners of her mouth as she smiled, at her lips pursed or moving in speech, and at her hands floating gently, sometimes, in pantomime, he felt a rush of love and contentment that he then had to suppress.

He was good at suppression, having learned in Manhattan's expensive neighborhoods that young, elegant, and beautiful women turned from the gaze of a man who, no matter how intelligent, worthy (perhaps), and admiring, had paint on his clothes, his watch, and his glasses, and who was dressed to work with his hands. And he could suppress his desires because he was an honorable man. And he did, though, aware that he was studying her and forcing himself not to look too hard or too long, she had, to her own surprise, no objection.

A pound of oyster crackers was already in a basket in front of them. "That's a great deal of food right there," she said. "I'll have a small fish chowder and a glass of white wine."

"I'll have the same," Fitch told the waiter, "but with a beer, not wine." He opened his briefcase to take out copies of the contract. "It's ready for signing. We can get that done today."

"I can't," she told him. "I didn't transfer funds or bring a check."

"You don't need a check."

"What about the deposit? Don't you require a twenty-five-percent deposit?"

"No."

"What, then?"

"I don't need a deposit."

"You don't? What about materials?"

"We're coming off other jobs," Fitch said. "We're hardly short of funds. Don't worry."

She had not done enough of this kind of thing to know how unusual this was. Her father would have been—and would be later—very suspicious, but she was not.

"And, about materials, that's another thing I wanted to talk to you about. We have a warehouse where we store our materials, tools, and trucks. We do a lot of expensive projects, and most of the time the clients have no way to use excess material, so they ask us to take it. Because we bring particular types of marble, tile, fixtures, moldings, whatever, from job to job, most of the time this is to our advantage. But if we go to another kind of job where we don't use that exact set, we have no room in our warehouse for the things we might need."

"So you want to offload it on me?"

"No. We can sell it back, but with the restocking fee and prices for broken lots, it works out to the same thing as buying new material at a lesser quality, and it's an accounting nightmare. After your place, we're going to U.N. Plaza to do two entire floors, and the materials are specific to that job. We've got to empty our warehouse, so there may be opportunities for advantageous substitutions."

This was totally untrue: his warehouse was too well managed to be overfull. He simply intended to give her, at his own expense, a far better job than she could afford, and he did not want her to know that he had done so.

"I've made an extensive list, with cut sheets and full specifications, of these potential substitutes. It has only upgrades, as you'll see. And if you don't like anything, we'll pull it out and go with the original."

"You can do that?"

"There's no structural work. We can do that."

"But you might have to repaint a room, or redo a floor or something. Wouldn't that injure your profit?"

"No," said Fitch, quite honestly, for on this job he would have no profit as commonly understood. He would have, as commonly understood, a loss. "You'll see in the contract that if any substitution, or all, will not meet your approval, you can require us at absolutely no additional expense to install the original, to meet the contract specifications exactly."

Taking out a little leather portfolio, she opened its red Florentine cover and, shuffling the pages, said, "I'm going to be away until Monday, March eigh-teenth. You might put a lot in, in a month, that I might make you pull out."

"Not to worry," Fitch told her. "In a month, we'll be mainly setting up, doing demolition, the systems rough-ins, framing, and administration—permits, ordering, receiving, inspections, all that kind of thing. It's a five-month job."

"My father said six months. Can you do it in five?"

"I'm going to put a lot of men on it. You'll see that there's a penalty clause. We'll have to refund to you five hundred dollars for every day past the completion date."

"And what do I pay for every day that you're early?"

"Nothing."

"Nothing?"

"That's right."

They were looking at one another directly, eyes locked as if purely be-cause they were in the crux of a business negotiation. Anyone viewing them from nearby, however, might have thought that they had fallen into the lovers' traction that one sees so often in New York, mainly in restaurants, as gardens and bowers are scarce.

"It sounds so disadvantageous to you. It makes me nervous. Do you un-derstand?"

"Of course I do. Look, I don't know what happened to the country, but everybody tries to screw everybody else. More so than in my father's day, more so than when I was a child, more so than when I was a young man, more so than ten years ago . . . more so than last year. Everybody lies, cheats, manipulates, and steals. It's as if the world is a game, and all you're supposed to do is try for maximum advantage. Even if you don't want to do it that way, when you find yourself attacked from all sides in such fashion, you be-gin to do it anyway. Because, if you don't, you lose. And no one these days can tolerate losing."

"Can you?" Lilly asked.

"Yes," he said.

"Tell me."

He hesitated, listening to the clink of glasses and the oceanlike roar of conversation magnified and remagnified under the vaulted ceilings of the dining rooms off to the side. "I can tolerate losing," he said, "if that's the price I pay, if it's what's required, for honor."

"Honor," she repeated.

"Honor. I often go into things—I almost always go into things—with no calculation but for honor, which I find far more attractive and alluring, and satisfying in every way, than winning. I find it deeply, incomparably satisfying."

"How do you stay in business," she asked, "in *Manhattan*?"

"We do a lot of work in Brooklyn," he answered. "Look, although I'm not as rich as some other contractors, I always have a steady supply of work, and usually it goes well. Sometimes we have a loss, but we're paid back in reputation and in pride in what we do and how we do it."

"I know," said Lilly, "from last time."

"Take the contract home. You don't have to sign it now. Bring it to a lawyer."

"My father's a lawyer."

"That's perfect."

"But, listen," she said. "I don't have to bring it to him. I can read it right here, and sign it. I trust you."

"No," he insisted. "I want you to give it to him. If he wants, we can modify it. I want you to be absolutely confident, absolutely reassured."

"Why?" she asked.

"I want you to be happy."

Moved by this, for many reasons, some of which seemed even to her to be mysterious, Lilly looked away—at the long sweep of the bar at which they sat, and the blur of waiters and barmen in white, moving like the crowds in Grand Central, even busier, and the noise like that of water and ice flowing in a rock-strewn brook.

"Tell me why you value honor," she said.

"I'm fifty-three," he answered with analytical detachment. "My father died at fifty-nine. What good is money? If I have six years left or thirty, it makes no difference. My life will be buoyant, and my death will be tranquil, only if I can rest upon a store of honor."

"There are other things."

"Name them," he challenged.

She met his challenge. "Love."

"Harder than honor, I'm afraid, to keep and sustain."

This startled her into silence.

"YOU'RE AN IDIOT," Gustavo said, as he and Fitch were measuring in Lilly's dust-filled duplex. The first day after the permit, the demolition had been finished in record time and removal and cleanup were under way, with nine men moving about like the builders of the Panama Canal. Gustavo was insulting only when he was frightened. "Here, because there are so many people with Ph.D.s, they have to drive taxicabs and mix drinks."

Fitch wasn't entirely sure what Gustavo was trying to say. Nonetheless, he answered. "But Gustavo," he said, "that's why we're a great power. It's how we invented the blender."

"You can't throw away the whole business for one crazy thing."

"Who's throwing away? Everyone's getting paid."

"From your pocket."

"So?"

"How are you going to retire? With the materials you're going to use here, and this kind of detail, it will cost us half a million dollars. No profit, and two hundred thousand dollars from your pocket."

"No," Fitch said calmly. "Five hundred thousand. I'm not going to charge her."

Gustavo put his clipboard down where he was kneeling, and straightened his back. "That's everything you have."

"Don't worry, Gustavo. We're going into U.N. Plaza on the eighteenth. We won't be late. We'll be early."

"The eighteenth of what?"

"March. Monday, the eighteenth of March."

"We'll finish here in less than a month?" Gustavo was stunned.

"I'm going to call in as many subcontractors as we need, pay overtime, work day and night myself. It'll be done by that date. When she returns from California she'll come back to the most beautifully done space she's ever seen—in pristine condition, clean, quiet, safe, complete—with a Fitch Company bill that says, 'No Charge.' That's what I want."

"Why?" Gustavo asked. And, when Fitch was not forthcoming, Gustavo commanded, "You've got to tell me why."

"If you could see her . . . ," said Fitch.

"I saw her when we did the kitchen. She's pretty. She's beautiful. But she's not that beautiful."

"Yes, she is," said Fitch. "She bears up, but I've never seen a more wounded, deeply aggrieved woman. It's not because she's physically beautiful. What the hell do I care? It's because she needs something like this, from me, from us, from everyone. Not that it would or could be a substitute, but as a gesture."

"A substitute for what?" Gustavo asked.

"Her husband."

"Her husband left her?"

"Her husband was in the south tower when it came down," Fitch said. "For Christ's sake, they'll never even find the bodies. Vaporized, made into paste. What can she think? What can she feel?"

Gustavo looked away to his left, at the wall where he had drawn some lines and written some letters. "How old is she?"

"I don't know. Early thirties? Middle? Her parents are old. The mother has that look in her eye, as if she knows that her time is close. I'm doing it as much for the parents as for the child."

Still on his knees, Gustavo closed his eyes. After a while, he rose to his feet. "To me," he said, "you cannot pay anything. Don't protest. Nothing for this job. I'll work with you day and night. Let me talk to the men."

"No, don't tell them. They have enough troubles of their own. They're not in a position to do this. I am."

"Fitch, they have honor as much as you. They'll decide for themselves. And that fucking Scotsman, he owes it to everybody and the world.

"Listen up!" Gustavo called, a colloquialism he had embraced with great enthusiasm, and that he spoke with authority and promise.

THE RHYTHM OF THEIR WORK in the month that followed was like a rolling wave. In hour upon hour of tedium, of scraping, sanding, sweeping, measuring and remeasuring, driving nails, turning screws, drilling holes, fitting things, smoothing plaster, and running wire, Fitch saw himself, as if from a trance, atop a wave rolling across the sea, the wind lifting droplets from curling edges and blowing them back like a scarf trailing in the slipstream of a car.

Their normal conversation was curtailed until they said almost nothing. Even the Scotsman, whose chief work requirement was to argue with Fitch, Gustavo, and everyone else, was quiet. He let his paintings stand enormously in his cold loft until the smell of linseed oil and turpentine was taken by the drafts and pinpoint leaks beyond the loft and blown over Long Island and out to sea, and as the paintings rested in darkness, the Scotsman worked in Brooklyn Heights.

The only respite was when something was setting or drying, or materials were late in coming. They scheduled the bathrooms in such a way that one was always available for use. They scheduled the rooms so that they never lacked a place for a row of cots. One man's job was purely cleanup and housekeeping. He took food orders, served the take-out meals on two doors resting on sawhorses, and carried out construction waste and debris twenty times a day. So that the food would be varied, he went round-robin from one type of restaurant to another. He bought compact discs and ran Fitch's music system, brought from Chelsea, like a disc jockey, taking requests. They might have a Greek dinner and afterward work to Celtic music, or a Japanese lunch followed by an afternoon of rock and roll. Everything was possible, because some of the people on the floors below were away, and the others were almost deaf.

Another man did nothing but deliver materials. Whenever he arrived in the truck, as many men as needed would come downstairs to unload and carry. It went fast, and he would set out again. When Gustavo was not supervising, he did the fine-work. Fitch set up a desk, his two cell phones, a bank of battery chargers, a computer, and a neatly shelved library of plans, telephone directories, catalogs, and ledgers. To get a break on materials, he would, while in the physical presence of the supplier, state the purpose of the job.

For example, he might walk into the marble place, which was in northern Queens and surrounded by chop shops and piles of salt. He was a good customer, but nothing like the big commercial contractors who did floor after floor of new office towers. "Deansch," he might say.

"Hey, Fitch, how are you?"

"Great, Deansch, great."

They liked him. Among other things, although he knew costs and never had to overpay, he did not have the power to make them slice so thin that they couldn't eat, and he always paid instantly, something almost unheard of in the contracting business. Now, however, though they didn't know it, he did have the power to make them slice it thin, so thin, in fact, that it was inside out.

"What can I do for you?" Deansch asked. "Are you in U.N. Plaza yet?"

"Eighteenth of March."

"We've got the marble when you're ready for it."

"Now we're on a small job in Brooklyn."

"Whataya need?"

"The ivory Carrara."

"The best we have and the best there is."

"Two thousand square feet."

"No problem. We've got it."

"You have to cut me a deal on it."

"I'll consider it part of the U.N. Plaza pricing. That'll drop it from sixteen to thirteen-fifty per square foot. That's a deal."

"I need better than that."

"Better than that?"

"We're doing this job for free, all of us. No one is getting paid. We're working eighteen-hour days, sleeping there."

Deansch tightened. "For who?"

"For a woman who lost her husband when the World Trade Center went down."

"What's her name?" Deansch asked, already struggling within himself.

"Lilly. Does it matter?"

Deansch shook his head, rocked it really, pursing his lips as he thought. "No," he answered. Then he looked up at Fitch, and said, "Take what you need."

Fitch answered him with a quick nod, which was all that was necessary, and within minutes the trucks were being loaded.

IN THE DAYS OF FURIOUS WORK, and the nights, when they labored in the blaze and heat of lights, something arose that made it easy. It was not merely a rhythm or a sense of progress. Nor was it the unusual speed of the work, nor the caffeine, nor the music, both of which powered them on all of their jobs and neither of which was capable of sustaining them as now they were sustained, power and perseverance flowing so voluminously and steadily that they were lifted from their fatigue, lifted above their difficulties, just as Fitch had imagined, as if on a wave in the wind. Such waves can without effort lift even immense ships, because the power of the wave comes from the great mass and depth of the sea.

Without the slightest hesitation, Fitch's men had refused pay, committed to staying twenty-four-hour days, and started immediately. The weeks in which they would work this way would be weeks in which they would not see their families, and it was not as if they and their families had no troubles to speak of that a month without pay would make worse. Fitch had no children and therefore no need to keep what he had or to come out ahead. They did. These people, who had less power over their own lives than anyone Fitch had ever known, were the most generous he had ever encountered.

Wives, mothers, aunts, and cousins would show up to serve meals of rice and beans, fish, chicken, vegetables. The many children in tow, who were quiet, charming, brown-eyed, would take a turn at sawing, sweeping, or painting, their fathers' hands often guiding them. Fitch paid their fathers well, but upon seeing this he resolved to pay them better, especially now that he had rid himself, or would shortly, of his carefully accumulated savings and, following upon that, of the need or desire to save.

A lapsed but believing Catholic, he had not been to mass since mass had lapsed out of Latin, but what happened in the weeks of February and March made up for the thousands of masses he had missed. The mass existed, in his perhaps heretical view, to keep, encourage, and sustain a sense of holiness, and to hold open the channels to grace that, with age and discouragement, tend to close. Witness to those who had little sacrificing what they had, to their children contributing to the work in their way, and to the fathers' pride in this, Fitch felt the divine presence as he had not since the height of his youth. The less he had and the closer to death he felt, the more intense, finer, and calmer the world seemed. It had been a long time since he had been on the ocean on a day of sun and wind, but now he and all his men were lifted and traveling on the selfsame wave.

THIS WOULD HARDLY BRING BACK for Lilly what had been taken from her, and, knowing it, he would work furiously into March, as if it might. March broke with pale sun, spells of warmth, and respite from the snow and bitter cold. Sunlight now flooded in from the great airy spaces over the harbor and the mouth of the East River, from between the buildings in the financial district, from east, south, and west, and even by echo from the colder and bluer north.

For long periods they forgot Lilly and forgot their purpose, as if the driving force of what they were doing was merely what they were doing and its driving force, self-sustaining, self-feeding, and rounding in perfection. The work itself became the object, and never in their lives had they done better. Never had the walls been straighter or smoother, never had the plaster been whiter, never had the wood been closer joined, never had the joints been tighter, the colors more intense, the proportions more artful.

Georgy had been absent except to measure, and when he arrived with his cabinetry they had no need to comment as one might when someone else has made his best effort but not quite hit the mark, for what Georgy had done was so self-evidently beautiful at first sight that their quiet admiration was the greatest praise. And when they fitted it all in, something that normally would have taken four or five days but which now they did in a day, and when it was combined with the appliances that Fitch and the appliance dealer had bankrupted themselves to supply, the men kept on saying, "Look at that! Look at that!" because nowhere in New York or perhaps anywhere else was there a better job.

This was repeated in rosewood paneling, in limestone baseboards, in nickel, marble, granite, and unobtrusive plaster molding that physics said could not be whiter, purer, or more like snow in bright sun. It was apparent in the ironwork, brass work, and glazing. The solid walnut doors were two and a half inches thick, with the same brass hardware and hinges as in the White House, and they closed more smoothly and quietly than the doors of a Rolls-Royce. The lighting had been planned by a theatrical lighting designer who had worked for free and delayed a Broadway opening ("So what?" the lighting designer had said), and its effects seemed to double the space. It shone here or there with such clarity and purity, or softly and gently, that moving from room to room was like passing through the seasons.

Although these attributes, some massive, some almost undetectable, were of interest in themselves and had taken sacrificial labor and care to create, the remarkable achievement was that they were all subsumed quietly into something greater. In the place Fitch and his men built, the trees and the garden below were pulled in, as were the water and the light, and the openness of the view in all its intricacy. It was a refuge, and yet it was not closed. It was a fortress, and yet it was light and airy. It was luxurious, and yet it was modest and austere. Everything was in perfect balance, contending forces in abeyance, as had been intended, and when on Sunday, the seventeenth, they withdrew, leaving the surfaces polished and perfect, they knew much more than that the next day they would be going to the big job at U.N. Plaza and would once again be earning. They knew that they had made something beautiful, and, because of this, they were content.

ON MONDAY, the eighteenth of March, 2002, Lilly arrived at the apartment late in the morning. Her train into Grand Central had been delayed, and the Number Four to Borough Hall had sat on the track for twenty minutes, its doors opening and closing as inexplicably as if they were responding to radio signals from Mars.

The sky was delft blue, and broken clouds spread across it were touched with yellow as the sunlight passed through them. In the playground at the foot of Columbia Heights, scores of young children worked the swings and bars as if these were the machines in a factory run by monkeys. Half were watched by their mothers and the other half by nannies who took benches according to nationality, with the world appearing largely Jamaican. As Lilly walked by, she saw a little girl on a sprung horse, a child of no more than two, with round red cheeks and marvelously intelligent eyes. Her grief flooded in—for the husband she had lost, for the child they would never have.

She could not appear to Fitch with her eyes red, so she veered onto the Promenade. She would look up at her apartment to see if they had made any progress on the outside, although there was not much you could tell from the outside. When she got there, she looked first across the river at the sky-line, to the space that had been occupied by the World Trade Center, and where now there was only light. And then she looked at her building. They had done the roof garden. Instead of the rusting iron railing, now there was a limestone balustrade. She could see the tops of stone planters in which were rooted elegant topiaries. And where a toupee-like edge of crumbling tar had lapped over the roof, now there were heavy copper gutters and downspouts.

Was this her building? She had to check, counting from the big apart-ment house, remembering details from the garden and the lower floors. It was, but her windows had been replaced. They were beautiful, French. Fitch had not been supposed to replace the windows. She was alarmed, thinking that perhaps she had been cheated. And she drew in a sharp breath when, looking closer, she noticed that the sills and lintels, which had been wood in dubious condition and were supposed to have been painted, were now the same taupe limestone as the balustrades of the roof garden.

Almost in a panic, she made her way around the apartment house and then south along Columbia Heights. Out of politeness, she rang her buzzer to let them know she was coming. She saw that her mailbox was brass, the buzzer solid and new. Even her nameplate was elegantly engraved. No one answered. She rang again, and then, like someone who is worried and ready to be hurt, pushed her key into the lock. As she went up the stairs, she heard no ham-mering, no saws, no radios, no machines, the things that might have drowned out the buzzer, which, although she did not know it, was now a bell.

At her landing, she was shocked. She had certainly not ordered a marble floor, nor the beautiful millwork, nor the pinpoint recessed lighting, nor the coco mat flush with the floor and surrounded by a heavy brass rim. She stared at the door in disbelief. Where once a single door had been was a double door, and she could tell by looking at it that it, like the windows, had actually come from France. She didn't know what to do, because she hadn't called for the replacement of the existing door, much less for the opening to be rebuilt, much less for the importation from Paris of a paneled and chamfered walnut door that was so substantial and perfectly crafted that she guessed that it and putting it in could not have cost Fitch any less than fifteen or twenty thousand dollars.

She knocked. Then she saw the doorbell, yet another thing for which she had not asked, and rang it. As she lifted her key to the lock, she imagined that Fitch had spent all her money—then she realized that she hadn't yet paid him anything—on the roof garden, entry, and windows, and would now extort much more to finish the interior. She was sure that he could not have touched the interior, not in that short time, not with all that had been done on the outside. Holding her breath, she turned the key in the lock and opened the door.

As she walked from room to room, she trembled. This could not be. It was a dream. How could he have worked so fast and so well? She was practiced in the close reading of complicated texts, and here was a work of art, in every detail of which the essential condition of art—as she believed it to be—shone through, and that was a beauty that arose from love. She did not know where she stood, what she had to pay, or when, or how. She did not know why Fitch had done it, or at least she thought she didn't know. No matter what, it was too much for her now. Fitch was too much for her now. It was too soon.

But then she thought of the child she had seen in the playground, of her innocence, of her eyes, and she thought that for the sake of such a child nothing was too much, nothing was too difficult, nothing was too soon. This made her tremble even more, not helplessly but with something akin to resolve. And then she saw on the mantle—and what a beautiful mantle it was—the Fitch Company bill, standing like a pup tent.

She knew before she unfolded it what it would say, and as she unfolded it she was calmed. The lettering was unpretentious. It said, "Fitch Co.," and, in a universal typeface for this word, "Invoice." Paying no heed to the lines printed on the paper, Fitch had written, "No charge through completion, paid in full," signed his name, and dated it "Monday, 18 March 2002." Lilly's hands fell to her sides, the bill fluttering down with them.

FITCH WAS WALKING SOUTH on First Avenue in pale sunshine that had everything about it of spring about to break the siege of winter. He had many things on his mind. His men were happy and reassured. Now they were working for pay, and they had the quiet power of those who had done right. They knew, as he did, that their work would go beautifully now that they had turned a corner. He himself couldn't wait to get at the job. Down the long prospect of First Avenue, glittering like mica in the sun, the building was in sight.

He was standing on the northwest corner of Fiftieth and First, waiting for the light, when his cell phone rang. He thought it might be Gustavo, but was not surprised that it wasn't.

"Fitch," she said, "Oh Fitch, this is Lilly."

And then he stood in silence with nothing coming from the other end of the line, but he did not call her name or think that they had been cut off, and when he saw the light change he stayed in place, for he knew that she needed time to regain her composure.

A Brilliant Idea
and His Own

THE SUPPOSITION, reasonable upon its face, was that the enemy would neither suspect a parachutist during a bombing run nor emerge in any case, and
that the bombs would have burst before he floated down. Therefore, he
would parachute from the last Liberator to have released its ordnance over
a town that flowed across a hilltop, on a night with moonlight enough to
guide a parachutist's descent upon a landscape burned into his eyes by flares
and explosions. Were he to land safely he would find his way to a high place
overlooking the battle and there conceal himself amid rocks and brush to report upon the progress of events below and direct the fire both of naval guns
and the allied artillery beyond the river to the west.

He had written himself off and wanted to get it over with. The sooner he
could fly out the side door into the darkness, the less time he would have for
apprehension. Soldiers who have been blooded know that action is an instant
cure for fear, and when battle approaches their experience makes them long
for it to come quickly, even if, as in this case, the chances were not the best.

Certainly it was outrageous to parachute into an enemy area during a
bombing, gliding amid flack, in the dark, onto rough terrain, but it was a
brilliant idea, and it was his own. Even when he had first suggested it he
knew that he himself would end up doing it, for he could ask no one else,

and that it was one of those things that, having come into existence, would nag at the imagination of anyone who knew of it, until it was accomplished. How foolish then to have broached it. And how further galling to have to argue for it in the face of opposition, explaining away doubts and portraying the mission as he had designed it, or rather as it had come to him instantly. They had argued that it was an attractive idea, but that it would probably leave him dead, and the staff to whom he had proposed it had asked if he were a pathfinder in a parachute regiment seconded to intelligence, or an intelligence officer seconded to an airborne regiment as a pathfinder. Whatever he was, it would make a splendid show, and the way he thought of it was that, in throwing himself into a night battle, he might by clawing back the curtain as he fell make a track of light like the traces of a shooting star.

Such transcendence notwithstanding, in the Liberator he comforted himself with inventory, counting magazines and rounds of ammunition, noting the position and attachment of a knife, visiting the bulging pockets of his jumpsuit to remember the placement and existence of pouches and bundles, first-aid kit and maps, signaling mirror, flares, telescope, pistol, tarpaulin, and line. And in his pack, food and blankets, a radio, and grenades. Even a Lilliputian book of paintings, and a Bible of the same size. He had passed through university with distinction and had chosen to be a painter, and the Bible was a gift from his father, who had served in the First War. "Take this," he had said as he gave it to his son, "and bring it back to me."

But now he dared not think of either his father or his mother. Rather, he considered the design of the moment, the shape and color of webbing and patches, the chance and philosophy that had brought him to look as he did dressed in the uniform of battle. Much had been planned in a great hurry and produced with no less speed. Shortages of materials led to almost bizarre substitutions, and all that was new had the mark of pure function and the feel of emergency, whereas that which had lasted through time and other wars and had been worn smooth had the feel of elegance. A few things made in desperation for this war would last, but just a few, and then they would be antique, and then they would be gone.

Now, however, the things he carried were everything, fresh and new, and he depended upon them. His parachute—the color of mother-of-pearl, sheer, smooth, soft, and clean—that would in perfection of form billow with invisible air. The cord and webbing, so strong that even in thin sections it could hold the weight of automobiles dangling above the ground. The rifle, and its scope, about which the armorers had said that as long as a shock were insufficient to shatter the glass, it would be insufficient to disalign the one with the other. If the scope were whole and you could look through it, it was properly sighted. Pack, battle dress, helmet, and boots fit him comfortably amid the din of engines as the Liberator made a wide left turn and flew up the coast.

In ten or fifteen minutes, were he still alive, the sounds of engines, guns, and bombs would have been replaced by those of crickets, cicadas, and the flow of the wind. And the moon, in a thin crescent, would be dipping quietly into the sea.

MIDWAY OVER TARGET, in the buffeting of flack—after the sudden buoyancy of the aircraft upon releasing its bombs, and its insistent, duty-bound descent to jump altitude—the red light went on, and he stood. A crewman in communication with the navigator listened intently on his headset. Then he raised his hands and pursed his lips as he watched the heavily laden soldier step to the door.

Let's go, the soldier's heart said, and when the signal came he jumped into the night and flew past the plane like smoke. In falling, fear vanished. In its place came alert expectation. Gravity worked with perfection, but his complete surrender to it was also his temporary victory over it as its effects disappeared during a few angelic seconds, only to return in the softest modulation as the chute began to open. Then the slight tug, always less than in the simulator, that signaled the beginning of a smooth descent.

He twisted his head and saw that the Adriatic was covered with light skeins of fog and smoke in which the moon and its weak reflection were tangled and lost. He pulled the lines until he was crosscutting the path of the bomber, as he had wanted, taken by the wind.

To the right, in a crescent south and east of an immense hill, was the port, dimly illuminated in the fires of the bombing, as if by embers. To the left, as the hill fell back down and curved slightly to the sea, was the "new" town, begun in the days of Rome. There the last of the bombs were falling. First they would flash, and seconds later the shock waves would swing him like a pendulum and tickle the inside of his lungs. Behind him, in the dark, were the enemy lines, between the hill and the river. And beyond the river were the allies: British, Americans, Canadians, Poles, Australians, New Zealanders, Indians, South Africans. Except for the Poles, they all spoke English, and if not invincible they were at least colorful. They were the empire of English-speaking peoples, something toward which since birth he had directed a great deal of affection, and in the contemplation of which he had always found pride.

Ahead and coming ever closer, the ridge at the top of the hill was dotted with clusters of buildings and old fortifications. Beyond, a crescent of beach connected the two parts of the town, and at sea out of range of enemy gunfire was the allied fleet.

The higher on the hill he landed the less walking he would have to do in the dark. But over the top of the ridge, falling away to the beach, were cliffs, and were he to overshoot, not only would he fail to gain his objective, he might be blown over the beach and drowned in the Adriatic. But the wind was just right, and as he calculated and recalculated, working the parachute toggles, the vector of his descent promised impact in a dark patch, probably a ravine, beneath a small saddle at the top.

Ravines were not good cover throughout, as patrols tended to follow the crease while moving up or down them, but the sides of a ravine, if thickly overgrown, were paradise for anyone who might hide. No one walked along the sides: it was unnatural. This place toward which he was heading seemed to him to be perfect, though he knew that all he was doing was moving toward a dark spot on the correct side of a hill.

Cautious by nature, he braced too early for the landing, and then had to relax, brace again, and relax, but he was so close that he could see the outline of the buildings in the saddle, and the shadows of the curbs on the road. He was coming in high, but would still land a hundred and fifty feet or so below the houses. Then he would have to descend to make sure of concealment. At least it was better than going up. Seconds remained. He was coming in higher than he had thought. He emptied as much air out of his chute as he could, which made him go so much faster that he dreaded the impact against the side of the hill.

Then he felt a puff of air. A gentle breeze ordinarily was a lovely thing as it traveled softly through the night, but not only did this push him forward faster, it rolled up the side of the hill like water overflowing the bank of a stream and lifted him like a balloonist, giddily, until he was higher than the ridge, higher even than the tops of the buildings, and then, momentarily still, like a roller coaster at the peak of its run.

"Oh no," he said as he began to descend rapidly to the east. Far ahead was the always alluring sea, where his mission would fail and he might be lost. The beach was too narrow, and the part of the town between the base of the cliffs and the strand was heavily garrisoned with Germans.

He pulled vehemently on the toggles to let air out of the chute so that he might land in a safe place, and in the seconds as he descended he realized that he was headed for a building. He would just overshoot it, and its blocking of the wind would then, perhaps, allow him to float straight down onto the road that ran along the top of the cliffs. All he had to do, given his track, was nothing, and it would happen.

But then, instantly, he decided to recast his bad luck and land on the flat roof, surrounded by a low parapet, just ahead of him. From there he would be able to see clearly in every direction, and spot not only for the artillery west of the river but for the naval guns that he could direct onto troop concentrations in the town. He could observe military traffic on all the roads. He could, like an observation plane, but invisibly, relay the exact details of each enemy action.

In a split second he had realized that the inhabitants of this building had to have sought shelter from the bombing, and that therefore no one would hear him land. Perhaps he could last up there for the whole battle, or at least for enough time to serve as intended. He pulled the toggles as if to collapse the chute, so as to be sure he wouldn't glide beyond the roof. The capture of such an observation post would be a triumph, but as with all things potentially triumphant, there was no way to be sure which way it would go, if his path would slam him against the side of the building or land him neatly on its roof. There was not enough wind in the game any longer to take him beyond. All he could do was wait, and he didn't have to wait long.

Until the very impact he could not tell which it was going to be, the roof, or the wall. Had it been the wall he would be out of the battle. Had it been the roof, the battle would perhaps be his. It was neither, but rather where the border of the one met the border of the other. Flying at great speed toward the edge of the parapet, he put out his arms to seize it so that upon impact he would not fall straight down the side of the building.

His momentum and the weight he carried pushed him hard into the masonry. Before he felt anything he heard a sound like that of breaking reeds as his ribs on the right side snapped like bread sticks. All the air was knocked out of him, and as he hung on to the edge of the parapet he realized he couldn't breathe. He thought he would never breathe again.

In shock and pain, against his own weight and that of a hundred pounds of equipment, with a poor hold, a parachute that dangled toward the ground in a long trail behind him, and no air, no breath, he tried to pull himself up and over. He couldn't. The more he pulled, the greater the agony. He dared not try again without lightening himself. To get out of his pack, hanging first with one arm crooked over the parapet, and then the other, was so painful that somehow the pain itself created the strength he needed to do it.

The pack dropped. He was lighter but weakened from having shed it. He thought about what was at stake and what he had to do. If he fell back he would probably die, and so would a great many others who, were he to get to the roof, might otherwise live. But he might die anyway, and he was in such pain that falling back would be a relief. Still, because the roof was right there, only inches away, he would concentrate all his strength on the one chance of lifting himself over the parapet.

He had never known how to do such a thing. As an athlete, he had never been able to pour all he had into whatever action he had tried to make the object of his will. This time, however, he had to know, and it came to him at the last.

He had to override his natural limitations, extend his initial burst of motion, and stay in the battle. He could not even think of falling back. He pulled up in the first surge, rising until his solar plexus was resting on the flat of the parapet, and here, where all logic said he had to fall back, he pushed further, his face impossibly contorted, with no air remaining, and got to the point where he could lean forward and throw all the weight that he could over and onto the roof. In this pivoting, his broken ribs were crushed further and moved to positions most unnatural. He landed with a clatter that was the strangest sound he had ever heard, and then, not having breathed in a while and frightened that he was going to die, he blacked out. At that moment nothing was left to him, neither judgment, nor movement, nor plan, nor pain, nor even a ray of light.

He awoke not knowing where he was. First, he understood that he was lying on his back. Then he understood that straps and buckles were pressed between the hard surface and his flesh. And then he remembered where he was and why, and what had happened. Still, he felt that if he were pulled again into the irresistible traction of sleep he would wake differently, somewhere else, perhaps in a hospital, or at home, so he closed his eyes and slept, but only for a moment before he was awakened by what seemed to be a war raging in the midsection of his body.

Was it he who was breathing? At times it was less breathing than flailing. Some apparatus within him that he could hardly feel had taken over and was moving his chest independently in quick shallow breaths that brought blood upwelling from his mouth as thinly as soap bubbles. His right side felt as if swords had been run through it. He moved his right arm below the elbow, and slowly ran his fingers over his rib cage. His tunic was wet with blood, and one of the ribs was protruding half an inch from his body. He could feel, through blood-soaked khaki, that the rib had splintered.

He regretted deeply the many times he had broken wishbones and held the shattered ends in his hands. The poor chickens, he thought, but at least they were dead. He felt genuine remorse about having eaten chickens and other animals without thought of their sacredness to God, who created them, and underneath this thought he thought that he was thinking this probably because he was going to die, and that when one thinks one is about to die, thoughts come of such delicacy that they can be offered only to God, and that though to those left behind they may seem disconnected, illusory, and unsupportable, they are the thoughts that, despite their weakness and unsupportability, may be the keys to heaven.

Each time he had been in such a state, he had, of course, not died: when he was thrown, by the explosion of an artillery shell, through a closed glass door, and, arteries severed, had nearly exsanguinated; and when in Norway he had been shot in the shoulder and left to die on a snowbank that had turned red with his blood. He was embarrassed to think that he might die, in case that he might not, and nervous that were his life to end, so would his mission. But perhaps he might do something before he died, if he could pull himself up, if he could still see, if he could speak, if he could gather his wits, and if he could last into the morning. Though he was in too much pain to think clearly, he tried to take stock.

He wanted to proceed in a military way, to make a plan that he might yet execute by holding through, but found that even before he could begin he was interrupted by contemplation. He was surprised that he felt a profound sense of relief in the knowledge, or the presumption, that he was going to die. He had one more job left, in this battle, on this high platform, and upon this he would concentrate, and if he were able to do the job at all he would be doing it heroically. Certainly that was a lot better than half a century of failure, doubt, and declining health in the shadow of Raphael and Dürer, if only because, modest by nature, English painters are as unassuming as English light. Nor did he want to make a spectacle of himself to mine attention from eccentricity as a trick for selling paintings.

He spit out some blood, and said in garbled words that no one would ever have understood, "Get on with it, then."

HIS POSITION COULD BE IDEAL. Unobserved upon the roof of the highest building on the ridge, he would be able to see a distant horizon on the water, almost everything in the town, and west to the Apennines. Were the other observers killed or captured, he could fill in for them. He could direct fire to all areas, find the German guns, shatter them with salvos from the sea, discover the tank emplacements facing the river, and strike them, too. To win a battle with such perfectly controlled strokes would be worth dying.

Though not a spot of red was to be seen, dawn was obvious in the lesser sparkling of the stars and the change above from black to almost royal blue. In attempting to look at his watch to see the time and calculate the hours ahead, he discovered that moving his arm to where he would have a good view of the illuminated dial was something his broken ribs found too painful to allow. He would have to ration all movement. Only the essential could justify the seeming electrification of his already taxing pain and its elevation into heights that, as he dropped away from them, were the only things that afforded him moments of relief.

He was still strapped into his parachute harness and lying on his rifle, but so great was the pain in his chest that he hadn't noticed. It would be better if he could get out of the tight harness and roll off the rifle. Not only would he be more comfortable, he would have a weapon. With immense effort he was able to unbuckle the buckles, but until he could get off his back he would have to stay in the harness. He lifted his knees. It hurt, but he could do it. By raising his thighs and pushing, he could move alligatorlike a few inches at a time in any direction. Now he was off the rifle and with it he could defend or even, at some inconceivable later stage, attack. The scope was intact, a bullet was in the chamber, the rifle was beside him. And nothing can cheer a soldier like a loaded rifle easily at hand.

He could get to the pistol, too, posted on his thigh, with its ammunition. He was very thirsty, and he managed to bring his belt canteen to his mouth and lighten it by half, thinking that water, most of which was in the pack, was bound to be a problem, but that with his loss of blood he had to drink. There were two days' rations in pouches and pockets, a first-aid kit, maps and compass, a mirror, and a telescope. Everything else was in the pack or had been strapped on to it: the rest of the food and water, magazines of ammunition, the submachine gun, and, most importantly, the radio. Though he could signal with the mirror, not only might the imprecision of his wrist, especially now, bend the light to alert the Germans, but to signal a group of coordinates in Morse would take forever, and anyway the ships were over the horizon.

The radio was essential. Assuming that he could stay alive and raise himself to look over the wall, a number of possibilities immediately occurred to him, though even if he did manage to retrieve the radio, after its fall of several stories it might no longer work. His first task was to determine if he could move, and if he could keep himself alive. He would have to wait for the light. He put his fingers on the protruding rib to see if the blood still flowed. It had stopped and was thickening as it dried. Falling in and out of sleep, he could not tell fact from dream. But underlying even this was an alertness to the approach of the enemy.

THE SUN STRUCK the eastern parapet and infused its whitewashed rim with an almost electric glow. As the section nearest him turned rose-colored the light descended until it struck him, too, warming as it moved from color to clarity. Before the light, German reveilles had echoed through the town. They sounded, at a mournful distance, like gramophone music, and this had transported him momentarily to London. He believed that the greatness of a city is a condition of mood, its first prerequisite that one is able to lose one-self in a seemingly infinite vastness that protects it from the flow of time. He believed that time dashes off a great city like rain from a glass dome.

The last time he was in London, in the spring, the light stood still, the mist that rose from the Thames seemed animate, and even the most profane music, wretchedly reproduced on a Victrola, was able to join past and pres-ent with unwitting fidelity. In London there were so many garden gates and so many girls standing behind or passing through them that the one you picked might stay with you forever, quite content to be lost with you in a row of houses in a mews hidden behind a little-known square. You could walk in the evening with someone you loved, and no one would recognize you and no one would care, which is, perhaps, one definition of peace.

As soon as the sun was high enough to be out of the eyes of the allied gun-ners they laid their fire on German posts newly established in the hours of darkness, and the sound of explosions clipped the wings of his dream. Like a geographer with deep knowledge of the complex relation of simple things, he knew that even though the ground beside him was covered in blood, he had bled no further, for he was not light-headed, and the chill he felt was only that of the October morning. His clothes were stiff with the blood that had fastened him where he lay, but with a shift and a shudder he broke loose.

He breathed with a wheeze and a soft clacking noise, and each breath reminded him that a piece of sharp bone still protruded from his side. This told him, like the hands of a strange clock in a strange dream, that if he had to go more than a few days without attention they would be his last. But if he helped to win the battle and the battle were won quickly, he might live.

He surveyed the roof. At the northern end, toward which his feet pointed, was a square water tank fashioned of concrete and terra-cotta block and elevated on a steel frame. Extending from it for watering plants in pots now plantless was a ragged hose with a brass nozzle. A small puddle from an imperfect seam told him that the tank still held water. If he could get to the hose, thirst would be no problem. A door at the south end, behind his head, led into a stairway, and as it was firmly closed he guessed that it was latched from the inside. Boards and terra-cotta block from the supply out of which the water tank and perhaps even the building itself had been constructed lay in the lee of the eastern parapet, and from the flat of the whitewashed roof projected four lanterned skylights, each about a foot and a half high with open louvered sides, in a square pattern that suggested they were ventilation caps for four lines of flats, or perhaps the skylights of interior bathrooms on the top floor.

Nothing else was on the roof except him. Its emptiness was promising, in that it seemed that it was little visited and months might go by before the door opened. No one came to feed doves or tend plants. There were no sun chairs, no athletic equipment, no toys, no bench, no stand for a telescope, no place where someone came to smoke and left bits of his cigarettes. In a battle, especially, with shells and bullets whistling through the air, it was not likely that anyone would come up to get a better view, or that anyone even remained in a building so prominently exposed, though the enemy, too, sought high points from which to observe, and this was the highest.

BEFORE HE COULD GET STARTED or collect his thoughts he heard tanks moving toward him from south on the road. That is, he felt them, for the pitch of their engines was so low that they were apprehended first in his lungs, which shook, and only then in his ears. In fact, he might have sensed them first in his hands had his fingertips been resting on the timpani of the roof. It would be advantageous for the defenders to move a platoon or two of tanks to the sea side of the ridge just beyond the top, where they could add their voices to the other German artillery, shelter spotters, and wait for the inevitable assault on the ridge itself, except that in what they might think to be a sheltered position they would be vulnerable to the naval guns over the horizon if he could spot for them.

In planning the mission it had been assumed that the Germans, understanding the potential of naval gunfire, would do all in their power to keep their formations in flux, put up heavy flack to bring down observation planes, and comb the hills for spotters. But brush-clad hills are hard to comb, especially if they are covered with sharp thorns. The roof was another thing. If the battle turned, they might very well come onto this roof, which meant that for him the sound of trucks would be more ominous and arresting than the sound of tanks.

Once the tanks had passed and gone a little farther north he heard them idling before they pulled off the road and dug in, and, after a few moments, the air was filled with shouts, commands, the changing of gears, gunning of motors, and clinking of treads. Then, one by one, the tanks turned off their engines. He wanted to see them before their crewmen finished positioning and would take stock of what was around them. He would have to peek over the parapet, and even had his head been no bigger than a woodpecker's its appearance above the perfectly regular line could be seen from a great distance.

He began to get up in the normal way. Fit young soldiers hardly think of the byzantine conspiracy of muscle, tendon, and bone required for moving the live weight of a body in defiance of gravity. The muscles of the abdomen and the back are linked to an interdependent frame that, if partially shattered, will not move without considerable protest. The pain that came from the first lifting of his head and the partial twist of his shoulders—merely to raise himself as he had done tens of thousands of times without a thought—pushed him back as if it were gunfire. Though it was sharp, its remnants were dull and pleasantly hot, as if to announce to him what he had not realized before, that he had a fever, the second stroke of the peculiar clock that had been set to ticking when his body struck the wall.

He had to teach himself how to rise, but first he had to determine the appropriate moves. He knew that he had to roll almost into a facedown position, and that to do this he would have to go left. He understood that, to go left, he had to move his arm out of the way. But that, too, was anything but simple. The pain was bearable when he moved the lower arm, using the elbow as a stiff pivot, but unbearable when he stretched the upper arm into an angle forty-five degrees from his shoulder. Breathing hard, he lifted his right arm over the protruding rib and let it hang limply across his chest. Next came a roll, using the arms as a weight that would help to pull him over. There was no way to do it other than to strain the torso, and for that he paid dearly but found himself on his left side.

With the feeling that his right rib cage was like the ice breaking up on a river, the force of moving water shattering it repeatedly, he pulled his right leg up and rose first to one knee, then the other, and hobbled to the wall. But this was the west wall, and the tanks were to the north, so he stood, using as a rail the very wall that had wounded him. As soon as he was up, he shed the parachute harness, though not without a cost in pain as he crossed first one arm and then another, dropping his shoulders alternately and stepping out of it like a girl shedding her slip. He walked slowly to the north end of the roof. There, looking out from beneath the water tank, he counted twenty-three tanks arrayed, just as he had imagined, along the saddle of the ridge.

When he turned to go back to the spot where he had fallen, he saw a blood trail. Though he had hardly begun his task, the hands of the clock had moved forward.

He returned to where he had been lying, not because of any preference for the spot itself but because it was where his parachute hung dangerously over the side. When, by moonlight, he had drifted in, the night shutters had been closed. After the moon had sunk into the sea there were hours of darkness when no one who might have remained in the building, and no one nearby, could have seen the parachute. Even now, with the east light flooding against one side of the house and the parachute roughly the same color as the sunbleached walls, it would for a time be invisible in the shadows.

As soon as it was observed, he could count himself captured or dead. And yet, not having pulled it up, he had dropped to his knees and stretched out. Though it would be hard to rise, and with the increasing light he was ever more likely to be discovered, he lay down and slept. If the pack failed to ride up in the sack formed by the chute, he would have to fabricate some sort of hook, and fish for the pack straps, something that in his condition might take all day. He hadn't the strength for two pulls. If he brought the parachute up first he had no guarantee that it would bring the pack, but if he went first for the pack the parachute would come with it.

Loss of blood and the heat of the morning allowed him to sleep through the artillery exchanges that came with first light. As he slept, imprecisely directed shells flew overhead as they came in from beyond the horizon. The naval guns were restrained for fear that their projectiles would hit west of the river among the allied positions, so most of the shells struck nothing and to no avail, and many fell into the sea, raising huge plumes of white foam. The Germans would think that no spotters were in place.

He didn't know that the tanks had held their fire or that the barrage had started at all, until he was jarred awake by the concussions of the bombardment. As soon as he saw that the sun was disconcertingly high he realized that he would be fishing for his radio in full light and full view, and that every second the parachute was draped over the side of the house he was at risk of discovery.

A hook, he thought, from what can I make a hook? He had no wire, nothing to bend, nothing already properly shaped. Then he thought of crossing his bayonet and cleaning rod in an x with long legs and short arms, affixing the parachute cord to one of the short arms, and using that, but the pack weighed more than seventy pounds and he had little confidence that the x would not collapse. A hook was such a simple thing that he had never given it a thought, but now he had to have one, or many men would die.

In the hot sun, high on his hill overlooking the sea, and under a vacantly blue sky, it was as if the cloth shutter of a camera were released to glide across his mind and memory. Bright light came in without obstruction, and then was obscured. Something made him close his eyes. He went from the open rooftop that shook with the explosion of shells, to an uncommonly high-ceilinged room where his tutor had always received him politely before an inadequate fire.

He felt the chill of the room and saw the darkness above. The tutor used to sit close to the fire, next to a small table upon which, without fail, was a book or a manuscript in an obscure language and about a neglected subject. And yet the tutor would give it his full and remarkable attention in the dark autumn afternoon, in the "new" building at Magdalen College, Oxford, while a protected herd of reindeer moved apprehensively through the mist and among the oaks. This room was filled with paintings that in the gloom seemed black.

He remembered as vividly as if time had hooked back on itself how his tutor had said that when facing what seem to be intractable problems the mind quickly comes up with answers that, as if out of modesty, it veils because they are insufficient or incomplete. He was told to look to the failed answers to find in them a route to success. Return to what you have done, and there, very often, you will find what to do hiding among the ruins. He had always thought this technique too Tibetan for an Englishman, and making a hook was a lot more prosaic than, for example, teasing out a subtlety or two of Fra Angelico's use of light, or understanding at the deepest level how Raphael, propelled by mystic force, used the language of color to embrace the love of God. This was just a hook, after all, a simple hook.

He went back to the idea of the crossed rod and bayonet. In his imagination he crossed them again, and then, just as the tutor had said, he knew what to do. Were he to attach a line to the rifle sling where it curved just past its point of connection to the underbarrel, the six inches of muzzle would be the point of the hook, and the point of attachment would serve as a fulcrum for the countering force of the rest of the rifle's weight. If the straps of the pack were to settle within two inches of the line, the mechanical advantage would enable eight pounds—the weight of the rifle centered twenty inches along its length—to lift one hundred sixty pounds. Without any rigidity at all in the attachment of such a hook, it would hold the weight of a man, and affixing parachute cord to the sling, if done with care, would not take more than a minute.

He lifted the rifle over him from the right side to the left and began the ritual of getting up. Moving his arms was sufficient to take his breath away, but he could not turn onto his left side. His shoulders were pinned to the roof as if a wrestler had been sitting on them. He thought to rest and try again.

After the pain had flared and settled, he moved in carefully deliberated stages in which he nonetheless invested every bit of force he could bring to bear. First the right arm, up, bent stiffly at the elbow. He could do that. Then the left, stretched once again at an angle forty-five degrees from the vertical line of his body. Then the lunge to the left that would turn him onto his side. Nothing. In response to the pain, he was paralyzed.

But he was still alive, and in an inimitable position for the observation with which he had been tasked, and he had devised a method for retrieving his essential equipment. He had already discovered tanks on the saddle of the ridge, and, given an hour's work of observation and reporting, he could direct fire from the ships to destroy or disperse enemy artillery, antiaircraft guns, tanks, and concentrations of infantry. Eventually, the town would fall. This had to be the logic of events, the closing of the ring, but every hour of delay would bring death and broken hearts.

He tried once again so hard that he was thrown back unconscious, awakening soon thereafter, breathing as if he had just run up a hill, his heart racing and weak. Though no physiological reason for this seemed clear, he felt that if he moved, or even if he remained without treatment for a day or two, something that was happening inside him that he could neither see nor understand would kill him. Still, he was not regretful that he hadn't landed in the ravine, for this high and excellent spot held the promise of victory.

"ALL RIGHT," he said to himself out loud, in a voice that, had he heard it other than in his present state, he would hardly have recognized, because it croaked like a frog. "I have the hook, I have the position, and I'm unobserved. How am I going to move?" After a few seconds, he knew that he had known the answer before he had voiced the question. "This is how I'm going to move."

The sun had already passed its zenith. Breathing like a sick man, he swung his right arm toward his thigh, raised his right leg to bring it closer, and let out a little cry as the shattered rib cage compressed. To reach his thigh pocket, it was unavoidable.

He unbuttoned the flap and pulled out the first-aid kit. Unfolding it was difficult, but he managed nonetheless, and pulled out the morphine. Three injectors lay on the whitewashed roof. As much as he wanted it not to be so, they were to be his clock of action and contentment. They would free him from pain and allow him to move, but he had only three of them, and after relying on these he would be in more trouble than he could possibly imagine.

He had been taught that what appears to be the easy way is often the hard way. The ease of drink led to difficult suffering. The softness of luxury brought one to one's knees. Surrender to what was most beguiling was surrender to what was most cruel. The consistency of the effect was well known, and could turn people of individual and idiosyncratic will into mere mechanisms that had lost their souls.

It was not easy for him to discard the needle cap and plunge the syringe into his thigh, and he did so with disgust. But he did so with urgency, for to retrieve the radio he was now willing to sacrifice his life, and had an injection of strychnine allowed him an hour of unencumbered action he would have injected it.

Even as the needle penetrated into his thigh and he watched the morphine disappear with the steady advance of the piston under his thumb, he felt a sense of immortality surging through him. He had always imagined that morphine was slightly buff-colored, but it was clear. It had just enough of whatever was in it for the light to pick up its viscosity. No matter, now he was immortal, his body a hindrance that he had left behind. Never completed calculations of orbits and angles, and music riding on backlit plumes of light and spray, filled the world.

From beyond subdued ecstasy that seemed to have neither beginning nor end, his lifetime of discipline reached him, and he thought, I don't want this lovely, gravityless thing that I am entangled in, that's like kissing a beautiful girl when you're twenty and so is she, but I don't want it.

He forced his eyes to roll right and roll left. A blinding sun moved in nauseating arcs as he looked at the wall, the rifle, and the roof. A drop of sweat caught in the golden glare sparkled like the heart of the universe. He could have accepted this freedom and pleasure, and died. He would have died prepared for death, content to go, with a longing to pass completely out of gravity, to lighten entirely. In the vestibule of death where he lay he was lightened only in part, and yet he floated like the sun upon the sea.

Rolling over and standing up, he could hardly feel what was happening inside him—not because there was no pain, but because pain had become a simple thing from which it was easy to feel remote. He stood outside himself, and yet he stood, aware that the greater his exertions the faster he would metabolize the morphine.

Looking over the parapet he saw that his pack had not landed within the folds of the chute but lay next to them almost upright in the brush. A cooling breeze came from below. The day was extraordinarily blue even for Italy, and the evening would be one of those evenings of golden autumn, when all the stonework took on the color of honey. He wanted to be alive at evening.

He was clearheaded enough to calculate that he could reduce his effort by half were he to cut the lines from the harness, which lay at his feet, attach the rifle, and let it fall, pulling the parachute up toward him as the line played through his hands. This he did, and when the rifle went flat in the brush, he pulled in the billowing panels of the parachute and its tangle of cord, and stuffed them between himself and the parapet, for a cushion.

Undoubtedly he could be seen from the valley, but there the enemy would have reason to look only west. The tanks on the ridge were out of sight, and would not see him. Nonetheless, he moved as fast as he could, pulling the rifle until it rose to a forty-five degree angle and pivoted on its butt plate.

With a few minor maneuvers, he moved this heavy marionette until it closed on the pack. Then he let it settle. The muzzle projected into the air and the rifle lay trigger guard up, as if a soldier had taken a break during a march and arrayed his things just so. After a moment of rest, it was easy to lift the rifle into action again, lower it, and in three or four swings hook the pack straps with the muzzle.

Immediately he began to haul the lines. They went smoothly over the parachute silk at the top of the parapet, but still there was friction. The distress of hauling eighty pounds surpassed even the magic of morphine. He could feel the action of his body surrendering to destruction—like beams shearing, roofs collapsing, or cables snapping.

The pack came even with the top of the wall. He pulled it over and fell back to where he had been, still breathing the ethereal breath of morphine, there to lie until the next things he saw were stars in air that had grown cold.

THE DRUG HAD LARGELY WORN OFF, making him queasy and his pain more treacherous. The morphine side of the equation, in which he had floated in awe, was an illusion with a price. As the night breeze came from the west, carrying with it the smell of burning brush in aromatic clouds of smoke that enveloped the city on account of fields that had been set on fire by stray munitions and the phosphorous of battle, he took from within his pack a canteen of water, some cheese, crackers, and a bar of chocolate. After eating a day's rations all at once, he felt much better. He pulled out the submachine gun, and removed the radio from its wrapping of blankets and a sweater. Once it was switched on, it had only one button to press and release. The monitoring station was in the trees across the river, not even two miles away. He had found his route back to the world, and he prayed that it would still be working.

"Furious to Glorious," he said. "This is Furious, calling Glorious. Come in Glorious."

Though the radio itself seemed to be in order, at first there was nothing. Perhaps they had stopped listening. He had been out of contact for a long time, although he was unable to remember exactly how long. He hated not being able to connect.

"Glorious, this is Furious calling. Glorious, come in, please."

Clicking to receive, he listened to a sea of static, until over the static a voice was carried. "Furious, we haven't heard from you in how long?" They were testing him.

He didn't know exactly, so he said, "Since you made me a munition."

"What's the first password?"

"Just a minute." He himself had made up the passwords, but they did not come to him immediately.

"Password," they said again.

And then he remembered: "I'm the man who broke the bank in Basutoland."

"Isle of Skye," was the response, so each knew that the other was real. "Have you had tea?"

"Yes. And I can tell you next time about the birthday parties of everyone in the company, in every platoon." This meant that he was so situated that he could call in strikes against targets in any cell on the map, each one of which was marked by a date, from nineteen hundred to the present, picked at random to fill the two-thousand-cell grid.

"When?"

"When the trucks come with the new barrels." This meant at next light.

"Very good, Furious. Stay well. Glorious out."

"Furious out."

Alone, as soon as the static disappeared from the earpiece, he felt a surge of contentment. He moved his watch so close to his face that it seemed like a wall. It was two in the morning: he had four hours to go before he could acquire a target. He would make a list, call it in, and fine-tune each salvo. The four night hours would be morphineless, as he would need the morphine for getting up and to stay standing.

It was cold, but wrapped in blankets he was fairly warm. He tried to sleep by following the streamerlike remnants of the morphine into the dark, but he couldn't, because even though he was injured he was well rested and alert. This led him to believe that perhaps he would heal. At least when he was still he could entertain such a thought. Any movement brought so much pain that he was forced to reassess. He may have been bleeding internally, with a dangerous infection in a dangerous place. The allies would have to take the city within a day or two, he thought, or, like so many Englishmen before him, he would be buried in Italy.

Stars pulsed and meteors flared now and then across the sky. The scent of fields afire carried on the air, and echoing off the west parapet, as if in a Brighton seashell, came the sound of waves. No matter what would happen to him, to those he knew, to England, or to the cause for which he fought, the stars would remain untouchable and active, the colors of light constant, the laws of nature immutable. Had the universe been still, he would have had no comfort, but the universe moved as if it were alive. The sun sailed perpetually and the earth forged ahead through space in a never ceasing silken glide. Comets tore through the settled systems in surprise, intruders and dissenters whose broader orbits made those of the planets seem tame. The asteroids jingled like ice, and far away the gorgeous mass of galaxies and distant stars blazed in a rhythm that had begun at the beginning of time.

He was content on his rooftop in the midst of battle while the stars burned like phosphorous flares. One death would not shake this eternity of motion. And if he could hang on until morning and force himself to rise, he would bring upon the enemy a fire of such magnitude, precision, and vigor that the Germans, who had asked for Götterdämmerung, would get it.

And then as if by magic his concentration upon distant light was cut short by a soft, muted shine when an electric light was switched on beneath the lanterned skylight closest to him. Probably no more than thirty or forty watts, it glowed from within, flickering occasionally with the uneven current, the only light to shine from within the building.

Just underneath him, someone had returned to his flat during a lull in the shelling, and turned on a light. The soldier on the roof found its glow enormously touching, so weak was it, so tea-colored, blooming unexpectedly in the dark, and hidden from everyone except him. He wanted to imagine who it was: a civilian, or perhaps even a soldier quartered there, but a soldier who had put down his weapon and taken off his heavy belts and ammunition. In other times, he would have let his imagination complete the scene, but suspecting that he might not live another day, he refused to imagine anything. What he had at the moment seemed more than enough, even overwhelming.

He had the lantern, glowing, and beyond it, over the parapet and out of sight, encampments with fires flickering dangerously despite the tendency of artillery to home in on light. He wanted to speak to whoever was within. The language spoken was not important; whether it was a man or a woman was unimportant. There, close to him, was someone yet living, perhaps the last imperceptible touch he would have with another life. He was already hovering above this person, unseen, like an angel.

Then the water came on. Through the vents in the lantern came its sparkling but languid sound, rising in the pipes, issuing forth, floating in air, tangling down, splashing at the foot, and running away with almost the sound of bells. The slight hiss of falling water was a cousin to the sea, the stars, and the static on the radio. Without any sense whatsoever, it all made sense, as if it had been orchestrated, but he wondered if these sounds would have seemed so carefully arranged and perfectly in harmony if he had been on a bus in Camden Town, worrying about small things. Suddenly, everything was benevolent.

Billows of steam began to float from the vents, coming quickly into the sharp night air. Soon they smelled sweet, and the water was held, and then dropped, in quantities that were remarkable. How had the water been suspended but in a woman's thick hair, in long coils carefully lifted from the nape of her neck to catch the flow?

He had no idea, of course, who she was. Nor did she know that he was above, and she probably never would. He managed with great difficulty to move off his blood-soaked square of the roof and travel, before too long, to a point close enough to the lantern to hear every drop of water, to see the steam on the opaque plate of glass, to inhale the sweet moist air, and to touch his fingertips against the vents as if in doing this he were embracing a woman that he would love for the rest of his life.

WHEN THE INHABITANTS of even the busiest cities are rising, the soldier about to do battle has long been up. In the absence of hot water or heat, he pulls as much life and warmth into his body as he can by moving, if he can. And he is able to feel action before its impact, as if the coming battle were a train speeding toward him in a tunnel, pushing a breeze miles ahead of its arrival.

As dawn struck the German encampments east of the river, soldiers moved about and circled the fires. Their bodies bent and dipped as they folded blankets. They stepped into the sun, and looked around. They shouldered their weapons. Messengers drove from one strongpoint to another, on motorcycles or in trucks. Officers stared through binoculars at the clearly illuminated allied lines.

The river was hidden beneath a low wall of mist that the sun soon made airborne and broke into shards through which shone the tops of the Apennines in pale reds and gold. Smoke that had risen in dark columns from a hundred fires was bleached into transparency by the sun, and even the waves rolling in from the open Adriatic seemed pushed down by flat trajectories of light fired from the semifinished crags of the Balkans.

When the sun was high enough the allied gunners began their volleys. These, for want of the kind of information he could give them—other spotters were in other places, but none had his comprehensive view—were poorly directed. Two observation planes had been shot down the day before he was parachuted in. Though many guns had exacted a toll, they needed, above all, guidance.

For the second time on the roof he awoke in heat and glare, and when he heard the shelling pick up he stirred, eager to get about his work now that he could. He was sick, and wanted to stay still. The slightest movement was painful and nauseating. Though his fever had partially abated, even in the absence of the morphine he was not quite himself. He knew that it was best not to move, that he had to let things settle, and the prospect of reopening his wounds by strain contradicted every natural impulse.

But upon going into battle—at the instant he volunteered, in the moment he accepted his orders, when the plane had left the ground, and when he had stepped from it into explosions and flak—he had already written himself off in the quiet way that allows soldiers to do their duty even unto extinction. The more he presumed he would not last, the better he was able to take satisfaction from doing what was required. The delight of honor unknown to anyone but himself would have to substitute for a life that no longer lay ahead.

Injecting morphine, raising himself, finally standing, and taking his telescope, radio, and maps to the parapet was for him as meaningful as the coronation of a king, for like a king who has taken a solemn oath, he had abandoned his private self.

After bulking up the parachute silk again to soften his contact with the parapet, he began to observe. So many targets were gathered before him that he chose what looked like the most influential ten, and called them in with great care. In a perfect world he would have called in many more and let the command choose what to hit and in what order, but, then again, in a perfect world he would still be in All Souls Library. As imperfection ruled, he did what he could: three concentrations of tanks, waiting to sheer off the first allied columns to penetrate in depth; four hidden strongpoints filled with infantry; an ammunition dump; a group of a dozen howitzers and 88s; and the tanks on the ridge. He would start with these, wait for redeployments, attend to them, and then, assuming that he still could, call in targets during the crossing and the battle.

First, he brought in a target with his telescope, in which what he saw was compressed, clear, and laden with intense color. When he had determined that the target deserved bombardment, he looked for landmarks, and then, after difficult deliberation, assigned it to a cell on the map, to which he added a red-penciled number. The cell *20 Dec. 04*, for example, became number one. He then determined where in the box the center of the target rested, and marked it with a red dot. Each cell was divided further into four quadrants and a bull's-eye where they met.

In an hour, he had marked his targets and called them in, reading clearly as fast as he could, so as to stay on air for as little time as possible. Anyone hearing a list of any sort broadcast prior to a battle would know it was a spotter no matter how ingeniously the transmission was embedded in ordinary radio traffic. The weak signal did not come from German radios, and yet it came from within the German lines. They would home in on it if they could.

The first call, delivered crisply despite the morphine, was surprisingly short: "One: twenty December, nineteen four. Q two, toward center. Two: four February, nineteen thirty-six. Q four, corner. Three: eighteen April, nineteen twenty-one. Q two, center. Four: thirty June, nineteen ten. Q one, top . . ." until he signed off, "Furious, out."

Monitoring this, if they had, the enemy would not rush to move every unit and reform every concentration. Had they been so willing, it would have been easy to scramble them. They would sit unknowing and uneasy, until the barrage came through, and even then they would do nothing but seek shelter. Only when the pattern of incoming fire appeared to tighten would they scatter. He had seen it before. He had caused it.

Preparation for firing would take at least half an hour and perhaps much more. His signal had to be translated into map coordinates for the gunners, they had to ready and aim, and the firing had to be timed for the assault. It might begin as soon as technically possible, or not until nightfall.

The morphine had begun its work but with less effect than the first dose. Semifloating, nauseated, he made his way back to his resting place, hoping the nausea would not increase. For someone to whom each breath seemed an agony, the prospect of prolonged retching was a serious threat. He imagined that it might kill him with much pain and no glory, and after dropping to his knees he lay once again where he had lain.

In the morning the guns went silent. The heat and quiet, the morphine, and the wind-carried sound of the waves put him in another world. He saw his life as if in stained glass, the streaming light through each section of glass providing an ignition of color. Though not every scene came to him it was as if every moment had a delegate in one vivid image or another. The panels were silver and gold, as blue and purple as grape, as warm as rose, as white and clean as a chalk cliff, or azure, or emerald, or gray, and they deepened with every stroke of his heart. He rode through black air above the earth in immense machines that Milton might have imagined, and flew from them to descend, under benevolent stars, to a world consumed in war.

Morphine and fever pulled him toward the bounds of life. Content to have drifted off without ever again knowing the sober feel of gravity, he was brought back by a great blast of naval gunfire rolling unobstructed over the sea. Then came the secondary thunder of high-explosive shell finding its mark after sailing many miles and plowing deep before it burst. Everything shook in half a dozen different kinds of bass vibration. His fingertips jumped. His lungs felt like drums. His eardrums popped in and out with the concussions as if he were rapidly changing altitudes.

At the parapet it was difficult to peer into the blast areas, not because of ballistic debris, which did not reach him, but because of the shock waves, which did, and which were as unnerving as sea flowing over the deck of a ship. His face was distorted by these blast waves as if by g-forces, and when he tried to direct fire more precisely he found it difficult to move the telescope, change position, or read the map.

Like a pilot who struggles against gravity and disorientation, he struggled against the detonations to make his best determination of where they were and how far off target. Then he dropped below the sheltering parapet and called in corrections. When they were made and his reports of damage given, he told Glorious that he would try again, but that he wasn't sure how long he could last. "Wounded," he said.

The radioman to whom he was speaking replied, "Well done. Keep at it as long as you can."

LYING HALF PROPPED UP against the wall, without the strength to crawl back to his place, he heard a vehicle stop on the road. Looking at the door to the stairs, he realized that even if it meant aggravating his wound until it would kill him, he had to get across the roof, climb the ladder to the water tank, and drop in. Although he only assumed it, soldiers had begun to search the house.

Remembering that no incoming fire had hit near, he lifted himself, looked over the north parapet, and saw that the tanks were moving to the top of the hill. The allied assault had begun, and they were driving to their firing positions.

"Glorious," he said through the radio, his energy gone. "This is Furious."

"Go ahead, Furious."

"What about number nine? You haven't hit number nine. It's moved west two hundred yards."

"Sorry, Furious. Busy. Will do, I'm sure. Over."

"That's all," said the soldier on the roof.

"Thank you, Furious. Glorious out."

To cross the roof, he had to crawl. Holding the submachine gun by its web strap, he dragged it as he went. His passage was loud, and the gun pulled up whitewash, leaving a trail that would give him away. With neither the strength nor the time to deal with it, he abandoned it where it lay.

War was like a series of windows, each narrower than the one preceding it, until in the end nothing was left of light or choice. How wide the world had been in the last days of civilian life before he had had any notion of enlisting. As soon as military service became a possibility, the passage began to narrow, and with each step it grew tighter and tighter. A hundred choices and a hundred chances later, he was crawling across a whitewashed roof as fast as he could, hoping to drop himself into a water tank.

Concealing himself inside the tank, as unpromising as it may have been, was better than simply lying in plain sight and dying in a single volley of automatic-weapons fire. Still, he was moving so slowly that when they would burst onto the roof he might be right in front of them, and he regretted that he was leaving a trail of blood.

At the foot of the tank, from his position flat on the roof, the ladder looked amazingly long and narrow. The wood was solid enough, but the twenty rungs or so seemed to call for a base more than just a foot across. Nor was it secured at the top, although on either side of the rectangular opening that gave access to the interior were long iron handles that, should the ladder move from side to side, would confine it.

He used the ladder itself to help him get up enough so he could start to climb. Every movement of his arms or legs was agony. His ribs opened the wound and cut into him from within. In a few minutes he was at the top, grasping the iron rails. Each step up had been a betrayal of his body, he thought he was going to bleed to death just from the climb, and not only was his position impossible, it was at the end of a trail of blood.

The water was four feet below him, and on the interior wall was a ladder of iron rungs that led into it. In the best of times, bending through the opening and positioning oneself on the ladder would have been a feat of acrobatics, especially since it was so high in the air, but in his condition it seemed impossible. He took another step up, until his waist was level with the bottom of the opening.

Using his arms to lift himself as he twisted and entered was out of the question. As precariously as he was positioned—and he might have fallen not just onto the roof but over the side of the building—his arms hung down limply at his sides. He hoped that something would happen that would allow him not to enter in the only way he thought possible, which was to pitch himself forward.

He was not going to do that unless and until the door to the roof opened. Even then he would wait for an instant, hoping to hear English. What he heard was not English, nor indeed any language, but the sound of naval gunfire and the transit of huge shells closing in from miles away. In groups of two and three only seconds apart they began to explode against the hill, along the top of the ridge, and amid the tanks he had targeted. Though the blasts almost threw him from the ladder, which rocked and twisted, he held fast to the iron rails.

One shot against the building and it would all go down, one shot nearby and the shock might blow the water tank from its spindly perch. How in the midst of deafening explosions would he hear the door open? He wouldn't. So he decided to go back down. But after taking two steps, he saw that the door already was open. With their backs to him, weapons extended, three Germans were going through the drill of assaulting a roof. They had seen no one at the base of the ladder, and now, just a few feet from him, were about to discover his abandoned equipment. Then they would turn, and there he would be.

He climbed up. When he reached the opening, amid the explosions, he pitched himself in. Hitting his head against one of the iron rungs, he landed on the water flat on his back, which pushed him toward the wall, where he hit his head again. "Fuck," he said, before he went under. It was as if the three blows he suffered had been delivered by a sentient being. The water was freezing, black, and, at the bottom, where beams of sunlight ended a short transit from cracks above the waterline, were waving patterns of gold and green. As soon as he broke the surface and breathed he tried to mute all sound. The echoes inside were extremely loud, but the sound was contained, and in the midst of the barrage even had it not been contained it would not have been heard.

The water was cold enough to banish some of his pain, but he knew that it would encourage the bleeding. In forty-five minutes, he thought, he would be dead. Being naturally fastidious, he was horrified at the thought that if he died there the residents of the building might not know it and would drink the water for months. The window of war seemed very narrow indeed.

He was now close enough to the end to sense the all-forgiving grace in which enemies no longer exist. In the eternal quiet that lay perhaps minutes away, the noise, exertion, and passions of the moment—all hatred, ambition, and the divisions among men—would be left behind as if from a fast express rocketing from a crowded station into the open countryside. In whatever might lay ahead, the fact that he died in an elevated water tank, high on a ridge, during a battle by the sea, would be something just to note, yet another of the sadnesses of the human heart, all of which, somehow, he would know.

Growing more and more content, he felt himself—and all else—slipping, but he felt something new and great, a comforting presence. How was it that, bleeding and cold, with perhaps only minutes of life left, he was pain-less, calm, and enfolded in an all-embracing love?

And yet he did not want to die. Half unconsciously, he pulled himself to the iron rungs that went below the water, and tilted his head up. At the first blockage of the light as a man appeared in the hatch, the first disappearance of blue from the rectangle above, he would push himself under and hold his breath, hoping that whoever looked in would need time for his eyes to ad-just to the darkness, and would neither notice the unavoidable ripples on the surface of the water nor look for too long. He expected this position, with his head turned up and his eyes filled with a rectangle of pure blue light, to be his last.

Then the barrage stopped, and it was quiet except for a few tanks speeding off the ridge. Soon they were gone. The field artillery had ceased. Nor could he hear small-arms fire. He was light-headed and thought that perhaps he could no longer hear. He looked at his watch. He had been in the water for more than an hour, and hadn't bled enough to die. He wondered if he would have the strength to climb the ladder and get out without falling. He tasted the water, which didn't taste like blood, and began to climb.

Sometimes he would black out on the way up, but he locked his arms around the rungs, and when he came back there he would be, folded against the iron, ready to take another agonizing step. There were only four steps to the opening, and he managed them all. The air outside, heated by the sun even as the battle had tried to scramble the physics of existence, was warm, sweet, and full of October light.

Through the quiet he heard the rumble of armor once again, and looked to his left along the ridge. A column of tanks and half-tracks drove toward him. And at the top of their long flexible masts that rose ten feet in the air were Union Jacks stretched out by the wind from the sea.

Vandevere's House

A YEAR OR TWO BEFORE MELISSA LEFT, Vandevere had fallen into the rhythm of making the house better, day by day. At first it had seemed that merely buying such a house would have been sufficient, splendid as it was in itself, but little things called out. The mailbox needed relettering, relocation, and to be set in a limestone plinth. The Bar Harbor juniper had to be thickened, trimmed, and fertilized. The stones of the long drive were neither round enough nor of the proper sandy color not to match but rather to suggest the sunlit glow of the beach beyond the dunes. The list he made in regard to things like this had more than four hundred entries, in a hand so small and precise that they might have been written-in by a mouse. The house loomed enormously large.

Apart from its unassailable beauty and the fifty-six acres of carefully tended farmland, lawns, and trees that rose to a rampart of heather-covered dunes and then swept to a wide beach unsurpassed by any in the world, what provided inimitable satisfaction to the owner and excited envy in others was that for at least a mile in three directions, and without limit in the direction of the sea, it was protected. Each of the few estates around it was of high station, indivisible, sacrosanct, and serene. Each was watered by fonts of money that sprang from banks and brokerages in Manhattan in such strength as to employ armies of immigrant maids and gardeners, pay taxes, and replace roofs . . . forever. Unlike things that were fleet, the value of these houses would hold, in perpetuity, 'til work be done, 'til kingdom come.

Twenty million had been too much to pay, but then again it had not, for even if the value of the house were to decline for a year or two or a decade, something inherent in it, like a mysterious engine that patiently worked through difficult times and good times equally, would keep and build its worth in an upward spiral. Vandevere had been able to buy this. He owned it. And it was worthy of its absurd excess valuation. Whereas most properties were certain to decay, this one had the spark of life in it, and seemed, somehow, to regenerate itself and all who came to it. It was the spark of life that he had bought, and for which he had paid. Money was a thing that could never come to life, despite the many illusions invested in it. No one ever thought a nickel was alive, and though some believed otherwise, even the breathtaking mass of twenty million was dead. It had been a good trade. As the nineties rolled off their middle, saturated in optimism and deals, he had thought this was the best he had done.

He had then put fifty million away in a fund that with only conservative growth would be more than enough to provide the wherewithal to maintain the house and pay its taxes ad infinitum. And after that he still had a hundred and thirty million left to live on, though he would be melancholy for the rest of his life because the partners in the most lucrative IPO of his career had conspired with the lead investment bank to insert a clause, in minuscule writing that even he had not read and that his lawyers could not properly interpret for lack of factual knowledge about the business, which clause, by its effect and irrevocably, notwithstanding any other clause to the contrary, and according to the laws of the State of Delaware and the State of New York, screwed him out of seven hundred million.

Shocked by his own carelessness and ashamed of the contribution he had made to his lasting defeat, he wanted only to live modestly and unnoticed. No longer in the newspapers as were his former partners, no longer a source of capital or ideas, he would remain as if motionless in his very lovely garden, in the midst of freshly watered hydrangea, geranium, spruce, and peach. Just over the protective dunes, which did not protect his regret, the

Atlantic, supremely cold and navy blue, broke into white foam and salt spray that carried on the wind and sparkled in the sun.

IN 1912, they had built Vandevere's limestone Georgian to fairly modest proportions that now appeared almost glorious but nonetheless were everywhere perfectly understated. The way almost a hundred years had weathered the stone and slate said that this house had not been built by an IPO, but its newly revised detailing made it clear that an IPO could not be totally excluded.

Though you could not see them, the things you could not see were flawless. The plumbing supply lines, for example, were made of an alloy used in United States naval ships to coat areas subject to the greatest corrosion. When water ran to sinks and tubs, you could not hear it coursing within the walls even with a stethoscope, and when it drained it cascaded inaudibly down stainless-steel pipes with sides two inches thick, themselves encased within walls as heavy with plaster as the White Cliffs of Dover.

The water was hot the instant it flooded from its English nickel fittings into the light of tiny high-intensity lamps set in the marbled bathroom ceilings and walls so as to make every bath sparkle like the Aegean. Because Vandevere took his vitamins with mineral water, he placed in the travertine wall next to his sink a refrigerator specially constructed by the Sub-Zero Company to mimic a feature Vandevere had observed at the bar of a hotel in Prague. Two dozen little bottles of Badoit were chilled silently and without condensation, ready to roll into his hand one at a time.

As the bathrooms were as big as kitchens, the kitchen too was overwrought. It had not only every excellent, unnecessary, heavy-duty commercial system, but also mechanisms designed to augment each one. The cooktops and ovens had digital thermometers that read out in a continuously moving display as if they were stock prices. Things like mixers and blenders rose slowly from nowhere on silent, smooth-running elevators. Because Vandevere did not want dust to accumulate in gray drifts beneath or behind his refrigerators and Agas, at the touch of a button they all moved at once toward the middle of the vast kitchen, like circus elephants on Pentothal, to reveal white ceramic runs that could be polished with a mop and chamois before the appliances were commanded back to their stalls.

The pantry, or what his chef called the *garde-manger,* was alphabetized. Under *G,* for instance, you could find Greek malted milk balls (made with goat's milk) in a glass canister with the date of purchase in calligraphy beneath the identification entry. You could also find, among other things (such as grape leaves and ginger), guacamole, gaufrettes, galichons, gooseberries, and gayettes. The shelves were of woven stainless steel, the baseboards limestone, the floor marble, the moldings from a renowned workshop in Flanders. In temperature- and humidity-controlled air, with its own window (most of the closets, too, had their own windows), the *garde-manger* could and did hold enough food to feed Vandevere, his staff, and guests, for three years. A special room, always dark and cool, was for the storage of olive oil in two-hundred-gallon glass-lined tip-flasks with nondrip ceramic stopcocks. Although Vandevere did not drink wine, his wine cellar held ten thousand bottles carefully arranged by region, château, and vintage.

The distribution of electricity, the heating of water, and the generation of auxiliary power from a two-hundred-thousand-watt, propane-fed generator that could run independently for a year, were accomplished underground, a hundred feet from the house, in a clean, well-lighted, Teutonic bunker. Even in a winter storm when the power was out and all the neighboring estates were dark, Vandevere's house glowed with light, heat, and good order.

The interiors were so beautiful that people who saw them for the first time were stunned into silence. In some places the colors were rich and in others perfectly austere, but each room was proportioned as if by magic to make its occupants feel both fully awake and wonderfully at ease. He had had paintings from the very beginning, and now he had more. Even the lesser ones from his earlier days were cleaned and restored, and all were perfectly lit, framed, alarmed, and insured—Gainsboroughs, Monets, a big Caravaggio, and others. The formal garden that led eastward from the pool was a reproduction of the garden visible in a corner of the Caravaggio. And the fence surrounding the property—with the exception of its sensors and surveillance aids—was a reconstruction of the iron fence described in Ser Brunetto's dream of the monastery in which he imagined that God had imprisoned him forever and without explanation. Along the inside of the perimeter ran a wide gravel walk with stone curbs behind which were dense evergreens.

HE HAD HAD THE OLD POOL FILLED IN. It was neither big enough nor deep enough and was in the wrong place, having been set between house and ocean by a dentist, the previous owner, whom Vandevere called, although Vandevere was not a dentist, "the previous dentist." This man had become wealthy, in the seventies sense, by inventing a kind of implant. No pool should be made to compete with the ocean and have as its backdrop ramparts of white sand ground from rock over a span of a billion years by the fierce blue water that covers two-thirds of the earth. So Vandevere built a new one, eastward of the house, in a place where in July and August the shadow of the chimneys began to move across the pool decking, as on a sundial, from six to seven in the evening. He made the new pool 105.6 feet long, so that fifty laps were a mile, which is the distance he swam every day. The water shone blue in a foil of white marble set in classical Italian gardens, and, in honor of Melissa, the water was, at one end of the pool, forty feet deep.

In May of 1967, Vandevere, a Harvard sophomore whose academic career was soon to be interrupted by the draft and a year on the DMZ, had gone with some friends to swim in the abandoned granite quarry at Quincy. Neither courageous nor foolish enough to jump from the highest rock platform, which the locals called *Rooftop,* and take the eighty-foot plunge into a lake of aquamarine water hundreds of feet deep, he had leapt instead from fifty feet, and was floating about after the shock of collision with the water, when he saw against the sun a blaze of something purple and gold that had appeared at the highest level and flown out with no hesitation. It fell like a meteorite and landed next to Vandevere as if it were a projectile from a sixteen-inch gun. The water foamed like the cataclysmic circle of a depth charge, and then, from the crown of white and aquamarine, like a leaping dolphin, up rose a girl.

Her hair stayed blond when wet; her eyes were green; her shoulders broad. She was the kind of woman who, in a sundress, looks nine feet tall, and when she breasted the foam Vandevere was struck by how sharply her nipples showed through the violet leotard in which she was barely dressed. There in the water next to him, as fresh as rain, was his destiny, for in her, and in him, and in time, were his children. As he and this beautiful young woman, the water running off her golden hair, floated in the quarry, they were immediately attracted and ready to be drawn to each other, and it might not have seemed unnatural had they fused like lizards on a rock.

He thought at first that she was a town girl who had found her way into a leotard (the summer uniform of Radcliffe), and he youthfully determined that he would marry her despite this. He would marry her even if she did have the hyena Boston accent, even if her father owned a luncheonette, and even if she had never been to France—because no matter what she was, she was pure force and life. To have leapt so heedlessly from eighty feet, she had to have been a town girl.

"You jumped from Rooftop," he said, full of admiration.

"I did," she answered, smiling with arresting beauty. The wind rippled the blue water around her.

"You could have been killed."

"Yes, but when I saw you jump from fifty feet, I had to do it . . ." she spoke beautifully and very unlike a hyena, "because I was mad at you."

"You were mad at me?" he asked, treading water furiously.

"I was."

"Why?"

"I couldn't stand the way in Hum Two you asked Finley questions about what we were reading *in translation,* to show six hundred people that you knew Greek. And not just once, but every goddamned day. I thought you were an ass." Her eyes narrowed as if she were still angry.

After a long silence, Vandevere simply said, "I was." And they studied each other while floating.

Though he wanted to ask her right then and there if she would marry him, and right then and there she probably would have said yes, as she was to say yes soon thereafter, he held himself in check, as he often did. "Let's swim to shore," he said, and offered his hand to her. She took it. In that first touch was their marriage. And they swam together through the opalescent waters of the deep quarry, shaming any royal procession that ever was.

. . .

THE PROBLEM OF HER LEAVING was insoluble in more ways than one, some minor but intricate nonetheless. Left with a double bed, for example, he could sleep symmetrically neither on one side nor on the other. Nor could he sleep in the middle, as that would have meant moving one of the pillows to the center and doing God-knows-what-else with the other. Three pillows, an odd number, would be as out of the question as would be one. To sleep in the center of the bed, he would have to go either distressingly asymmetrical with an even number of pillows, or symmetrical with a distressing odd number. A single bed would not harmonize with the proportions of the room. Double singles (or, as the consultant he hired called them, *twins*) would simply restate the agony of asymmetry.

So every night he slept on a different side, but this, too, was offensive to symmetry in that there were seven days in a week and 365 days in a year, and even the Pope could not change that. Vandevere sometimes wanted to drown such problems in scotch, except that he did not drink, because once you opened the bottle it was no longer whole. The only thing to do was to get married again, but how could he know whether or not the woman he chose to marry was simply concealing her messiness during the seduction phase, as most women did? Women were absolutely pristine and symmetrical until, after a few months of marriage, it was as if tornadoes emerged from their purses and ripped up the ordered fabric of life.

Philosophically, Melissa had understood the argument that, as death and dissolution are unavoidable, life when it can be chosen should be the assertion or creation of an aesthetic order. Even the dissolution that followed death did so according to the absolute laws of nature. Within decay was order. Molecules linked and unlinked with more precision than cabooses in a freight yard. Streams of particles followed perfect trajectories and rose from what had once been a body, joining with the great oceans of air in an inconceivably complex ballet of fluids. Even with burial came a balanced transformation, a model of infinitude, a textbook case of gasification, combination, oxidation, mineralization, et cetera.

Vandevere wanted order not in the sense of control or imposition, but in

the sense of a painter who orders his colors into a painting. Buying and selling companies was more like directing traffic than making something of
beauty, but, then again, in the abstract what was so different about directing
the traffic of colors and directing the traffic of sums? Perhaps if he had
stayed with some of the businesses he bought, instead of tossing them away
in frenzies and bubbles, he would have been less in need of another order to
make. Most of the businesses he bought, however, were in the larger scheme
of things suitable for sale only in a frenzy.

Thus, the house, and the need, when the children were gone, to make
perfect gardens; to store the best olive oil; to mount, construct, build, perfect,
and refine; to anchor things, and keep them, consuming as little as possible
and laying in as much as could be stored and preserved.

Melissa understood philosophically, but, despairing of argument, she
could not agree. To him, his meticulous approach and unvarying discipline
seemed redolent of life. But to her they seemed always to freeze things in
place, and were like death, which is why she left. But she still loved him, and
he loved her, and while he dreamed that she would come back, suddenly
neat, she wished that he could break free from what she considered an all-
consuming tyranny, and that then they could remarry.

IN SEPTEMBER, East Hampton can be the most beautiful place in the world,
when the ocean, brimming over with a whole summer of sun, surges to and
fro in clear light, finally warmer than the air. Beaches newly empty of
bathers and haze reflect in the far distance like gold, and cicadas make a
hypnotic white sound that almost holds back time. Only a Mercedes or two
passes down the beach road or climbs up from Napeague. Seagulls wheel in
the air, relaxed, landing anywhere, unafraid of being chased by boys who,
now, as white foam crashes onto warm and brilliant sand, are trapped in
prep schools from Maine to Manhattan, sweating in their blazers, doing
sums, and learning Latin.

Sometime in the last week of September, in late morning, Vandevere sat
in his east garden, the Italian one. Both he and it were exemplary of what he
had long undertaken. Although fifty-four years of age, he was in perfect
health except for a slight deafness on one side, the consequence of having

been a rifleman without earplugs. Early that morning he had run six miles, done calisthenics, lifted weights, and swum. His exercise clothes, washed and ironed, were back on the polished blond wood shelves of his airy closet. He had read the *Washington Post,* the *Wall Street Journal,* an article on naval operations in narrow seas, and an essay by Friedrich Hayek. At a breakfast table set with Copeland china, George III sterling, and Austrian crystal, he had dared eat a peach, some fat-free yogurt, and a piece of dry toast.

After breakfast he had dismissed the staff for a day off. During their leave he would cook his evening meal over a fire of driftwood he gathered on the beach, and, having washed and put away the dishes, he would read until the fire went out and the stars blazed in the wind. And although in these quintessentially lonely times he was less lonely than people who cannot do without the incessant presence of others, he was lonely nonetheless.

He sat in the garden, which had been gardened for six hours before the staff departed. Six hours is a lot of time for several professional gardeners to garden, and not a blade of grass was out of place. Nor was a hair on his head out of place, except for some that blew perfectly golden in the breeze, as if by design. The September sun was warm and weak, the wind pleasing, the light pure, and the sound of waves thudding onto the beach now uniformly timed as if to match the steadiness and glory of the weather and the slow even beating of his heart.

As lean and strong as a man his age could be without being a fop, Vandevere wore brown English walking boots polished to a Royal Grenadier sheen. His shorts, tailored in London for Africa and not quite pressed, were clean and unwrinkled; his belt, of bridle leather, was buckled on the second hole. His lightweight polo shirt was of navy-blue silk. As was his custom, he had set his reading glasses over a pair of polarized sunglasses that made everything seem cool and blue.

Removing the reading glasses, he rested them carefully folded on the closed volume of the journal he had just finished. East-southeast, in the direction of the sun, were peach trees, flower beds, caramel-colored sandstone walks, lawns, a sapphirelike pool set in a flat unwindy place, fields of corn and alfalfa, vegetable gardens, a riding ring, and the dunes. This was the way it should have been, except that Melissa should have been sitting beside him in all her settled and spectacular middle-aged beauty.

His bank accounts, investment accounts, and REITs were perfectly tended. Monthly summaries came to him in leather folders, weekly in heavy blue paper trimmed in gold. Experts kept the accounts growing, and in their reports they rounded to the thousands. Experts also had cataloged his extraordinary library, the envy of anyone who might envy a room. His desk drawers were a marvel of organization, and all the linen, one-thousand-two-hundred count, was tucked in without a wrinkle. Even nature was cooperative across its many spectra, of sun and surf, and the lighter blue of the bay, and hay waving in the wind like water heaving on the surface of the sea. Vandevere was as happy as could be expected, and resigned to his life and his death. An almost magical ordination of all physical things seemed to bless his choices and his well-being as his luck continued to hold.

He blinked and stared ahead, breathing slowly in the slight trance that comes after exercise, and rather than think of anything at all he just watched everything that lay before him. What was left, and what to do? Much as he was compelled to it, the pursuit of material perfection weighed heavily upon him. Perhaps he would travel, or have a beautiful sailboat built to put him on seas that in their immensity and danger would bring him the liveliness of youth one more time. But whatever he might do, as long as he kept the house and refused to disengage from it, Melissa would not return. Nor was he able to leave it, as much as his inability to go to her would break his heart.

HALF ASLEEP AND HALF DREAMING, he smelled fragrant dry smoke. He assumed, as he awoke, that it came from the brush pile at the Maidstone Club. Now that it was September and the wind was coming off the shore, the gardeners there would burn the huge pile of pine boughs that had been drying since their deaths in a storm in late May. Though its source was half a mile distant, the smoke would come to him when the wind shifted eastward, as it did from time to time.

In fact, all the land windward of the fire was swept with a resinous scent carried on a haze of white ash, so that it seemed like Italy in the early fall, when farmers burn the stubble on their fields and sweet smoke is everywhere. He had never understood exactly how the chains of fire, orange at night and white by day, could regenerate the land over which they burned, so that in the spring it would be green again and bring forth rich crops. But the tranquil scent of these fires told him in its calming sweetness that after destruction a new beginning was assured. By what mechanism he did not know, but he knew that it was so.

He thought that the wind coursing in a straight line from the Maidstone pine boughs would now be visible in air that had filled with smoke until it was a gauzy white. If they were home, the people who lived between his land and the club would probably complain. If they were absent, their staffs would not, as maids and gardeners accepted such things far more readily, being used to forces and currents that shaped their lives and carried them from place to place with neither their consent nor their desire.

Should he himself complain? He loved the scent of the smoke, but the smoke was now almost alarmingly heavy. It had thickened so much that the peach trees seemed to be standing in fog, and when its white shroud reached the dunes, it compressed and accelerated, speeding over their tops like a magician's silks.

Anxious about how densely this Maidstone smoke was covering the rest of his property, and wanting to know if it had enveloped the house, he turned around slowly and was surprised to see that the hayfields closest to the Maidstone Club were clear. Continuing his turn, he saw that the lawns immediately west of the house were clear as well, and that the smoke was coming not from beyond the house but from it—from his own house, which was burning.

Sometimes, when confronted with momentous things, he did not move as quickly as might have been expected, but stayed still to think of what was true, what was right, and what was required. He stayed still now. Then he calmly stood, rotated his chair, and sat down again facing the house. Flames leapt from places that he never would have believed flames could leap from—from beneath copper gutters and seemingly from solid walls. How many minutes, precisely, he watched this he did not know, but as he sat, the conflagration built.

Vibrating with restraint, he went through in his mind all the things that were now dissolving in flame and combining together in a serpentine of gases and smoke, in a ballet of uncountable particles each behaving with a precision to which he could never even aspire: paintings; suits; books; metals and silver; things of ivory, leather, and silk; furniture of cherry and mahogany. The heat was such that even the porcelain might melt. He felt this heat, but did not move. Nor did he want to move even as all he had built and worked for over so many years vanished before him at great speed.

For he had already left it behind, and his spirit had been unlocked, and his soul freed, in a gift that had come on the wind. All that Vandevere could think of now, as white smoke swirled around him like snow, was his wife as she had been at the quarry, and her face, and the water running off her hair as she had bobbed up in the foam.

Prelude

GOD KNOWS, I was young enough to be excited by the World's Fair of 1939, and many of my friends were as impressed as if it were the prelude to Armageddon, which, as it turns out, it was. But I did not allow it to haunt my days and nights, as it did theirs. For them it was one and the same with coming of age, but for me such things would have to wait, though not for long, and when they did come they were carried on the crest of the breaking wave that was the war.

I was repulsed by the modernist theories and ideology of the Fair. I didn't like them on their face, and didn't think that buildings and cars should be shaped like torpedoes: it was bad enough that torpedoes were shaped like torpedoes. Overwhelmed by the richness of the world and impassioned with what I had, I thought it would take a lifetime of effort to understand even the smallest part of it, and did not fancy that it be reformed or discarded before I had even come to know it. I did not want my street to lose its trees and dappled light so that it could be the bed of a streamlined conveyance that went at blinding speed from one nowhere to another. I did not want the form of things to change, nor my parents to grow old and die, nor to lose the comfort even of familiar imperfection. I wanted neither a revolution of the proletariat, nor a thousand-year Reich, nor even a radio without static, for in my radio with all its static I could hear, over and above Beethoven, the progress of a lightning storm a thousand miles away. My great desire was to achieve rapturous and complete physical unity with the most exquisite woman in the world, to whom I would be devoted for the rest of my life, which was the very least that would have been required to accommodate the infinite number that I imagined of the kind of ecstatic kisses—each lasting for hours—that I had yet to kiss.

A general sense of oncoming destruction may have been the reason why all around the country so many mementos were sunk in so many corner-stones that it was not at all unusual to see a man hurrying down the street with a time capsule tucked under his arm. Into these stainless-steel-and-glass cylinders were rammed the wrong things—evening papers and monthly magazines; reels of movie film; small products of civilization such as cameras, coins, and electric razors; the kind of things that come and go and do not last. But if one of them would in fact last ten thousand years, who then so far off would care more for a spool of thread, a telephone, or the classified section of the *New York Herald Tribune,* than for the portrait of a physician or carpenter staring out in time, or the inner thoughts of a girl in Paterson stitching shirtwaists, or the cri de coeur of an operator of machines, or any one of thousands of such scenes.

They put in time capsules that which should not endure but does. They choose what is interesting over what is profound, the charming over the beautiful, the nimble over the true. It was only eight years ago that time capsules were so much in fashion, before the death of some fifty millions placed the urge to preserve ephemera in a somewhat different light. In a world of balance and counterbalance, and laws that cannot be abridged, the echo of the war must come. Such violence, as it flows through all things, must flow back. And yet peace seems long lasting and everything has begun anew. The soldiers are home. This summer in Manhattan there are a vast number of baby carriages in the street and a vast number of babies in their mothers' arms. Although it is summer, Friday, the 27th of June, 1947, it feels like spring, when grass sits lightly and evenly upon the fields, and trees are so green and delicate they seem to float up with the light.

If I go to my window and lean dangerously over the sill, I can see Grand

Central at the end of the street, and in the opposite direction, framed by converging lines of brownstones, a patch of blue, the East River. You don't have to look long before a ship, tug, or barge rushes across it and disappears from sight. The street itself has the unusual quality of midday blackness topped by shattering silver light, which New York shadows make at the base of straight stone walls. Like stage light, it changes very fast and the shadows are theatrically velvet. When I arrive in the morning, and when I leave at five, I walk in this light like a bather in the surf. The pigeons are the foam that scatters on the top of the waves, as they fly up in glistening flashes that ride the air. Throughout the day as I sit by my window supposedly filling out my ledgers, the combined roar and glare of Manhattan becomes a whisper and the light of dusk, and the music goes faint and shifts to a minor key, as if I am looking on from afar. This sensation sets a seal on time like a press that fixes the incessant motion of words upon a page. To see the present in the clear, one must see it as if from the future. I watch the ships glide across the narrow slot at the end of the street, and though they pass quickly, they are frozen against the blue forever.

I work for United States Steel, at a steel desk. For the past six months I have been transferring data from tens of thousands of index cards to thick fifty-column ledgers. Someday they will have machines to do this, but now I am the machine that organizes the health records of a rolling mill in Ohio. For reasons that it did not share with me, the management has decreed that they be abstracted in a particular form. It is no secret that in tabularization and cross-tabularization many statistical operations are rendered possible, and although after my first day here in January I was bold enough to suggest that instead of using ledgers they put the data on punch cards for key-sorting, they, or, rather, he, Mr. Herman Bleier, had not heard of key-sort, and Mr. Herman Bleier said to me, "Ledgers will do."

I have not seen Mr. Herman Bleier since early February, and was told by the receptionist on his floor when I had a question for him that if I had a question I should write to Mr. Bleier in care of United States Steel, Oakland. I don't have any more questions, at least not for him, and I pray that he has forgotten me. As my salary comes in, my benefits accumulate, and I receive modest periodic raises in pay, I am unsupervised, having fallen into the cracks of an immense corporation that seems not to know that I exist. I work in an area of unused offices, where no one ever comes, and I do not know a single person at United States Steel, which means that not a single person at United States Steel knows me. Even the receptionist of whom I inquired of Mr. Bleier's whereabouts thought I was from another company, or at least another division.

This is just. Since I entered the army, in 1942, I have been a servant of steel—moving it, dodging it, shooting it, ducking it, and, now, making it. As steel should be for our purposes, and not we for its, my present situation must be part of the natural balance of the dominant forces of the era. But the days of steel, even steel, are numbered, as all metals have their age, and then pass from the scene. Thus, this billet cannot last, but it serves for now. I have even tried not showing up, and no one notices. I have no one to whom to report my sick days, so they go unrecorded. But I do come to work almost every day, because I want to finish the job—albeit at a leisurely pace— within five years.

The nature of my workday would probably cause management some concern if they knew about it. From eight to nine, I do ten cards. From four-thirty to five-thirty, I do another ten. At this rate I will be finished in 1952. The root of this is that Mr. Bleier told me to wait for him to collect my work. When I asked when it was due, he replied imperiously that he would tell me when it was due when he was ready to tell me when it was due. That was our last conversation.

At nine, after my first intense burst of labor, I go to the Y, when the morning swimmers have left for their jobs and the pool echoes with ripples that have not quite disappeared by the time I dive in. I swim a mile, do twenty minutes of weights and calisthenics, shower, and then go on my break. There would be no point in returning to the office and then going out for a break, so I combine efficiencies and sit in a café that I found in Murray Hill, where I have a light breakfast and begin to read the paper.

Back at the office by eleven, I finish the paper and do correspondence that I have brought from home. At half past twelve I then go out for the lightest of lunches—broth, mainly—and return precisely at ten of one, but because my lunches are so short I feel justified in taking a nap until two, which I do. Refreshed and in a dreamlike state, I awaken and begin to write upon my legal pads. I do this for two and a half hours, with the greatest pleasure and satisfaction, until four-thirty, when I go back to the cards for an hour, working late every day.

Whatever one might think of what I do, it is nonetheless true that I am following instructions, working each day, doing my work with meticulous care and attention, taking only twenty minutes for lunch, arriving early, and leaving late. I am the model employee. And I am also staying at the peak of health. My conduct is consonant with well known generalities. The United States is far and away the leading steel producer in the world, United States Steel is first among steel companies in this country, and, as far as I am concerned, I am part of a winning team, even if they don't know it.

Furthermore, my experience in the military leads me to believe that of the tens of thousands of employees of United States Steel, I am not the only one who is writing a novel. Most likely, in the warrens of vast buildings converted to subsidiary use or idleness, at mills around the country, are forgotten rooms in which superfluous employees pour their hearts out upon paper or spend the hours drinking-in from books what their predecessors poured out before them. Probably in offices in Oakland, Ohio, or Kalamazoo, someone is taking a great deal of time in a clerical task and stealing from United States Steel, as am I. The pity of theft is not only the damage of loss but the corruption of the thief as he justifies his actions, slithering all over the map of what is right and what is wrong, in the slime he excretes to break his own fall.

On the other hand, and I hate to do this, because it smacks of the rationalization I have just descried, officers of this corporation are paid a great deal more for doing a great deal less than what I do, and in far greater luxury, just as there are those in this company who, for less, risk their lives and work to exhaustion—just as in the army I was in an infantry platoon that was landed in Sicily, Salerno, and Normandy, and the sound of gunfire was as familiar to us as the sound of polo mallets was to some soldiers who never left California, and the sound of the surf to those who manned coastal defenses against an enemy who never came. I used to dream of serving my enlistment in riding a horse from Amagansett to East Hampton and back on the beach, over and over, with rifle, wind, and waves.

In the uneven distribution of rights, privileges, and luck, who am I to challenge this accidental posting, relief, and rest? If in fact I have not paid already for this interlude, then I simply have yet to pay. When my father was dying, we sold most of what we had, against his protests, to pay for what he might have needed to suffer less than he did. I left college. The house disappeared. My mother became a cashier. And then, when she died, nothing was left at all, I had just crossed the Rhine, and I came to her grave two months after she was put in it.

So I accept this covert and undeserved award, in behalf of my father and my mother and the men who died beside me and who doubtless would say that the spark of life is brighter even than the shield of morals, who would say that before they died they had wished for luck, and that luck, by definition, is seldom just. Men who die beside you are like climbers who fall away into an abyss. On the battlefield you do not have the time to be moved, such are your responsibilities. What you feel is shock, which spans the valley of death like a bridge and spares you from dying more than once. I intend with all my might, clerk or no, cheat or not, to die only once, and at the end.

And yet though what I am doing here may not be a mortal sin, it is nonetheless dishonest and dishonorable. In that sense, its pleasant nature has become unpleasant, its advantages taxing. The only reason I haven't disengaged is that I have been leaving behind the things that broke my heart. I had thought that I might need a full five years, but not now, no longer, for something has happened.

A few weeks ago, just after Decoration Day, I went one morning to visit my mother's only sister, who lives on Staten Island so near the ocean you would think it was the coast of Ireland, where she and my mother were born. I go there not just to see how she is, but to present myself to her as if she were my mother. It is as if—and she, too, feels this way I know—her eyes become my mother's eyes, and when I report to her what I have been doing I am not really speaking to her, and she doesn't expect me to, but to my mother. I stayed for a lunch of salad and iced tea, which was all I could take in the heat, and when I left I walked on the beach road toward the Narrows, with the sun beating down.

When at last I reached St. George, and sailed into the shade of the ferry terminal, I had the feel of someone who has been by the sea in the sun, which is what June can do for you even close to Manhattan. In the cool darkness of the ferry hall, I listened to the echoes of gates closing, engines turning over, and the sound of footsteps on the stairs, heel taps, and muted conversation.

I had read the newspaper, had no book, and was pulsing from the sunburn of the road, when the gate was pushed back with the call for the next boat. Moving forward, my glance was averted by the sight, on a bench to my left, of a woman of about my age—had she been much older or much younger it would not have mattered, for as she lowered her newspaper, folded it, rose, and swept toward me, I fell in love with her.

Having done with the paper, she dropped it in a trash can as she moved past, crossing my path not a yard from me and on her way up the ramp. She, too, looked as if she had been out on the ocean, perhaps the day before, and she was as full of summer as a woman can be. Dressed in white, somewhat tense, with buoyant blond hair, she moved ahead of me as gracefully as a skater. And on her left hand, which I thought she held as if she knew that I was looking, were no gold rings, not even one.

When she chose the port side, I dared not follow, if only because I wanted to so much, and I went to the starboard side and stepped into the sunlight. As the boat pulled away and the water churned and upwelled beneath it, I began the terrifying imagination of how I might approach her and what I might say. If I said the truth, it would be too forward, but anything else would be almost a lie. I have never known how to solve this problem, which is why I have so many memories of girls and women in places where I lost them without a word. But this time was unlike any other.

What the world calls a pretty face seems to me most often to be vacant, doll-like, self-conscious, and grasping. Women who are told that they are beautiful and come to believe it not only lose delicacy of soul and sharpness of wit, they forfeit the appealing privacy and loneliness without which real beauty cannot exist. They hardly reflect, as everything reflects upon them, and this makes them dull.

The woman on the port deck in the shade was someone—this I knew from having looked into her eyes for only an instant—of a spirit both tranquil and profound. Perhaps, I imagined, what I took on faith to be her great intelligence has made her lonely, but not too lonely, for she is too graceful for that, grace having brought her the companionship she needed. Perhaps she is not what I think she is, but, no, I can see in her face the qualities for which love comes not only easily but even, as now, almost explosively.

Halfway across the harbor, I had not come up with an answer. There is no good way to approach a stranger with whom you have fallen in love. At Governors Island, I grew anxious, and leaned over the rail to estimate the distance to South Ferry. Five minutes, I judged, and I've lost my chance. Here I was, a slightly trembling coward, not even a real clerk for United States Steel, who had seen a beautiful woman who was standing on the deck opposite and would get off the ferry and disappear into Manhattan forever.

I thought timidly that I might see her again, even later that day, and thus be able to approach her, saying, "I saw you earlier on the ferry." But in Manhattan what would the chances be of that? I was going to have to go to her even though I could think of nothing to say, to begin my halting conversation with the words "Forgive me." I had to do something. Almost faint with love and fear, I leaned back in, about to propel myself—with a chance of knocking people down—through the cabin and to the other deck, and there she was, next to me, just a foot and a half away.

"Jesus Christ!" I said. Being so close to her was like being hit by a tremendous sunlit wave that had rolled from the South Atlantic onto the Amagansett beaches.

"I beg your pardon?" she replied, smiling slightly, but looking at me with doubt.

"You were on the port side."

"So I was."

"And I was on the starboard."

"You still are," she said.

"I am, but I no longer have to come up with a pretext to talk to you."

"Why would you need a pretext to talk to *me*?" she asked.

I hesitated. I could see that she was watching with interest as I tried to be exact.

"Without a pretext, it would have been too forward."

"It would have. That's always the problem, isn't it."

"I saw you in the terminal, when you threw away your paper. I thought that the motion of that—of your having thrown away a newspaper—was beautiful."

This was for her truly arresting, and she stared at me.

"Even if you walk off this boat," I said, "and I never see you again, the sight of you, back there, in the terminal, in the dust-filled air, will never leave me."

I loved her all the more because she remained guarded as, ever so slowly, as if, in wading across a channel, she let herself be taken just slightly with the current, judging every footfall and still in control, but ready and wanting to float.

"I saw you, too," she said, the saying of which did to me what, apparently, I had just done to her, "and I came over to the starboard because I was tired of looking at the Statue of Liberty, and wondered if perhaps I could see you again." It was no small thing for her to have said that.

I love the way she speaks, I love the beauty of her features, and the grace of her hands. She had been dropped at St. George after sailing in from eastern Long Island, where her parents have a house, and her fiancé keeps his boat. He went to Harvard, as I did, but ten years before me, and he was able to finish. In the war he went in as a colonel and came out as one. I went in as a private and came out a captain, rising purely by battlefield promotion. One more year of residence in Cambridge and I can have my degree. He works for Morgan, and of course, in my way, I work for United States Steel.

Tonight I meet her at Penn Station. We are to take the train to East Hampton, where I will be a guest for the weekend at her parents' house. They may have to get used to the fact that I'm not wealthy, that for a year and a half after my decommissioning and my mother's death I've been biding my time, and that for the sake of the dead—the inert, the immovable, the invisible in their graves—I will not be rushed. I intend to live up to her expectations, to exceed them, which is why I have remained here, to judge the moment precisely, so that I may say, this is where I am, and this is where I'm going, and this is why. I will follow only what is true, good, and real. Despite what I have seen not so long ago, I will not lose my faith, for in her multiple beauties she herself is correction and compensation for what is sorrow and brokenheartedness. "Let's be practical," she said, "about love. But not too practical." I'm willing.

It's Friday, the 27th of June, 1947. I don't know what lies ahead, but the city is hot and the sky is cloudless. In quiet offices like this, many clerks, both men and women, are working in the heat, in the breeze of a fan, in the whirring of electric motors and the distant surflike noise of traffic. Barges and ferries are skidding across the bay trailing silver wakes backlit in the golden afternoon. Out to the east, the beaches of Long Island are still largely empty, for the season is only just about to begin. There the water curls into foam and thuds against the sand, and the wind will not tolerate in the dunes even a single tree. But inland are estates and farms and fields of summer sparkling in the heat and mist.

The trains that make the trip out there were troop trains not long ago, and in the evening as they rush from Center Moriches to Montauk their open windows glow yellow in twilight as ropes of steam and spark splay out against a cobalt sky. The train stations are of stone, and even close to Manhattan you see hayfield after hayfield. This is all going to change. Things are bound to get faster, lighter, and less substantial. The world, which is going the way of glass, will leave many fine things behind.

But so be it, for it leaves behind the dead as well. I came through the war and into the clear, and this is the clear. On this day in June, without a cloud, no doubt in the vast countryside that surrounds New York as an ocean surrounds an isle, hawks are rising into the blue, and as they circle and are held in apparent indecision by the ever-expanding view, they only seem to idle.

When the current that lifts them subsides, they will have seen all that is around them, they will have judged their moment and chosen their destination. And then in air both buoyant and invisible they will find their support, and, as the sunset cools the world, will begin their great glide toward the pure color of night. The last that they see other than the stars will be a distant band of violet and blue, a target of perfection they will never reach, but toward which they will have been aimed like arrows.

Perfection

EARLY IN JUNE OF 1956, the summer in New York burst forth temperate and bright, the colors deep, the wind promising. This was the beginning of the summer that was to see the culmination of a chain of events that had begun, like everything else, at the beginning of the world, but had started in a practical sense in March of the previous year, when the Saromsker Rebbe opened the wrong drawer.

A heavy wet snow had snapped some telephone lines in Brooklyn, many of which at that time were carried on poles above the ground. When these went down, the magnetic effect coursed its way through the webs of copper and steel in the telephone exchanges and made oceans of static that flowed like backwash into every telephone in Brooklyn. The Saromsker Rebbe had intended to use the telephone to propose a meeting with Rabbi Moritz of Breel, who lived on Ocean Parkway with his followers, who trimmed their hats in mink, whereas the Saromskers lived in Williamsburg and trimmed theirs with sable. The Saromsker Rebbe wanted to discuss a theological difference that now appeared reconcilable.

The Saromskers had taken in many survivors of the Holocaust, mostly children who had been babies when their parents had been murdered. Their devotion to mothers and fathers they had never known was fiercer and more concentrated than anyone might have dreamed, except perhaps for the parents themselves in the very moment they were parted from their children. Their prayers for the union of souls, and their silent and intense petitioning of God had the strength of all the winds of the world, of its invisible magnetism, of oceans and seas. But they were petitions that, for all their power and urgency, and though perhaps answered in time or beyond the limits of time, were not answered then.

A few of these children had been old enough to remember, some even to have begun serious study before their world was destroyed, and to these the Saromsker Rebbe would listen when, on a point of division, they held that things had changed, that movement was possible, especially in the New World and in the eyes of the young. Thus, soon after the war, the Saromsker Rebbe had swallowed his pride and begun to speak to Rabbi Moritz of Breel, who had also taken in a number of mysteriously intense young refugees. Theological reconciliation moves at a pace that makes the advance and recession of glaciers seem like the oscillation of a gnat in the golden light of a summer evening. Braced for a lifetime of cautious exchanges, the two rabbis had discovered that the telephone, more urgent even than the telegraph, was the most complimentary way for one to get the full attention of the other.

But because of the snowstorm the telephone was not working, and the only thing audible within it was something much like the experimental music then in vogue, of which neither rabbi had even the slightest inkling. The Saromsker Rebbe held the handset and tapped at the little button on the left side of the base, first three times, and then five. "Hello? Hello?" he said to the static. He repeated this six times over the space of an hour and a half, after which he gave up. Instead of talking on the telephone, he would do what came naturally and what was holy: he would write.

He wanted to write a short note, but with fountain pen in hand the Saromsker Rebbe was a dervish. Possessed of undying momentum and driven not by his own hand but by the ancient operation just of picking up the pen, he filled it, applied it to paper, and began moving it about. It then began to drag him after it like a plowman who had attached himself by a strong harness to a gigantic young plow horse *before* hitching it up to the plow, which horse was then stung by a big and very angry bee, and had run until he had crossed all of Bessarabia—through rivers, over fields packed with wildflowers so that the plowman emerged looking like a huge bush in full bloom with windmill legs, in long flights off cliffs, through startled towns, breaking fences that exploded like wheat on a threshing floor, through houses, skipping across the decks of boats, following the sun so that its light fueled him and he pulled the plowman without exhaustion. The plowman as he ran shouted prayers, and the horse, having long forgotten the sting, raced the sun as if to overtake it. Horses cannot be expected not to have such notions, or rabbis not to write all night.

In the morning, when the snow had fallen off the wires because of strong winds from the Ramapos, the Saromsker Rebbe found himself with forty densely imprinted pages that left him vibrating like a piano wire and that had to be delivered as soon as possible to Rabbi Moritz of Breel. Shaking not from fatigue but from having followed his pen all night, the rebbe rang his nickel-plated bell, and one of his students, who had just started the day shift outside the study door, instantly appeared.

"I have written a little letter to Rabbi Moritz of Breel," the Saromsker Rebbe said, holding the forty pages up to the light. "It must be delivered to Ocean Parkway as soon as possible. Who is the fastest and most nimble of our students? Who is smart but not so immersed in his studies that he would be crushed by a truck? Who knows the map, and will be able to come back? Who speaks English well? And who will make a good impression on Rabbi Moritz of Breel?"

The student said, "It's simple."

The Saromsker Rebbe knew that nothing is simple. "Really?" he asked.

"Yes."

"Who?"

"Roger."

"That's a name?"

"That's his American name—Roger Reveshze." Stepping forward, the student said, "Rabbi, he's so fast he bounces off the walls. He speaks English perfectly, and he will impress Rabbi Moritz of Breel. He's one of the ones from Majdanek."

The children of Majdanek were the cause of many problems. Like other children of other camps they had their terrors and incurable sadnesses, but, for whatever reason, they even more so. For whatever reason, Majdanek was worse.

"He spends a great deal of time praying for his parents. He was just old enough to know them. He might study more, it's true. He could be a better scholar. . . ."

"Who are we to say?" the Saromsker Rebbe asked. "When he prays, is it recitation?"

"No," said the student. "When he prays, white light bathes the walls. You can see it through the cracks."

"Why did no one tell me this?"

"It just started. He's only fourteen. We wanted to let him calm down before we told you. He's a kind of wild man."

"And you want me to send him to Rabbi Moritz of Breel, a man of ninety-six?"

"Rabbi Moritz will know if he's a *baal shem tov*."

"Maybe."

"Shall I send for him?"

"How is he at maneuvering through traffic?"

"Nothing can touch him. He could be a snake fighter."

ROGER Reveshze had run through the halls and up the stairs, his robes and fringes trailing him like battle flags in a strong breeze, and when he presented himself to the Saromsker Rebbe so excellent was his blood oxygen that he did not breathe hard. Many people can do physical feats and afterward suppress the need to take deep breaths, but Roger, who did not need to suppress an urge he did not have, stood quietly before the rebbe, his eyes semiskeptical.

Like many fourteen-year-old boys in Hasidic costume, he had the sweetness of a lamb and the mischievous air of an owl. At the same time, though possessed of a slight and awkward body that had not yet solidified as it would in time, he seemed to have extraordinary gravity, or perhaps, the Saromsker Rebbe thought, I am just imagining it.

He was not imagining. In Roger's wild eyes, big ears, and big teeth, was a face, framed by blond *payess,* that led with instant speed to the Pale of Settlement the Saromsker Rebbe had known in his childhood. He merely had to look in the eyes of this boy to see the heart of eastern Europe, and there, rising against a field of black and gray, came a fume of gold in which, like smoke, souls in transport spiraled upward.

Roger had something about him forever sad but forever indomitable. The rebbe decided to ask a question or two. He allowed them to spring whence he knew not, like an egg coming from the mouth of a magician.

"What is your Hebrew name?"

"Elchanan ben Moshe ben Arieh."

"What do you see, Elchanan ben Moshe?"

"You."

"When you close your eyes."

This was for Roger an emotional subject, but one with which he was familiar on a daily basis, so he closed his eyes, raised his arms in a gesture of surprise, for what he saw was different every time, and said, "I see a courtyard in falling snow, people wrapped in blankets and shawls, wood that is broken and steps that are worn, a man standing in a square. He is dressed in black silk robes, his *shtreimel* almost covered with snow, his beard white. My heart cannot convey his expression. And I see houses that are lit weakly but brightly, their windows glowing yellow."

"Do you imagine this?"

"I don't imagine it, it exists."

"Still?"

"Still."

"Do you pray?"

"Of course."

"Who generates the prayers? Do you?"

The boy smiled.

"And what happens when you pray, physically?"

"I twirl."

"You don't daven?"

"I begin to daven, and then I twirl."

"Like a dancer, spinning?"

Roger shook his head in the negative. "No, head over heels."

"Head over heels," the rebbe repeated, "no gravity."

"I'm blinded," Roger reported matter-of-factly.

"By darkness?"

"By light: white phosphorus, pinwheels, stars on a field of fire. It's an illusion. An ophthalmologist could tell you why. Nerve endings."

The rebbe was not convinced. Vision and skepticism are man and wife, bride and groom. "How do you know it's an illusion?"

"Because."

"Because why?"

"Because I prayed for the life of a bird that had flown against the window and was dying on the sill, and though I was swept up beyond the world, so was he. It's an illusion."

"Maybe it was supposed to die."

"I didn't want it to die."

"Since when is what you want central to the scheme of things?"

The boy nodded in acceptance. These matters would have to be deferred, and the rebbe decided to return to the business at hand. "Roger, please take this letter to Rabbi Moritz of Breel, on Ocean Parkway. Do you know how to get there?"

"Yes, we went there two times."

The Saromsker Rebbe put the forty pages in a Manila envelope. Then he opened the top right-hand drawer in his desk and took out a box of matches and a thick candle. He lit the candle. In his left hand he held his seal and in the right the end of a little stick of saffron-colored wax. But, as the wax melted, he burned his fingers, and he withdrew the flame. "I lost my tongs," he said.

"Tongs," Roger repeated, fascinated by the word.

The rebbe went to get a fresh stick of wax from lower down, but he opened the wrong drawer. As soon as he saw what was in this drawer, he slammed it shut. Flushed as red as if he had just climbed a sixty-foot rope, he found the saffron-colored wax elsewhere and nervously started to soften it in the flame.

"What was that?" Roger asked.

"What was what?"

"What was that in the drawer?"

"Wax for sealing envelopes."

"In the other drawer."

"What drawer?"

"The one you opened before you opened the one with the wax."

"Nothing."

"I saw it."

"Saw what?" The rebbe's eyes were now beady.

"The box."

"What box?"

"In the drawer."

"What drawer?"

"What is *Lindt?*" Roger asked.

"What is Lindt? What is Lindt?" the rebbe repeated.

"Yes, what is it?"

"I don't know," the rebbe said, now looking at Roger with panic.

"Oh."

Roger successfully delivered the Saromsker Rebbe's letter to Rabbi Moritz of Breel, whom he did not see, and who could, therefore, make no judgment as to whether Roger was a *baal shem tov*. Everything settled down and returned to normal, except for one thing.

WHAT WAS LINDT? Roger's teachers, all *unter rabbis* and *nachmollers,* didn't know, and his classmates didn't know, either. He went to Rabbi Eisvogel, who was second to the Saromsker Rebbe, and his designated successor.

"Rabbi Eisvogel," Roger said, captivated by birds perching on icicles hanging from the eaves of the rabbi's study, "What is Lindt?"

"Lint?" Rabbi Eisvogel asked back. "Lint is cloth shavings or other material, little fibers that collect and combine. Why?"

"No, not that. It was written on the box—L-i-n-d-t."

"What box?"

"I don't know."

"But you saw a box?"

"I don't know."

Rabbi Eisvogel asked, "Did you see a box in a dream?"

"Maybe."

"Are you all right, Roger?"

"I'm all right."

"Good. Lindt, whatever it is, I'll think about it," the rabbi said.

Roger thought that he would never find out what it was. The world was full of mysteries, and he had much else to think about, having been immersed in moral questions day after day, like metal annealed, since he was three years old. He returned to his studies and forgot about what he had seen in the Saromsker Rebbe's drawer. But, then, when the next Sabbath was over, a lighthearted Rabbi Eisvogel, in the presence of students and disciples, asked the Saromsker Rebbe point-blank, "Hayim, tell me, what is Lindt?"

The Saromsker Rebbe's face turned as red as the flag of the Soviet Union. "I don't know," he said, with a Cheshire Cat smile, "but it may be a kind of Swiss chocolate."

Rabbi Eisvogel said, "Ah, I see. Is it kosher?"

"How would I know?" asked the Cheshire Cat, disappearing into the semidarkness, where, amidst chanting and singing weakly illuminated by the light of only a candle or two among the coal-black sateen robes and dark sable hats, a passage had opened to the East, and such questions disappeared in a dim whirlpool that shattered time and revived the life of a hundred generations rising like a bonfire. The black coats, sable hats, and hallucinatory prayer were a stage setting in which light and darkness were intertwined for the coaxing, temptation, and entreaty of countless spirits that, somewhere in the closed and darkened rooms of time, existed still. And though these were as shy and delicate as fawns, they did come, in the mind's eye. And, when they did, they floated before the speechless scholars, not in whitened afterimages but with the strength and color of figures in Renaissance paintings, for it was not death that had been summoned but life, and life came as if the sun had risen and shone through the blackness of night.

. . .

ROGER THOUGHT that only he knew the Saromsker Rebbe to be imperfect. Though the Saromsker Rebbe was constantly making protestations of imperfection, Roger now understood that these were only a cover to shield from the eyes of his followers the real imperfection. The Saromsker Rebbe had lied, directly and by omission, and with what the Sage of Minsk, the Koidanyev *Gaon,* called "dreadful unholy serpentines." Lying was an unsolicited insult to the divine order.

And he ate something that wasn't kosher—not once, not twice, but over time. He concealed sin. He hid evidence. He misled his followers. Although because of the nature and scale of the offense all these things may have been morally forgivable, aesthetically they were not. The balances of the universe are precise and delicate. Depending upon the consequences, lying may be morally condemnable in varying degree, but aesthetically it is impossible in the absolute. One uncourageous lie destroys the core of the imagination. Roger hated lying, and knew that it was the outrider of malevolent forces, which come first with a lie so that they might not have to fight to subdue you. They declare what is true, how to order the elements of truth, and what is false. They ridicule, oppress, and—if you do not bend to them—they kill you. Roger would never yield to pressure, to false commandments, or to threats, for he had something for which he could gladly die, something that he would proclaim without embarrassment, that was the root, the rock, and the holy place of his life. This was the truth of the death of his mother and father and of so many other people's mothers, fathers, children, wives, husbands, brothers, and sisters, in the holocaust into which he was born and to which he would, until the end of his days, bear witness—even as others might forget, ridicule, dismiss, or demean it.

This was the hook with which the small, slight Roger Reveshze grasped at the robes of God in the hope of holding Him accountable. And though he was told not to, though it was illogical, a presumption—perhaps a blasphemy and a sin—Roger Reveshze knew his position and held fast. For him, this holocaust was a barrel in which the whole universe rolled. He cared little but to look forward to a life that might in a single place touch upon perfection as confirmation that blind persistence and love would lead to eventual reunion.

THERE WAS no great consequence in defying the Saromsker Rebbe: Roger had his compass, and nothing could turn him. But now he could no longer trust the Saromsker Rebbe to sense an impending holocaust, which was part of the rebbe's responsibility as the leader of a community immersed in the study of ancient texts and without the time to read newspapers and journals. Perhaps the rebbe's regular reading of the *New York Times,* the *Herald Tribune,* and the *Forward* had led him to nonkosher chocolate, but, despite the risk, now Roger had to read them, and to study the politics of nations, as he could no longer trust the Saromsker Rebbe to do so honestly. This required as well occasional listening to the radio. What radio? And the newspapers, being so thick, were almost impossible to conceal. You could hardly slip them between the pages of a book. Why was so much space given to advertisements for malted milk balls and brassieres—the claims for which obviously were self-serving lies—when a psalm or the Ten Commandments could be written on a diaphanous piece of parchment the size of a postage stamp?

For a boy who was used to four-hour exegeses of a paragraph, a sentence, a line, or even a single word, the prospect of reading every day a newspaper the size of a life jacket was terrifying. Perhaps, to ease his way into such things, and so he would not be faced with the problem of hiding such a big bundle of paper, he would start with the radio. He had heard radios when he passed by open apartment windows. Once, he had stopped short before an unattended parlor as a Brahms string quartet flowed like an invisible river past curtains lifting in the wind. He had not been allowed to listen to the radio, because nothing on the radio stayed still, and a lie could appear and disappear before anyone could know. A country that listened to the radio would have no way of knowing, therefore, what was true. Roger understood the reason for the prohibition, but now he had his own dispensation. And not only did he have a dispensation, he had a mission.

"Luba," he whispered to one of his classmates, another lamb-and-owl combination, "where is a radio?"

Luba found this entrancing. "You want to listen to the radio?"

"If I could ask a Jew a question, and not have it answered with a question . . . ," Roger began.

"You would be the czar. There's a radio in the butcher shop," Luba said like a Roman conspirator. "Schnaiper can't turn it off."

"He's possessed?"

"The switch is broken. It plays day and night."

"Why doesn't he pull the plug?"

"It's plugged in behind the giant refrigerator where he keeps the liver. If he pulled the plug he would have to move the refrigerator, and if he moved the refrigerator he would have to take out all the liver."

Roger nodded. "It's on all the time?"

"Day and night. The cats listen to it when he leaves the store. And he can't change the station, or he doesn't want to. Roger, he listens to . . . *boogie voogie.*"

"The tubes will burn out," Roger said authoritatively.

"No, they won't," Luba answered. "It doesn't have tubes. It has new things called *trahnzeestores,* which never burn out. It will go forever."

"He'll sell the liver."

"Not as fast as he puts new liver in."

"How can that be? Eventually the refrigerator would expand until it was as big as the universe."

"No, sometimes he puts in an onion," Luba said. Luba had been born in a town, recently wiped from the surface of the earth, where logic was not held in the highest esteem when it was held at all.

"How do you know all this?" Roger asked.

"On *erev Shabbos* I get the *gribenes* and other chicken stuff from Schnaiper. In the morning the truck gets the meat, but the *gribenes* is never ready then, so in the afternoon Rabbi Eisvogel sends me for it. I carry twenty-five pounds of it in a wicker basket strapped to my back."

"That's what that is," Roger said, "and that's why it smells that way."

"Yeh," Luba said.

"Can I take your place?"

"For how long?"

Roger thought. "Five years."

Luba's eyes crossed, and he rocked his head from left to right.

"I'll give you all my hamentashen."

Luba raised his eyebrows and looked to the side.

"And half my jelly doughnuts," Roger added.

"All of them."

"Three-quarters."

"Okay," said Luba, "but you'll have to wait until May. I have a subdeal with gizzards. I bring them to Rabbi Glipsin of Foin, but in May he's going to Neshville."

"Where's that?"

"I don't know."

SCHNAIPER THE BUTCHER looked up. "Why suddenly a new boy? Where's Luba?"

"He's in training."

"For what?"

"To become a polar rabbi."

Schnaiper narrowed his eyes.

"Canada," Roger said, pointing straight up. "Completely full of ice."

"So?" asked Schnaiper. "We have winter, too. What would a polar rabbi have to know?"

Roger slowly and intolerantly moved his head, as if to say, "What an idiot," but, then, instead of jumping forward with an explanation, he said nothing, and let the butcher beg for it.

"What? What would a polar rabbi have to know?"

Roger laughed.

"Tell me," Schnaiper commanded.

"You're a butcher, right?" Roger asked. This was a carefully plotted question to ask a man, in a white apron, with a huge knife in his hand, standing at a giant butcher block next to a case filled with ten tons of chicken liver.

"What do you think?"

"So, tell me, Mr. Butcher," said Roger, "walrus."

"What walrus?"

"Walrus. Kosher for Passover, or not?"

Schnaiper's eyes darted. "How am I supposed to know?"

"I'll tell you." Roger beckoned for him to lean forward, and the butcher did. "Ask a polar rabbi. He would know. At this very moment, Luba is deep in studies of precisely this kind of question. Penguins."

"Who's his teacher?"

"Rabbi Eisvogel."

"Eisvogel. Good man. Still wants twenty-five pounds of *gribenes?*"

"Yes."

"It'll be fifteen minutes. I apologize for the radio. I can't turn it off. It's *goyisheh,* but if you daven you can drive it out of your mind. I myself like it. It has pretty music called *boogie voogie.*" He went to package the *gribenes,* taking the wicker basket with him like an alpine guide.

Left by himself in the ice-white interior of the butcher shop, Roger lifted his eyes and listened. The radio had been on of course, as it was an eternal radio, when first he had walked in, but it had been just noise. Now he cocked his ears to listen and decipher. He expected to hear, perhaps, an interview with a famous rabbi. No. He thought the next most likely thing would have been an interview with the Pope. No. News about wars, Germany, ships at sea, the president's health. No. Whatever it was, however, it was as slow and deliberative as a Talmudic exegesis. In fact, he was pleasantly surprised by the unhurried pace, for he had expected thoughtless gushing, and this was careful, tranquil, with long calming spaces between the words.

"Two on," the voice said. "Two and one ... Miller at bat. You know, Mel, it's been a long time since we've seen ... the pitch, low, ball three. It's been a long time ... since a rookie, like Miller ... winding up ... ball four, he walks. Bases loaded."

This desultory conversation, the epitome of a summer afternoon, and one of the most soothing things Roger had ever heard, went on and on. "A three-two pitch to Hollins ... line drive ... base hit. The pitch was up and Stanky jumped to get it. So he has a lead single in the bottom ... in the bottom, of the third. He was zero for four ... in last night's game. The pitch, swing . . . on the way to Allen. Foul over the Yankee dugout. Allen came to the majors by way of Richmond, Virginia—a good place to play ball. . . . The pitcher winds up. Ball, low on the outside."

In the spaces within the narrative Roger heard a lovely and persistent sound, like the sound of the ocean, and within that sound were others. Sometimes the speaker would get excited and the ocean would roar, and then, uncharacteristically, he would yell numbers and say how great it was, or how dangerous. For fifteen minutes, Roger listened to this, mesmerized, with absolutely no understanding whatsoever of what it was. Then Schnaiper returned, his pluglike body hauling the alpine basket of *gribenes.*

"What is that?" Roger asked, pointing up.

"On the radio?"

Roger nodded.

"That? That's the best part. You could listen all day. I do."

"But what is it?"

"It's baseball," said Schnaiper, "from the House That Ruth Built."

"From the House of Ruth?" Roger asked, stunned.

"*Live,*" Schnaiper said.

"Where is it?"

"The Bronx."

EVIDENTLY, rabbis kept certain things from their students. Wonderful things. Exciting things. If Schnaiper could be believed—and never had he overweighed a chicken—there was a place in the Bronx that—Symbolically? Actually? Miraculously?—was a direct link to the Israelites. Roger knew that such places could be found in *Eretz Yisrael,* but never had he heard that they existed in the Bronx. Immediately he wanted to go there, to see. The problem was that he did not understand its language, which seemed as dense and impenetrable as his studies in the Talmud, which, after all, had not come on the instant.

So he inquired of Luba, because Luba had been fetching *gribenes* from the outside world for so long, "Luba, what is the House of Ruth, that's in the Bronx?"

"The House of Ruth?" Luba closed his lamblike eyes. He had no idea what Roger was talking about, but as a direct descendant of Rabbi Vogelsblume of Hivnis, he didn't have to know. He closed his eyes, spread his arms, and waited for the answer. This was the way of the Jews in countries where for lifetimes they had been forced to the ground, where fact was never better than dreams. Later rationalists, even among the Jews themselves, mocked this, because they had never been so long in extremis, and did not understand art, ecstasy, or the parting of seas. They did not understand that, for those who have nothing, dreams are real. Luba began to speak as if possessed: "The House of Ruth . . . is in the Bronx."

"I told *you* that," Roger protested.

"Did I say you didn't? It's a palace bigger than the temple or the baths of Babylonia. People dance in the aisles, and its four-hundred-foot-high walls are hung with gold and purple draperies. Lit by divine light that showers down from heaven, beautiful women work in a field in the middle, harvesting wheat, like their great-great-great-great-great-grandmother Ruth. In galleries as high as the Empire State Building, legions of rabbis read the Talmud, and klezmer bands in the vast celebration areas play for dancing as in Simchat Torah. And the food! The food! Vegetables! Roasts! Fat pieces of halvah! Poppyseed cakes! Wine. Every day at sunrise and at sunset the rabbis dance on the wheatfields with the Ruths, like daughters. And, someday, the students will marry the beautiful Ruths, and have babies."

Luba was still vibrating with longing when Roger asked, "How many women work in the wheatfields?"

"A constant supply. As fast as boys are born, so are girls. They come together as the rivers flow. That's the way it is. But there's a catch."

"What's the catch?"

"You can't go there."

"Why not?"

"You just can't."

"So what's the good of it?"

"After you die," Luba said, opening his eyes, "you're taken there on a holy sled."

"Luba, it exists in the world. I heard it."

"But you'll never get there," Luba said, holding his finger up the way Rabbi Eisvogel did when he drove home a point, "unless. . . ."

"Unless what?"

"Or," Luba said.

"Or?"

"Unless you die, or they are in peril and need a champion to save them."

"What kind of peril?"

"Defeat. Such a place is always under siege, but sometimes a champion prays and prays, and then maybe the Holy One, blessed be His name, allows him to champion the House of Ruth. But the champion must have great virtue, for he will carry in his hand the very staff of the Lord."

"How will he know that it is the staff of the Lord?" Roger asked.

"It will be passed to him in the fields, and it will be as if of gold, and it will shine in the light."

UNTIL THE NEXT *erev Shabbos,* Roger dreamt of the House of Ruth. He knew in his American mind that what Luba had said could not be and that no such place could exist, just as he knew that people, even the holiest mystics, could not fly. But in his Eastern mind he knew that the ancient rabbis of Breel and Talakreblach actually did fly, even if in earthly terms they did not leave the ground. How was this? To say that they flew, they would have had to have made, in defiance of gravity, a vertical distance between themselves and a point of reference. When Rabbi Vimy of Breel and Rabbi Canopy of Talakreblach concentrated, their point of reference was not the mere earth. They envisioned the limitless universe, in which they floated as freely as sparkling fish. And was it not true that they did float amid the phosphorus-glistening stars? That the earth came between them and what kept them otherwise afloat was a fact and not a dream, but it was not much of a fact in comparison to the gravityless infinity in which it existed. The earth was just a speck, less than a speck, and Rabbis Vimy of Breel and Canopy of Talakreblach were, in fact, flying at blinding speed through space, as are we all, but at the time of their visions they were the only ones who both knew it and felt it, which is why they did fly, and which is why Roger could picture the

House of Ruth in the Bronx: a place that, even were it not real, God—having hinted to trusting imaginations—would be obligated to make real in one way or another, such as by having Ruth build it.

The rabbis let Roger be—even Rabbi Eisvogel, who was something of a cold bird. When a student suddenly didn't pay attention and fell off in his work, the rabbis looked carefully in his eyes. If his eyes were as eyes usually are, they brought him back around in various ways. But if within the eyes they saw a fire, they left him alone. In fact, they asked him what he required—food in his room, a certain scroll, time to pray, a trip to the ocean, music, a conference with a mystic—and they tried to supply it, to breathe air into the fire for the express purpose of keeping it alight.

Rabbi Eisvogel asked the question, inquiring about what Roger might need.

"I want to go to the butcher's and listen to the radio," Roger said decisively.

"Which butcher?" Rabbi Eisvogel asked.

"Schnaiper. He's the one with a radio."

"Go," Rabbi Eisvogel told him, trustingly. "We'll keep your book open where you left it."

FROM SCHNAIPER'S RADIO, which had never ceased playing, came the same, languorous, slow, Southern conversation once again. "Do you know what they're saying?" Roger asked Schnaiper, who was very busy.

"What?" Schnaiper asked back.

"This conversation on the radio."

"Baseball," Schnaiper said, cleaving a veal chop. "You know, the game."

"Do you understand it?" Roger asked.

Schnaiper rested his cleaver on the butcher block as if he were a stork resting a broken leg. "Of course I do."

"Tell me how it works."

"The whole game? The rules?"

"Yes."

"It's simple. I've never seen it, but I know from the radio."

Roger nodded.

"First, there's a *peetch-hair,*" Schnaiper said, breaking into their exchange of Yiddish with an English word.

"A *peetch-hair*? What's that?"

"I don't know, but without the *peetch-hair* they can't play the game. I heard once how a *peetch-hair* was hit by a flying object of some sort, and they stopped the game until they brought in another *peetch-hair*. From this, don't ask me."

"But what do they do?"

"Well, they run around *besses,* and sometimes they steal the *besses.*"

"What are *besses*?"

"Puffy white things they stick in the ground."

Roger was nowhere. "So what's the point?" he asked. "And what are all the numbers for?"

"I don't think the numbers mean anything, really. Anyway, I pay no attention to them. The point is that there are two teams, and the winner is the one that can stay the longest."

"What prevents them from staying?"

"When they miss."

"Miss what?"

"The ball."

"You never said anything about a ball."

"Oh yes, there's a ball. They throw it at each other, and hit it with a stick."

"What for?"

"I don't know. They don't know either: ever since I got the radio, they've been losing."

"Who?"

"The *Yenkiss.*"

"The *Yenkiss,*" Roger repeated.

"That's one of the teams. They used to be the greatest team in the world, Mel said. Now they're dying. They won't win this year, even with Mental."

"What's *Mental*?"

"Mickey Mental," Schnaiper replied, knowingly.

"What's that?"

"A person, the greatest baseball player of our time. But Kansas City, unless a miracle will happen, is going to kill them."

"Really kill them?"

"You bet."

"What could help them?" Roger asked.

"Nothing. One more game and they're finished. But for next year, if they had a champion, another one like Mickey Mental, but better, well, that would be a different story, maybe."

FROM THE TOP FLOORS of the building where Roger lived, and through the gaps in ocher and brown buildings and within the steel cage-work of bridges brushed with cool sunshine, the East River was visible in wide segments of blue. From the roof, the blue patches were larger, for one could see over some of the buildings that had blocked them from below. And from the top of the stair shed yet another story over the roof, the river was freed. You could see all the way from St. George on Staten Island, along the cliff faces of lower Manhattan and Midtown looming rocklike in the day and sparkling like galaxies at night, to the Triborough Bridge. River traffic arrived suddenly on the swift current and departed with equal speed, or fought north as slowly as a man carrying a desk. Sometimes Roger saw a boat gliding out into the harbor at dusk, its stern light bobbing in recession until it became a star. The lovely light making its way into the vastness of the ocean, like the dead in their quiet departures, grew ever fainter.

That fall and winter when it was neither too wet nor too cold, he ascended the incline to reach the small rectangular space at the top of the stair shed, and there he spent many hours in prayer. He recited nothing. He sought nothing. His prayer was the hopeful resurrection, in his heart, of those who were gone. It was the dissolution, in his mind's eye, of all elements, colors, and sound—until, lighter than smoke, they formed a picture as full of glory as the patient astronomical photographs that he had never seen and that, in later years when he would see them, would bring to his face a smile of recognition. All was grace and perfection there, all just and redeemed, all prayer answered, ratios exact, rhythms perfect, laws obeyed.

He had known such things, somehow, since infancy. And he understood that, as he grew, his responsibility was to make sense of them: not to adopt them for his purposes but to take a tiny fraction of the light of perfection for use upon the imperfection of the world, like a match that for an instant brings a little daylight to a dark hallway.

Between the Yenkiss' loss of what Schnaiper called the *Verld* Series to Kansas City, and the opening of the next baseball season, Roger concentrated upon a single obstruction that he wished to burn through, a single request, a single question. It did not come, and it did not come, and it did not come. The fall's lucid shadows deepened the colors of Brooklyn and Manhattan, and its cold air enlivened the stars. Winter froze all emotion. Sometimes he would sit in the cold until his heart hardly beat and he was blind, and he would strain, sweeping the darkness in search of a blaze of power, but he would find nothing, he would see no light. Spring came violently and ended in soft air suffused with the scents of flowers and warm brick. Baseball season had started in April. No one was happy. Then came summer, promiscuously scattering great volumes of light, dashing it up streets that had long been in shadow, touching the undersides of bridges as if the sun were boiling in the rivers beneath. Nothing happened, but he refused to give up, and then, on the fourth of June, something did happen.

THAT DAY, as sunburnt as a strawberry, Roger came down from his perch for the last time. Upon seeing him, they went to get the Saromsker Rebbe, for Roger had the pellucid eyes of a *tzaddik,* and the Saromsker Rebbe, whose eyes were unclouded with age, was the only one who could properly look into them. He knocked on Roger's door. Inside, the boy was packing a small suitcase.

The Saromsker Rebbe closed the door behind him: there were many people in the hall breathing respectfully.

"I'm leaving for a while," Roger said, "but I'll be back in a few months."

"Where are you going?"

"To the House of Ruth, where a miracle will come, a splinter of light, a flicker."

With everyone following him, the Saromsker Rebbe hurried through the halls. A thousand people packed into the assembly hall, where dust was dancing in beams of sunlight. The Saromsker Rebbe stood on a high platform. "It could be," he said, "that there is a *baal shem tov*."

Before the instruments were taken from their cases and the locks pulled on the schnapps cabinet, Roger carried his butterscotch-colored suitcase down the brownstone steps and disappeared into streets that had begun to darken and glow red with alien neon. Never had he been to the Bronx, he had no map, and did not know the subway, but he was carried as if on a puff of wind through roaring tunnels and white-tiled stations full of the temptations of kosher hot dogs prepared with nonkosher utensils. While the express idled with open doors in the green curve of the Fourteenth Street station, he listened to a saxophone. The notes for which the player of this instrument was reaching and would never attain were the notes Roger had just heard, and even after the doors closed and the train rumbled uptown, he heard them still.

THAT NIGHT, Roger slept on the roof of the 161st Street IRT station, under faintly visible stars that would have blazed but for the emanations of electric light that make the sky above the City of New York the color of a jonquil. He slept neither on a park bench nor on the pavement, because had some Irish bullies tried to beat him silly, it would not have been a mitzvah for Roger had they been struck by lightning. The air in his resting place was relatively cool and dry, and he was so young and flexible that the washboard indentations in his back vanished ten minutes after he left the corrugated roof.

Soon the sun was high and people were streaming from nowhere to the aquarium-dark spaces under the El to buy puffer-fish-shaped fried things the color of apple pie that were filled with potatoes and cheese, triangular slices of pizza (a new thing) from which the ingredients had tried to slide and been killed during their escape, armies of nonkosher fried chicken parts arranged in golden ranks as in the Napoleonic Wars, and candied apples that you could buy only if you signed a statement stipulating that you wouldn't sue after you ate the paper that stuck to the flat place on the top, had all your fillings pulled out, and were stabbed by the stick. This offered neither the prospect of lunch nor any other meal for a boy whose idea of bliss was herring and dilled potatoes. What did it matter? He wasn't hungry, and he stepped from the shadows of the El into the bright sun, where the House of Ruth loomed as white as chalk, a Pleistocene cliff against which swirled the gray-black exhausts of the Major Deegan Expressway.

Hours before the game, he approached a ticket booth. "Is this the House of Ruth?" he asked.

"This is it."

"This is it, just like that? This is her house?"

"His," the ticket seller said.

"His?" Roger asked.

"His."

"Ruth was a woman," Roger stated.

"Ruth was a Babe, but he wasn't no woman."

"That's not true," Roger said, "but it doesn't matter. I've come to save the Yenkiss."

"From what?"

"Defeat."

"You still need a ticket."

"I shouldn't just go in?"

"You have to buy a ticket even to save the team. But you're in luck. If you buy even a cheap ticket now, you can go to the best seats for the pregame practice. Mantle is batting this very minute."

"Mickey Mental?"

"Yeah, Mickey Mental."

"He's the one I'm supposed to replace, I think."

"He'll be so disappointed!"

"He can be on the team. I'll just hit for him."

Not having any money was no discouragement for Roger, who pivoted away from the ticket booth, faced the massive concrete walls and iron gates, and, with Moses and Joshua in mind, threw out his arms. His chest was expanded (which wasn't saying much), his fingers spread, and his face upturned in expectation of a miracle, but no breach appeared in the walls. So he repeated the gesture, and said *"Liftoach!"* Curiously, no breach appeared this time, either, or any of the dozen times thereafter. Still, Roger had no doubt that he had been commanded upon a divine mission.

Like Joshua, he circled the walls. Unlike Joshua, he came to a truck bay into which vendors were carrying trays of freshly baked pretzels, jelly doughnuts, and other things. Stepping up to an immense Armenian who was carrying sacks of roasted peanuts to a baggage trailer inside, Roger said, "Mickey Mental sent me out here to help you because he wants all these beans inside before it rains."

"What?"

"Mickey Mental. He sent me."

"Mantle?"

"He can't do it. A pain in his back, from playing the violin. Get those beans in right away. You know what Rabbi Belknap of Mazlow says about beans in the rain."

The Armenian looked at the slight, blond, Hasidic Jew, and said, "Rabbi Belknap. . . ."

"Let's go!" Roger commanded.

In a kind of trance, the peanut czar of Yankee Stadium agreed. "Okay. Let's go! You take these beans from the truck. Go ahead! Take them. Take the beans!"

After working for half an hour, Roger was in. Not only had he found the House of Ruth, he had breached its walls without slinging a single stone or slaying a single Boabite. Gliding up a ramp in search of June daylight, he came out on the first tier near left field. Looking east toward the bladder neck of the Bronx and into the vast right-field decks rising unto the crane of his neck and topped by rows of flags and formations of lights like the radars on a cruiser, he realized that although it did not fit Luba's description exactly—gone were the purple hangings, the maidens, the grapes—it was close. You could fill it with every rabbi in the world and you would still have room for more. He looked at rows and rows of seats as neatly folded as laundry, lacquered hard and beerproof. Remembering the oceanic sounds on Schnaiper's radio, he filled in the crowd. In his vision of what he heard, he saw whole steppes of people whose faces were like seeds peering from sunflowers, and whose changes of position and sudden cheers were like wind sweeping high grass. Legions disappeared in the shadows, from which a roar echoed like a hurricane. How many places like this, he thought, would it take to hold six million people, and his answer, quickly calculated, was one hundred twenty. Stadiums packed with fifty thousand people could be placed in a line down both sides of Manhattan from Washington Heights to the Battery, with no space in between, and if the souls within could break their silence, the roar would be unlike anything ever heard.

"One foot at a time," he said to himself, with no idea why he said it. "One foot at a time." He sighed. If only his father and mother could see him, standing in Ruth's house, about to save the Yenkiss. They would not know of either of these things, but if only they could see him.

A young Hasidic boy in black robes and a fur hat on a hot June day had no idea how to save the Yankees, but his moving feet carried him to the rail. At the elliptical center of the field a man in a white suit stood on a barrow of dirt and would periodically throw something at two men who faced him. One of the men was in turtlelike armor, squatting. The other stood, with a weapon.

When the thing that was thrown at the man with the staff would come at him almost faster than the eye could see, he would strike at it, and there would be a crack as in the breaking of a cable, after which the thing that was thrown would fly out into the air, along varying trajectories, and land in the grass. Then someone would throw the man on the dirt a new thing, and the process would continue. Sometimes the man who held the weapon missed, and the thing that was thrown was caught by the turtle, who threw it back. Who knew? But this was baseball.

On the back of the man with the weapon was the number 7. This meant, according to Schnaiper, that he was Mickey Mental. It was a good place to start. If you are going to help the needy, help those in most distress, and those in most distress are those who have fallen furthest. Roger was sure that it was no accident that the only thing between him and Mickey Mental, the greatest baseball player of the age (according to Schnaiper), was a hundred feet of perfectly clear air through which sound could easily carry.

THIS WAS AT A TIME in the morning when the field was most like what a field is supposed to be, swept clocklike by golden legs of sun stilting across it as time progressed, insects busy in flight against the huge foils of black shadow. A white blur that is not mist but a condition of the light, a lost and miscellaneous glare, covered the empty stands and bleachers in which, to Mantle's delight, virtually no one had yet appeared. And those who had come early kept as respectful a distance as pilgrims in St. Peter's who have stumbled upon the Pope in the dry runs of investiture. Fragrant breezes from the field alternated pleasingly with cool downdrafts of leftover night air rolling off the second level like a waterfall. It was the perfect time for the great player to concentrate on the attainment of perfection in hitting the ball. To allow his gifts free rein, he needed something like the flow of a river. In the mornings, when Yankee Stadium reminded him most of the fields his forebears had farmed, that river flowed best. He was deep in concentration, and doing very well, when he became aware of a distraction.

From behind, from the left-field fence out toward third base, came a kind of squeak. At first he thought it was a bird or a cricket. Then he realized that it was an imploring voice. Once every great while, coarse people got into the stadium before a game and stood at the rail calling out his name, hoping for acknowledgment, a conversation, or an autographed baseball. This he had learned to ignore.

But though he tried, he could not ignore the squeak. He screwed up his face, rested the bat against his shoulder, and held up his left hand as a signal to the pitcher to hold off. What was this squeak? He lifted his head, hand still held out, and squinted, which was what he did when he wanted better to hear something behind him. He heard the calling of his own name, after a fashion. "What?" he said, as if asking why the perfect morning had to include this.

Roger had been squeaking as regularly as a tree frog in heat. For ten minutes, without even a hint of self-consciousness—indeed, with miraculous happiness—he had been calling out: "Mickey Mental! Mickey Mental! Mickey Mental!"

Convinced that he was being mocked, the champion turned his head somewhat like an ostrich and stared over his own broad back as if it were a wall. He was expecting to see a large disorganized lout with a face oriented in many directions at once, or possibly a bland-looking idiot with eyes only inches from his hairline. But he saw nothing, because he was looking too high. When he dropped his aim a fraction he spied a small, funny-looking thing in black. Not budging from the plate, he leaned back slightly on his heels and focused on the object, laboring to understand what it was, while all the time it squeaked at him, shouting, "Mickey Mental! Mickey Mental! Mickey Mental!"

By this time the turtle had stood and removed his carapace. "What is that, Mickey?" he asked. "It's not a monkey, is it?"

"Monkeys don't talk, Yogi."

"Maybe it's mechanical."

"It's making fun of me," Mickey Mantle said. "I've got to take care of this." He strode angrily toward Roger, bat famously in hand, as irritated and as polite as a steambath attendant. Halfway there, he saw that his tormentor was a boy in Hasidic robes and a *shtreimel.* The face of this boy was, in fact, oriented in many different directions, but lucidly so, so intelligently in fact that it gave Mantle pause, for in Roger's young eyes was a depth that, even though they were young, Mickey had never seen except in the eyes of the very old. Roger had stopped squeaking, and was smiling, because everything was going according to plan.

A foot taller than Roger, Mickey bent forward, squinted with his left eye, opened the right very wide, and said, "Are *you* . . . calling *me?*"

"You're seven," Roger said in his accented English.

Mickey nodded.

"What a number! What I could tell you about that number!"

"Is that what you wanted?"

"No."

"Why did you call me that?"

"What?" Roger inquired.

"Mickey Mental."

Roger shrugged. "That's your name."

"What's my name?"

"Mickey Mental. Isn't it?"

"Say *Mantle,*" Mickey commanded.

"Mental," Roger said.

"Mantle," Mickey repeated.

"Mental," Roger echoed. He could not hear the difference, and wondered at this strange form of introduction.

"Mickey Mental," Mickey said. "Are we done?"

"Oh no," Roger said, "not by a lung shot."

"Not by a lung shot? Look, kid, I've got batting practice. Do you want me to sign a glove or something? I'll do it, but leave me alone."

Roger looked at his hands. "Glove."

"Whadaya want? I'll give you a minute."

Now, like clouds dappling the sea, the thinking moved perceptibly across Roger's eyes. "I've been sent to help you," he said.

He spoke with absolute seriousness, with a gravity of unknown but arresting origin. Mickey forgot the passage of time. Thinking that he was losing his mind, he asked, "Who sent you?"

"*Boruch ha Shem,*" Roger said, which means, "blessed be the Name."

"*Boruch ha Shem,*" Mickey Mantle repeated. "Who's that?"

"It's forbidden to say the Name."

"But you just said it."

"No I didn't."

"*Boruch ha Shem,* right?"

"*Boruch ha Shem.*"

"So, you said it."

"I would never say it," Roger said, "*Boruch ha Shem.*"

"Well, you tell *Boruch ha Shem* that I'm not interested."

"I wouldn't say that," Roger said, in a way that indicated a nervous apprehension and his absolute certainty that one dare not do such a thing.

"Okay," said Mickey, "your time is up. That's it." He turned and began to walk back to home plate, hoping that he would hear no more squeaks and that the next time he looked back Roger would be gone and would not appear again.

But he had taken only a few steps when Roger shouted, "God. I can say it in English."

Mickey stopped, turned around, and went back. "God sent you?"

Roger nodded.

"He Himself, personally."

Eyes closed, Roger nodded unambiguously.

"To do what?"

"To lift you from the darkness of defeat."

"And how, did He tell you, are you to do that?"

"I was not told how," Roger said. (The problem for Mickey, as he himself saw it, was that he believed Roger.) "Specific instructions I didn't get, but I was watching, and as usually happens, it came to me."

"Okay," Mickey said, "save me."

"I will," said Roger. "You were repeatedly hitting that object which was thrown at you, with that axe."

Mickey looked at the bat and rolled his eyes.

"And I noticed that you hit the object out to many different places, and that people expressed approval or disappointment depending upon where it landed. Is there an ideal place to which to direct it?"

Mickey laughed to himself a little like a crazy person. "Yeah," he said, "there is an ideal place to which to direct the object."

"Where?" Roger asked.

Mickey took the bat in his left hand, turned his head to the right, and extended his right hand, pointing up and away. "You see that clock over there, above the sign?"

"That says *Longeens?*" Roger asked, pronouncing it with a hard *G*.

"Longines," Mickey corrected. "The ideal place to which to direct the object is over that clock. No one's ever done it. No one's ever directed a ball out of this stadium."

"I'll show you," Roger said.

"You'll show me."

"Yes, I will."

"Kid, we have the best batting coaches in the world. I'm supposed to be the best batter in the world. How can you show me?"

"Listen," said Roger, losing his patience. "That's what I was sent here to do. Let me show you, and if I can't, I'll go."

Mickey stared at Roger. "What is this?" he asked.

"The goat can butt because he has horns," Roger said, as if that settled it.

And, as if it did, Mickey said, "You wait here. I'm going to see."

"See what?"

"Talk to my friends."

"Okay."

Mickey walked quickly back to home. Roger prayed. Davening, he was pulled into the clouds of galaxies and stars, the explosion of suns united and uniting, the greatest glory bleeding perfectly into the smallest thing, the smallest thing assuming effortlessly the greatest glory. It was not that he imagined this or summoned it to appear, but, rather, that his prayer was that the curtain be lifted.

AN AGITATED MANTLE took up the batter's position and tapped the plate with the end of the bat. Berra pulled down his mask. Mantle raised the bat and made eye contact with the pitcher. To dispel his confusion, he wanted to hit one into the stands. The pitcher, Martin, wound up, released, and a slow ball came down the chute, precisely in the middle of the strike zone. Mantle swung to smash the ball, and didn't even touch it.

"Stee! Rike!" Berra said.

"Shut up!"

Knowing that his friend didn't talk this way, Berra flipped up his mask. "What's the matter?"

"That kid. He's got me shook up."

"What did he want, an autograph?"

"No. He's come here to save us. God sent him. He says he can show me how to hit a ball over the clock."

Berra thought. "Let him come to the plate. That's what he wants. Let him hit one. Why not? What can you win?"

"You mean, 'What can you lose?'"

"No. 'What can you win?' It means, 'Grab the bell by the broom.' Maybe he can save us."

"How can *he* teach *me*? He's a kid. I don't know, twelve? He's a hayseed," by which the great slugger meant *Hasid*.

"Mick, maybe he knows."

"I don't think so, Yogi."

"You were a hayseed before you got into baseball," Berra said, expressing the almost universally held impression that Mantle was, somehow, the paradigm of American agriculture.

Mantle looked sharply at the catcher. "I was *not*."

"Sure you were. Everyone knows it."

"A hayseed?"

"Yeah. Ask any baseball fan in America."

"With the hat, and the sideburns and everything?" Mantle asked.

"That's right," Berra said, thinking of straw hat and rural aspect.

"I was not!"

"Yes you were," said Berra, bobbing his head up and down in confirmation. "You've got it written all over you."

Mickey thought this was a dream. "How come no one ever told me?"

"Because it's so *obvious*."

"It is?"

"Yeah."

"How?"

"In the way you dress, the way you talk, the way you look. Your accent. Your face. It's part of why you're such a hero. I'm Italian. People look at me differently. It's a different attitude."

"Wait a minute," said Mickey, "wait a minute." He turned to the pitcher. "Hey, Billy," he shouted. "Billy. Do I strike you as a hayseed? Do I look and talk like one?"

The pitcher said, "Yeah."

"Seriously?"

"Yeah."

"How come you never told me?"

"Why should I?" the pitcher shouted back. "Who am I, your girlfriend?"

Mickey stared off into space.

"Mick, get the kid," Berra said. "Bring him out onto the field. We'll put the guys in position; it'll be the thrill of his life. Look at 'im. There's no one with him. If you're alone, you're all by yourself."

"Yeah, but he doesn't know anything about baseball. He calls the ball an object and the bat an axe. He says that he doesn't know how, but that God will provide."

"Get him anyway."

"You believe him?"

"I'll get the guys," Berra announced.

As MICKEY MANTLE lifted Roger over the fence, the Yankees loped out onto the field. Maintenance workers looked up. What was this? The whole team, in an empty stadium, set up for a game?

"How much do you weigh?" Mickey asked Roger after he set him down and they were walking—Roger's black costume flowing with the breeze—because the airborne Roger had seemed to Mickey to have had no weight.

"Thirteen and three-quarter *shvoigles*," Roger answered.

"How many pounds is that?"

"I don't know. There are eight *beyngaluchs* in a *shvoigle*."

"Did you ever play baseball?"

"Until a little while ago, I never heard of it."

"Well, here on the field, awaiting your direction, are the New York Yankees."

"You know," said Roger, almost at the plate, "God shifts an untold number of birds twice a year from the top of the earth to the middle, and from the middle back to the top—geese, herons, *fingelehs,* robins, chickens, starlings, woodpeckers, *kibniks, stvittles,* albatrosses, sprites, doves. . . ."

Mickey awaited what was next.

"If He takes the trouble to shift a goose from the North Pole to Havana, He could easily have set me in proper motion to end up here, and He did. Here are the Yenkiss, all spread out, as He intended, and here am I. Hand me the axe."

Mickey gave him the bat. When it came into his hands, the sun, purely by coincidence, hit it in a peculiar way, and it appeared to glow. Roger held it almost at arm's length, like an upraised sword, and stunned the Yankees as he swayed back and forth and twirled around, for the bat seemed to them— as it seemed to him—to be a staff with a power beyond that of the maker or the wood. That he would dance so, in front of them, as if unaware of their presence, or not caring, they found extraordinary. He was, in fact, momentarily unaware of them, because his thoughts had been seized, and flowed in only one direction, where the staff pointed, up. The only thing in his heart at that moment was love, and the only thing before his eyes a verse from the book of Ruth: "May the Lord deal kindly with you, as you have dealt with the dead." What the Yankees did not know was that this boy who knew nothing about baseball had come into their midst to test an ancient compact that of late had been broken. The Yankees did not know that their stadium had been turned into a court of justice in which the prosecutor was an odd little boy and the defendant was the creator of the universe. In Christian theology—and the Yankees were Christians—this is inconceivable. God does not appear in the dock. He does not dispute with those over whom He holds absolute sway. In Jewish theology, however, He does.

When he finished, Roger looked about and realized that everyone was staring at him in absolute silence, and that now he had to do something big. Praying internally nonstop, he stepped into the position in which he had seen Mantle, and tapped the plate with the bat.

"What do you call the object that is thrown toward you?" he asked of anyone. At a distance, he had not seen that it was a ball.

"Ball," said Berra, leaving out the article, dropping his mask, and crouching into position.

Roger looked at Berra's segmented armor and said, "You must be *trayf*." Then he turned to the pitcher and said, "Throw ball!"

"Hit it above the clock," Mantle said matter-of-factly. After all, they had discussed this already.

Roger nodded, but Wylie, one of the coaches, who was mean and small of soul, mockingly said, "No, first knock off the hand."

"Which one?" Roger asked.

"The minute hand," Wylie answered, delighted. The clock read 10:20.

"Okay," said Roger, choking up naturally on Mickey Mantle's heavy bat.

Martin began to wind up for an easy pitch—he didn't want to hit a small Hasidic boy—but Roger stopped him, and turned to Mantle. "Mickey," he said, "when I knock off the minute hand it will fall to the seats below. It's pointed and it must weigh many *shvoigles*. The sign on the left," he said, meaning the sign to the left of the scoreboard, "says '*Anyone interfering with play subject to arrest.*' Does that mean me?"

"No," half a dozen people said in unison. This broke the spell. Now they realized that he wasn't even going to connect with the ball, and they began to think of ways—such as biting their lips—not to laugh at him so as not to devastate his pride, although they knew Wylie would.

"Hey Mickey," someone said, "after the kid finishes, let him keep the bat." "Okay," Mickey said. It was a good idea. The kid wouldn't feel so bad.

Roger pointed at the minute hand. This was so much what like Babe Ruth used to do, uncannily so, that even though they thought he was imitating (which, never having heard of Babe Ruth, he was not), they were troubled. They assumed that the strikeout would take quite a few pitches, with Martin kindly throwing a ball or two, and they shifted from foot to foot.

Martin wound up relaxedly. He was hardly going to throw fast or fancy. He leaned back and threw.

If you had seen it in slow motion, you would have seen a baseball traveling like a planet in orbit, precisely and languorously, though behind its sharpness the rest of the world would have been a blur. Then you would have seen the bat moving back ever-so-slightly, like the hammer-cock of a Colt .45. And you would have seen Roger's left foot elevate minutely above the ground. Then you would have seen the bat itself making an arc as certain and as powerful as a comet's, and you would have seen the flow of his muscle and the light in his eyes, and the astronomical powers fed from the billowing fringes and folds of black cloth into the almost-glowing staff. You would have seen, in Roger's face and eyes, a battlefield look, an expression that comes only when impossible outcomes are guaranteed. And then you would have seen the impact—so tremendous that the ball shattered into a hundred thousand minute particles filling the air with a cloud of dust that disappeared on the wind.

The Yankees had never seen anything like it. No one had.

"What happened?" someone asked.

Berra flipped up the mask. "The ball was pulverized. I saw it. I've seen the skin come off a ball, but I never saw a. . . ."

"Was that a trick ball?" Coach Wylie yelled to Martin.

"It was the ball that Mickey hit into center," Martin answered.

No one spoke.

"I'm sorry," said Roger. "I guess I hit it too hard. Next time, I'll hit it more gently."

"He hit it too hard," Mickey said to himself, dazed.

The coach got a ball, inspected it, bounced it against the plate, and threw it out to Martin. "Try this one."

Now no one breathed except Roger. The pitch was thrown. The same astronomical conjunctions occurred. The bat connected explosively with the ball but, this time, just under the limit beyond which the ball would have been destroyed. Leather was stretched as far as it would stretch, thread too. It traveled in a straight line, leaving behind it a brief trail of orange flame and then a hardly perceptible line of white smoke.

Mouths dropped open and bodies froze as the ball slammed into the minute hand of the clock that said *World's Most Honored Watch* and blew it from its axle so that it windmilled through the air, corkscrewing, eventually, into the ground in front of the wall that had written on it the challenging notation, *407 Ft.* The field of Yankee Stadium, with the Yankees standing upon it, was still.

Even Roger stared at the javelin- or propellerlike minute hand stuck perpendicularly in the ground. A seagull dipped down to examine the broken clock, and then, taken by a gust of wind, rose like a rocket and disappeared into the clouds.

"THAT DIDN'T HAPPEN," Wylie said. "It was a trick. I've seen it a million times."

"Seen what a million times, Wylie?"

"They put an explosive charge in the clock, and somebody watching with a telescope pushes a button, which sends a radio signal to the detonator, which explodes the hands off the clock. It's the oldest trick in the world."

"And you've seen it?" Mantle asked.

"I saw it in the minors in North Carolina. I saw it in Florida. I saw it all over. You know, they do it."

"I hit the object, truthfully," Roger stated.

"I'll bet you did, kid. Let's see you do it again."

"He can't, the hand's down already."

"Now that the charge is gone," said Wylie, "let's see you knock off the other one." He had to believe his own theory.

Roger tapped the bat against the plate. He had a grim, insulted look. "Throw ball," he said to Martin, who was already on the mound.

Before the pitch, Wylie shouted, "Don't go so easy on him this time!"

Martin shot back, "What's the difference? It's how he hits."

"Anybody can hit a slow pitch. That's just giving it to him."

"Throw ball!" yelled a peeved Roger.

"You say, 'play ball,' or, 'pitch it in,'" Mantle told him.

"Pitch it in!" Roger shouted.

Martin wound up, and the ball came in toward the plate fast but straight. Now that the motions were familiar, Roger was unconcerned about missing, and looked forward to the sharp crack of the bat. He worried only about hitting the ball gently enough not to pulverize it. Once again, he connected. Once again, the ball smoked toward the clock and struck it, this time breaking the hour hand off at the base. It fell, bumped against the scoreboard, and landed flat on the bleachers.

The Yankees were awed, but wanted reassurance nonetheless. Knowing that there was no wind, and that the field was dead silent, Mantle almost whispered, "Kid, can you put a hole in the clock?"

"Sure," said Roger. "Where?"

"At the two o'clock position."

"Pitch it in!"

The ball came in, and left like a recoilless rifle shell. A crunch sounded shortly after a hole appeared near the two.

"Get Stengel," Mantle commanded, his voice almost shaking (Mickey Mantle's voice never shook, at least not in Yankee Stadium). "I think the kid's just about to hit the ball out of the park."

In no time at all, Stengel emerged from the dugout. He had already been on his way, having been told by a choking assistant manager that Babe Ruth was back, reincarnated as a kid who was fresh and could do things the Babe had never done. Stengel believed this to be an elaborate joke, and he didn't have time for jokes. "What's going on here?" he asked belligerently. "Why're you guys on the field? It's not enough that Kansas City is going to completely run over you, you want to be tired, too?"

Mantle shook his head. "Casey, this kid is going to hit the ball out of the stadium," he said, and then laughed like a deranged person. "Really, he is!"

Stengel focused on Roger for the first time. He tried to speak, but the sight of Roger, so small and slight, in black Hasidic robes, a *shtreimel,* and *payess,* made him unable to. Then he said, "All right. You got me. Now let's get back to work, okay?"

"I'm serious," said Mantle, a little angry and a bit trembly.

"Have you been drinking, Mickey?"

"He destroyed the clock," a Yankee said. "He did. Look."

Stengel looked up at the blasted clock. "Who did that?" he asked.

"He did," Mantle said.

"It's a trick," Wylie shouted. "I saw it in the minors."

"Okay, jerks," Stengel said, never known for being unimpulsive. He paraded back and forth for a moment or two, thinking. "If that kid can hit a ball out of this park . . . gimme a break, will ya . . . if he can do that, and he's gotta do it more than once [the businessman in Stengel could be cautious, too], I'll sign him for a million dollars a year and I'll double your salaries, every single one of you."

The Yankees were ecstatic with the prospect.

"But," Stengel went on, "if he can't—in fifty pitches—I won't sign him for anything, and I'll cut your salaries in half for a year." Stengel loved this. Unlike his current season, it was win-win.

"All of us, Mr. Stengel?" asked an outfielder who had just risen from the farm team and had a baby to feed.

Now Stengel nearly glowed. "No, you've got a choice here. Everyone who thinks the kid can hit it out, get behind the third-base line. Everyone who doesn't, get behind the first-base line. If you're behind the first-base line, your salary stays the same, no matter what. If you're behind the third-base line, it's double or half. Ha!" He was sure that not one member of the team would walk north beyond the third-base line. He had brilliantly transformed their joke on him into a joke on them.

For the next few minutes, the Yankees were deep in thought, and no one moved. Then Berra stood up and, with his left hand, removed his mask in the practiced gesture that he had accomplished many thousands of times. Stengel thought he was giving in. But Berra took a breath, pulled the mask back to his right shoulder, and hurled it like a pie plate beyond the third-base line. "That stands for me!" he shouted, and squatted down, confident that he would not have to catch the next pitch.

Mantle smiled the smile of someone who, though he may be about to lose grievously, will feel a deep satisfaction even in loss—as if the things that people do, all the hundreds of millions of different things, were measured not merely in the visible and apparent accounts of the world, but in another ledger of far greater import. He crossed the third-base line, and waited. Just standing there made him feel like his ancestors who had crossed oceans, knocked down forests, and fought wars.

Then the others followed suit, until only Stengel, the new outfielder, and Wylie were left behind the first-base line. Stengel was irritated beyond measure, but delighted as well. "Wylie, you don't even count. You're not a player, get away from me." He looked at his team. "Okay, nuts, you want to mutiny? Okay. You're outa your minds. But, look, I like it! You know why I like it? I like it because it's justice. You're doing so badly, you deserve a cut in pay. That's why."

He turned to Martin, still on the mound. "What about you?"

"I'm with them," Martin said, pointing to the team.

"And so am I, goddamit!" yelled the new outfielder, crossing over.

"You mustn't say that," Roger scolded as the outfielder ran by him.

"Let's go then," Stengel said. And then, to Roger, "Did they put you up to this, kid? Did they pay you?"

"No one ever paid me anything," said Roger, "in my whole life."

After assessing Roger, Stengel turned to Martin. "Billy, don't hurt him. Gentle pitches, nice and easy, all of them."

"You haven't seen him," Martin said.

"But I have seen him. He's standing right there. Look at him. Can you believe it? Kid, if you can hit the ball out of the stadium once in fifty pitches, you can have as many more pitches as you need to hit it out again, and then I'll sign you as a Yankee for a million dollars a year."

"It has nothing to do with money," Roger said, and tapped the plate with the bat. "It can't have anything to do with money. I don't want the money. I just want to teach you," he said earnestly, "to hit these objects, these . . . *balls,* with perfection."

Because there was no other sound except the dim roar of traffic on the Major Deegan, even the slight luffing of the flags in the June sky was audible. The Yankees knew that what they expected was not possible, but they believed that they were going to see it.

"What lies behind the wall, past the tall white building?" Roger asked.

"The Bronx," Berra answered.

"And what lies beyond the Bronx?"

"Long Island Sound."

"Are there many boats in Long Island Sound?"

"On a day like today," said Berra, "there are."

"Beyond Long Island Sound, then?"

"Long Island."

"Of course," said Roger, unhappily. "And then the ocean."

"Then the ocean," Berra confirmed, "like water off a duck's back. Why?"

"I wouldn't want to hit anybody," said Roger. "Play ball."

As Martin wound up, Stengel was filled with joy, because, if Roger could do this, doubling salaries would be nothing compared to the revenue that would pour in. To see a ball hit out of Yankee Stadium, people would come from Borneo. If Roger couldn't do it, the pay cut would free up funds for hiring some new players with blood in their veins. But, most of all, Stengel, like his team, like everyone, loved being at the threshold of great events.

The ball flew in, expressly. Roger now had the look of a professional, the Mantle look, the forward-oriented, concentrated gaze, the ease, the love of action. It was the attitude of the kind of racehorse that lived above all to run. *Shtreimel* tilted, he stepped forward and leaned gracefully into the pitch. The bat connected with the ball, this time with a sharp up-angle that every experienced batter and all the coaches deemed impossible for propelling the ball over the wall. It was simply too steep. Even had Ruth hit a ball so steeply it would have flown gloriously high but not even reached the bleachers.

This ball, however, left a faintly white trace and seemed to accelerate as it climbed. Everyone except Roger shielded his eyes and followed the trajectory. The ball made no parabola, but kept going up. They waited for it to lose power and head down, plopping into right field, but it didn't. Only when it disappeared from sight did they realize that it was not going to come down in the stadium. They didn't know where it was going to come down. It was gone.

It had never happened before, and no one knew what to do. So Stengel dropped to his knees and said "Holy cow," more softly than people usually say holy cow, and he kept repeating it, as if he were in conversation with himself, a conversation limited to those two words spoken with different emphasis and intonation. It went something like this: "Holy cow. Ho-ly cow. Ho-ly cow! Holy cow? Holy . . . cow! Ho-ly . . . ca-ow! Holy? Cow?" and so on, quietly, madly.

The Yankees gave no thought to their new wealth, for as Roger hit four more pitches, one after the other, into the distant Atlantic, and Casey Stengel made an opera out of just two words, they could think only of how lucky they were to be there at that very moment.

ROGER TURNED TO STENGEL and said, "You see?"

"I see," said Stengel. "I see."

"I have a suggestion," Roger went on.

"Sure, we'll do it."

"I was watching Mickey hit the balls here and there."

"Yes," Stengel said. (Not "Yes?" but "Yes.")

"Three people wait out in the grass to catch them."

Stengel nodded as if seeing the game through new eyes. "That's right. They do."

"They shouldn't. The one in the middle should stay, but the others should come closer in."

"Who would cover left and right field?" Mantle asked.

Roger pointed to both, and said, "The one in the center can go to either."

"Uh," said Stengel, most timidly, "we've found that, given the depth of the field, the most a man can cover is a third. You see, the most he'd have to run would be a sixth, which would then give him a chance to cover the field back to front." Stengel paused. "You have another way?"

"Yeh," said Roger. "Cover from the center. I'll show you. Give me one of those kreplach," by which he meant a fielder's mitt. (They wouldn't have known had he not held out his left hand and slapped it with his right fist, as he had seen Larsen do with his glove.)

"Get the kid a kreplach!" Stengel barked, and Mickey Mantle—Mickey Mantle—ran to the dugout as eagerly as a batboy, and emerged with his own kreplach to give to Roger.

Roger jogged to center field. He didn't go particularly fast, but he seemed to rise as high with each step as if he were wearing kangaroo shoes. Mantle took the bat that had just made history and positioned himself to hit pop-ups.

"Hit one right to him. See if he can catch it," Stengel commanded.

"What?" Mantle asked. "He just hit a ball out of the park, five times in a row, Casey. You think he can't do what he says he's going to do?"

"He's probably never caught a ball," Stengel insisted.

"So what," Berra said. "The start of the middle is the end of the road for the beginning."

"That may be so, Yogi," Stengel said, "but let's make sure to start where he is."

"I'll do that if you want," Mantle agreed, and hit one toward Roger. Mantle was so good that Roger didn't even have to shift his feet to position himself for the catch, which he accomplished swimmingly.

They weren't expecting what happened when Roger threw the ball in. Never having thrown a baseball, or even held one, he overthrew. The ball sailed into the back of the upper grandstand. "This has gotta be a dream," Stengel said.

"It isn't," said Berra. "You know how, when you're dreaming, there's a sign that says, 'You're Dreaming'? There's no sign."

"Yeah," said Stengel. "You're right. There's no sign, so we know we're not dreaming. Okay, Mickey, let's see if he can do this. Hit him one as far back on the third-base line as you can."

"I have a feeling he can do it," Mantle said, hitting with newfound strength.

The ball went deep into left field, and Roger followed—no, preceded—it with inexplicable speed. His run had nothing about it of gravity. He just burned across the grass, like a fast train, and waited for the ball to come in. This was astounding, but not impossible.

Stengel continued to direct. "I want to see this. He's standing on the third-base line. Hit one right along the first-base line. If he can cross the field . . . if he. . . ."

The ball went high into right. Roger kept his eye on it as he ran. He ran so fast that one of the players said, "Look at that! Look at that!" and Roger arrived in right field in time to catch the ball.

They motioned for him to come in, and as Roger glided toward them along the first-base line, this time carrying the ball with him, Stengel turned to the team and said, "This is a whole new situation."

BECAUSE OF THE MANY complications that ensued, Stengel knew it wasn't a dream. Dreams are notable not for their complications but for their lack of them, which is not to say that they aren't complicated. Precisely because it wasn't a dream, everyone who had seen what had happened had to be bribed, threatened, begged, or cajoled into silence. This meant the Yankees themselves, including a few coaches and assistant managers, four grounds-keepers, and a hot-dog-roll contractor who witnessed the remarkable events while wheeling in several thousand pounds of hot-dog rolls. Stengel (who, as Berra said, was the smartest jerk who ever lived) enlisted those in the conspiracy not only with huge amounts of money but with roles to play. The hot-dog-roll man was retained at $5,000 per week to provide covert transportation for Roger in a hot-dog-roll truck. The groundskeepers were promised, if they kept mum, new lawns and new houses. The Yankees themselves had everything to win.

The problem of secrecy wasn't overwhelming. The real trouble was that Roger would have to quit a week before Rosh HaShana, which meant he couldn't play in the World Series. This was unbearable, and as the Yankees played—brilliantly, if losingly—against Kansas City that afternoon, the conversation in Stengel's office went as follows:

"You've got to play in the Series, Roger. You can have anything you want. What do you want? Money? Broads? A car? A trip to Israel?"

"I want the Yenkiss to win."

"So do I, Roger. That's why you've got to play in the Series."

"I can't."

"Roger, this is important here, really important. Who exactly says that you can't play in the Series?"

"God."

"I understand. You want to be a good guy. You want to be devout. You want to follow the rules. But God wouldn't mind if you played in the Series. I'm sure many famous rabbis would uphold my statement."

"He would mind, He told me."

"What passage says that? We'll get the best rabbis to look at it."

"There's no passage. He told me."

"He told you directly?"

"Yeh."

"I mean He actually . . . He . . . told you Himself? You spoke to Him?"

"I always speak to Him. But this time He came down to the roof."

"Symbolically."

"No."

"No?"

"Mr. Stengel"—which Roger pronounced "Stengeleh"—"I weigh thirteen and three-quarter *shvoigles*. I'm two *yumps* tall. How do you think I hit the ball out of the house? Do you think I could do such a thing alone? Who do you think is in charge here? You? Me?"

NOT ONLY WOULD ROGER have to quit a week before Rosh HaShana, because of study requirements and holidays, he could play only in five games. Also, he had to have kosher food, and a place to live. Even had Roger been willing to accept money (Stengel foolishly told Mantle that the Yankees would have signed Roger for $10,000,000 a year—contingent on performance), the Yankees would have put him up in the presidential suite at the Carlyle anyway. As they didn't even have to pay him, this was almost effortless. No one in the world, Stengel reasoned, would ever make the connection between Roger Reeves, the new rookie fresh out of the Carolinas or possibly Georgia (who knew?), and Winston Wilgis, a neurotic and reclusive rubber heir whose aides paid the hotel staff large amounts of cash to be discreet, and who was never seen and never left his room, although his adopted son, a Hasidic teenager who sometimes wore a baseball uniform, came and went regularly in a hot-dog-roll truck that pulled up to the loading dock.

Roger had bodyguards—two huge couches in bulging suits and bowl-like haircuts, whose enormous Magnum revolvers were like giant swellings under their coats. They stood in front of his door whenever he was there, and checked the rabbis who brought carts of kosher pancakes and chocolate milkshakes for milk meals, and Bessarabian shish kebab and chopped-liver sandwiches for meat meals. They shook the Cel-Ray celery tonic bottles to make sure they were not bombs (which, when Roger opened them, they were), and kept all maids and waiters in total ignorance of the occupant of the hotel's best accommodations. Roger was rather alone.

The first night he was brought to the hotel, after ten hours of unwritten-contract negotiations in which he was totally inflexible and got exactly what he wanted, he was tired. At his insistence they had stopped at a delicatessen at 100th Street and Broadway, where he ate like a cow and drank six bottles of Cel-Ray, his favorite drink in the world, that he had had only once before in his life, during a raucous and disorganized Simchat Torah when he had mistakenly grazed at the rabbis' sweet table.

They popped him into the hotel room as if he had been in a hotel before, which he hadn't, and there he was, in the presidential suite of the Carlyle, on the day that he had hit five balls out of Yankee Stadium, but luxury meant nothing to him, and this kind of glory little.

The furniture was so European that Louis XIV might not have noticed had he by some miracle been transported to the Carlyle from his own time and place. The carpets were soft and dense, the walls smooth and solid, everything clean and well lit, the colors bleeding into one another like wounded comrades in the French foreign legion. Roger wandered from room to room, but only in the living room did he fully realize what was happening, for there, as high above the earth as an airplane, huge banks of whistle-clean windows opened out on Manhattan, which roared and glowed, fading into the distance in never-ending avenues of a million flares, draped with necklaces of bridge lights, and banked high with massive buildings twinkling like starshine on a lake. Someone else standing in the same place, a president perhaps, a tycoon, a movie star, or even a baseball player, might have felt a feeling of power and vindication. To be high and to see the world marked out below you in cool fire is, after all, the dream of angels, but Roger felt neither pride nor vindication. Instead, his heart swelled at the great expanse of lights and a blood-red pennant left in the sky by the setting sun. He had no thought of what he had accomplished or where he had come. Looking over the miraculous work that stood before him he saw no reflection or reminder of himself, but only the kind of high glory that rides from place to place and time to time on a shower of sparks.

June was hot, perfect, and strange. It started magnificently and was slowly transformed into the initial bakery days of summer, tolerable for their novelty, when the beaches are as hot and white as molten glass but the ocean is blue and numbingly cold. A day of prairie heat would surrender to a northern European evening with cool breezes veering off the Hudson and sailing down the avenues like Dutch sloops. Morning fogs as thick as cotton could burn off in a minute, leaving behind them a newly shining world. It was a gorgeous month, but its brilliances were a foil for many peculiar things.

For example, a Mr. Winston Wilgis, rubber heir and recluse, called the Hotel Carlyle front desk to ask for a complete set of the Babylonian Talmud and sixteen cases of Dr. Brown's Cel-Ray Tonic on ice. The next day, he asked for deep-sea fishing equipment, and if you had been walking on the street below his suite and had had occasion to look up, you would have seen, at various times, tarpon lures, bagels, socks, and a banana flying with dampened grace ten feet above you, a pendulum suspended by semi-invisible line.

As much as he caused others puzzlement, Roger himself was puzzled. Worked with great skill into a fruitwood enclosure in the living room of his suite were two televisions and a high-fidelity radio. One television played in black and white, the other in experimental color. Neglecting these wonders on his first night, Roger awoke early the next morning and turned the knobs. He had never seen a television. At first, nothing happened, but then a white dot appeared in the center of the pudding-gray glass, soon to move and intensify like a supernova, and then, like the opening of an umbrella, to expand into what became a picture accompanied by a hardly bearable tone. The picture was of something that looked like a spiderweb, and had written in the corner, *WPIX-TV, Channel 11.* Utterly useless. The one in color was not much better, though it looked like a Herschel Trixie, the only abstract artist Roger had thought he had heard of, though he had actually not heard of any.

The radio played more than just one station, and because no liver-filled refrigerator case interfered, you could turn it on or off whenever you wanted. The quality of its sound far exceeded that of the butcher's radio, and the first time Roger turned it on the most extraordinary music filled the room, music such as he had never heard. He listened in wonderment as someone sang a lyric that sounded like, *A wop bopa loobop a pop pop pop, a hop poppa loopa, a wop bop pop,* and so on, with a pace and excitement that, though entirely foreign, seized him and made him dance around the room in abandon. Not even a Memphis lounge lizard could have done a better number, or swiveled his hips, bit his lips, and raised his cheeks until his eyes were slits, than did Roger, who, when the song ended and was replaced by a jingle that went, *Brusha brusha brusha, new Ipana toothpaste, healthy for your tee-eeth!,* stopped dead in delight.

Roger was not the only one that June to be astonished as both the sports and rabbinic worlds were thrown off balance by inexplicable changes to the New York Yankees. The only plausible explanation, that the Yankees wanted to draw new fans from the perhaps-underrepresented Orthodox Jewish community, was fairly unsatisfactory in that it did not actually explain the extraordinary measures. First came the announcement that hot dogs sold at the stadium would be only kosher. They were mainly kosher anyway. Then the revelation that on "ice-cream days" (a new term in baseball), hot dogs would not be served, and vice versa. This caused quite a stir.

At the press conference called to announce the food plans a reporter asked Stengel if and when peanuts would be available. "I'm told that peanuts are parve, and will be available at all times," he answered. Most of the reporters thought that "parve" was a Stengel word (perhaps picked up from Berra, who was always inventing new ways to say things) that was the equivalent of the beatnik "cool," or the now dated "swell." This quickly infiltrated the sports press, and announcers began to talk about "the really parve double-header," in Baltimore, or Y. A. Tittle's "parve new contract."

The nation became aware that now before every game in Yankee Stadium the stands echoed with Hebrew prayers, and that Hasidic rabbis stood behind the umpires at each of their positions. Disputes that had once taken seconds or minutes now sometimes took hours, with boys in black silk running to and fro to fetch or return leather-covered tomes for support. Stengel began to pronounce his own name with an "eh" at the end, and no longer referred to his team as the Yankees but as the Yenkiss, with the last syllable pronounced as in the last syllables of "hocus pocus."

Speculation was that all of this was an inexplicable commercial strategy of the management, and as long as people credited the theory the inexplicable seemed explicable. Even when the team refused to play on Saturdays, everyone thought it was simply a disastrously stupid move somehow designed to increase attendance. But the changes were not solely the work of management. Some of the players now wore what everyone in New York called *yamakas,* a strangely Japanese way of referring to what Roger called *kipote,* or, in the singular, a *kipah.* When the press finally got up enough nerve to ask Eustis Jackson Jr., the second baseman, why he was wearing such a thing, he said, with some heat, "I'm a colored man, this is a free country, and I can do what I want."

When Berra was asked, he responded with a long and phenomenally disjointed essay about freedom of speech, the free-enterprise system, and his ancestors. What did that have to do with his wearing of a *yamaka?* With a twinkle in his eyes that the press never saw, he said, "They would, had they could, because the least obvious reward for labor is hard work." But that was not the end of the encounter.

"Hey Yogi," a reporter said. "What are those threads, those, uh, fringes, sticking out of your pants?"

Yogi tucked them in, saying, "Frayed threads. It happens when it's washed a lot."

"Yogi," they asked. "What is all this stuff, suddenly?"

"What stuff?"

"All this Jewish stuff."

"What Jewish stuff?"

"You know, kosher stadium food, Hebrew prayers, rabbis behind the umps, *yamakas,* fringes. What's going on?"

"Jewish stuff?" Yogi asked. "As Eustis said, it's a free country, right? Look, guys, when you have a choice, there's only one way to go."

They accepted this, and went on. "But closing on Saturday is nuts. Aren't you worried about attendance?"

Berra laughed. "Just be there for the game against Kansas City."

THE REMATCH AGAINST KANSAS CITY was also a home game, as the A's played solely away games that June because their field had been invaded by locusts. In New York at the end of the month it was hot and nearly everyone was either at work or at the beach. That the stands were half full might have been worrisome to management as a sign that the Yankees had lost their touch, but they were worried only about Roger.

Roger was fine, had kept up his extraordinary record in numerous practices (although, to keep the strategy secret, he hit balls out of the stadium only in the dark), and assured them that the presence of a crowd and the press would have no effect on what he could do. But they had seen too many confident rookies turn to swamp mush at the roar of the crowd, to be reassured, and they breathed apprehensively all through June, especially Stengeleh, who thought that perhaps he was having an epic dream.

Just striving to imitate Roger had made the Yankees hit better, run faster, and throw harder. They were losing by lesser margins, and although no one expected them to get to the Series, there was hope that they might hold their own enough to come back the next year. In fact, the sportswriters hoped for the agonizing comeback that would give them a great theme for the rest of the season. In the bottom of the ninth inning in the Thursday game against the A's, the score was Kansas City 3, New York 0, which wasn't so bad, and might be good for stimulating eight hundred words of drivel about a Yankee revival. The radio announcers, however, were used to filling dead air in any circumstance, albeit with a languor that would have been the envy of Oblomov. No matter what, they would broadcast their perfectly timed descriptions in wonderful baseball-afternoon bursts.

Thus, Red and Mel—Red from Alabama, and Mel from Alabama, Red thin and Mel stocky, Red red-haired and Mel blue-black, Red high-strung and aristocratic and Mel what you might call a garage guy, Red a prima donna and Mel a prima donna, and both as comfortable to American ears as the sound of the lines whipping against a flagpole on a windy day. Red was looking forward to catching the train up to Briarcliff, and Mel was going to dinner that night with a broad. They thought the game was more or less over. So, apparently, did a lot of other people, who were headed to the subway and the parking lots. The voices of the announcers, arrowing over the air, conveyed a yearning for scotch on the 5:06 as the sun beat off the brackish Hudson, and the anticipation of the relaxed clink of glasses and ice at '21.'

After some light opera in service of Rheingold Beer, Mel summarized: "Yankees versus the A's, Yankee Stadium, bottom of the ninth." The word *ninth* had an upward intonation, like a rising pheasant. "A's three, Yankees nothing, Koswick on third, Miller on second, two outs."

"Folks," said Red, "there are two outs, and Mantle is up. Or will be . . . in a second. What do you say, Mel?"

"It's pretty clear, Red. Mantle has to go for a homer, and Zelinka has gotta walk him."

"And strike the next batter out. . . . There's potential drama here, Mel. Mantle has been hitting well."

"You're right, Red. If he hits now the way he's been hitting in practice, the Yanks may have a chance today."

"I know what you're gonna say is strange, Mel," Red interrupted.

"You've seen it, too?"

"I have. He'll hit one into the bleachers, and you'll see a pained expression on his face, as if that's just not good enough."

"That's what makes a champion, Red. Never satisfied."

"Okay, Mantle is up. Zelinka can't take the chance. He's gotta walk him."

"There's Mick. He brushes the dust off his left leg. A few practice swings."

"He looks intent. He's gotta hit for the bleachers. Look, people have stopped leaving the stadium. They're poised at the ramps, their feet toward the exits, their bodies twisted so they can look over their shoulders at the field."

"I'll tell you, Mel, I would not walk out of this ballpark if Mickey Mantle was up at bat, or, if I did, I'd stop just like these folks."

"The pitch," said Mel. "Ball one. So far on the outside that maybe it was for the Dodgers."

Red added, "Some people are booing Zelinka."

"Zelinka doesn't care. The game could ride on this. He can't let Mantle drive in three runs and go to dangerous extra innings."

"Zelinka hasn't fared well against Mantle in the past. He knows. . . . He winds up . . . the pitch."

The pitch was a slow boat to the outside, so far to the outside that it had to be slow to give the catcher time to get to it. But that was not something to be taken for granted, as the pitcher and the catcher had. Most uncharacteristically, Mantle ran after the ball.

"He's running!" the announcers shouted. "He bunts! Oh boy! He's halfway to first already, and there's no one there to pick up the ball!"

Koswick, the runner on third, started toward home but the third-base coach called him back. "I coulda made it!" Koswick said. The coach just looked away, as did the rabbi behind him. Meanwhile, the catcher went for the ball and found himself in the middle of the infield while Zelinka rushed in to cover the plate. The catcher frantically threw the ball to Zelinka, who almost didn't catch it, and, when he did, stood on the plate in a state of shock, looking out at bases loaded and knowing that his options were getting fairly narrow. As he returned to the mound, the fans at the exits went back to their seats.

The radio announcers forgot what they had been thinking of, because here was what they lived for. Bottom of the ninth, bases loaded, three nothing, two outs. Of course they and everyone else hoped the next batter up would go to a three-two count, the ultimate precipice of baseball, but even without that, what they had was good enough. A home run would win the game, a triple would tie it, a double would put the Yankees one down, a single or a walk two down. They were still alive, and no one knew what would happen.

"Morgan is up next, Red. With his batting average. . . ."

"The only question, Mel, is who will be the pinch hitter."

There was a delay, during which an argument in the Yankee dugout was overshadowed by the inevitable Kansas City conference with Zelinka, which was very animated.

The announcers commented on the pressure, and set the scene for their audience across the nation. "It's been a really hot day in New York. The first subways, windows open, are rolling past, taking home those lucky enough to have gotten off work early. A shadow has just begun to move across the field, and although it's an ice-cream day in the stadium, you can smell hot dogs and hamburgers cooking in the restaurants beyond the fence. The question remains, ladies and gentlemen, who will hit for Morgan? Mantle's not moving from first. It was a strange thing to see him bunt."

Then, over the radio, in every town and minuscule junction in America, from Caribou to the Everglades, Norfolk to San Francisco, came the following question: "Reeves? Who's Reeves?"

THE SOUND OF PAPER being shuffled was heard across the nation as Red and Mel pulled out the back pages of the roster.

"Roger Reeves," said Mel. "A rookie out of Georgia. His first day in the majors. This is unbelievable, Red."

"It sure is, Mel. I've never seen it . . . in all my life. Reeves has never played before a crowd this large, never faced a pitcher like Zelinka. The Yankees . . . well, something's come over the Yankees."

Mel had been reading. "He's only eighteen years old," he said, astonished. "He played for half a season. On a team called the Milledgeville Crab Legs. That has since been disbanded."

Red hushed down into his portentous voice. "All I can say, Mel, is that I'll bet this boy is seven feet tall and weights two hundred and fifty pounds."

"Southern boys are short, Red."

"What do you mean?"

"I mean they're short and light. Look at you."

"A lotta colored boys are Southern boys, and they're big, Mel."

"Yeah, Red, but this is a white boy."

"How do you know?"

"Because there he is."

Roger walked onto the field, with the crowd primed for the most generous cheer of their lives, but the cheer was drowned in shock.

He was not even five and a half feet tall, he was so gangly that it seemed
he could not have weighed much more than a hundred pounds, and his
quaquaversal gait and quaquaversal eyes made him look like someone who
might indeed have been on a team called the Milledgeville Crab Legs. As a
physical specimen, he was easier to associate with a hospital than a major-
league baseball team. Even from far away you could see how thick his
glasses were, how white and delicate his hands. The baseball cap capped his
head like a mixing bowl, but did not stem the wild flow of *payess*.

"You know he's from the South," Mel said, "because he's got those
Johnny Reb sideburns. But he's so small. Why is that, Red? Why are people
in the South so small?"

"They aren't."

"Yes they are. What is it, nutrition? The Civil War?"

"They aren't."

"Yes they are. Look at Reeves."

"I think Reeves will acquit himself well," Red offered, "no matter what
the impression you have of him." As far away as the docks of Galveston, they
could tell over the radio that Red would have killed Mel but for the fact that
a baseball game intervened. It was strange, in that both were from Alabama.

Roger took his position and raised his head to look at the huge stadium,
now completely silent and still, with tens of thousands of people looking
back at him. He looked left, and there was Zelinka, three times his size,
smiling with contempt. Even the rather large Orthodox Jewish contingent
in the right-field stands was quiet. They knew in their bones that Roger
Reeves of the Milledgeville Crab Legs was one of them, and their overwhelming emotion was fear that he would be the reason for the defeat of this
otherwise invincible gentile team (they were somewhat behind the times),
and that this might result in a pogrom.

Zelinka decided to drive a fastball right down the middle, square in the

center of the batting picture. He had done this many a time before to rookies, who always had swung after the ball was in the catcher's mitt. When
pitched without complication, his fastball was so fast that no inexperienced
player would ever be able to connect with it. And given Reeves's size and
weight, even if he did it was possible that the force of the ball would push the
bat back, rather than vice versa. In the few cases of this that Zelinka had
seen, the batter was shocked to find himself, absent his own volition, back in
the ready position. The only drawback was that such balls veered up or
down, and sometimes bounced off the catcher and rolled into play without
anyone realizing that the batter hadn't hit them. It didn't matter. Zelinka
wanted to make every pitch to Reeves a rifle shot. He was enraged that they
would put such a batter up against him, and wanted to make the ball smoke
on its way in.

The stadium was like an ocean of angry rabbis. The whole world at that
moment seemed to depend on Roger, and he had no confidence that he
could hit a baseball, much less one thrown by an enraged major-league
pitcher, much less send it out of the stadium and thus make in the world
of baseball an explosion like that of a hydrogen bomb. Roger could not even
see the ball. He had no illusions. What was he? Nothing. He was, as gentile
and nonobservant Jewish children of the era called each other in derision, a
"spastic." True, he could run, and his reflexes were live wires, but, from hitting? Jews couldn't hit, never could. Their job in the mystery of things was
to take on the kidney a baseball thrown by a tall Irishman or a giant Pole like
Zelinka—people who were not afraid to punch, or jump off a waterfall, or
ride a bicycle on a rope stretched between the Woolworth and Municipal
buildings.

It didn't matter. Not only that, but what no one ever knew or could know
was that, after the pitch, Roger always closed his eyes. It was then that he felt
the arms, fluttering and feathered, golden and shiny, reach from behind him
and slowly, viscously, take hold of his hands on the bat. The joy that this
brought him, knowing that it was not he that held the bat, but an angel,
made him float. No one ever looked at a batter's feet at the swing, but had
anyone peered stereoscopically at the photographs of record, he would have
seen that Roger's feet were held a quarter of an inch off the ground. He

floated, and was happy. An angel supported him in his arms and gently held the bat, and, with eyes closed, Roger would swing with the angel.

He felt that, even were he betrayed, even were he to be abandoned, even were he to be humiliated in front of fifty thousand gentiles, it would be enough that he had had so intimate a discovery of so unpredictable a God. It would be enough that he had been promised, even were the promise not kept. It would be enough that in the House of Ruth, he had been clasped by an angel's wings and raised from the ground.

"The pitch!" Mel and Red said to the nation simultaneously.

Even with eyes closed, Roger could see the ball coming in, as white as the foam of a tidal wave, moving like a cannon shell, a piston, or a comet, with a power that made the air around it roar. Then this ball slowed most graciously into an almost rhythmical stillness. It glowed, pulsed, and seemed to grow to the size of the moon, and then dutifully stopped one foot in front of home plate, with glistenings, luminous rings, showers of ice, pinwheels of diamonds, and leaping sparks spinning from it. "Hit me!" it shouted, in the visible language of stopped and floating baseballs. "Hit me!"

Feathers pressed in unison against the limitlessly powerful wing, and the bat moved like a jet as the wings grew taut to slow it lest the ball be hit too hard, and when the two connected, the ball fled like a cat on fire. It went just slowly enough so that everyone in the stadium could track the flame, and track it they did, up at the angle of a useless fly, but so far up that its trajectory seemed aimed at the huge daylight moon loitering impudently above the Bronx.

Fifty thousand people dared not breathe. Their heads lifted and their eyes opened to the maximum as the ball flew from the stadium, clearing the flagpole by *six hundred feet,* headed perhaps to Africa or Rio de Janeiro, over Orchard Beach. And as everyone followed it, Roger began to walk quietly toward first.

As the Yankee runs came in, the crowd grew hysterical on account of the frail unknown Yankee who brought up the rear and ran from third to home with uncanny spastic grace to win the game for the Yankees by one run, the only one of its kind in history. In the stands the gentiles shook the pillars of the world with their shouts, and the Jews prayed silently, thankful to have been spared.

. . .

SOMEONE BROUGHT CHAMPAGNE to the locker room, and it was spilled wastefully over everyone. They picked up Roger and, dancing between the benches, carried him from place to place. One of the team held the bat and kissed it; then he elevated it above his head and marched around in triumph. They chanted in unison: "Ro-ger! Ro-ger! Ro-ger!"

Roger squiggled out of their grip and slid to the floor. "No!" he said, retrieving the airborne bat. "No!"

"No?" they asked.

"No," he said, pausing to regain his breath. He held the bat out in front of him on display. "This is the bat of God," he told them.

"The bat of God," they repeated in awe.

"No!" he said again.

"It isn't?" they asked.

"It is."

"Is it," they asked, "or isn't it?"

"It is," he confirmed, "but you may not worship it."

"Why not?" Berra asked. "God! It's the bat of God!"

"Yes," said Roger, "but you can't. If you worship it, you are worshipping only a thing that He made. He didn't even make it, He caused it to be made."

"So?"

"He made everything, so if you worship only one of those things, or any of them, or all of them, you are worshipping your own choice, and thus you are worshipping yourselves, which you must not do."

"What the hell are we supposed to do with the bat of God?" Mantle asked.

"Treat it," Roger said, remembering a song he had heard on the radio, "like a lady."

As the Yankees tried to assimilate this, everything was frozen, and amid the stillness, the doors of the locker room began to stretch inward with wavelike changes of pressure against them in advance of the sports press, which no force in the world could stop.

"Quick, Roger," Mantle said, "jump in the laundry cart."

Roger flew into a wheeled canvas hamper, and the Yankees covered him with towels. Then the doors burst open and what seemed like a thousand men with tickets in the brims of their gray hats flooded in like the tides of Fundy.

"Roger! Where's Roger Reeves!" they screamed.

"Who?" the Yankees asked.

The great crush of press was driven into a kind of seizure, which the Yankees much enjoyed. "Roger Reeves! He's a legend! He hit a ball. . . ."

"Yes?" Mantle asked.

"He hit a ball . . ." the reporter repeated, sweeping his left arm across an imaginary horizon, "out of the . . . out of the. . . ."

"He went home for the weekend," Berra said. "He wants to spend the weekend with the former Crab Legs."

"In Milledgeville?" they asked.

"Yup," Berra said.

The wave that had burst in now evacuated with a sucking sound of withdrawn air, and the rest was silence. Roger popped up from the towels like a chick breaking out of an egg, and said, "I've got to get back to the hotel; I'm way behind in Mishnah."

"If this is a dream," Berra said, "then let it be your wishbone."

ROGER REFUSED to play away games, not only because of the difficulty in getting kosher food (which, like kosher food itself, was surmountable), but because he wanted to hit balls out of Yankee Stadium each time he was up at bat. He suggested, and Stengeleh agreed, that this might be good for the Yankees. The whole country was already in a fever, the press had ravaged Milledgeville and come up with not even one former Crab Leg, and the greater the mystery the more people wanted to know. There was no Roger Reeves in Milledgeville. Never had been. No one knew him. Who was he? Was he a robot? Had Roger Reeves shown up in public, anywhere, he would have been torn apart by gushing hands, but Roger Reveshze was free to walk about, entirely ignored.

As the fervor built, the Yankees played at Detroit and Roger rested for a Thursday game against Chicago. Every seat in Yankee Stadium was sold, and scalpers were disposing of tickets for a premium of one thousand percent. The front pages of the tabloids for that entire week would be devoted to Roger: *Who Is Yankee Miracle Boy?; Reeves to Field Thursday; Never Again?; Stengel Says, "Watch!"; Reeves Unknown in Milledgeville;* and so on. Pictures of his face, many times enlarged, like photographs of the moon, appeared in the newspapers. Television ran slow- and stop-motion films of him again and again. Industries were born putting his name on mugs and cards, though not his image, for which they needed his permission, and would have paid dearly had they been able to receive it. The president was asked about him at his news conference, prompting the normally good-natured general to snap, "How the hell do I know? He's not a secret program. He doesn't work for the government. Why are you asking me?"

Such fame, even pseudonymously, might have worked upon anyone other than someone who had received as the answer to his prayer the embrace of an angel. This coursed through Roger's veins like life itself. It put the world in a very clear light, even literally, illuminating in the texts Roger studied, for example, each Hebrew letter as if it were caught from every angle by miniature suns shining on it like spotlights. This gave the letters depth, and never had the texts themselves seemed so profound, brilliant, and beautiful. He was astounded to discover that these readings, which normally were only words, were now accompanied by music. The letters and words on the page, formerly black and black-gray, now shone like bright sun on burnished brass.

Though Roger had not seen the angel, he had felt its embrace and sensed a coolly burning orb. He guessed that this would be surrounded by souls of similar perfection gliding gracefully and unseen throughout their days.

THE WHITE SOX were a repulsive bunch of taciturn midgets whose throwing arms seemed attached to stolid blocks of steel. Whereas most pitchers were like supple human fly rods, the White Sox were like trench mortars or dough-nut machines. They never looked anyone in the eye, they had flat heads, and although they did everything to win, as long as they belched forward like steam shovels they really didn't care if they won or lost, which was lucky for them, because, after Roger took to the field and single-handedly prevented a single ball from touching the grass, they had to decharter their airplane and go home on a bus. The final score for this, Roger's second game, had been Chicago nothing, Yankees 147.

The Yankees were regretful but too stunned by the whole situation not to accept that Roger would play only three more games. Sure to lose him, they yearned to know how he did it, so Stengel gingerly asked him if he would hold a clinic for the rest of the team.

"A clinic?" Roger asked.

"A baseball clinic," Stengel said. "You know, teach them how to hit, how to field, how to run. You're only going to play three more games, and we thought, well, it'd be great if you could leave behind some of what you brought. We're doing okay now—I mean, look at the score against Chicago— but you never know. The way we were going this year, before you came. . . . We could lose it." He laughed nervously, not daring to bring up money, which he knew Roger would refuse.

"I don't know from baseball," said Roger, "not a thing."

Stengel bowed his head. "Really," he said, in awe.

"No."

"Then how did you . . . how did you. . . ."

"That?" Roger asked.

"Yes, Roger," Stengel said politely, "that."

"I could tell them what I do know."

Stengel looked at Roger, who was illuminated in fading reddish-brown light. He was less than half Stengel's size. He didn't know the rules of base-ball, much less the subtleties. By rights and the laws of physics he should not have been able, even had he connected with the ball, to have hit it beyond the diamond. A child of his size and underdevelopment would not be able to throw the ball from home to second, much less leap twenty feet in the air (as he had done in the White Sox game) and then get the ball off on a flat tra-jectory to burn into the catcher's mitt at home plate before the thrower was back on the ground. "Yes," said Stengel, "tell us what you do know."

"Okay," said Roger, "but I'm telling you, I don't know anything."

That was not quite true. He had begun to think about the game. For example, he liked very much that the ball was an object descending from heaven, and he thought of it, therefore, not as an object to be captured for the glory of the captor but as a gracious gift that brought with it in train a bit of the loveliness of the sky.

FOR THE SEMINAR, the Yankees went to their secret practice field at Lake Honkus, near Mohonk, in the Shawangunks. The Yankees had bought a secluded estate and set up a baseball field on what had been a cow pasture, where they could practice in secret their surprise plays and coded signals. The lodge where they stayed was filled with wrought iron, Indian blankets, and buffalo heads. In fact, in Roger's room, he and a moose had a staring contest for at least an hour.

The next morning, Roger and the Yankees put away a huge breakfast, during which Roger discovered that the maple syrup the Yankees used on their pancakes was kosher, and made an interesting sauce for pickled herring. Then they went outside and sat on benches facing a portable blackboard. The weather was wonderfully cool and clear at Lake Honkus. Stengel brought Roger up to the front, stood him next to the blackboard, gave him a piece of chalk, and said, "Kid, we're totally secure."

Roger looked at the Yankees, who looked at him expectantly. What could he possibly say that would enable them to hit a ball out of the park or jump twenty feet in the air?

"From baseball I know nothing," he began, "but what's a lock?"

"What's a lock?" Mantle echoed.

Roger nodded.

"You mean like a lock on a door," Larsen asked, "or a lock in a canal?"

"Both," said Roger.

"A door lock is a metal thing with a lot of really smart junk in it," Berra said.

"Okay," said Roger, "and the lock of a canal?"

"A chamber for raising and lowering boats, with water from the river or canal to run it."

"Yes," said Roger.

Time passed. The Yankees stared at Roger. More time passed. Then Roger said, "Both illustrate the mechanism of the world."

The Yankees inched forward. No clinic had ever begun like this.

"God is perfect," Roger said. "His creation is perfect. It doesn't seem so to us—we who suffer and die, who must live with sadness and terror—because we can't see it in its entirety. If we could, we would see that it is in perfect balance. The counterweight for which we long—to right wrongs and correct injustices—is sometimes far away from us in space, time, or both. But, taken as a whole, from far enough afield, all is in balance, all is just.

"Good. What does this have to do with baseball and locks? As set out in the teachings of Rabbi Pepper of Biloxi and Rabbi Goldfinch of Barnevelt, the modern-day disciples of Rabbi Yoel ben Isaac of Zamosc, and his grandson Rabbi Yoel ben Uri (whose last names I will not say), each a *baal shem*, and their descendants, et cetera, in God's eyes, in fact, and in truth, all souls, absent the deficit of sin, are equal. For example, a wise and brilliant king has no higher rank in the view of the Almighty than a beggar who has not even the comprehension to speak his own name. At the final judgment, both souls can glow equally in the same circle of continuous light."

The Yankees nodded slightly. They understood; they had all deeply loved those who were far from perfect.

"Okay," said Roger. "So here is the question that Yoel ben Isaac put forth and Yoel ben Uri answered. If these souls occupy the same level at the end, equally beloved of God, and if God's creation is perfect, how can an imbalance exist in their lives on earth? How can one suffer all the miseries of this life, and the other know all the glories, if in the end every account is to be reconciled and they come to the same reward? In a perfect universe, how can such a shortfall exist? How can God allow it?"

Not even the entire Yankee lineup could answer this question, though they strained to do so. Roger again challenged them. "Tell me, how can God allow it? Do you know?" He surveyed them. They didn't. "I'll tell you, then. It's simple. He doesn't. What is equal in the end is equal also in the beginning and in the middle. There is no deficit even on this earth, even in the smallest picture, the tightest section of view. But how can this be? The king and the beggar live vastly different lives. Ah! That's what you think. That's what may be apparent. But it isn't true. Why? Because," he said to the Yankees, their eyes unblinking, "the mechanism of creation is like a lock."

The Yankees waited. How was it like a lock, both kinds?

"Both kinds. The metal lock has a cylinder that, for the door to open, must turn. This cylinder has a row of holes drilled in it, in which rest pins. In the barrel inside of which the cylinder turns and is encased, is a line of holes spaced exactly like their counterparts in the cylinder, with its own set of pins. In the locked position, the pins from the barrel fall into the holes in the cylinder and prevent it from turning, because they cross and block the interface. When the key is put in, it raises the pins exactly to the points—at a different level in each hole—where the barrel pins are above the line and the cylinder pins are below it. If all the pins were raised indiscriminately, sometimes the cylinder pins would block the interface, and sometimes the barrel pins would. If they were not raised at all, the barrel pins would block the interface and, thus, the rotation. To allow the turning, each pin must be raised according to what it requires. Some are raised more, some less, which is why the key is jagged. In the end, its unevenness makes a perfect equality that allows the lock to open.

"And a lock that lifts or lowers a boat is a mechanism that gets its power from the urge of all water to find its own level. Only that way can things flow, rivers run, and the world function—when the disparate forces of the universe are conjoined, and rest easy in an equality of perfection. Every force that exists is held in balance by a counterpart with which it must be united, and with which it is united, even if the connection be not apparent to us.

"Like the pins in a lock, the beggar and the king are lifted by God variously and invisibly, but equally, even in this world, so that the perfection will not be broken, for, by definition, the perfection *cannot* be broken. They ride unseen waves and are held aloft by unseen supports. Were they not so lifted, the world would not work.

"Only those who have suffered can know the strength of the compensation they acquire. The emissary that comes to them is all-embracing, and though some may deny or mock this, it is many times more real than the world itself, for next to this working of perfection the world itself seems only a tinsel of the imagination. God compensates even in this world. He must. He does. And the reception of His compensation, like a quantity of physics, is the certain though insubstantial thing we call holiness. Those who would deny it would do so simply from lack of having received it. Perhaps the king, gifted in other ways, has no knowledge of holiness, while for the beggar with no gifts, it is overflowing. You may wonder what this has to do with baseball."

They nodded.

"It seems clear to me," he said, as a breeze brought resinous air from a thick pine forest that bordered the practice field as evenly as a crewcut. "I have been able to do what I did because my arm was guided, my strength supplied, my speed achieved, by the ever-present will of God for balance and perfection. Perhaps a Phoenician ship listed too much to port, thousands of years ago; or it was too cloudy, for too long, over a glacier in the Himalaya; or a woman's heart was broken for a day by her suitor in Montana. I don't know. I do know that it is important to know that such balances exist, and that, if I didn't know it, I wouldn't have the heart to continue."

"Can we hook into this stuff?" Berra asked.

"Not if all you want to do is win games," Roger answered.

"But wait a minute," Berra demanded. "Let's say someone cheated in Chinese checkers a thousand years ago in Peru. If I could hook into that, I could run twenty feet back to the plate even though Zelinka is just an inch from it, and put him out, right?"

"No," said Roger. "It doesn't necessarily work that way, and God is not fond of games."

"Even baseball?"

"Even baseball."

"Why?"

"Games can become, because of their closed set of rules, an independent universe, a distraction from the seeking of perfection. If they are taken as a universe in themselves, what a meager universe that is. This offends God, who worked for six whole days to make the universe we have. Can you imagine what would come of the work of an omnipotent being for six whole days? What is the infinity of detail, the infinity of extent, the infinity of connectedness, and the infinity of surprise, times six?"

"It doesn't apply to baseball?" Stengel asked, not quite sure of exactly what *it* was.

"If your object is merely to play baseball, it doesn't."

"What's your object, then, Roger?" Mantle asked.

"Because of the imperfection I have seen, I live for the hope of restoration. That's all I live for, even if it be a sin."

"What imperfection?" Stengel asked.

Roger's expression was incomprehensible to the Yankees as anything but some sort of nervous ailment, because boys his age who are not afflicted with a crippling disease do not show on their faces the pain of old men. "I was born during the war," he said, to answer the question, "in a place called Majdanek. I knew nothing else. The physical privation of this place, the terror of the selections and the frequent killing of people around me, seemed natural. Until I was three, I existed in the aura of my parents' love. I don't know what they did to keep us alive, but I know that whatever it was it was done for me. I stop abruptly when I begin to imagine what they must have suffered, especially my mother. For this I pray with love and gratitude, every day. I wish it were they who had lived and I who had died, although that would have taken from them what they wanted most.

"Just before the liberation, when I was three, we were marched out and made to stand at the edge of a pit. In the pit were thousands of bodies. Bulldozers had compressed and shaped them. They were as white as snow, and beneath them was a lake of blood. Even among the crushed forms and severed limbs, some people remained alive, though not for long.

"My mother and father told me that they loved me. They tried to shield me with their bodies. When the firing began, the force of the machine-gun bullets caught them and the other adults and they were hurled into the pit as if a wind had blown them away. The firing had been over the heads of the children, who stood on the rim untouched and unable to move. The guns were not lowered, because bullets were scarce.

"A soldier came by and picked me up by both ankles. My head hit the ground, and then he swung me around like an ice skater swinging his partner. I remember the blood rushing to my head, and the world blurring into blue and white. Even as I was twirled, the soldiers were laughing. After I was released, for a moment, I flew. Undoubtedly, I passed over my mother and father, and though I thought I was going to fly forever, I fell into the center of the pit, face-to-face with a dead woman upon whom I had fallen, whose mouth was open.

"I thought I was dead, too, until the bulldozers drove over us. The sound of bones breaking was like the sound of burning kindling. Many times, the bulldozer drove right over me, but though I was too frightened to move, I found myself each time between the treads. Then I was caught in a wave of tumbling bodies that, pushed by the blade, washed up at the edge. The bulldozer no longer came near me. I lay quietly as it worked, and then slept.

"After nightfall, I was awakened as I was wetted with gasoline. Choking on it, I climbed over the rim and walked into the darkness. I thought that this was death and that I was dead, but when I looked back and saw the huge blaze of the fire in which my mother and father were burning, I knew that I was still alive. I knew the difference. I wanted to die, I wanted very much to die, but, not knowing how, I lived.

"That is the imperfection I have seen," he said, "and all I want from the world is some indication or sign that, forward in time, or where time does not exist, there is a justice and a beauty that will leap back to lift the ones I love from the kind of grave they were given."

THE POOR ORIOLES. They had no idea what was going to happen to them when the Yankees took the field in Roger's third game. Though they knew to be concerned with Roger himself, they had closely studied the first two of his games and saw hope in the fact that in these the other Yankees had been only marginally better. If they could isolate Roger, the rest of the Yankees would still be the Yankees Brooklyn had beaten in the Series the year before. Their rivals in the Bronx, they thought, still lacked focus.

But when the Yankees returned to the Bronx from Lake Honkus they did have focus, albeit of an unusual sort. They appeared to be bent on a certain kind of vengeance that was entirely alien to and had never been seen in baseball. True, baseball had its fierce moments, and sometimes teams were arrogantly knit together into bands of primitive warriors who pressed their case in a way that knocked the wind out of their fans. When the outfielder Whitey Koski was deliberately struck in the head, or so it seemed, by the pitcher Chick Perkasky, so concentrated and angry were Koski's teammates that they burned up the rest of the game. With home run after home run, and fielded balls thrown back with the force of cannon fire, they astonished the spectators, of whom they had become totally unaware.

When Doug Little and Kevin Small, two Giants, were attacked by drunks hurling coconuts during an exhibition game in Sarasota, the Giants came alight with heavy hitting and flame-thrower pitching. For two weeks they beat every team they played, and then, when their anger dissipated, they returned to their losing streak. Such things were expected of teams whose players had been struck by fastballs or kneed when sliding, but why the Yankees? The Yankees were in the midst of the most spectacular rise baseball had ever seen. Why would they be angry? Why would they be grim? No one had suffered indignity or abuse. If anything, they could be expected to be sheepish and self-conscious about their inexplicable good fortune and the fact that now they all had Cadillacs.

This is, anyway, what the Orioles had been counting on. Nonetheless, the Orioles saw out on the green lawn the faces not of baseball players but of soldiers. When he didn't smile, Berra looked even more like a turtle, and he refused to be engaging. The Oriole batters felt pure concentration emanating from him as he crouched at the limit of their peripheral vision. Mantle looked no longer like a farm boy but rather like the ruthless head of a giant steel corporation. The boyishness in his eyes had disappeared and been replaced by a metallic coldness. Larsen didn't bother to touch the brim of his hat or adjust anything before his pitches, each of which seemed designed to break Berra's wrists. All the Yankees—except Roger, who remained mild (because the world into which they had just entered, and in which they would stay for only a short time, was his forever)—had an intense impatience that changed their timing to something such as no one had seen. Baseball is like a clock, in that its wheels turn at different speeds and all its moves require waiting. Eventually, everything pops at once: the detents lift, springs decompress, arms rise, and hammers strike twelve times, even if only twice a day. Most of the time, however, is spent waiting for one wheel to align with

another. So it is with baseball and its glorious pauses, which cannot be
rushed and which even the announcers mimic with genius. Were the empty
spaces to be compressed or done away with, the game would die.

Driven by emotion, the Yankees played a game with few spaces, little
hesitation, and no rest. To describe just a small part of the Orioles' nightmare, which took place within the span of a hot-dog transaction, Larsen
pitched without a warm-up, firing the ball across the plate at a hundred
miles an hour. The batter swung late, and before he was finished with his
swing Berra had thrown the ball back to Larsen as fast as a pitch. Immediately after the ball ploughed into Larsen's glove, he pitched it, and the batter,
who had barely taken up position, swung again. This was repeated, and,
within twenty-three seconds of the first pitch, the batter was out and gone.

When the next Oriole hit a fly to third, Rocky Babis, a new guy covering
the base, harvested it and instantaneously rammed it across the diamond to
first, where the Oriole Brutus Evans was tagged before he got back to base,
making three outs. At the instant Evans was tagged, the Yankees sprinted
in, and the next Yankee up stood impatiently at the plate before the Orioles
were even out of their dugout, which, not surprisingly, gave the Orioles an
incurable case of the heebie-jeebies.

The *Daily News* now referred to the Yankees as "the Invincible Engine."
Although Larsen was not pitching perfect games, his pitching was astoundingly quick and deadly. As a team, New York had become the model of a
grim and efficient army that fights an unspeakable enemy and is reconciled
and devoted to its tasks. Roger's last three games and quite a few afterward
were played not as games but as tributes. The Yankees no longer cared about
their standing in the league or their chances for the Pennant or in the Series.
They did not care about their salaries and bonuses. They did not care that
children ran up to them in the streets and women watched glowingly as they
passed. They did not even care about winning: winning, for them, became
joyless. They wanted only to play to perfection and to rush it on, as symbol
and sign, to speak directly to God, and to face like men the fact of evil and
sorrow in the world.

And they played so beautifully, so well, and so apparently with something higher in mind, that the announcers really did not know what to say—

except that they would always remember, and that something had turned that summer to gold.

ROGER'S LAST GAME was in late September, on the dry cloudless day that confirmed to all that summer was finally over. October would bring some heat now and then, but this was the signal that New York's bejeweled fall had begun, when sharp shadows brought depth and reflection, and because of the declination of the light the rivers looked their bluest. Sounds, too, were sharper, and better sustained on the cool dense air, and no longer was everything blurred by the summer vapor that fills-in the channels of sight and sound.

Everyone knew that the Yankees would be on Detroit like a tidal wave. Bookies were giving odds of ten thousand to one. And for a team on its way to face a firing squad, the Tigers were in a festive mood. They looked forward to the exhibition, to watching Roger hit balls out of the park, and to winning, perhaps, if not the game, a rich pool based on the point spread: the most daring Tiger had placed his stake on a spread of nine hundred runs.

Buoyed by the summer's place in history and coffers overflowing from the unprecedented gate since June, not to mention the miraculous improvement of the team and the likelihood of its coming back to beat the Dodgers in the Series, Stengel simply announced that this would be Roger's last game. As Berra always said, "The middle is the end of the road for the beginning," and Roger was going back to the South (Milledgeville, Stengel had confessed to the public, had been a feint), to a small town that, to preserve his and its privacy and peace, would remain unknown.

When people heard this, they ached. Although the sports press had never stopped trying, Roger had never been interviewed, and the public had exactly the image of him it wanted. He was the ideal and paradigmatic American—lanky, side-burned, taciturn, unmarried, young, rich (they thought), mysterious, and devout. Had he run for president he could have won by a landslide even in a nonelection year, and that fall the presidential campaign was in full swing. Harvard invited him to be its president, the treasury to be on medallions, Wheaties to be on the box. Commercial offers were so lucrative that, had he taken all thousand of them and bargained well, he could have been the richest man in the world.

But all Roger wanted to do was go home, where no one would know anything about what had occurred in baseball that summer—except that a Jewish player had been a brief sensation. Even Schnaiper would not grasp the significance of what had happened, and would not in any case realize that its agent had been the new boy who fetched *gribenes* for the rebbe. The Yankees would keep his secret and never call on him, content that he had helped them this one time, because this was what he had asked of them.

After the game, he would stay in the locker room until early evening. Dressed again in Hasidic clothing, he would shoulder the books he had not already sent home by book post, and walk out of the deserted main gate, as obscure as he had been when he walked in. He would get on the subway and go back to Brooklyn, where he would continue doggedly the task of his life. But there was one more game to play, the most unusual game ever played in the history of baseball.

The Yankees were up first, and because everyone knew the Tigers would never come in from the field, before the first pitch chairs were brought for every Tiger player except the pitcher. Next to the chairs were little tables with ice buckets, bottles of Coke and lemonade, and snacks. A hundred thousand people filled Yankee Stadium, double its capacity, and in the South Bronx and upper Manhattan millions had gathered, packing the avenues, cramming into all the empty spaces, their faces turned toward home plate, even though the three television networks were broadcasting live. Inexplicably, the rules had been changed, and Roger would pinch hit for everyone on his team, even Mantle. After the national anthem and ten minutes of prayer, Roger walked onto the field.

He was greeted with the longest, loudest, most extraordinary cheer that had ever been raised, a hundred thousand voices amplified by the hornlike shape of the stadium, and a million more following on in the street. Though he knew he deserved no such thing, he was pleased nonetheless—because he understood that they were not cheering for him even if they did not know it—and he bowed his head to honor what they were cheering. Not mistakenly, they thought that this was a sign of humility, which set alight a self-sustaining, self-replicating, waxing roar that rose for half an hour and tumbled from the stadium on waves of thundering air that could be heard from Kingsbridge to Canarsie.

Mantle gave the bat to Roger, who walked gangly-legged to the plate. When the umpire shouted "Play ball!" the cheer went up again and did not die for fifteen minutes. Then, when all was quiet, Roger turned crisply to the pitcher. The pitcher wound up and sent a hundred-mile-per-hour fastball screaming at the umpire, for the catcher, who was eating poppyseed cake, sat on a chair off to the side.

The ball that came in at a hundred miles per hour left at quadruple that speed, whining briefly through the air before it disappeared in the pure blue forty degrees above the top of the flagpole. The fans were wild, but then settled in to simple euphoria as Roger hit pitch after pitch high over the Bronx toward Africa and the South Atlantic. The pitcher was supplied with one ball after another by teammates standing next to huge bins of baseballs on the sidelines. After a hundred desperate throws, his relief came onto the field and stood behind him, and when his arm gave out the relief pitcher took over so as not to break the rhythm of Roger's drives.

Roger was lost in the soundless incantations that affirm the truth of truths. The pattern of the vast numbers of baseballs streaming over the wall was like a cloth of ghostly white threads, or seeds sown in a light and helpful breeze. Four-hundred-mile-per-hour baseballs pierced the air and whistled over the Bronx in a song, while the announcers said virtually nothing. "Let's just look on as this unfolds," they had said, forgetting that they were on the radio and that people listening could not see what they saw, "for it will never be this way again." And, then, counting under their breath, they joined their audience in subdued amazement as the balls flew by in steady procession, like raindrops speeding sideways in a gale. Two thousand of them were shot from the stadium that day. There might have been more, but Roger stopped at the even number, which he thought might be a record. It was.

The players, the management, the professionals, the sportswriters, and the fans were aware that, before Roger, they had never seen a ball hit from the stadium, and that they never would again. To see two thousand in a row, without a miss, without hesitation, pause, or variations in path or timing except those that he willed, was as if God had chosen that moment to make His presence known, and they reacted accordingly in wonder and delight. For the moment, at least, they felt as if the deepest circles within them had been squared, their ragged doubts knit smooth, and the world were ablaze with the light of perfection.

ROGER HAD LONG SINCE tired of the suite in which he lived in deadening luxury on the Upper East Side. It was now empty, as it was empty before his arrival, a rosewood and alabaster tomb without even a body, a columbarium without ashes. In that neighborhood it was fairly easy to get a Fabergé egg but almost impossible to get a kosher chicken. True, the dwellings were well kept and well appointed, they often were as high as birds' nests, and you could look out and see half a million windows and not a foot of fire-escape iron, but the difference between this place and where he lived in Brooklyn was like the difference between a wool suit on a hanger, and a lamb. There were those who would instinctively choose the suit, and those who would instinctively choose the lamb. It was not for Roger to criticize anyone who would take the suit, but he himself would gather the lamb into his arms.

So with the place where he lived, a jumble of ancient brick in a basket weave of black iron that lay upon the tenements like fishing net sprawled to dry across a city of crates. The streets had no prospect and were tight and twisting. Only from the rooftops could you catch a glimpse of ships and blue water, and the trees, being so few and rare, were achingly beautiful.

Roger's affection for the awkward and homely way in which he lived had not diminished, and it began to enfold him graciously even as he headed out the stadium's main gate. It was the way his parents had lived, and the way their parents had lived, and so forth, and so on, very far back. But it would be a sin to carry on habit for its own sake, or to venerate the old merely because it is old. After all, given the expanse of the infinite, all that occurred did so within less than the duration of a spark, so everything was new and had to be judged for what it was. Tradition was an illusion, an afterimage—comfortable, yes, but unjustifiable in itself.

The ancient ritual, the black coats, the way of speaking, the languages, the revelations and commentary, the candles, the cuisine, the marriage customs, and the fur-rimmed hats, were things as new as if they had just burst upon the world like the first rays of light. Pop. There they were. To think that they were old would be only a mistake of perspective. What made them what they were, and so different from everything else, was that each one carefully and deliberately put the things of the world in their place. Each was a declaration and vow, each the outcome of a battle in which reason strictly assigned them a post. And thus subdued, the things of the world were sweet, and the world rose, like a planet in ascension, to its proper position.

The subway, inexplicably elevated aboveground, rolled down its track, taking Roger home. It made many turns indirectly in directions different from the one in which he was headed, but the sum and subtraction of the departures would constitute the precision of the aim, and had the train gone merely in a straight line, it likely would have missed. It went noisily amid the appearance of a million gently burning lights that gradually took the place of the bright scales with which the setting sun had armored the face of every building. It went left, it went right, it lurched north, south, east, and west, but then it began its last dash toward Brooklyn like a dog following a trail.

Roger closed his eyes, and a world that once had been came alive in all its tender detail. His mother lived again in moments so taxing to him that it threatened his young heart. His father lived again. They moved in color and dimension, and as the train rushed forward the world doubled back upon itself, twisting immeasurably, confounding time. In these moments, when it was as if he were observing them, unseen, they were, somehow, observing him. He could neither explain nor understand, but he was sure they knew.

When the train rose gracefully onto the bridge and sped with immensely complex clacking over iron rails in an open box of steel held in the wind a hundred feet above the river, the sound made Roger open his eyes. There was the world clear in the night, its sparkling towers piercing a band of brilliant orange light. For a moment, and just a moment—for he had work to do—he thought about what had happened. What had happened was but a single, lovely note in an always urgent song that he had been brought up to sing, like those before him, in protest of mortality, hope of survival, and love of God. It had happened here, in the New World, and why not? If Ruth could, among the alien corn, begin the line in Judah that led to David, then what was not possible here, and what perfection would be disallowed?

Sidney Balbion

EACH HOUR OR SO, the waiter who in his starched white jacket looked like a rhesus monkey left his station to sweep sand from the single tennis court. Though in the end this was less economical than erecting a barrier at the edge of the windblown dunes, the hotel was just scraping by and had neither the capital nor credit for building walls. Every effort was directed instead to making the guests happy. Perhaps their memories of the unexpected luxuries visited upon them in this splendid, sunny August would spur them to book for the next season and to tell their friends, so that the summer of 1940 might see the full occupancy that had not been achieved since 1929.

Accordingly, the hotel in the dunes east of Het Zoute sparkled through the night, steady in the wind but for the Japanese lanterns on its terraces riding the air and staying lit long after everyone had gone to bed, just so that if anyone did venture onto the beach in the dark and turned back to see the hotel, he would see something brave, beautiful, and standing alone.

The laundry worked overtime, for the greatest part of the hotel's luxury was its cleanliness and the quality of its linens. The silver, more than one would expect at a resort with only two stars—though at the turn of the century it had had four—was finely polished and, because of the sea air, frequently. The chef was French, and very good. Flowers were brought every day from the polders, and at the porte cochere a row of intensely colored flags snapped in the blue as in a Manet.

The more expensive places were grouped farther west along the coast. That was merely fashion, for here, east of Het Zoute, were the most wonderful dunes, ten stories high and a mile wide, and the beach was empty. But something about a hotel standing by itself at the end of a sand-colored road was forlorn, and fashion finds nothing more repellent than the forlorn. Nonetheless, in what it did not know was its last season, the hotel had by its extraordinary efforts become once again a place of luxury, and it deserved to have had its stars doubled, although not only were they not doubled, they would vanish forever after the building itself, having become a German post, would be destroyed by naval gunfire.

But now, in August of 1939, this was unforseen. At ten a.m., breakfast was still being served on the terrace, because there had been a dance the night before, and though sparsely attended it had lasted, in surprisingly balmy air, until three in the morning. The waiters were peacefully serving *complets,* ushering like dance partners their white ceramic pitchers of coffee, tea, or chocolate, and pushing carts laden with fresh croissants and brioches. Without success, the sun shone on the glass and silver jam pots as if to pale their pure reds and yellows.

There was only one record for the Victrola, and the young waiter who swept the tennis court had to play it over and over: Fred Astaire, singing "They Can't Take That Away from Me." But there were no protests, for everyone had seen him sing it in *Shall We Dance,* a film that, with French subtitles, was playing at the cinema in Zeebrugge, and the song itself seemed to fit the moment so perfectly as to demand repetition.

MRS. LAWRENCE and her daughter Angelica had come to the edge of the polders, by the sea, because they had heard from a neighbor how beautiful this Belgian seacoast could be, though the neighbor had formed his opinion in the trenches close by, when, in Flanders during the war, his heart being broken, he was prone to seize on even the most insignificant beauty as if it were illuminated by the world's most golden light.

Even now in a time of peace, it was much like it was then: quiet, deserted, the wind almost constant, the waves never ceasing to greet the shore with a seismic thump and a rush of foam. Even now, twenty years later, horrendously transformed corpses disinterred by the Yser and the Lys and sent to sea would wash back up on the beaches, unidentifiable and grotesque, but not so long ago the beloved of those who, carrying on after two decades, working at a desk, tending the garden, taking a bath, bicycling through well kept streets, would never know how the waters had lifted from the mud their husband, father, or child.

On the polders back from the beach they grew carrots and potatoes, malt, barley, oats, tobacco, flax, and wheat, and a great deal else, in rich and undisturbed tranquillity. At Het Zoute you could get ten days full board and a room overlooking the sea for what you might pay in Brighton for three days in a room above a shopping street, and Mrs. Lawrence and Angelica had six days to go. Then they would get on the Ostend boat and cross the Channel, and then by train to London and cab to Brent, refreshed for the year. It couldn't have been better.

"How do they make such magnificent croissants?" Angelica asked. Of a perfect figure at nineteen, she could eat as much as she wished and never show it, and with as much blood-red jam.

"It's the butter," her mother answered. "They have better butter than we do."

"Why can't we import their butter, then?"

"It's the water."

"Whatever it is," Angelica said, "I like it."

Suddenly, Mrs. Lawrence, whose face was long and built like a camel's, went absolutely quiet. Her daughter felt the change.

"Do you know who that is?" Mrs. Lawrence asked with delighted excitement.

"Who what is?"

"The man," Mrs. Lawrence said in an undertone and, ventriloquist-style, without moving her lips, "to your right. Don't stare. Just move your eyes."

"Him?"

"Yes."

"Who?"

"Sidney Balbion."

"Who's that?"

"Have you never heard of Sidney Balbion?" the mother asked. The question sounded like a lyric out of Gilbert and Sullivan.

"Of course not. Who the hell is Sidney Balbion?"

"He's like Harry Lauder, although not as big, of course, but he's very good. He's quite good."

"Music hall?"

"Yes," said the mother. "He was most famous during the war."

"That was more than twenty years ago. That was before I was born."

"And from time to time he would be billed in London, at the top of the bill. Well, if not at the top of the bill, then second or third, and if not in London then in Slough, where I saw him once."

"What songs does he sing?"

"Lots. Wonderful songs."

"Like what?"

"There were so many. I can't think of them."

"What about just one?"

"'Laura O'Banion'? 'Lara O'Banion'? 'Lucy O'Banion'?"

"I'm sure that was a real toe tapper."

"No no, he was good, really. He entertained the troops. Your father saw him after the Somme. He used to dance with *two* canes. That was his . . . trademark. Yes."

Sidney Balbion, a man of about sixty, simultaneously closed his eyes and lifted his face to the sun as it came into the clear between the entangled white clouds over the sea. He was tall and, for a man of his age, unfattened. The hair that was left to him in a bathtub ring around the side of his head was jet black, as were his large, rich eyes, his beetled eyebrows, and his heavy beard, which he had to shave twice daily. His teeth were as white as new piano keys, his nose excelled in prominence, and his forehead exaggerated the contrast of his features in a way that could easily be discerned from far in the back of even a major theater.

He had the air of someone who once had been frequently recognized and who, though now hardly recognized at all, was prepared to be charming and responsive to anyone and anything—even a crossing gate, a door slammed in his face, or a shop girl who thought he was an animal cruelty inspector.

"I'd like to talk to him," Mrs. Lawrence said.

"Why don't you? He's not doing anything."

"He's sleeping."

"No he's not. He was reading his paper, and when the clouds parted he turned his face to the sun."

"He's in his bathing costume."

"He's wearing a robe."

"It wouldn't be right. Oh, look, that man just sat down. He's an Englishman. You can tell. They're talking. I'd be interrupting them."

"Who cares?" the daughter asked.

"But I tell you what we can do: we can sit behind him and listen to what he says. He won't even know we're there."

"And that would be right?"

"He's famous. We won't tell."

"He's not famous, and you will tell. You'll tell everyone."

"*I* want to know. That's the point," said Mrs. Lawrence, who then gathered her things, crossed the terrace undetected, and slipped into a chair directly behind Sidney Balbion's, there to listen and knit. She was soon joined by her daughter, who tried to read a newspaper in German and had to give up after the first paragraph, which was also the first sentence. And there they sat and listened to the other man and to Sidney Balbion, who once had sung for the king.

"Have you heard anything from the Farkases?"

"I don't hear anything from the Farkases, Nigel, except what comes through their solicitor. It costs a great deal of money to hear from them, and as it's always a demand, a threat, or an accusation, the more I don't hear from them the better."

"Even Herman? Herman's the good one, isn't he, and Willi's the bad one?"

"No, Herman's the bad one, and Willi's the bad one. There's no difference between the two. Herman likes to pretend that he's a decent chap, but he isn't."

"Herman's the one who met Hitler, isn't he, not Willi?"

"Nigel," Sidney Balbion said, with the beginnings of impatience, "neither of them has met Hitler. Herman claims to have met Hitler but never has. Willi makes no claim about Hitler, as far as I know."

"Why didn't you just keep your mouth shut about Hitler, Sidney? You've got to learn to be more diplomatic."

"To the contrary, Nigel. I'm an entertainer. I make my stock-in-trade the truth. Oh yes, everyone thinks he knows that nothing we do is real or true, but that's the point, you see, that's how we convey the truth, by letting it ride under the belly of the ram. I didn't make speeches. I spoofed him. It was better."

"You killed your career, that's what you did."

"What does it matter? Hitler will pull the whole world into war, once again. In light of that, what does the career of one music-hall singer mean?"

"It means a lot to you, Sidney. And if you're right you can go back to entertaining the troops."

As the waves broke sharply, Sidney Balbion looked at his friend askance, hesitated, and then said, in the most evenly delivered lines, "I already have entertained the troops. I am now forgotten enough so that I would not again be asked to entertain the troops. And I would not abstain, merely to put myself in a position to entertain the troops, from trying to forestall a world war."

"What war, Sidney? We have peace. I know a violinist. . . . Hitler is interested at most in the German-speaking areas that surround Germany. The violinist heard him say so, privately, at a reception."

"Well, then there's nothing to worry about, is there? Nigel, never trust what famous people are overheard to say in private. They have been attuned to audiences all their lives, they know as if by magic when others are listening and when they are not, and they think like a fox."

"The prime minister, the whole British government, press, and people believe this, but not Sidney Balbion. That was your ruin, Sidney."

"I've been injured by that, yes, but it hasn't been my ruin. I was ruined by time, as is every one and every thing, eventually. I just passed through at excessive speed, and am dead before I've died. And there's nothing I can do about it."

"For example," Nigel went on, "everything beyond the German areas, beyond Austria, the Sudetenland, and Silesia, is filled with Jews, millions and millions of them. Hitler wants the Jews *out* of Germany, obviously. He would have to be insane to invade a lot of countries where there are scads of Jews. What could he possibly do with them? That's the guarantee, iron clad, that he won't go much further than he's gone."

"Even if you're right, Nigel, this is not the cause of my ruin."

"No," said Nigel. "You were playing . . . what? . . . Birmingham? Bathgate? You were doing all right."

"I last played Birmingham in 'twenty-eight, Bathgate in 'twelve. My last engagement in England, Nigel, was in Reading, in nineteen thirty-four."

"I don't understand. The Farkases have theaters everywhere. You have a contract with them."

"I do."

"Why aren't you playing in their theaters?"

"They don't like my act, and won't book me anywhere."

"Then why don't you go someplace else?"

"There is no place other than anywhere."

"I mean to another organization."

"They won't let me go, except to play limited engagements elsewhere, for which, understandably, no one wants to book me, and I wouldn't want to sign. Ballet. Have you ever heard anything as absurd? I can hardly get out of bed in the morning, when I ride in a train it's hell to get out of my seat, and the Farkases say I'm free to do ballet, which I've never done in my life anyway. The contract says that if a new act I present is comparable to what I've always been doing, the Farkases have to put me on, but they won't. That's why I've brought suit."

"How long will it take?"

"A lawsuit? Aeons. Ages. Epochs. Light-years. Because of litigation, I now, finally, understand infinity. You know, they improperly tallied the box office (in their favor), and reneged on their obligation to publicize my appearances. In Reading, I suppose they thought I wasn't worth it, so they spent only half of what they were supposed to spend. And then, when the theater didn't fill up as it might have, they blamed me, and now they won't book me anywhere."

"How are you supposed to eat, Sidney? It's a crime."

"I was paid a goodly sum in advance, but that was fourteen years ago. I made the contract with Lord Lyons, but then he died and everything went to the bloody Farkases. Now they want the money back. It's been fourteen years, in which I turned down scores of offers. The money's run out. I gave them fourteen years of my life. I worked up four completely new acts, big ones, and now they won't book me and they won't let me go."

"What do they want?"

"The money; they're Farkases."

"How do you exist?"

"I'm using up my savings, and my contract does allow me to entertain at private parties."

"Ah! Aristocrats have huge affairs, don't they? The Riviera, yachts, country houses, and all that. Could be quite lucrative."

"Not those kind of parties. They don't want the music hall in those places."

"What parties, then?"

"Birthdays, mainly. Children's parties."

"Oh. But still, only the aristocracy could afford the musicians and the sets for that sort of thing."

Sidney Balbion sighed. "I don't do music hall, Nigel, not at children's parties. Children are different: they wouldn't appreciate it."

"Yes, but their parents . . . What do you do?"

"The clown. I do children's birthday parties, as a clown."

Nigel did not suppress an explosive burst of laughter. He would not have been able to had he tried. He was much relieved when Sidney joined him, and they laughed, as good friends can, until they had tears in their eyes. Mrs. Lawrence cleared her throat so she would not give herself away by following them, and took up her knitting with faux furiousness, as Angelica read a French fashion magazine, oblivious of everything.

After a while, during which the wind shifted slightly and, with unusual clarity, brought the sound of the surf pounding the strand, Nigel said, "The Farkases are crazy."

"The Farkases are not crazy. They are, however, malevolent. They will gain nothing by my ruin but pleasure, which makes them malevolent. On the other hand, they are quite right that there is no demand for what I do. I can't blame that on them, I can only blame them for the way they're handling it. Though the times have changed many times in my life, I haven't. I've always done what I do. I started when I was a little boy. I used to. . . ."

"Would messieurs like something to drink?" the young tennis-court-sweeping waiter asked.

"Nigel?"

"Yes. Very. *Citron pressé,* with a dash of gin."

"Two *citrons pressés,* one with gin," Sidney said, and the waiter swooped backward and walked quickly toward the bar, where the bartender was shaking a drink in a silver repoussé shaker.

"I used to dance with a stick. I would do it for sheer joy and in imitation of a performance I had seen—Terry Fisher, remember him?—and I loved it. I would do this alone, with a great deal of passion. Lots of entertainers see what people like and then do exactly that to please them. I was always the other way 'round. I did what I did, and then, purely by accident, it pleased others, and I was able to earn a living, and a good one, for a time. Then things changed and I didn't."

"But why not, Sidney? That's the way of all life. You change, and if not, you die. Why didn't you change? Why can't you change?"

"I think," said Sidney Balbion, "that some people can't change merely because they're not agile enough. I'm agile enough. Some don't change because they object to the new. I don't, really. I have no objection to talking pictures, or Fred Astaire. I admire Fred Astaire. I wish I could dance as well as he."

"Then, why?"

"Affection, Nigel, affection. And loyalty. The music and the dancing, and the conventions of the music hall—the bright light and roseate makeup, the pastel-colored cities painted upon the scrims, the girls in gorgeous costumes—I have affection for all that. I wouldn't leave it for something new. For when I was a boy, and spending long hours teaching myself the routines, I was alone, and they saved me. I'm grateful to them, and they have become the storehouse of my emotions. It was as if the songs and the dances were a recording mechanism upon which all that I loved was etched. Loyalty, loyalty to remembrance, at the very least. Oh, I change. My acts are never the same. But the core remains, the heart of the matter, and that never changes. The world bribes you, threatens, and cajoles you. It wants you to betray your affections and your loyalties. I won't."

"That sounds rather silly coming from the man who is famous for 'Lara Olive's Lacy Lingerie,' Sid."

"I know. But it's like loving a baby. Let's say you had a child and it was unattractive to the world because the world could not see past a less than interesting face, or a bent physique. Would you love that child any the less?"

"Of course not, but, 'Lara Olive's Lacy. . . .'"

"I realize it's not Bach, Nigel, but when I sing it there's a great deal wrapped up in it—memory, all the people who listened over the years, the faces of the soldiers at Arras, who appreciated it as if it were the most beautiful song in the world, and then filed out in a thunderstorm of artillery, so many of them to die. Still, I make no claim. It's not my place to make a claim of one sort or another, only never to betray, and I will not betray."

The rhesus-monkey waiter, who momentarily would return to the tennis court yet again to sweep away the sand, appeared with the *citrons pressés*. They took them, thanked him, and drank them.

"Would you care to join me for dinner tonight at l'Espalier, Sidney? It's not far down the coast, and the jitney is very pleasant in the open air."

"I'm leaving," Sidney Balbion declared.

"When?"

"Four o'clock train."

"The Ostend boat will have left."

"Not going to Ostend, going to Berlin."

"Berlin."

"And then to Poland."

"Poland."

"I'm going to tour."

"As a tourist?"

"As an entertainer."

"Poland, Sidney?"

"I open next week in Przemyśl. Then, for various lengths of run, Sosnowiec, Piotrków, Kalisz, Bialystok, and finally, assuming that all has gone well and my reception justifies it, Warsaw."

"Sidney," Nigel said, "the Poles will receive you in utter bewilderment."

"I suspect you are right."

"They won't have the slightest idea of what you're doing."

"Why should they? They're Poles."

"The theaters will be empty."

"And I will be in them, singing."

"But I thought the Farkases could prevent you from going on?"

"Not in Poland. The contract says that I'm committed to them exclusively in Great Britain, and that in those countries where I'm neither a subject nor a citizen, I must obtain their express, written consent. There was always Italy, the factory towns, and they would not consent; and there was even Germany, and they would not consent."

"They let you have Poland?"

"No, they can't stop me in Poland. I'm a British subject but also a Polish citizen. I was born there, in Tarnow, near Czechoslovakia. Might as well have been born on the moon."

"I knew you had some Yiddish, but not Polish."

"Not a bit. My parents never uttered a word of Polish after they came to England."

"I can't imagine, Sidney—forgive me—that a tour of those cities would be very rewarding. I mean in a monetary sense."

"It isn't, but it's something."

"At least it proves my point."

"What point?"

"About Hitler, about your view of the whole thing. You are in fact in agreement with me if you, Sidney Balbion, a Jew and—little did I know—a Polish citizen, are going to Poland, now. Obviously, you don't believe that Hitler will invade."

Sidney Balbion was amused.

"It would be suicide. You don't believe it, do you, I know you don't. You can't."

"Nigel," said Sidney, after a pause in which Mrs. Lawrence had ceased to knit and even the waves seemed to have held their breaking in abeyance, "I do."

"Oh no," said Mrs. Lawrence under her breath, her fingers motionless around her knitting needles, "oh no."

And then Sidney Balbion stood up to his full, impressive, music-hall height, and in his robe he looked regal. "Honor, Nigel, honor," he said. "It's the only thing left, and it leaves you with happiness. Come, let's take a walk on the beach. I want to look at the sea before I go."

As the two men took the path between the dunes, Mrs. Lawrence said to her daughter, "Look, Angelica, look. There goes Sidney Balbion."

Her daughter did look up from her fashion magazine, and she said, "I told you, Mother, I've never heard of him."

Mar Nueva

To ME, nothing is as vivid as the Mar Nueva, though in the more than fifty years since my summers there I have lived in other countries and seen great things. And, then, there are the little things that in their mass can dim other memories. I've sailed in glass-bottom boats, joined glacier parties, and slept in tiny huts on the veldt, but when I went back to the Mar Nueva last December for the start of the summer season, I found that the intervening half century had robbed me very little of remembrance, which is not to say the recognition of maplike details. In those years, some beaches had been washed away, while others were born of hurricanes. What had been the main road is now merely the coastal road, both fashionable and crumbling. Further inland, on what used to be cane fields, divided highways cross in cloverleafs, and middle-aged businessmen who were not born then speed along in air-conditioned cars to summer houses three times as costly as the old estates and no bigger than their potting sheds.

Nor by remembrance do I mean the precise identification of landmarks, for individual trees are down, fences have long since vanished, and this time we were going south to hills that once I had seen across the bay from our house, hills that distance and tropical air had stripped of detail and painted sullen, massive, and blue—so there was nothing specific and arresting that I might have seen even if things of that nature had the good grace to last.

I mean by remembrance only my utterly clear recollection of the light on the surface of the sea, the color of the sky, the way the waves rolled in, between parcels of the sweetest silence, and how the entire sea moved, surging and falling back without breaks or whitecaps, in transparent contours that rose and fell like the chest of someone who is asleep.

Our acceptance of an invitation for a long weekend had been carefully qualified—only three or four days, I said, and we may have to return early. I wouldn't have accepted at all if our hosts' villa hadn't been on the other side of the bay, almost around the point. My wife knows of my aversion to this place. It is why we have traveled so much abroad.

I thought that half a century would have been enough, that I could simply lose myself in the indolence of the Mar Nueva—something for which it is justly famous, and something which once I knew well. After all, I'm a grown man, my children live in several foreign capitals, and now that I'm older neither delight nor sorrow come as easily as they used to. We arrived in the middle of the afternoon, and went to a terrace overlooking the sea to have something to drink and greet our hosts, knowing that quiet days by the sea lay ahead. It should have been delightful. We made jokes. I felt nothing.

But when I sat down and looked across the bay, my eyes went right to the unshaded northern promontory. As a child, I used to look over the dazzling sea in the middle of the afternoon as it shone brightly in a confusion of light. Now I had the north light, and the air above the sea was as clear as ether.

I excused myself, and went down a steep path to a deserted beach. The waves were strong, exactly as I had remembered. When they broke upon the sand, colors and sound bloomed from them, and when they retreated they sighed just as they had always sighed when they sought refuge in the cool blue currents. Across the bay, still sitting in a private forest of orange and lemon trees, was a huge house with a roof of red tiles. To the left, poking through the branches, its own roof no more than a dot, was our house.

MY FATHER and my father's parents before him had come to the house on the Mar Nueva since 1880. They had been guests at first, and then rented, until 1904, when Señor Alvarado died and his sons broke his vast holdings into a dozen pieces. My family bought the beach house and a small grove of mixed citrus. Every year, we were overwhelmed with lemons, limes, oranges, and grapefruit. We supplied our friends and relatives, and made gift hampers for my father's business acquaintances. For that reason we had an enormous supply of wicker baskets and excelsior. As a boy, I grew expert at packing the fruit and circling the baskets with a wide red or magenta ribbon. My sister and I learned to tie bows as symmetrical and voluminous as water lilies.

When I drove to the Mar Nueva last December it took three and a half hours to get there. Except for some broad curves where the coast bends inward, the road is now straight. We used to drive in a touring car that could not go much faster than a bicycle. If we left before dawn, we would arrive at about nine or ten at night.

The car was open, as big as a small swimming pool, and as high off the road as a reviewing platform. We always had a breeze, or crosscurrents of wind when we rounded a bend. I would stand in the back and pull down branches that hung over the road. I wasn't supposed to do this, and I tried not to, but when a branch came winging by overhead, something vital and automatic in my legs always made me leap up. Never once was I cut as I instantaneously stripped down the vegetation, and because the leaves were crushed as they flowed through my hands, we never arrived at the Mar Nueva unperfumed by their fragrant oils. Once, by accident, I grabbed a snake. I had it right in the middle, and it started to curl around my arm. Probably just as surprised as I was, it didn't hiss or bite. I think it must have been poisonous, since what else would it have been doing hanging in a tree? After my shock had dissipated, I screamed, and threw the snake from the car. No one else had seen it, and I was too scared to say what had happened. I screamed a few more times.

My father stopped the car under some palms. "What's the matter?" he asked, after setting the brake. I burst into tears.

He turned to my mother. "When we return to the city," he said, "we must take this child to a physician."

I thought this was funny, and began to laugh. To allay his anxiety, I tried to explain what had happened, but managed only to say the word "snake." I was then overcome by the kind of laughter that takes precedence over breathing.

Frightened that I might die of a convulsion, my father picked me up, ran from the car, and dunked me in the sea—clothes, shoes, a book in my pocket, and all. I will never forget my mother and sister, waist-deep in the waves, watching gravely, and then gradually beginning to enjoy the opportunity of standing in the ocean at midday, fully clothed.

On the way to the Mar Nueva we always found a beach and stopped to have lunch. Once, we saw a campesino trying to fly a kite. The peasants then had neither kites nor the time and energy to fly them, so this was unusual. Although the kite had a good tail and was properly constructed, the campesino couldn't get it off the ground. Despite strong winds—that day the waves kicked up enormous amounts of foam that blew back over their crests—each time the kite rose it would upend and dive at the sand.

This man was about my father's age, and my father seemed to want to join him. We got through lunch and swimming, and still the kite had not risen. As we were drying off, ready to get going again, not very happy about putting on our clothes over the salty residue of the seawater, my father took out *La Prensa* and opened it to the center page to read first, as he always did, the weather reports. Not only was he a cotton broker, who had to know the rainfall and humidity in Cairo and Khartoum and in Birmingham, Alabama, but he used to say that the weather was the only real information you could find in *La Prensa,* at least about our country. Though this was obviously a true statement, and everyone knew it, it was dangerous for him to say it out loud.

Anyway, as soon as he opened the paper an explosive gust of wind ripped it from his hands and propelled it down the beach at the speed of sound. Three or four sheets temporarily plastered themselves around the campesino, slapping him in the face, and then took off again. They curved up and were rocketed into the sky with such great speed that they became little specks faster than anyone could make a comment. They rose straight up, higher and higher, until they were buried in the clouds, at which point the victim of the newspaper attack slowly came over to us, stared into my father's eyes in wonder and defeat, and quickly handed him the kite, as if to say, "The rich have all the luck."

I mention these things to show that a full day's drive then seemed faster than a three-and-a-half-hour drive now. We always stopped at least a dozen times—we had to fix the car a lot, and we went swimming whenever the sea looked inviting.

But even had we driven last December on the crumbling coastal road, I do not think it would have moved me to remember the way I did when I first saw my house—from a great distance—after half a century. I must describe it, because its physical characteristics are somehow close to the heart of the matter.

IF YOU WERE GOING SOUTH, you turned left and drove into a tight space between the dark, glossy leaves of two orange trees. Perhaps because everything these trees had was expressed in their marvelous foliage, they didn't bear fruit. We had to trim them back every year, my father said, or they would scratch the car. My father would get up on a ladder and round them as if he were a professional tree barber, and I would do the lower parts, after which he would go over what I had done to make it even.

After lurching through the citrus trees, you pulled onto the cobblestones, where we parked the car. From there you could see right through the center of the house to the sea beyond. The sea close in was blue-green, but it had such a bright quality that it almost seemed white. And on the other side of the reef it ran dark blue. It was so inviting that I would run right through the house and sprint across the lawn to the beach, where I would stay by the water until my mother called me for dinner. She always had to call several times, for I was able to sit in the wind and watch the waves for hours. I imagined that somewhere within them, immediately close, was another world both infinitely tender and forgiving, where every doubt would be set to rest, every contradiction explained, and every fear disarmed.

I remember with much affection the details of our last summer at the Mar Nueva. Everything was bound up with the sea. Sometimes on my way to the beach I stopped in the kitchen and took a beer from the icebox. It was hot on the Mar Nueva and as a child I drank enormous amounts of the kind of beer that has no alcohol. We were told that the United States had prohibited alcohol, and I accepted this with the same puzzlement as I would have the statement that Britain had prohibited oxygen or that France had prohib-

ited wood. But whatever the United States had done, it resulted in shiploads
of alcohol-free beer delivered to the Mar Nueva in December and January,
when people here were thirsty in the heat and Americans were drinking hot
cocoa as they stood on frozen lakes. Always proud to sit down with an ice-
cold beer in my hand, I was ostentatious about it in town, with the object of
entrapping someone (preferably a priest) into reprimanding me, so that I
might point out with an air of offended innocence that all the alcohol had
been carefully removed by the manufacturer before I refreshed myself. The
dark-brown bottles were great objects to retrieve in diving, because they
were so much unlike every other color in the sea. You could throw them far,
they sank quickly because they were so heavy, and they often settled upright
on the gold-flecked sands.

Our inner courtyard had a small fountain. Though the bedrooms and the
winter living room were off the courtyard, we spent most of the time on a
veranda that overlooked the lawn and the sea. Here we had placed awnings
so that even in heavy downpours or blistering sun we could eat our meals,
talk through the afternoon, or read. Here also we had a radio that played
classical music and static. I have always associated the two, and a Beethoven
symphony seemed to me neither authentic nor profound if it did not carry
the sound of the nocturnal winter lightning storms over which the radio
waves from central Europe had to rise before gliding into our warm summer daylight.

Each bedroom had a bed, a chair, a ceiling fan, and mosquito netting
(though the veranda was just windy enough to keep away the insects, the inside of the house was not). I had been given a butterfly net. Mistaking a
Latin word for an English phrase, I was enthusiastic about chasing "leopard
opera" and having a collection of their jewel-like wings, but I could never
pin them. I tried to get my father to do it, and he refused, saying, "If you
want butterflies, you have to pin them yourself."

We played croquet and badminton, we swam and dived, and I climbed
trees even when they had no coconuts. I skinned my knees and elbows, and
learned that no matter how tired you get near the top of a palm, you can't
let go, because, if you do, you fall. Most often there was a reward, too—
coconuts. At age nine or ten, I was a happy blond monkey.

There are a few other things I must mention about the Mar Nueva before I tell what happened there. About two hundred meters down the beach, just at the border of our land and a much larger citrus plantation, was a short wooden pier. It was able to withstand the sea in winter because it was made of joined and bolted lignum vitae, and the columns upon which it stood were tapered to cut through the waves passing underneath. I fished and (when my father was there) dived off this pier. It was so solid and high that in all but the worst weather I was allowed to go there alone.

The sea was warm and buoyant. You could stay in it for hours at a time, and when you did you forgot everything but the bands of color in which you floated, the grace and speed of the rainbow fishes, the rhythmic laxity of the sea fans, and the surging of the water to and fro over the reef. You became part of the sea after just an hour. You thought like a fish, you hardly thought at all. I have never forgotten the small waves that lapped at my back, the wind and spray that caught and broke the light, and the contrasting smoothness and consistency of the deep swells. I have never forgotten, and I will always retain my confidence in the sea as a place to rest, if need be, forever.

Although today to have a villa the size of our house on the Mar Nueva would mean that you were able to fly around in your own jet, and play polo, we were not rich. As a cotton broker, my father had his ups and downs. It was a matter of the weather not just in our country but everywhere in the world. Perhaps because he was completely dependent upon the elements he did not have the false pride of someone who imagines that he has broken from nature and is not subject to its laws.

OUR LAST SUMMER at the Mar Nueva started out much the same as any other. I managed to escape my part in unloading the car (there was nothing in it anyway but groceries and clothes), and ran through the house to the beach. I remember how elated I was to stand at the edge of the breaking waves and watch the wind twirl and depress the water. This was in early December, and every day until March the sea would do the same thing and I would be in it. I imagine that no general ever felt as satisfied or vindicated, no matter what his conquests, as I felt then looking over the sea.

I went down the beach toward the pier. When I was halfway there I stopped as surely as if I had seen a saint suspended in the air before me, glowing like the peephole in a blast furnace. I ran back to the house and cornered my father.

"What is it this time?" he asked.

"A wall," I said.

"What wall?"

"On the beach. By the pier. It runs back into the trees, and it's tremendous. It must be bigger than the Great Wall of China. It's at least five meters high. Maybe thirty. It's made of stone, and it stops at the beach and then it goes on. It goes into the trees. I don't know where it stops. I didn't look."

My father took both my shoulders and gave me one of his piercing looks. "Are you sure?" he asked.

"I'll look again," I said.

"Claudia, why don't you go with him?" my mother suggested to my sister.

I was about to resent that, but Claudia had already disappeared into the kitchen. I ran like crazy through the citrus trees, thinking that I had imagined the wall and that I might go all the way to the point and not see anything. Then I would have to come back, though if I walked slowly it might all be forgotten. I remember that I wished I had imagined it, even at the cost of my own embarrassment.

I nearly ran right into it, for it was in a place that had once been perfectly open. It *was* five meters high, and it was made of stone. I ran along it, inland, until I no longer felt safe, and then I ran all the way back to the beach. There I checked to see that it came almost down to the pier, as I had reported, and I looked around it. On the other side were now three or four little houses, booths, lined up along the beach. Back from them were the orange trees that had always been there, and the beach grass.

"There are little houses," I reported breathlessly to my father.

"Bungalows?" he asked.

I didn't know what a bungalow was, but it sounded right, so I said, "Yes, bungalows, lots of bungalows all over the place, everywhere you look."

My father was downcast. "People from the bungalows will be walking all over our beach. Maybe it's for the better that they have a wall. But why such a big one? And how could they have put it up so fast? Let's go see." I darted ahead of my father, and when he reached the wall I was already standing on the pier.

When he joined me, he shook his head. "That wall must have cost twice as much as the land itself." Then, as we stood over the waves coursing between the pilings, he turned and said, "Those aren't bungalows. They're sentry boxes."

For the next few nights the wall and the sentry boxes were a main topic of dinner conversation. At first we thought they were part of a military base. But why a military base? My father said there was no possible reason for a military base there. A prison? No. The wall of a prison would go all the way around.

A few days later, when we had had to go into town to get more groceries, we stopped on a high point on the road and my father pointed to the enormous tiled roof. "It's just a private house," he said, and we started off again, wondering what kind of private house had risen so quickly and so splendidly right next to us in a single winter while we had been in school and my father had been trading cotton. No one in town knew anything about it, which was hard for us to believe, because those people seemed to know the name and life story of every lizard on every rock in the Mar Nueva.

On the way back, my father told us that it was a villa, just like ours, but that it belonged to someone very important. "I could scout around inside," I volunteered.

"Don't you dare," he ordered. "I absolutely forbid you even to cross over onto their beach."

"But the pier is half on their property and half on ours," I protested.

"You can go to the pier," he said, "but don't go beyond it. Sentry boxes mean sentries, and sentries have guns."

"Maybe they're swimming houses," I speculated.

"Swimming houses," my father said, looking at me with disdain. "Stay out of there. The place belongs to someone very important, someone close to Santos-Ott."

CHILDREN THESE DAYS do not understand—not even my children in their day knew—what it is like to live under a caudillo. All life is a contest between the caudillo and everyone else, and the caudillo must win. He must successfully intimidate every walker on every street; every sitter in every café; clerks at their desks; lovers in hotel rooms; skiers on mountain slopes; peasants in the fields; and children in their classrooms, ever mindful of his stern portrait next to the flag.

You must fear even to think in opposition, lest you talk in your sleep or carelessly insult him in the presence of one of his agents. When I was six years old, a shopkeeper on our street in the city lost his wife in an automobile accident, and fell into despair. In a democracy he might have had to shoot himself or jump off a bridge, but under Santos-Ott he merely brought a phonograph to his shop and played the music of an exiled composer. We were at lunch on a spring afternoon when we heard the music. The moment my father recognized it he ran to the window and pleaded with the shopkeeper, for his own sake, to turn it off. As the music played, the street emptied. The shopkeeper, who sold vegetables and eggs, had put the phonograph on a table and pointed the horn into the air. He sat on the stone step leading to his little shop, with a glass of wine in his hand and tears in his eyes. My father put on his jacket so he could go downstairs and see what he could do, but by the time he got to our front door the music had stopped and the store was shuttered. Within a week a shoemaker had moved in. Once, I mentioned the name of the man who used to sell vegetables and eggs, and my father said, "Just forget him. Put him out of your mind."

Santos-Ott dressed in white summer uniforms or, in winter, in a long military coat. His portraits were executed only when he was in this coat, so that even in late November as we sat in class fanning ourselves with our exit cards he looked down upon us coolly, with not a bead of sweat, absolutely motionless in the ten-kilo coat. It had two rows of buttons and a black collar with silver oak leaves. I know, because I stared at it through a thousand boring lessons. It was monumental, and he himself was tall. His peaked hat, with a visor and many more leaves, helped to make him seem like a giant.

I used to see the coat also in the pictures of him in *La Prensa Color*. It was not quite tan and not quite gray but, rather, the color of a Weimaraner dog. This, and the fact that Santos-Ott himself had absolutely blue eyes, gave rise to a universal comparison that never could be spoken but that never needed to be.

Though Santos-Ott had the typical dictatorial attribute of always receiving flowers from exemplary little girls in the national dress, everyone in the country looked in the little girls' eyes and could see that, even at four or five years of age, thinking that they might trip or hand over the bouquet incorrectly, they were numb with fear.

My teacher dared not criticize him. My father did not speak ill of him even at home. He seemed to me to be like God. I imagined that his children, if he had them (we never knew), would be more frightened than anyone else. Until the revolution, in all my life I had never heard a single soul but one speak against him—no strong man, intellectual, priest, or peasant, not even foreigners, who soon learned to bite their tongues. Only my sister, Claudia.

I WILL KEEP FOREVER and with great affection a vision of her, at seventeen, on a fall day when the air was so cold and clear that we had to wear sweaters. Our father had gone to Norway and brought back sweaters that he said were from a special batch made for the Norwegian royal family: because he was a cotton broker, he had contact with textile manufacturers and weavers, and we always had the best clothing, although it almost never fit well.

Claudia was tall and had not yet filled out. Because she moved her long limbs as if they were already heavier, she was awkward. Sometimes she would become so frustrated with herself that she would cry, and then my mother would take her in her arms and tell her that it would be just a matter of time until everything came into balance.

Her hair was the color of white gold, her eyes bluer than the eyes of Santos-Ott. The boys in her form shunned her, merely because they imagined that she would not even consider them. But anyone who cared to look closely could have known how lonely she was, for although in repose she was formidable and off-putting, as soon as she moved or spoke her animation and charm turned the burnished colors into soft allure, as if she were overjoyed just by the fact that someone was talking to her. At seven years her junior, I thought of her as a grown woman.

I remember that the pattern of her sweater was entrancing, especially as her long shining hair moved across it in soft sheaves, parting here and there, so that you wanted to brush it aside to see how the animals were placed in the flowers. A band of white and blue crossed the top of the yoke, and the yoke itself was so resolute, deep, and detailed that it seemed like a patch of mountainside. Mine was different. It had a herd of reindeer with a forest of brown antlers floating above them.

In 1932, a group of colonels on the Altiplano attempted a coup. It didn't make sense to start a coup from the Altiplano, and their efforts brought them a short civil war in which they were quickly driven into their sanctuaries. Even on their own ground they behaved like amateurs, and when the army closed in on the provincial capital, they fled on foot. Santos-Ott, commanding his own troops, had known their character. Anticipating that they would flee, he waited with two massive cavalry columns on a field between some high ridges along the route the plotters had hoped to use for their escape.

This became the Battle of Rosario, in which two thousand disorganized, retreating rebels were met by eight thousand men on horse. The action was much like that of an exercise at the military academy. The cavalry made diagrammatically perfect sweeps and charges on just the right lines, with little worry about being shot off their mounts, as only half their opponents were armed and those who were armed had little ammunition. The newspapers spoke of a pitched battle that had lasted for days, but still the truth got out. There were almost eight thousand survivors, the victors. They told their families. Their families had tongues.

Santos-Ott was quick to realize that those men who had been trapped between stone cliffs and ranks of cavalry and slaughtered at leisure over a period of ten or twelve hours had presented his opponents with two thousand martyrs. After dark, cavalry units had crisscrossed the field, crushing the wounded under their horses' hooves, until the drop in temperature relieved them of that task. Patrols circled the battleground to prevent families from coming to the aid of the defeated, and to shoot anyone alive enough to move. The victorious army made camp on a plateau not too far away, and a thousand bonfires kept them warm as those wounded rebels who still hung on slowly froze to death. The image that captured the public imagination was of men dying of cold while looking at the glow of the orderly fires around which their enemies were drinking hot tea.

Though Santos-Ott knew that two thousand martyrs are not nearly as ef-

fective as one, he moved to protect himself. Abandoning his pride and vio-
lating the tenets of dictatorship, he appealed to the public in a carefully
mounted political offensive. For us, this rarity consisted of an army lieutenant colonel addressing the assembled student body of our school. One
morning, a month after the battle, he appeared at the lectern of the assembly
hall and nervously tried to assure us that everything was fine: the government was not merely firm—and correct—but desperately necessary, and
good in its heart.

Though he wore the same kind of tentlike coat as did Santos-Ott, and
the same kind of hat, and was roughly the same age, he had the face not of a
hardened soldier or a cold political functionary but of a tobacconist who has
spent the greater part of his life sitting in a kiosk that afforded him most of
the sorrows and none of the glories of a man who is shot from a cannon.

Perhaps the lieutenant colonel would not have been intimidated by guns
and sabers, but he was intimidated by a sea of children's faces. The adoles-
cents and younger children stared at him with a kind of lunatic freshness,
and with a skepticism born of freedom and almost total ignorance. Even in
our authoritarian school, where the nuns were always rapping us on the
knuckles, we moved from place to place in an uncontrollable tide, numerous
fat children were always unable to stifle their giggles, and we had half a
dozen semiprofessional anarchists. How does one deal with untutored spirits? Teachers have difficulty. An army lieutenant colonel was at sea.

When he stood to address us he had the cautious, amazed air of someone
in a monkey house. Though each child was confined to a seat, there was so
much writhing and fidgeting that it was like a storm blowing through the
jungle.

He introduced himself, and stated that he had come to stress the need for
vigilance after the Battle of Rosario. For political reasons, enemies of the
state would seize the opportunity to spread falsehoods, but he had come to
describe the incident solely according to the facts.

Then he began his falsified account of the battle—falsified, we knew, because it was exactly parallel to the descriptions in *La Prensa*. The more he
went on, the more relaxed he became. In describing the maneuvers and their
classical antecedents (Santos-Ott was a great admirer of Napoleon) he won
the majority of the boys over to his side, as an engineer might have in ex-

plaining a marvelous machine. I myself have always been strongly drawn to objective beauty, and I delighted in the decisiveness and power of which he spoke and which he claimed to represent. And we, after all, the boys of a private academy, were the stuff that made up the officer corps.

When he finished, he was confident enough to ask for questions. Indeed, boys as young as eight were jumping in their seats, wanting to pose questions about flying wedges, crossfires, saber charges, and what have you.

The girls, however, had not been enthralled. In their stubborn and infuriating way, they were undoubtedly thinking about sewing or pastries. I wondered how they were content to dismiss things of great excitement, how they could insist upon looking at the world as if the most important part of it were the little kingdoms of which they were the queens. Nonetheless, my sister, who was in the next-to-last form, seemed surprisingly agitated. From the way she was moving around in her chair, and from her expression, I was sure that she was about to speak, but she did not raise her hand. I suspect that she felt obliged to stand and question him on behalf of those who had died. Everyone thought she was hard and pure, and she often rose to the part with great courage.

Mind you, I was not analytical then, not capable of understanding what moved my sister to be as impetuous, outspoken, and daring as often she was (she would, for example, at great risk to her standing among the teachers, flay alive any nun who dared to come to class unprepared). But I have remembered, and as the years pass, even though I have—I think—long understood her, I am surprised. For me, the power of recollection has always seemed sadly and inversely related to the power of action. My memories grow more intense, as if they had a life of their own. And if I close my eyes I see the pattern of her sweater in the most exact and luminescent detail, the way you see something bright that you have apprehended from the dark. I see her hair shining under the light. I have trouble recalling her voice, at seventeen, but the words are there, exactly.

ALTHOUGH THREE HOURS in the sea then seemed as long and expansive as the years now seem short, the weeks of our vacation passed quickly. The Mar

Nueva could have been another planet—a sea planet—where no unpleasant things existed, where you didn't have to study logarithms or dress in a suit, where your parents were always nearby but you were old enough to go off by yourself, where gravity was annulled for much of the day in astoundingly transparent water that, either blue or green, glowed as brightly as an electric light.

In February, when the cities were unbearably hot and strangely empty and yachts glided across the Mar Nueva as quietly as moths, I determined that I would help my father struggle against the vagaries of his profession by providing food for the table. I decided to become a fisherman, and much to my own surprise, for I have never had much confidence in my own resolve, I did.

I fished single-mindedly from dawn to late afternoon. Though I knew that my parents and even Claudia were as disturbed by my devotion as they were impressed, I aimed to impress them until they had forgotten what had made them uneasy.

On the very first day I caught three bluefin, of which we ate one and gave away two. When I got better, and could cast as far as a grown man, when I knew what kind of bait to use with different tides, and when the fish were running, how they ran, how to drop a hook right in the middle of churning water far offshore, and how to get a fish in fast enough so that I could hook another from the same school, I did so well that my father had to take me into town every night to sell my catch.

At first we stood by our car in great embarrassment, with the fish resting in a box of ice propped up against the running board. It took a long time to sell them off, and my father didn't like all the driving, so we struck a deal with a man who had a stall in the market. Every day at four o'clock he arrived in a truck that steamed with dry ice, and pushed a wheelbarrow to the pier, where my catch was strung, fresh and alive, riding the promise of the waves but never able to break loose.

I provided the main course almost every night, and with the money I earned supplying fish to a market strained by the needs of the summer people I provided the rest of our food, too. I was sinfully proud of myself. In the long hours I spent casting from the pier I frequently imagined that every girl I liked in school was somehow able to see me, and I often moved as if I were fishing in front of an audience. I was ashamed if I failed to cast beyond the point where I could actually see my lure as it splashed into the waves, and delighted if I could throw it temporarily into oblivion. The critical observers I made up for myself slowly forced me into expertise, and I caught an overwhelming amount of fish. I remember that often when I whipped the lure off one of my long surf-casting rods I looked ahead nobly and said, "Rosa!" Rosa was a little girl who was not very pretty, I loved her like crazy for years, and she grew up to be extraordinarily beautiful.

I was at the pier every day from dawn till four. After the fish man came I brought the money to my father and took the best fish I had caught into the kitchen, drank some fruit juice, and went into the ocean until dinner. The waves in late afternoon have an exhausted quality. I have noticed in many places all around the world that beaches empty at about four. Everyone has had enough, even the ocean. The light is too bright, the wind too steady. But underwater it was the same: the temperature was constant, the light was only slightly different, and the fish did not go back to their villas to shower and eat cherry ices.

SOLDIERS APPEARED in the bungalows. My father had been right about them: they did have rifles. When I looked in their direction, they didn't look back. Except for an officer who came out of the bushes and asked me what I was doing, who my father was, and how long we had lived there, they did mainly what I did: they scanned the sea. And the officer had refused to tell me who lived in the huge villa sheltered among the trees.

Soon I was as indifferent to the guards as they were to me. In the capital every other doorway was guarded by a detachment of infantry, and soldiers with rifles slung across their chests stood on street corners all day long looking at the women who passed by. I concentrated on fishing.

Claudia hardly ever came to the pier. My father visited often to check the fish, to sit and talk, and to bring me pitchers of ice water. Even my mother, who walked in tiny steps and hated to go through the bushes, came to visit a few times. But Claudia was in a sulk because she longed for the social life of the town—a sun-bleached extension of social life in the capital, which, though much less formal, was just as self-serving. I think she wanted the boys who had just left school, or were perhaps a little older than that (though not by much), to lose their breath as she passed by. She wanted to be noticed, and, of course, she would have been: she would have been a sensation. But in that regard my parents were unambitious. They never went out, they didn't sit in cafés, they had a small circle of friends—cotton brokers, unknown journalists, businessmen who didn't do too well, and some people whose strength and troubles prevented them from settling into any one profession. And relatives—my mother's brother was an inventor who invented a thousand things, not a single one of which was ever patented or produced (who needs a shoehorn that doubles as a drinking straw?).

My parents were grateful that Claudia was still with us, and they patiently endured her outbursts. After all, she was almost eighteen, and would soon be marrying. "She is undergoing a painful transition," my mother said. I used to stare at Claudia and wonder about this transition. She spent so much of the day reading Russian novels that her ears were red where she had rested her head on her hands. Reading in winter always seems to me to be rather businesslike; in summer, it puts you in a trance and makes your bones ache.

Anyway, one day in the third week of February—the seventeenth, to be precise—I was sitting at the end of the pier. There was a breeze, and the waves were rolling in slowly. They hardly broke, except on the beach itself, where they quietly tucked themselves in. It was before lunch, and the sun was high. I was casting into the wind, trying to close in on a big school of fish that had me praying for them to veer shoreward. These were mackerel, which belonged in the open sea, and the water around them looked like the rapids in a river. They had no business where they were. They should have been out deeper in the blue, and as they passed inshore I was able to cast my lines farther than ever before. My four lures fell short of the fish, but I was enthralled anyway, and I shouted into the wind for them to come closer.

They didn't. They vanished beneath the swells, leaving me with beautifully taut lines drawn by the power of the sea. I turned around. Right next to me, practically on my heels, was an old man dressed in sandals, a bathing suit, an open shirt, and a peasant's straw hat.

I almost fell into the water. "Sorry," he said. "You couldn't hear me because of the wind, and I didn't want to interrupt you when you were going great guns. I saw that school, too. I thought I'd come over and see if you could pull one in."

I knew I had a volatile imagination. I was the one who claimed in near hysteria to have seen a prehistoric bird. Still, I was terribly afraid that this old man, who was unusually tall and wore impenetrable sunglasses, was actually Santos-Ott. I wanted to run home and say that he was Santos-Ott, and to be convinced of it, but for him not to be Santos-Ott.

How could it have been Santos-Ott? The soldiers were still in their bungalows and he was alone with me. He wasn't in a general's white summer uniform, and he seemed shy.

I think I knew that he was indeed Santos-Ott, but if I had admitted it to myself I would have fainted, so I pretended that he wasn't. This is just an old man who's going to go on and on about fishing, I thought, as deep within me alarm bells were going off, flames were licking the back of my lungs, and choruses of the damned were singing, "Caudillo! Caudillo! Caudillo!"

"I have four lines out," I began, breathlessly. "Each line is two hundred meters of Permafil with a rated strength of seventy-five kilograms. I can cast sixty or seventy meters with the wind, but if there's a riptide it will carry the line farther and deeper. That's why I have so much line. The big fish are in the blue."

"Check the lures," he said. I began to reel them in.

BY THE TIME I had retrieved the lures, my heart had slowed down to normal. I would have been very proud if I had pulled in a big silver mackerel, but unfortunately I had no fish to show the old man. Now I know why I had calmed down. Very few people who get to be chief of state lack the ability to put others at ease. And, then, he was not in his coat, he was deferential and truly interested in my fishing technique, and we were out at the end of the pier, on the sea.

"I thought that, for it to work, you had to be pulling a lure through the water all the time," he said. "What's your method? When I was a boy in the mountains, we would put a lure in the stream and the water flowing past it would keep it alive. You can't do that in the ocean, can you?"

Everyone knew that Santos-Ott had been a boy in the mountains. It was part of the national mythology: I had heard and read the phrase "a boy in the mountains" applied to him hundreds of times. "Often, you can," I answered. "It's because of the point. The currents sweep along the coast and then are deflected straight out to sea by the point, so it's like a river, only it curls back in a circle and hits the shore again. If you throw a bottle over the reef it will head straight out to sea, but in a few hours it may be washed up on the beach. Sometimes the riptide is so strong that I think I have a strike. But mostly it's gentle enough to carry the line out slowly, and then, after you brake the reel, to hold the lure just below the surface."

"Why doesn't the lure come back, like the bottle?"

"Because it doesn't go far enough out. To make the full circle, something has to touch the open sea."

"How do you know all this?" he asked. "You talk like someone who has been on the Mar Nueva all his life."

"I have," I answered. This made him laugh. "And I know about what happens to a lure, because we went out in a boat and found it. It spins around and goes back and forth, just like a fish that's holding its place."

"Do you catch a lot of fish?" he asked, as if he were thinking about getting some for himself.

"Enough for us to eat, and I sell the rest. I've been paying for our food," I stated with obvious pride, and then added, "this summer."

"But it isn't necessary for you to do this, is it? What does your father do?"

"He's a cotton broker."

"A cotton broker can do very well."

I didn't want to tell him that my father worried about our savings as they dwindled in the heat, or when the weather was too wet, or too good in America or Egypt. And besides, our tuition was what did my parents in, and in that sense I did feel responsible for helping my father, even if he didn't need it.

"Where are you from?" the old man asked.

I knew he could tell from the way I spoke that I was from the capital (and not many people from anywhere else had villas on the Mar Nueva), so I told him the district.

"Where, exactly?"

That meant he longed for the city. I told him the street.

"It's not far from my house," he said.

His house! I was sure that his house was the Presidential Palace. Inside the fence were a polo field and a golf course that you couldn't see from the boulevards even had you been willing to risk arousing the suspicion of the guards by looking toward them. Yes, his house was near my street. If you wound your way through the Sixth District to the bottom of the hill, crossed the park, and then crossed the Boulevard of XX September, you'd be right at the gate.

Some time passed, and to end the silence I allowed myself an indiscretion. "I'd like to go in your house sometime," I said. "I've never been in a house with four hundred and fifty rooms."

"Four hundred and fifty-six," he responded, without the slightest trace of emotion or irritation. I knew, at that moment, that his power lay in the complete control of his emotions, and that, unless he wanted to, he felt no emotion whatsoever. It was clear to me on the pier. He was intelligent, inquisitive, and pleasant. He made you admire him in the same way that you cannot help but admire a good watch or a Swiss cable car. Everything in him worked without inhibition, and he wasted neither time nor words. He was virtually an embodiment of pure forces: the laws of nature could not have been more cold or precise.

But he ruled my country for forty years because he could, at will, quickly develop within himself passion and resolution that were unparalleled and astounding. When he spoke he temporarily converted even his staunchest opponents and brought to tears crowds of men who had resented him all their lives. He fired up old women and grandmothers until they wanted to join the cavalry. With complete control, he could go from passion to reserve, at will, from light to dark and dark to light, like lightning flashes in a thunderstorm. Some men have oratorical ability and a great heart, and some think so coldly and well that they turn roiling problems into smooth ice. Santos-Ott was both.

"May I come from time to time to watch you fish?" he asked.

"Yes," I said, hardly believing that the caudillo had asked for my permission.

"Perhaps you'll even give me a fish," he added.

"Of course," I said, with daring familiarity. "It's half your pier. I owe you rent, I think."

"I have a colonel who can plank fish the way they do in the mountains. I'd have him cook it for me." He thought for a moment. "He says he can plank fish."

"Would one fish be enough?"

"Why not?"

"Don't you have big dinners, with ambassadors and ministers?"

He shook his head. "I eat alone. If you let people under your tent they come to the conclusion that they can throw you out."

"Oh," I said, only half understanding, because our tent had a cloth floor, and I imagined people crawling under it, making huge hills of canvas.

"I played that game for twenty years," he added, "and then I realized one day that I didn't have to play any longer. But you're too young to remember what it was like then. You weren't even born."

I smiled. It was a disadvantage not to have been born then, but it was also an advantage, and I knew it.

He didn't smile back. "Let's see you cast those lures out to blue water."

I looked over the reef. "I can't," I said. "It's too far."

"Clear the reef," he commanded.

I picked up the first of my poles and leaned back. Arching my body, I cast out the lure, extending my arms like a ballet dancer. The lure kept flying through the air until it landed in the blue band. Elated because I had never cast so far in my life, I picked up the other rods and sent three more lures, one after another, with strength newly discovered, right into the blue.

When I turned around, he was gone. Perhaps because the sun was so hot I was not sure that I hadn't dreamed him up in an extended hallucination. But I continued to feel a sense of power and motion, and for a moment or two I was sure that I was destined for great things, and I would not become the kind of ordinary man that I have, in fact, become.

These sensations were so strong that I had to doubt them. Then I looked at my lines and saw that they were fixed solidly and skillfully in the distant band of deep blue.

KNOWING MYSELF THEN, and now, I would think that my immediate reaction to an encounter with Santos-Ott would have been to run home proclaiming it in half-insane breathless squeals. Adults at that time were either members of the Institutional Party, subversives, or scrupulously apolitical. My father was the last. In many ways the neutral ground was the most dangerous, for the subversives were enough under control for the authorities to be vexed mainly by the apolitical, whom they always suspected and for whom they had the greatest contempt.

My father, being carefully undeclared, did not betray his real views even to his children, probably for fear that we would blurt them out and bring upon ourselves some terrible disaster from which none of us would ever recover. We knew that he had contempt for *La Prensa,* but so did everyone else. Even Santos-Ott, in the famous speech during which he laughed, had said, "Do you think I am so stupid that I believe what I read in my own newspaper?" And the whole country laughed with him, and loved him for having told the truth.

So I was left at an impressionable age to judge for myself questions of which I had neither knowledge nor understanding. I knew that Santos-Ott was a terrible figure, intimidating and cruel, but I knew as well that being in his presence was exciting. Perhaps alone among all the people in my country I was able to talk with him as if he were a mortal man. I have long since forgiven myself for imagining in a boyish way that because I was such a good fisherman he would take me under his wing and make me his successor. Though I would continue the practice of looking out at everyone from photographs of me in a Weimaraner-colored coat—and here I rejoiced that my eyes, too, were blue—I would be kind, I would allow *La Prensa* to say anything it wanted, and we would live not in the Presidential Palace but in our house, more beloved than feared.

Above all, I would return to the Mar Nueva every summer with my family, and although soldiers would stand in the bungalows and people would line up on the road to see me as I passed, I would fish from the pier, with Rosa by my side, leaving the affairs of state to run themselves after the first gentle push from my all-encompassing benevolence.

That afternoon, when the fish man paid me, I laughed at the crumpled currency with the picture of Santos-Ott, thinking for some reason that together Santos-Ott and I controlled hundreds of millions of neatly pressed linen bills in closely guarded vaults in the capital. The fish man asked me what was so funny. Didn't I like his money?

"Ah, money!" I said. And then, looking at him portentously, "When you have the means of production, then"—I nodded my head—"you see."

"You see what?"

"Ha!" I said.

"You should wear a hat," he told me as he climbed onto his truck. "Always wear a hat in the sun."

That night I sailed in to dinner, a demigod. Instead of reaching for the pepper grinder I simply held out my open hand as if it would fly to me of its own accord. My mother passed it my way without a word, and I chuckled without noise, like the villains in films.

"Did you eat any strange fish or floating thing?" my father asked tentatively.

I laughed and shook my head.

"Fermented fruit, moldy bread or cookies, unfamiliar seeds or gourds?" He sounded like a customs inspector.

"We have no moldy bread or cookies," my mother said indignantly, as I shook my head slowly, tolerantly, back and forth.

"Perhaps he found them on the side of the road, or they were washed up on the beach," my father ventured.

I tipped my head back and laughed like an African chieftain, with more depth and percussion in my lungs than I knew I had. This really stunned them.

"It's the sun," my sister declared, while my mother reached out to feel my head. "You can't stay in the sun all day long, day after day, and not . . . you know."

With her many recent outbursts and tears in mind, I said, quite royally, "So sayeth the cuckoo, from deep within the clock."

"Enough!" my father insisted. "You behave, or you'll spend the next four days in your room rolling marbles around in the shade."

A look of vindication passed across my sister's face.

"Both of you," my father said in a way that betrayed the existence of his many pressing problems, "have been behaving like inmates in an asylum. Let me remind you that you are privileged to be here, that we may not be able to afford this place next year, and that the Sixth District in February—something you have never experienced—is so hot and miserable that cast iron gets as soft as gutta-percha and the drinking fountains become steam vents.

"I know you don't have friends, and are isolated," he said to my sister, "but you should swim in the sea sometimes." And to me, "I think it might be a good idea for you to stay indoors at midday. The fish don't run then anyway."

"Sometimes they do," I protested.

THE NEXT DAY began like any other. I arose at five-thirty and found my sister reading in the living room, never having gone to bed. After crushing the scorpions on the kitchen floor, I took some bread and fruit juice, and left with my fishing equipment to pull in the fish as they fed.

In early morning the sea and the light ran together. The water surged with great energy as if to show that it had been refreshed during the night. And in the privacy of dawn, the sea and the beach coexisted without argument—no breakers, no sparkle in the sands. The tide was up, and blue-green water glowing almost white on its surface moved gently under the pier, quite close, hissing occasionally as it was forced through crevices in the pilings.

I attended to my rigging and ate breakfast. When I finished I looked up and saw the gleaming blue band, the first part of the sea to take the sun. I cast my lures and watched them fly. They landed in the cold blue, and the lines stretched taut. The morning tide took them out where I couldn't see them.

In the deep and luminous world of the sea, fleets of huge fish circle the globe, neither breaking the surface nor touching bottom but suspended in silent layers of shadowy green and blue, rising a mile or falling two, fighting noiseless battles in great societies of which we have never even dreamed.

Perhaps because of a change of season, a migration, or a war among the fishes, a vast school of bluefin passed by the Mar Nueva that morning. The waves were broken by their churning, and they crowded the entire bay, seething underwater for as far as I could see. For all I knew, the school was as wide as five days' sailing and as long as ten. Just an edge of it may have been enough to fill the bay.

In their excitement the bluefin took my lines as fast as I could pull them in and cast out again. They were the biggest fish I had ever caught, inhabitants of the open sea more amazed than I by their turn of fortune. They weighed as much as I did, and in two hours I exhausted myself. I ran to the house to get my father to help me, but he had gone with my mother and sister to town, so I took whatever extra lures and heavy line I had and returned to the pier.

The fish eventually swallowed all the lures, and then I was casting out empty hooks, on which they impaled themselves without thought. Though some got loose and others snapped my lines, by the time I had broken three poles and was too tired even to think of casting I had almost thirty bluefin tethered to the pier, each of twenty kilos or more, with some of at least fifty. They were so big that I was afraid to fall among them. I even wondered if they might destroy the pier, for had they been able to concentrate their powers, they undoubtedly could have.

I lay down, peering through the cracks at my catch as it circulated below me. My muscles were stiff and aching and I could hardly move. The wood upon which I rested was as dense as concrete, slightly rosy, almost coffee-colored, with a scent that complemented the scent of the brine. Each time the waves withdrew, they exposed the backs of the bluefin. When the bluefin crossed they sometimes had the leverage to part the fishing line, and when they did they would circle in confusion among the pilings until they found an opening to the sea and sped away. After some early losses, the tangling ceased as the distance between the fish increased, and I was left with more than twenty.

As the sun beat upon my back, I had a strong urge to let them go. Because freedom can be understood only as the absence of restraint, and the restraint I had known had always been benevolent, I valued freedom insufficiently for myself. But I could tell the difference between them and me. Their movements were so sad and aimless that I knew I had to cut them loose.

On the other hand, I had been trained over many long days to appreciate a strong bend of the rod, and the more fish you catch the more you treasure the feeling. Down below me was the equivalent in live currency of two weeks on the pier in the hot sun. If I didn't throw back a single mackerel, why should I release this herd, no matter how noble or powerful they seemed?

My answer to myself was that they had everything about them of the open sea, and I had never intended to capture the open sea. I turned to look for the thrashing of the school from which I had taken them. It was there, but fast disappearing. The mass of bluefin was part of something very great and beautiful, and I felt keenly that I had no right to powers over them.

Because the temptation to hold the wealth for which I had struggled was great, I put off a decision. As the sea moved beneath me and the bluefin grew quiet, I fell into an uneasy sleep.

I AWOKE, weak from the sun and disquieted by dreams that I could not remember. My sister was sitting beside me, her knees pulled up to her chest. Our parents had sent her to the pier to call me for lunch. Usually this was my father's job, but he and my mother had gone back to town to wire money to a bank. We were all to converge upon our meal at once.

"What happened?" she asked, referring to my three broken rods and a disordered tangle of lines, hooks, and leads.

"Look," I said, and knelt to peer through the planks.

She dropped down in imitation. Because she was wearing a straw hat that kept the glare away from her eyes, she could see better than I could. The water underneath was glowing, and the bluefin had become as patient and apathetic as dogs on a hot afternoon. But, unlike dogs, they were in a cool sea. They had lost none of their sparkle or bearing, and they remained exquisitely beautiful.

"How did you catch so many?" she asked.

I told her. And then I added, "I think I'll let them go."

Young girls, especially those who are troubled by loneliness, and who stay up all night reading Russian novels, can be so profoundly sensitive that passion springs from them quite easily, and though their love may be focused inexplicably, the love itself is as innocent and genuine as they are and can readily convince you of sentiments you might not otherwise adopt. Claudia was always quick to decide, and in this case I hardly needed convincing. "Cut the lines," she said.

With the aid of my pocketknife, we set about freeing the bluefin. I lifted a line to give it tension, and she snapped it with the blade. Just like the fish that had been freed before, those newly released circled once or twice and then propelled themselves with all their power toward the open sea.

Freeing the bluefin brought us closer. She was, after all, my sister. Our blood was the same. There was much that we shared in common without ever realizing it.

MY SISTER was staring through the cracks in the pier when I looked up and saw Santos-Ott coming toward us.

First I thought of pushing her into the water, but he would undoubtedly have come to her rescue and scolded me, and there they would have been, face-to-face, with my value as a mediator wasted. Then I realized that I didn't have any value as a mediator. He was used to dealing directly and decisively with everyone and everything, and so was she.

When he was halfway down the pier, I thought of pushing him into the water. I didn't have to think about it very long. I had seen quite a few unsheathed bayonets, and though at that age I had no fear of death, I made up for it with a dread of pain.

When he got to us, she was still staring at the remaining bluefin, and her straw hat covered her eyes. I bent down beside her and said so quickly under my breath that all the words may have compressed into only a few, "There's someone here. Don't say anything. Just shut up." And then I added, "Don't be a chatterbox."

"This is my sister," I said. I didn't need to tell her who he was, but I did anyway. "And this is Santos-Ott." I turned scarlet. He was amused.

When she looked up, and rose, I saw him change. Of course I can only speculate as to what moved him, but I believe that he felt admiration and goodwill for her youth. What is more endearing than a young girl on the verge of womanhood? For an old man, she lights up the world.

I was proud that she was so tall, that her eyes were bluer than his, that she was handsomer, and that she was absolutely uncorrupted and perhaps incorruptible. She put him in his place in a thousand ways, and he must have had to think hard of his fleet and his army just to be able to look her in the eye.

Even without my introduction she would have recognized him instantly, for, although I had hardly noticed, his straw hat and open shirt had given way to an admiral's arctic-white uniform. He had so many gold stripes and stars on his epaulets that compared to him the commander of the navy looked like a rating, and he wore a huge medal on a red sash. Only one kind of man will take a solitary afternoon walk dressed like five field marshals, a different kind of man from the one who had talked to me about fishing.

"I can hardly believe my eyes," my sister said without any sarcasm. Still, I thought this was disrespectful. So did he.

"How so?" he asked.

"Is it true?" she inquired, sliding gradually into the tone I had hoped she would avoid. "The caudillo is standing on my brother's fishing pier, alone, without guards?"

"I don't need guards," he said.

"Have you left the palaces unguarded?" she riposted, as quickly as if she had been following a script. "Will you walk through the capital alone, through the Fourth District, for example, because you are so beloved of your people?"

I believe that she was at him so fast because, after her initial shock, she was relatively unimpressed. Perhaps if she had had less presence the weight of his own would have constrained her. Although I was upset, I was not really surprised: neither of them was any good at wasting time.

I tried to stop her by interrupting about the fish, but he gestured for me to be quiet. He tensed the muscles around his mouth and narrowed his eyes. How ugly and terrible a fault he revealed as he faced a young girl as if he were confronting thousands of men, horses, and field guns.

"My object isn't to be beloved," he said, "or to court public sentiment."

"No?"

"No," he answered, shaking his head. "Each country on this continent is braced to come apart in anarchy but for the one man who holds it together, the man who is appreciated only when he is absent. Then they call for him. But the people have short memories. In your case, because you are a child, you have no memory at all. My father died in the last civil war, as did hundreds of thousands of others. To you, it is prehistoric. You cannot feel it. You don't even think of it. For me, it has never ended.

"And as for my courage," he said, stabbing the air with his index finger, "I will, if I desire, walk through any district in the capital, and any valley in the mountains, completely alone. You underestimate me. Long before you or your parents were born, I had learned many a hard lesson.

"Put me in the mountains today with nothing but a peasant's clothing and a sword, and I'll again raise armies, confound my enemies, survive, and prevail. I don't need those men," he said, sweeping his left arm toward the soldiers in the sentry boxes, who almost came to attention at the gesture, "and they know it. If I did need them, even one of them, I wouldn't be here. You know," he said, shifting tone in a way that offered her escape if she would succumb to the shock of his onslaught, "I don't have power because my portrait is on postage stamps. My portrait is on postage stamps because my power was born with me."

I felt oppressed by the consistency of what Santos-Ott had said, and I understood even then that no answer could obliterate his point entirely. But, to my great surprise, my sister answered him, and she did it without the slightest hesitation, for she, too, was able to draw on passion.

Whereas his had had identifiable origins, hers had taken form instantly. But, then, power grows from accident as much as from discipline. As she addressed him I trembled, but she was as steady as a stone pillar.

"Caudillo," she said, as if *she* were the chief of state, "you pervert logic for your own benefit. Perhaps because everyone is afraid of you, no one has corrected your error. Perhaps no one has even tried. Let me explain to you how you err."

Without doubt, no one had spoken to him like this in more than half a century. I knew that save some miraculous intervention my sister was going to die. She also knew, but she went on as fluently as a columnist in *La Prensa*. She neither faltered nor hesitated. Her voice did not break, her eyes did not leave his for a moment.

Though I was astounded and proud, I feared for my father and mother. I knew that whatever happened they would suffer most, and I began to cry.

"You present two alternatives," she stated, like a prosecutor. Where she had picked up the firmness and speed in her voice I do not know. "The first is anarchy, and the second is your absolute authority. You say that to avoid one we must have the other. What would you say, then, to an anarchist who put it in the same light: 'To avoid despotism, we must have anarchy'? Both of you will fight till kingdom come and, if need be, flip positions as readily as you flip temperaments. When the anarchist unseats you, he will be the strictest authoritarian. When you are unseated, how quickly you will become Santos-Ott, anarchist."

"Do you realize the cost of this outburst?" Santos-Ott asked almost tenderly, as if he had visualized not only what was going to happen but his regret as well.

"Yes, I do!" she shouted. "My life. So you'd better listen."

"I cannot believe that you have not been schooled deep within the opposition," he stated, coolly. "I cannot believe that you have not been raised on hatred and bitterness."

"Of course you can't," she replied, matching him in tone as if to show that he had no more self-control than did she. "If you believed any differently, you'd have to quit. Most people, Caudillo, do not oppose you: they are merely injured by you."

"Do you understand what you have done?" the caudillo asked, relishing the mortal blow he was about to deliver. "Obviously you could not have thought up such things yourself. Your parents should have been more careful."

"What do you mean?" Claudia asked. "Be clear."

I could hardly believe that my sister had instructed Santos-Ott to be clear.

He slowly nodded his head, as if he had confirmed his own notion, and he said, "I mean that revolutionaries should not keep parrots. That's what I mean."

He turned his back on us and walked away. No matter what his sins or powers, he had the air of a man who had been deeply hurt.

FOR A MOMENT we were stunned, but then, as if it were a way out of the bind into which Santos-Ott had put us, we began again to cut the bluefin loose. Each time a fish broke from captivity it circled in puzzlement with none of the easy grace it had had in the freedom of the sea. But when it got its bearings and knew exactly where to go it picked up speed and swam as straight and powerfully as a torpedo, cresting the foam where the breakers caught the reef and then disappearing into the ocean's comforting infinitude.

When we had seen them leaping in the open sea, and could see them no more, our momentary satisfaction gave way to fear. Neither she nor I felt like standing on the pier in full view of the sentry boxes and the soldiers, and we went into the groves on our side of the wall.

Sheltered from the midday sun, we stood in the shade and looked up through the branches of the citrus trees. Their leaves were dark green, as shiny as a newly waxed automobile. Not one was ragged or about to fall. Through them we could see the far more perfect deep blue sky. We were near a pool of light, and everything else under the trees seemed like black lacquer. It was cooler in the dark, and I felt as if my heart were beating as fast as the wings of the glistening insects that flew among the leaves like creatures of polished gold.

"What are we going to do?" I asked, not fully able to separate what was happening from what might have been had it been a game.

At first she made no response, and then she said something remarkable, in that it showed that she had already come to terms with her situation and with herself. She said, "What I regret the most is that I have never been in love with anyone who loved me. I thought it was only a matter of time. It probably was."

"You'll have it," I said, ashamed of lying to someone who could see so clearly.

"No," she answered. "I won't."

Then we heard footsteps. In my childishness, I thought it would be armed men. But it was my father, walking on the lighted paths between the trees, having come to summon us to lunch. Despite the heat, he was in a tweed jacket, the same one that he wore on weekends in the city. It was light in color, almost white, and with the sun shining off it I had to squint to look at him. He passed by, missing us in the shade. He called for us, and as he was calling my sister's eyes filled with tears. She ran out from the trees. "Here we are, Daddy," she said, and went to him, flinging herself into his arms.

This was strange behavior for a girl who had passed the summer in an adolescent sulk, but my father quickly embraced her, as if she were a child, for she was, after all, his child, his firstborn.

AND NOW I HAVE RETURNED, more than half a century later, to the edge of the sea where, a few days after we stood in the pools of light and dark under the citrus trees, my sister drowned herself. Though it is autumn now and I am sitting in the shade, in my house, in the Sixth District, I feel as if I am on the beach in full light, staring out at the water, right next to the waves. It is a very strange feeling. All I have to do is close my eyes, and what I see is more real than what is real.

In fifty years there has been no forgetting. All the trips to glaciers, fjords, and ancient cities have been to no avail, for somehow I have always been at the Mar Nueva. I might as well have gone there every summer.

Though we maintained superficial connections, I was driven from my father forever. Despite my youth, he could never forgive me for not warning him, and from then on he thought of me as intolerably stupid. But he was wrong. We would not have been able to leave the country, and if, as he had imagined, he had gone to the caudillo to offer himself as a sacrifice, the caudillo, I am sure, would have killed them both. The caudillo, after all, ruled all his life and died a natural death. Garcia, who had succeeded him, was overthrown shortly thereafter, but not Santos-Ott, for Santos-Ott knew best of all how to obliterate opposition—efficiently, almost automatically, irrevocably.

And he did. My sister died. My parents, who had never liked Santos-Ott but had never done anything to oppose him, were broken. They lived and died in defeat. Of course, he gave them every reason to go against him, but he was clever enough to paralyze them by leaving them their son. And what do you think that did to me? The answer is that I have remained a quiet man all my life.

Claudia drowned in the deep blue, but the tides brought her home. I found her early one morning, in the shallows, her back rising above the little waves, her hair all tangled as it moved with them, and now she has a grave. Still, in December when I returned to the Mar Nueva the first thing I did was to go down to the water and report to her there, for I believe her soul and youth are in the sea.

I told her how much my parents had loved her, and how they had never forgotten, not even for a moment. I told her of my life, and how I had lived it, and of my sorrow. And I told her of how, once, not long before her death, I had seen her when she thought she was unobserved, with her arms around herself as if someone were holding her.

Rain

In his endless grief, the deputy inspector of customs often thought about St. John's Park. For in the months before Mackie, at age eighteen, put a pistol to his head and died in his father's house on the tenth of September, 1867, St. John's Park had been torn up, and in its place had risen the Hudson River Railroad freight depot. The park had been as flat as a stone floor and full of widely spaced trees as straight as the white columns of St. John's Chapel. Fine houses separated by spacious gardens had surrounded it. In the winter, at dusk, the newly appointed deputy inspector and his son had sometimes walked through in the cold wind, while lamps and fires flickered in the houses on the perimeter. And when darkness settled they had broken the winter stillness with their difficult conversation. Mackie was troubled, and his father, who though he tried could not plumb even the shallows of those troubles, was frightened.

As long as the park had been inviolate, and as long as there were in the city itself so many quiet, empty streets, and a tranquillity like that of the Berkshires or the plains that feed cold winds into Albany, the deputy inspector of customs believed that the glory, order, and commanding silence of the past could come forward to smooth the roiled waters of the present in an omniscient velvet tide.

But the park had been broken in a season or two, subsumed in industry, the value of the houses surrounding it destroyed, the fortunes that had built them forcibly evaporated, and the memories that once had rested lightly on the snow-covered field buried as grimly as the dead they had kept lively in the souls of the living. Mackie, just eighteen, a clerk in an insurance office and newly enlisted in a National Guard regiment, somehow had felt such unbearable heaviness that he had put an end to everything.

His father, who for so long a time had had to face the deaths of his relatives, friends, and dreams, one following upon another and never seeming to cease, was now defeated utterly. The passing years made no difference to him as he waited to sail out, living gracefully when he could, but only for the sake of those he loved and not for his own, and to reflect as much as possible before the moment of his obliteration.

Reflection and contemplation had come easily and inescapably to him, like the flow of the Hudson past the town of Hudson, or the rise of the Catskill eagle on March winds: reflection and contemplation for their truth and nothing else. He was far less useful in almost any other way, though he was able to do things, and had done them capably. But what he had done, and what he would do, his immersion in the fires of activity, seemed only a distraction from the pull of infinite, actionless darkness. Reflection had been to no avail, for in the end he found himself swept on the same great current and as helpless and bewildered as the most unreflective man alive.

EVERY MORNING on his way to the customs house he passed a bookseller on a side street far from the crowds on the avenues and yet, even accounting for that, mysteriously inactive. Many stores manage somehow, day after day, to exist without customers, and so did this one. He had never seen anyone in it, not even once, although he himself had discovered there a copy of *Typee,* pushed back in the shadows, low on the geography shelf, damaged, spine out. Of all his books, this was the one that represented him least, and there it had stood for at least four years, and might stay forever.

In the window of this strange shop sometimes attended to by a heronlike balding man whose resentment of everything was flawlessly communicated even when all one could see of him was his back, was the *Bird's Eye View of the City of New York*. A highly detailed, hand-colored lithograph ten years out of date, it showed New York from aloft, gripped in the frenzy of commerce. Despite problems of perspective that made an unsuspecting horse near the Brooklyn Navy Yard as big as a five-story building, it was majestic overall. One could see at a glance why, with a great engine such as New York supplying the armies with shot, shell, ships, and men, the Union could only have prevailed in the War of Rebellion.

Ships swarmed at the docks, anchored in the rivers, moved out to sea, and came into the harbor. The plumes of white sail or steam that identified them for what they were, were matched in signaling power by billows of smoke from factory chimneys, running full out with the wind. And like the engraving itself, fading in the sun year after year, the clouds dispersed and went pale, their substance fleeting even as their motion was frozen.

On the way to the customs house every morning, quiet and inconsolable, he stopped before the fading lithograph to peer into the muted streets of Brooklyn. There, sometimes, on a winter morning, he had turned the corner on a prospect both empty and long, its buildings stolid and patient in the cold air and pale sunshine. With everyone at work or inside by the fire, these houses were as quiet as headstones.

ONE MORNING in the middle of September, after weeks of unrelenting rain and a hurricane, the air now sun-filled and clear to perfection, the deputy inspector of customs went down to Whitehall to retrieve an envelope of manifests, and then headed up West Street to the Gansevoort Docks. Anyone who must report to work and stay for a required time is bound to love an errand that for half a morning leads him through the free city that in those hours he normally cannot know, and his pace will be slow and his step deliberate, for everything he sees is a gift.

West Street and the docks were crowded with the rush of passengers and freight for boats departing that morning for New Orleans, Savannah, Baltimore, and Boston, almost every one a steamer and almost all capable of sail. The forests of mast, spar, and rope were like a single line of rain-darkened trees on an Appalachian ridge. Sometimes white captions bloomed from ships that had backed out to set sail in midriver, and when the boilers of steamers were lit, clouds of coal smoke distressed the air like an artist's charcoal.

West Street, though very wide, was packed with drays, horsecars, coaches, and immense wagons. People labored under bundles and carried crates on their shoulders. On the sidewalk that ran along a front of four- and five-story brick emporia and offices, well dressed women, bearded carters, foreign sailors, and men in top hats moved intently, booking tickets, buying things, having breakfast, visiting clerks, never ceasing, never stopping.

The North River—that is, the Hudson—was almost in flood, fuller than he had ever seen it, flowing south with the tide and now swelled with the outpourings of a dozen rivers and a thousand streams carrying off the rains of the Hudson Valley, the Catskills, the Berkshires, and the Adirondacks. By the time this immense volume of waters ploughed past Manhattan, it nearly lapped over the edges of the piers, it lifted the ships high at their docks, and it went by so rapidly and with such force as to suggest a mountain torrent. Some ships, unable to dock, stayed out in the river, anchor chains taut, anchors by no means certainly fixed. But this was the crest, and the sun seemed to guarantee that the river would rise no higher and flow no faster.

THE GANSEVOORT DOCKS were neither ordered nor neat, nor, in the daytime, ever quiet. The deputy inspector strode through aisles made by bales, crates, and stacks of lumber, and smelled the cacao and coffee of Africa and Central America, the tea of Ceylon, the cotton of Egypt, the cedars of British Columbia. Into stolid, orderly, Christian New York had come the crews of a legion of small ships—Fijians, Angolans, Portuguese, Samoans, Russians, Cockneys, Arabs, and Goans. Some were tattooed and in costumes that— even if no more outlandish than hoop skirts and corsets—had about them the breath of cannibalism. But none of this was new to him, as he was quite used to such things, having decades before left cold, white, and austere Albany to sail into the South Sea. Like other ex-sailors, he was not rattled by a man with a few bones in his nose.

After closing the door to the glassed-in office, and as the noise of the dock receded, he found himself in the midst of a dispute, which, when it would ebb, was a conversation.

"Pulling it up and loading it on a wagon . . . I don't know. Can't we just hold off?"

"She's been anchored for two days. How long must she wait?"

"What about borrowing the dory upstream?"

"They need it more than we do."

The deputy inspector of customs asked, "What ship is it?"

"The *Antrim,* a mile upriver. Bartleby should go. He's young, he can row against even this current."

"Tell him what Bartleby said," bid the other man. The deputy inspector waited to hear.

"Though it was a simple statement, his words were offensive to me. I could mark them down as insubordination, but they were conditional, and I don't know how to take them. He said. . . . I shall not repeat what he said, but he says he doesn't want to."

The deputy inspector nodded. "Sometimes a boy of that age gets it into his head that he just doesn't want to do what you want him to do. I think it may be that, very early on, as if the lens of time were distorted, he can see way over the fence, as if he's lived his life near to the end, in a kind of clairvoyance." They stared at him, wondering what he had said. Then a steamer blew its whistle. "Don't ask him again. I'll do it."

"You'll do what?"

"Row upstream to the *Antrim,* inspect the cargo, collect the duty, and glide back."

"What makes you think you'll live long enough, at your age, to row against this flow all the way to the *Antrim?*"

"A mile?"

"With the speed of the current, it would be the equivalent of ten, with a furious pace, unrelieved."

"I know that."

"You won't get two hundred yards."

They knew the deputy inspector had come by his job through some minor interference in the White House. They knew that he had written books. They knew that he had been a sailor, a whaler, and a farmer. They also knew that he was too old to push a mile against the North River when the North River was as desperately south-seeking and voluminous as it was then. It would be, they thought, his comeuppance for not accepting bribes, as they did, and for a maddening presumption of superiority, unconfirmed by position, that irritated them daily and beyond toleration.

"Just make sure," one of them said, "that you don't get swept out the Narrows. There are inns where you can stay on Staten Island, or Rio de Janeiro." Whatever a guffaw might be, they followed with it.

EVEN COMPROMISED by the forest of pilings that held up the piers, the massive flow of water was so great that the dory, tied up on the lee, stretched its moorings like bowstrings. His hands were soft, and he hadn't rowed hard in decades. The last time he had ploughed or hayed, or used a shovel, was long before. Where would he find his strength, or protection for his hands? What if his heart were not able?

His first task was to avoid being thrown against the pier a hundred yards south. As soon as the painter was let go, the dory rushed for destruction, and he had to row desperately not to be shot across the gap. Unless one rows every day, at the beginning of a row the oars must be swept slowly, to establish a rhythm that will keep the stroke smooth and efficient and allow the blades to dip into the stream without fighting or chopping it. It is as if the water is organized or has a soul, for when it senses respect in the proper rhythm, the timing, and the consideration of the stroke, it seems—contrary to physical law—to help the rower along.

He had learned this in whale boats in the South Sea, the Central Pacific, and in the Atlantic from Greenland to Cape Horn. He had seen the inexplicable liveliness of the water itself, which answers in response to recognition and is kind in return for the apprehension of its grace.

But between the piers, fighting the north-to-south current as he tried to exit west from the slot, his stroke was choppy and arrhythmic, slapping the water, badly balanced, slipping without power, exhausting him almost before he had started.

"Shall we throw you a rope?" he was asked.

In between breaths, he yelled, "No, ye shall not."

He would row straight west, and then, hard on the port oar, point north again to the pier, where his colleagues stood taking their ease, and rise on a course that resembled a saw tooth, a line of sharks' fins, or the depiction of waves in a musicale. And thus he propelled himself into open water.

While turning north he was swept south of the south pier, but then he found a clear course, north by slightly northwest, that would take him up to the *Antrim,* resting in midstream a mile away and impatient for inspection.

Though his stroke had yet to engage the aid of the river itself, it was smoother, and if it had not actually found the required rhythm at least it seemed to be seeking it. The sun had long before risen above the slate roofs and rigging-tangled masts along the west shore of Manhattan, and it shone hot in the blue, twirling as it ascended.

Releasing the oars, he shed his jacket so quickly that a shiny brass button was violently severed from the midcoat and flew like a honeybee over the gunwales before it dropped into the water and disappeared forever. The button, until that very moment a perfect little sun in color, shape, and reflection, now made its way into oblivion. But the other buttons on the coat of blue wool still gleamed in the light, and there was nothing else to do but row.

Row he did, his shirt darkening first in patches, then entirely, and then becoming as soaked as if he had been in a heavy rain. His breathing, though anything but easy, had settled down, as had his heart, and if not he would have died. His stroke was slowly conforming to the wishes of the water, the boat slowly making headway north, cutting against the current with increasing steadiness and balance.

As he moved into the equilibrium of old, that as a young man he had known so often and so effortlessly on warm and distant seas, he did not even notice the blistering of his hands, the breaking, and the blood, cherry red against the varnished yellow oars, flowing in straight lines down the shafts.

Now he was chasing whales once again, with everything ahead, with time as vast as the Pacific, horizonless, infinitely rich, and in his favor. Now he was more vulnerable, for the sake of his wife and children, than ever was any wife or child. Now his parents lived, and he had not watched them at their last. Now he was free to fight and communicate with the current and that which ran beneath, and thus to know and feel it, without doubt or the necessity of faith. Now his stroke was smooth, life in full flood, the city in motion, the sun rising, the river running.

ARRIVING AT THE *ANTRIM,* he shipped oars and briefly glided to the foot of the gangway, where a Malay sailor gaffed the boat and tied it fast. "I'll be up," the deputy inspector said, "as soon as I can put on my jacket." Realizing that the Malay sailor could not understand, he pointed up and then to the jacket splayed across the stern seat of the boat.

When he was alone, he removed his shirt and held it in the wind and sun, a wind that, like the current, had not been in his favor. Soon he himself was dry, and even the shirt, which he held in his hands like a bullfighter's cape, followed suit. At first in lighter patches, and then in whole areas of white, and then, after how many minutes he did not know, the shirt was dry in his hands and stiff with salt.

Though properly attired when he came on deck except for the missing button, he was the color of a hot rose. As his blood carried the heat of his body to the air, and his muscles ached as they had not in years, he felt accomplished and young.

And with the rush of blood he was alert to the world, his powers of perception working at the highest speed, which seemed to make everything go slowly. He felt his heart beating strongly and evenly, slowing gradually, having carried him forth and served him well, and not in danger of failing. Most pleasant was the heat that raced to his face, the scarlet that would remain for half an hour, signifying both what he had done and his capacity to do more.

"What have we got?" he asked the captain, an Englishman who, the deputy inspector thought, would mercifully offer him no bribes unless he did so only because he thought the custom of the country would require it. The deputy inspector wanted to show him that the custom of the country did not, that America was as upright, and more so, than England—even if the custom of the country, to the deputy inspector's great regret, was changing very rapidly.

"Fifteen hundred bales of china from the factory at Hankow."

"Are they uniform?"

"Absolutely, as you shall see."

"Let's open some." They descended into the hold, which smelled like willow: the stays of the bales were willow that had been cut in the summer. "You're bound for Albany."

"Yes."

"You'll need a good pilot especially now that the hurricane has lifted the river so high."

"We came through it off the Virginia capes. Worse than rounding the Horn. I'm astounded that we are here."

The deputy inspector turned to the captain, who continued. "We lost five men, all to deliver bales of china to Albany. I do hope Albany is in need of crockery."

The deputy inspector shook his head. "Most likely it will be barged through the Erie Canal to find its way west. We'll open ten bales, please." He walked down a long row, tapping five bales at random. As the sailors pulled them out he commanded them to go two deep and three deep at each one, alternatingly, to get five more. The sailors, who were English and Irish, understood without clarification, and moved as quickly and efficiently as if they were storekeepers who owned their inventory.

In kerosene light, the willows were cut, and the bales spilled their contents. The china came in sets for sale, each bale having the same number of sets, each set the same number of pieces.

"No serving ware, other cargo?"

"No."

"I need to count, and then I'll clean the manifest. I prefer to do that alone, if you don't mind."

After everyone had left, he walked slowly down the rows of bales, counting carefully, in the clean scent of willow, his face throbbing gently, his breathing deep. The count was satisfactory.

He left the hold and summoned the captain from his cabin. Better to accomplish the transaction in the open in full view of the crew and not even accept a drink while on board. This payment was by letter of credit. He would carry back no money, only banking documents. It went fast, the stamps were affixed, the papers put in their envelopes, and when he was done he wished the captain a good trip up the Hudson. "When you anchor at night, in the bays," he said, "if the sky remains clear the moon will be full. They'll be haying now, so the air should be sweet. I grew up on the Hudson. I love it as if it were woman or child."

"Why don't you come with us, then?" the captain asked politely.

"I'll be back there," the deputy inspector answered, "soon enough."

THE CURRENT carried him down the Hudson as fast as a horse could canter, but effortlessly, over sparkling and transparent waters that had the feel of glass and the lightness of air. Slightly melon-green, they were pierced and netted by lines of gold light like fractures in a vein of rock. Having risen, the river was wider, and despite its rapid flow it was flat and tranquil.

With nothing to do but watch, as the air around him was resplendent with sun, and Manhattan seemed to roll from south to north, he felt the charge of the waters that had come down from the place of his birth. He felt their power, their purpose, and their tranquillity. This buoyancy was the after-effect of rain, the clarity an after-effect of storm. Everything seemed perfect in the light. But then he put his hand against his jacket at the solar plexus, where only blue threads attested to the button that once had been sewn on strong. The others were still shining. He kept his hand where it was, close to his heart, as if in salute or blessing, and as the boat raced swiftly downstream, he bowed his head.

Passschendaele

CAMERON PREFERRED to keep from the eastern border of his land, because it ran along a ridgeline on high meadows that dropped away into the alluring darkness of Sanderson's pine-filled woods. The terrain was little different on one side of the ridge or the other. Soft clearings floated among the dark evergreens; long meadows on mountainsides stretched for benevolent mile after benevolent mile, covered with wildflowers in spring and deep snow in winter; and mountain streams cut through everything, tumbling down, roaring through small gorges, until they became the calm black water of larger rivers. And if not quite pacified, they were saddened, with the mountains behind them and no more white falls or breathlessly cold channels but just slow water that had run its course through air once blue.

The presence of a fence in such a place was hard to understand, as the land on either side was so much the same, except that one side was Cameron's and the other Sanderson's. But, for Cameron, Sanderson's clearings, meadows, and woods were magically animate and electrified, because he was in love with Sanderson's wife.

The near and distant forest across the wire was much like Mrs. Sanderson herself—beyond reach, oblivious of what he thought or felt, and extraordinarily, painfully, beautiful. The chance that he would see her on the fence line was remote: he never had, and expected that he never would. There were too many open miles, and the scale of things in that country, the Stanford Range in British Columbia, did not encourage incidental meetings, though it would have harbored easily a hundred million well protected trysts. It was only that the meadows led to her, the clearings and woods surrounded her, she had ridden through them, and they were hers. Even though he was in his middle age and she not far behind, he loved her without control or dignity, the way he would have loved her had he been nineteen.

Several times a year, Cameron had to repair the fences on the eastern side, because much of the wire was not new, and would rust to powder if left in place. Some of the posts were set in wet ground and tended to rot, staggering like the wounded, tilting the fence and tangling its wires. Sometimes a steer broke through, possessed, perhaps, with madness or fear. And bears tore up the lines, like raiders attacking a railway, so purposefully that their work would have been easy to confuse with that of a man, had they not always left behind their unmistakable tracks.

The eastern side was the higher side. That portion of Cameron's land rose in the direction of Mt. King George and Mt. Joffre, mountains on which were glaciers and perpetual snowfields. It was the difficult and slow side as well, because it was so inaccessible and high. He had to ride in on horseback and bring the wire along in a coil wrapped in rawhide. Any posts needed for replacement had to be cut on the spot, with an axe. If a hole had to be sunk, he had to do it with a folding shovel, since the gasoline-powered auger he carried in his truck was far too heavy to bring up onto the eastern ridge. All in all, the eastern side was difficult in many ways.

FOR THREE DAYS in June, Cameron had ridden the fence—leaving before the sun came up, returning home at dusk—and he had been lucky. There were only a few posts to be pounded in with the heel of the axe; a few dozen slipped wires, fixed with a bent double-headed nail and some hammer blows; and some partial breaks, mostly of the top wire, which was stressed more than the others by temperature contractions or drifting snow.

The fourth day, he judged, would be his last up there, and he might get home late in the afternoon instead of at eight or nine, knowing that he would not have to go out east again until the fall (to bring in the steers), when he was likely to see Sanderson on the other side of the fence, doing the same thing.

By one in the afternoon, he had risen to the higher meadows, where there were not many trees and he could see just about everything, including the valley that led eventually to Sanderson's house, and faint trails of smoke from Sanderson's fire. Or perhaps they were branding, curing meat, or burning deadwood. Ahead for six miles or so was the rest of the fence. It ended in the northeast, flat up against a vertical rock wall half a thousand feet high.

No mountain goat, much less a steer, could have bent his neck to see the top of that wall. Though they had no one to tell them about the danger of falling rocks, or lightning that slithered down the face, and though presumably they had no historical memory and could not conclude by either logic or deduction that it was dangerous, the steers wisely kept clear of the foot of the wall even though the grass there was richer and greener than it was anywhere else. And, for some unknown reason, perhaps because bears in high meadows are happier than bears in the woods, at this altitude they were content to use the baffles, and seldom tore at the wire. The last six had always been the easiest of the miles, and they were surely the most beautiful.

When Cameron was young, when it was still his father's place, and he had yet to marry, he had loved to finish riding fences at the sheer wall in the northeast corner. At that time, the adjoining ranch was owned by the Reeds, whose son, several years older than Cameron, was killed at Passchendaele.

"You know what?" young Reed had once said to the even younger Cameron. "Everyone's talking about how dangerous it will be in the war. But I'm not worried about that at all. I'm worried about the fact that a certain number of years after I come back I'll be so old that I'll be supposed to die. I don't like that idea, so I've decided that I'm not going to die."

"Ever?" Cameron had asked, wondering what the older boy was up to.

"Ever" was Reed's answer. "Or should I say never." And then he had smiled in such a way as to make young Cameron think that, even if his friend were excessively foolish, he was excessively brave.

Cameron himself had longed to go, but was too young; and, much later, discovered that he had become a man only when he stopped envying Charles S. R. Reed for having been killed in battle. During the First War, and for the many years thereafter until the Sandersons came from Scotland, the eastern side had been for Cameron a lovely isolated place with a life of its own. He would spend days in the forests there, or on the high meadows, and, if the weather was good, he would be taken up entirely by nature.

Fiercely in its grip, in the trance of youth, in the sunshine at eight thousand feet, he could go for days like an animal—not ever thinking, but riding, leaping, plunging into the ice-cold pools and glacier melts, stalking birds and game—with the same eyes and heart as a bear, an elk, or a horse. But only until the weather turned, for when it was gray and rainy, or sleeting in June, or when the great thunderheads with their accompaniment of artillery passed overhead to drench and freeze him, he thought and calculated with a city dweller's devotion to thinking and calculation. Nothing was what it was, simply, but became instead the symbol or part of something else. Time forced its own consideration. Ambition reigned, as did disharmony. When he was sixteen, eighteen, or twenty, however, such disturbances, like the storms, were dispelled and forgotten in one blue morning.

That was before Reed sold out to the Sandersons, in the middle of the Depression; not because he was hard-pressed but because he had never stopped grieving for his son. "There's nothing wrong with war," the senior Reed had said to Cameron, when young Charles S. R. Reed had been five months gone toward Passchendaele, "except that it destroys the ones you love. I fought against the Boer in South Africa—I volunteered to go because I was madly in love and wanted to be worthy. I shouldn't have spoken of it to my son. But if I hadn't, he would have gone anyway, for he, too, was in love. I just hope that he comes back to me alive."

It was said, on no specific authority, that the elder Reed disappeared to some city, where he was bitter and alone; that the Sandersons had paid him a good price; and that Mrs. Sanderson's family was wealthy enough to have given the young couple a wedding present of a thousand acres of the most beautiful land in the world. Their wealth, however, could not have matched the gossip, since Reed sold off the best three-quarters of his herd, and the

Sandersons lived until the end of the Second World War in a painful frugality that elsewhere might have been called poverty.

But, in Cameron's eyes, on those thousand acres there was no such thing as poverty, even if the lady of the house possessed only a single dress for summer, and a worn one at that. There was no poverty for them, even if they had few luxuries, no telephone, no electricity. And to wash they had had to take water from a stream, heat it over a wood fire, and pour it into a huge gold-rimmed porcelain bowl that, before it was chipped, had probably been a salad bowl in a hotel or railroad buffet, since on it in ornate gilt lettering were the initials of the Canadian Pacific Railway.

That bowl had come to mean something to Cameron the way material objects do to people in love. He remembered it because she had been standing by it, with her hand touching the rim, the first time he had ever seen her—on a cold mountain-summer morning in 1935.

SANDERSON had been in the mountains for a year or more before Cameron had encountered him on the ridge, mending the fence. Cameron rode up, dismounted, and watched in silence. No matter that for ten miles in any direction they were the only two beings that could talk. Neither spoke.

Every now and then, the recently arrived Scotsman looked up at the man on the other side of the fence, who stared at him in unexplained amusement. But he would be damned before he would speak first to an uncivil Canadian who had lived in the wilderness since birth and probably had little more in his head than would a bear or a wild ram.

For half an hour, Cameron watched his new neighbor diligently mend the fence. Either someone had shown Sanderson how, or he had thought it out himself, but his splices were good and would last as long as the steel. Cameron thought that if he could be forgiven for not speaking, he had found a friend.

Just as Sanderson finished and was about to mount his horse, Cameron said, "Will you send me a bill, then? Or are you a monk from some religious order, doing the Lord's work in mufti?"

"I beg your pardon?" the Scotsman asked in such a heavy accent that

Cameron immediately realized how he had known about mending fences: he, too, was a countryman.

"I was just wondering if you were a traveling monk."

"And why would you wonder that?" Sanderson replied coldly.

"It's either something like that or you're uncommonly generous. Anyway, you have my thanks."

Sanderson looked at the fence.

"Right," said Cameron. "It's mine."

"I've been working on it for four days now," Sanderson said bitterly. "Why isn't it marked?"

"It's not the custom here. You should have asked."

"Reed told me that I had to keep up the southern and western fences."

"No," Cameron said, shaking his head. "South and *east*. When you get into Alberta, the custom changes. There are people straddling the provincial border who don't have to worry about any fences: they're on the line where ways of doing things meet, and they reap the benefits. Of course, it could have been just the reverse, too, and I'm sure that in some places there are those who have to tend their wire in all directions. We're both lucky, though, in our way. We share the north wall. I've got a lot of river on my property as well, and there's no fence like a fast deep river."

"Now I know," Sanderson said. "You can take over from here. Maybe I will send you a bill."

"You can send it if you'd like. Doesn't mean that I'll pay it."

"Don't worry about it," Sanderson said, and got on his horse. Although Sanderson appeared to be in no mood to talk, Cameron believed that there was never a better way for a man to make a friend than in a fight of little consequence.

"Our eastern fence is mended, all but the last easy six," Cameron announced to his wife at dinner that night.

"How so?" she asked.

"Sanderson did it. He thought it was his."

"Did he put in much wire?"

"Plenty. I haven't seen it all, but he replaced it, just as I do, not only where it's broken but where you can tell it's going to break."

"You ought to give him back what we've gained."

"He didn't have to put it there."

"I've heard that they're having a hard time," his wife said. "Why don't you bring him some wire, and some beef, since they probably can't afford to slaughter their own animals."

"I suppose I could do that. He seems like a nice fellow. There's probably a lot he can learn from me."

"He may not think of it in quite that way," Mrs. Cameron said.

"I don't see why he shouldn't. Our family has been here more than half a century—he arrived a few months ago. It shows. He spent four days fixing a fence that didn't belong to him. But all right. When I go there," he asked, "do you want to come with?"

"No. But tell me about Sanderson's wife. If she seems nice, then I'll ride over, too."

The next day, Cameron found himself in front of Sanderson's house, screaming "Hallo!" to no avail. Though a rich volume of smoke issued from the chimney, no one answered. They were away and had left far too big a fire burning unattended, or they wanted nothing to do with him. And he had ridden almost twenty miles, carrying heavy coils of wire and another big package, and to go visiting had put on his best riding boots and a new Black Watch shirt.

He decided to leave the wire on the porch and the meat just inside, away from raccoons and bears. He wanted to write a note, and thought that they might have a pen or pencil somewhere near the door. He wouldn't have to go all the way in.

He took the leather off the coils of wire and carried them up onto the porch. When he stepped into the shade, he realized that on his way over he had been pleasantly sunburned by the June sun and the snowfields. "Hallo!" he said, rapping at the door. When there was no answer, he opened the latch and looked in.

The fire was ablaze. A large iron kettle hung over the flames, and was just beginning to steam. There must be someone here, he thought. And then, as his eyes fully adjusted to the light and he looked about the room, he saw that there was.

SANDERSON'S WIFE, her left hand clasped against her chest in fright, stared at him from across a wooden table. She was wearing only a slip, that was a pearly salmon color with a gray metallic sheen. To have been polite, Cameron should have turned away. To have been wise, he might have left for good.

But he couldn't take his eyes off her. "I called and called," he said. "Didn't you hear me?"

As if to establish his credentials, he pointed at the coils of wire on the porch and held up the large package of steak. "I'm your neighbor. I've brought your husband some wire and some beef. I wanted to leave a note, but I didn't have a pen, so I just stepped inside."

As he waited for an answer, he was free to look at her. She remained motionless, her right hand gripping the side of the bowl with the golden rim. Just her arms, hands, and fingers were enough to mark her as a beauty. Her eyes were lucid and green, and the thick soft hair that was piled atop her head and fell about her face in long wisps and exquisitely curling locks was a matte red so rich and subdued that it made him giddy. And her complexion, which showed, too, on her shoulders and chest, was a cross between mottled red and ivory. Cameron's paralysis was not lessened by her gorgeous expression of surprise, by her silver and gold rings, and by a light gold neck chain splayed across the lace trim of the slip.

She motioned for him to go outside. He moved back and looked at the bowl, trying to remember its smallest detail, down to the curl of the letters, for he wanted to be able to recall the scene with the power to renew it. Then he went out onto the porch, shut the door behind him, and stepped into the sunlight.

He wished that when she joined him in the daylight she would be ugly, and that the way she had struck him as so beautiful would prove to have been an illusion of the dim light—this for the sake of his lovely wife, whom he loved and did not want to wish to abandon, and because he was not suitable for Mrs. Sanderson. He imagined that a man suited to her would have to be many ranks above him, though Sanderson, it seemed, was not.

Since he could never have her, he would have to hate her for it. Even had she and he been unmarried, having her would have been out of the question. But, then, what about Sanderson? He was not a god. Perhaps she was as beautiful as she appeared to be only to Cameron. Perhaps, given time, she would leave her husband. Or, given more time, he would die. Perhaps, Cameron thought, his ride over the snowfields in the strong sun had been too rapturous. Then he remembered her face.

Having lost this debate with himself, he stamped his foot against the boards, sorry that he had ever seen her, bitter about the imbalance that the sight of her made clear to him, and angry that he felt so low when just that morning he had ridden across the high meadows, in sight of a line of snowy peaks to the north, feeling that there was no place higher that he or anyone else would want to go. As he was turning to leave, she walked onto the porch. She was in an old-fashioned flowered dress, and the sight of her made Cameron wish for Sanderson to come galloping in and distract him from her lacerating and untouchable beauty, which was even finer in the daylight than it had been in the dim interior of the house, where there had not been any of the blue glacial light that seemed to lift her off the earth and make her smile something not of this world.

She carried pencils and paper. "I don't need that now," Cameron said. "I was going to leave a message only if no one was in."

She shook her head to say no, smiled, and pointed to herself.

She's crazy, he thought.

Then she raised a hand perfectly adorned in rings, and tapped her left ear. When next she put her index finger across her lips twice in succession, he understood.

"You can't hear," he said, already moving his lips more deliberately, so that she might understand.

She nodded.

"You can't talk."

She sat down on the step in the sunlight and made room for him to follow. "I can talk," she wrote on the pad, in a firm but delicate hand, "but they say it doesn't come out very well, so I prefer to write."

"Do you talk to your husband?" he asked.

"Yes," she wrote. "Only to him and to my parents, who are in Scotland. I

also talk to the animals, since I am told they sound even worse than I do."
She smiled. "Please," she continued, as he drank in every movement of her
hands and eyes, "don't mention this to anyone. In all of Canada, you are the
only one who knows."

"Why?" he asked.

"I am ashamed," she wrote. She indicated emphasis and nuance with the
pen (by writing very fast or very slow; by bearing down hard; by returning
to underline or circle; and by drawing the letters one way or another, to look
shaky, flat, tired, or animated) and with her facial expressions.

"There's nothing to be ashamed of," he told her, "nothing."

"That may be so," she wrote quickly, "but long experience has shown me
that it's best this way. I've always preferred to keep to myself."

"But what if you have to go into Invermere? They'll know then."

"I've been there only once. If we have to, we go to Calgary to shop. It's
bigger, and no one knows us there."

"Calgary is a long way off," he said.

"Invermere is small," she wrote back.

"Well, I can't dispute that," he answered.

"Are you married?" she wrote.

"Yes."

"Then," she put down, "please don't tell even your wife. If I could hear
and talk like everyone else, I would talk no end to other women, and I suspect that I'm not unusual in that desire, except that I don't get to realize it."

"She wanted to visit," Cameron said. "When the pass is open, it's not that
far on a good horse. Would you enjoy that?"

"No" was the written answer. "Or, rather, yes. But, again, my experience
tells me that it would not be a good idea."

Cameron took a chance. "Because of me?" he asked bluntly, wondering
if she knew the effect of her beauty.

Evidently she did, for she nodded, and then, as if for emphasis, wrote,
"Yes."

"Isn't that a lot to presume?" He was bluffing. It wasn't anything at all to
presume, but he thought she might become interested in him if she imagined that he, of all men, could not see or did not care about her beauty.

"Experience," she wrote.

Because Cameron looked dejected, she added, "If you feel distraught, don't worry. It will pass."

"I don't think it will."

"Don't be silly." Her hand flew across the pad. "A man doesn't have his head turned forever. After all, you don't know me."

"And if I did?"

"I won't demean myself. But I do tend to draw men to me very strongly at first, only to see them drop away much relieved and delighted to go."

He wished that he had been more circumspect. But to have been so might have been a far greater fault. It was not the first time he had been defeated by great desire, and he felt completely inadequate, dismissed, rejected. He left abruptly, because he was sure that she wanted him to go, because he wanted so much to stay, because, quite simply, he loved her. He never remembered much about the feverish and unhappy ride home, or how many times he had dismounted to pace back and forth in agony and puzzlement. He did, of course, resolve never to see her again. And he was a man of strong and tenacious resolution.

LATE IN THE AFTERNOON, Cameron came to the meadows that led to the high wall. These meadows stretched for a mile and were dotted with stands of small pine that grew sheltered from the wind in depressions and hollows. At almost nine thousand feet, the horse moved slowly and breathed hard, and his rider found himself in a trance of sparkling altitude. The sky was flawless and still as Cameron inspected the last portion of his fence. Progressing slowly upward, he was sure that there would be no breaks. Where the final meadow began to rise steeply to the wall, he was going to check the fence from a distance, and turn around without actually making a ceremonial finish at the cliff—in touching it the way a swimmer touches the wall of a pool before he will credit himself with a lap. But he saw from the base of the meadow that a long portion of the fence was down. The wire was shining in the sunlight, spread in every direction on the field. The posts had been pushed over, snapped at the base, and scattered. With luck, if he had enough wire, and could salvage enough, and work fast enough, he might repair it by dark, and then ride home by starlight on trails that he could take blind.

He cantered over to the damage. He knew from the tracks that a grizzly bear had done this—or perhaps two, while the cubs watched. Either they had been too big to get through the baffles, which were untouched, or they had just wanted the high meadow to be completely open. Because the splinters were moist and the leaves of the moss compressed, he knew that it had happened while he was just a few miles away thinking placidly about his good luck. The bears themselves might be gone, or they might be taking a nap somewhere amidst the sunny boulders. Removing his rifle from its scabbard, he worked the bolt to put a bullet in the chamber, and leaned the weapon against a rock. It was not that he expected the bears to lie in ambush for him but rather that, in working hard, he might not notice them until his horse panicked.

They had pulled down sixteen stakes and broken eleven at the base, rendering them unusable. The wire was severed in two dozen places. Only a bear could have done that, even with the light steel that he had always used on the high meadows. His coil of wire was greatly diminished after the repairs he had made on the way up. If he had enough, it would be just enough, and still it would be hard to do it right. The splicing would be weak, with no tripled windings, and he would have to use fewer posts, spacing them farther apart than usual. But the fence might hold, especially if the bears were on their way to some distant, higher paradise in the north. He set to work.

First, he rode a mile and a half back into the timber. Although he could have used the meadow's little pines for posts, at that altitude they took forever to grow, and destroying them might have turned the upper pasture into a rutted and barren hillside when the rains washed the thin layer of soil off its base of rock and scree. In the timber, hidden from the world by distance, height, and the maze of a thousand pines, he used his axe to cut and trim half a dozen small trees. He was a very strong man, he had used an axe nearly every day of his life from the time he was a small child, and the axe he used was the best available, sharpened with a soft stone and oil, and kept, like some kind of strange one-legged falcon, in a leather hood. The trees went down in a stroke: they might as well have been celery. And he trimmed them of their branches with several sweeps close to the trunk. After a series of hatchetlike blows at the narrowing end, he had a sharp fence post soaked with its own resin as if it had been designed for placement in wet ground.

He tied the posts up in two bundles and dragged them out of the woods. Then he slung them over his saddle and walked the horse back to the break. If the break had occurred sooner, steers might have passed through, though it was early in the season for steers to have reached this altitude. But even then it would hardly have mattered. Sanderson would have pushed them back over, as he would have done for Sanderson's animals, with nothing said between them. In the twelve years since he thought one day that he had found a friend in Sanderson, he had seen him only half a dozen times along the fence or in Invermere, where Mrs. Sanderson had been forgotten and it was generally assumed that Sanderson lived alone.

Mrs. Cameron's warm invitation, a week in the mail even though the lands adjoined, was never answered. Now that his children were old enough to ride by themselves wherever they wanted, Cameron feared that they might ride east on some adventure and discover the great secret of his life. But, being young, they would not have been able to see her in the way that he had seen her. Perhaps no one did, although she had implied that at least some had; and she had known immediately that, as she put it, his head had been turned. Perhaps she had had children, had aged, and lost her beauty. He wished that she had, but knew that no such thing could ever happen to her. That her features had, accidentally, been fine and unusual had little bearing on the woman herself. If she had lost the accidental beauty of her form, it would only have served to accentuate the substance that form had been privileged to convey.

One of the things that hurt him most in his speculations east was the possibility that she had died or gone away, and that, without his knowledge, his life had been rendered meaningless. And he didn't know her name, something that was difficult to bear in light of the way he loved her.

After several years, he did not think of her very often. By the time England was again at war (this time he was too old), it seemed almost as if he had forgotten her. After all, his wife, too, was a beauty, with a softness that

Mrs. Sanderson did not have, and the luck of a pretty face and a graceful body. But she was not as deeply faulted as Mrs. Sanderson, or quite as radiant. And it had been the fault—not the deafness but the mistaken, unnecessary shame—that had driven deep into Cameron's heart.

As the years went by, he put her more and more out of his mind. But time proved immaterial, for suddenly, in the midst of a false peace, he would dream of her, and for weeks thereafter suffer intense desire. Then the desire would slowly fade, and he would continue getting older, waiting for the next potent and surprising reawakening. Were it not for this, he would have been a happy man. Perhaps he was a happy man even so.

THE POSTS had to be placed in rocky soil, and in sinking them he strained like the soldier he had never been, breathing hard and evenly, sweating, taken up by his love of the work, for only work could conduct away his unfortunate passion. Because of the new spacing, four or five new holes had to be made, and a similar number of broken pieces extracted from the ground. Some were easy, some not easy at all. How fine the task, though, of building back this fence, with all his strength, discipline, and experience. It was for the sake of the lovely woman he had married, for the children they had had, for Sanderson, for Mrs. Sanderson, and for himself—though he couldn't see exactly how it was to his benefit unless it were purely a matter of honor.

He pounded in the posts until they flattened against the underlying sheet of rock. His strokes and timing with the heel of the axe were perfect, and each downward blow married solidly with the posthead.

The second and last time he had seen her had been in Vancouver, during the war. The disarray of the cattle market had brought him to the coast seeking a better price for his beef. He never got it, and he never found out what she had been doing there, apart from bowling on the green, in a formal white suit, in the company of a lot of pretty old ladies who took the game very seriously.

He was resting in Stanley Park, at midday, watching the old ladies at their game, when she appeared and took her turn. A long time passed before he was able to believe that it was actually she, and then to summon the courage to rise. But when he did approach her, it was easy. He almost floated across the green, hypnotized, pushing the carefully placed shots all to hell with his feet.

She recognized him immediately, and when she turned to face him fully her expression was reminiscent of those days when strong sunshine and deep shadow alternate in silent breathtaking contrast. The emotion that swept across her face told him that he was not the only one to have spent the years in longing.

They stood in the center of the bowling green, oblivious of a growing stream of reprimands—she because she could not hear them, and he because he didn't care. The old ladies were incensed: not only had their game been spoiled, but they had been ignored. So they returned the fire and resumed play, paying no attention to the two wickets who stood, apparently insensate, staring at one another in the middle of the contest. Balls began to whiz about like shrapnel.

They didn't notice; they couldn't look away. With no words spoken, all custom was shattered as he put his hands on either side of her white waist-band, touching her gently. She extended her arms, and they found them-selves in a subdued embrace appropriate to a crowded Vancouver bowling green. But everything was said, at last, and in the silence that she had always known.

A ship began a series of powerful whistle blasts as it coasted through the in-let on its way to the war at sea. This, the deep steam whistle, was the one thing she could hear, or, rather, feel—a symphony for her, the one precious rum-bling sound of the world. It pushed through her chest and took her by sur-prise, moving her by its suddenness and power. She held up one of her hands and spread her fingers to see them vibrate, as the air itself was shaken from its sleep. He had told her that he loved her, and admitted it finally and forever to himself. At least he had done that.

AFTER THE POSTS WERE UP, Cameron began to string the wire. Not only had it been broken, but he himself was obliged to cut it in the stringing, and to replace rusted lengths that likely would not stand being stretched onto a new arrangement of posts and baffles. The skill with which he wielded the splicing tool was something of which he did not think to be proud. But he had the sure facility of a fisherman minding his nets, or a woman with years at the loom, and there was no tentativeness in his movements, which seemed to pull his hands forward as quickly as they would follow.

As he worked, his thoughts turned to Mrs. Sanderson. There were things in the mountains to make up for a love that was unfulfilled. When his tongue was tied, when he could not act, or in the punishment of forever parting, he had found compensations. And if the discipline that kept him from her had not been so sweet in itself he would long ago have jumped his horse over the fence and ridden down to the house at the base of the thin column of smoke. But having what he desired was not important, for the mountains would remember, and, once, in Vancouver, he had been lucky.

When he finished, the sun hovered red and gold above a sharp and distant ridge. The new wire looked like lines of silver and platinum, and the pine posts were solid and black. A pool of meltwater had formed in the middle of a patch of snow about a hundred feet from the fence. Cameron took off his clothes, walked across the snow, and threw himself in. The water was even colder than he had expected, but, wanting to get clean, he thrust his head under and rolled himself over. The pain of doing such a thing was pleasant, for, afterward, when he rose slick and sparkling from the ice water, he was warm and relaxed, and he could reflect pleasurably upon the half a minute or so of breathless cold when his discipline had kept him under and served him well. After he had dressed, he threw the saddle on his horse, cinched it up, and put back the bit. When his tools were gathered and tied on, and the rifle chamber emptied, he mounted. The wind was clean and cool.

He walked the horse from the first splice to the last, and swept his eyes over each new post and twisting of the wire, up to the rock wall itself. Then he veered across the meadow and wound down through patches of snow now blood-red with the declining sun. Several hundred yards west of the fence, he reined the horse around to face what he had done. It was a good piece of work, and undoubtedly it would hold. The wires now glowed like molten metal.

He was not a stupid man. He knew what he was about to do, he knew very well, and he finally felt a deep brotherhood with young Charles S. R. Reed, who had gone to Passchendaele of his own accord, and who, in his lack of wisdom, had perhaps been wise.

Cameron realized that the horse would want to canter, and that he would have to kick him into a gallop. As they crossed the quiltwork of snow and grass, the horse would begin to tense for the jump, and his rider would have to let out the reins. They would take the fence quite easily.

Whatever he did, his heart would be half broken. That was what Reed had risked at Passchendaele, for he had not gone to war except to come back to love.

Like the soldier he had never been, Cameron spurred his horse toward the ranks of glowing wire. They took the fence. They cleared it by at least two feet, and left it behind in the sunset, a very sad thing.

Jacob Bayer and
the Telephone

EVERYONE HAS HEARD of Rabbi Smilksteen of Pokoik. Everyone has heard of Rabbi Merman, the *Gaon* of Vitebsk. Everyone has heard of Rabbi Grittle of Havemayer. Everyone has heard of Rabbi Blottis of Geldenhorn. These were famous men, they wrote long books, they had followers, they occupied positions and directed institutions, they were sheltered by buildings, and cooks brought them food. But who has ever heard of Jacob Bayer, who walked thousands and thousands of versts and taught thousands of students, and slept on the hard wooden benches of the *hadarim*? Nor was he entirely unknown, although how he became slightly famous and what happened subsequently have not been recorded and are bittersweet, as events that are largely forgotten often are. If he had not been physically so huge, perhaps the biggest person in the Baltic and White Russia, no one would know about him at all. But when Jacob Bayer walked into a town, even horses turned their heads.

Before he came to Koidanyev he had been employed in a small *heder* in Pahzhilski-Dominitzin, which was one hundred twenty versts to the west of Minsk, whereas Koidanyev was to the east. The rabbi of Pahzhilski-Dominitzin had gone to check on the class and had come to an empty room. Running about in the summer heat with the physical symptoms of a panicked intellectual, he found Jacob Bayer and his students gathered at a fence that had been almost completely subsumed in dangerous brambles. Grasped in the fingers of each boy was a rose held as gingerly as if it were a bomb.

"What is this?" the rabbi asked, feeding delightfully on the shock of discovering an irregularity.

"What is what?" Jacob Bayer asked in return.

"These boys are holding roses!"

"Yes?"

"Why?"

"As we were reading the passage about the rose of Jericho, it became clear that none of them had ever held a rose. I'm teaching them the meaning of the word."

"By standing near a dangerous bush?"

"Rabbi Bing-trellis," said Jacob Bayer, "the word for rose was written to turn us to the rose itself. Without knowledge of the rose itself, the word is meaningless. *Vered,* as it is written, is beautiful, but the rose is more so."

The rabbi was so enraged and confused by this arrogant concretism and its resulting action—boys holding roses, by the thorny stems, in the sunshine—that the blood stayed in his head and made him the color of the roses themselves, though his neck was thicker than their stems, even if not by much. And although Jacob Bayer had been happy in Pahzhilski-Dominitzin and had begun to awaken in his students the love of truth, he was gone that night, heartbroken at yet another failure, another alienation, another expulsion, another going out. But as he walked under the summer stars—of June, 1913—his memory of the redness of the rose made his heart as light as moonlight, and floated him above all disappointments.

JACOB BAYER had been told by his father that Koidanyev was a pious and interesting place of low hills and tall pines, with a clear river that rushed through it freshening the air. In summer, people swam in the river, and the town that had formed along the banks was wealthy and beautiful. It had been known as the Switzerland of White Russia. Its metal and tile roofs, glinting above the blue-gray water, were famous throughout the pale, and the hills of Koidanyev caught the wind and afforded views over light-filled plains in all directions.

After a week on the road, a sunburned and lean Jacob Bayer encountered three Jewish peasants fixing an irrigation gate. *"Erev tov,"* he said, using Hebrew to impress them. "Where is Koidanyev?"

"Koidanyev! Everyone wants to go there," said one, quite sullenly, "because, because. . . . You see, in the distance, that flash of light? That's it." Five or six versts away, the goldenness of the town caught the sun.

Though most settlements of the pale were arranged along the road like the branches of a tree, not Koidanyev, because of its relation to the river. From the main highway a spur led directly to its heart. You entered upon this road and left on it. The road was bisected by the river, against which the citizens of Koidanyev had retaliated by bisecting the river with a bridge. When Jacob Bayer came to this bridge he saw two guards dressed in policemen's caps. They wore belts from which hung pistols, and they were sorry, they said, but Koidanyev was full.

"Full of what?" he asked.

"Of people who have come to get rich. The rooms are taken, the streets are crowded, the restaurants are stuffed."

"Then there will be many children who will need teachers, and rabbis who will need assistants."

"They don't do that anymore," one of the guards said.

"Don't do what?"

"Study."

"Torah?"

The guard shook his head from side to side.

"Talmud?"

"No."

"Anything?"

"Many things, but not these. They don't need to."

"How can that be?"

"They left all that behind," the guard said. "They have big thick doormats, and gold utensils. They have indoor plumbing, electrical lights, and fountain pens. They have English clothing, German typewriters, and the most beautiful leatherwork you have ever seen, not to mention furniture, automobiles, and glass windows. Everyone has servants. The servants have servants. The servants of servants have servants, and they have servants, too. There is no one who hasn't got machines. I have machines. He has machines," he said, pointing to the other guard. "And everyone, of course, has a telephone, which is what makes Koidanyev rich in the first place."

"A what?"

"A telephone."

Though Jacob Bayer knew half a dozen languages, he did not know Greek. He knew enough etymology, however, to parse the roots of the word. "Everyone has someone who can speak at long distances?"

"Not a person, a machine."

"Ah," said Jacob Bayer, "a talking machine. Good idea. I know only the telegraph. As a youth, I was much more interested in such things than I am now. Then that which was supposed to have been startling and new seemed to be only a variation of what had come before, and I realized that I had begun to pretend to myself to be amazed when I wasn't amazed at all. So now I do without them, as I do without most everything."

"They won't believe that, and once you saw Koidanyev you would want to be rich like them."

"I don't think so," said Jacob Bayer, remembering his consistent inability to do what other people did. "All my life I have done nothing but study. Had I wanted to be rich I would have sold dictionaries. Had I wanted to be powerful I would have been a rabbi. But I have no position and no power. I'm a nothing. Very early on, I was entranced by the notion of truth, and the more I concentrated on it the less opportunity I had to become a something. But although riches last for a generation or two, honor lasts forever. After you depart, your riches are divided, but your honor is indivisible."

"I'll tell you what," said the first guard, "we'll let you in if you wait until evening so you won't be seen coming from the road. At dusk everyone is so busy that no one will notice. But you have to promise that when you leave, if ever you do, you'll give us half of whatever you take with you. You see, they don't pay us, we have a deal instead."

"Every material thing," the second guard said, "that you haven't taken in with you, or that you have replaced at a higher value. In Koidanyev a teacher of the new things can have a whole chicken three times a day if he wants, buttered rolls with jam every morning, *gribenes,* chopped liver, *p'tcha,* oranges, boiled beef. That's what kind of place it is. Do you accept?"

Having little and expecting nothing, Jacob Bayer accepted. They took inventory: a leather bag, a willow bundle for the brushing of teeth, fine soap, a steel pen, two pencils, a bottle of ink, a *Tanach,* a dictionary, prayer equipment, a locket with pictures of his mother and father, his folding spectacles in a leather case, and a knife for cutting salami on those lucky days when he could get near one. Surveying this, they were sure that he would become just like them and everyone else in Koidanyev. How could he not? No one who came into this better world had yet chosen to love the old one more.

As HE WALKED through the abundance of Koidanyev in early evening, Jacob Bayer was seized with inexplicable melancholy. What objection could he have to prosperity that had arisen out of genius and hard work? Why did the unprecedented vitality here—perhaps the only place he had ever seen in all the Baltic and White Russia where the song of things had left the minor key—not lift him as it did others? A man of honor, he stood ready to condemn himself for envy. But he felt no envy, and, to the contrary, was grateful that the euphoria had failed to touch him and that he was neither as happy nor as confident as the people he saw. They, who had so much, seemed lost, and he, who had nothing, knew exactly where he stood. Was it possible that their happiness might be less even than his unhappiness?

On the road, he had now and then eaten apples, pears, and cherries, and he remembered each as exactly the rarity it was. In stalls on the streets of Koidanyev and in well ordered stores lit with electric lamps were every type of fruit he had ever known or imagined, and fruit of which he had never heard: all those of a temperate climate, of course; citrus of every variety, half of which he never knew existed; dates; currants; mangoes; papayas; bananas; kiwis; star fruit; breadfruit; passion fruit; and a hundred obscurities such as, for example, Chilean cat pears, which were the color of mourning doves and tasted like marzipan. They came fresh, dried, canned, jarred, candied, compoted, diced, doused, soused, and sugared. It was not enough to be a date. A date had to be a *medjool* date. And even that was not enough. There were "huge," "giant," "premium," and "extrastupendous" medjool dates. To further assuage the need for money to change hands, some of these competing dates came in magnificent containers of crystal, Bristol, sterling, and gold, and if that were not enough they accomplished their final conquest simply by being expensive beyond any reason or justification, which made them, somehow, and to some, infinitely desirable. And that was just fruit.

Of bagels the people of Koidanyev were so knowledgeable and libertine that they made them with things that had no connection to bagels, such as pineapple, tomatoes, mushrooms, cheese, and saffron. Of saffron they had so much that they sold it by the kilo, as they did truffles, caviar, and shrimp. "Shrimp? What is that?" Jacob Bayer asked a fishmonger in a silk suit with a perfectly snowy white shirt and gold buttons.

The fishmonger looked over his Scottish smoked salmon, his bluefish, his tuna, and his herring in Calvados. "Shrimp," he said. "If you wait until tomorrow we'll have the ones that are the size of chickens. They make a meal in themselves served on a bed of wilted arugula with a good Champagne."

"Aren't they forbidden?" Jacob Bayer asked. He knew they were.

"When the telephone came to Koidanyev," the vendor said, "we rethought all those things."

As Jacob Bayer made his way through the hive of commercial streets he noticed that the people walked as purposefully as soldiers. They laughed deeply and spoke fast. And they were healthy. Perhaps, like him, they had been in the early summer sun, and it was this that made them glow. More foreign to his experience than anything else was that they talked into black instruments from which they appeared to receive no answer, and carried on conversations that were half alive.

The talking was unearthly—faster, more uniform of tone, more insistent, with few rests or pauses, and a strange migration of the eyes as the head remained fixed in an effort to please the invisible. Even praying was not like this, but much more fluid and natural. This had the air of bad acting, and everyone did it. It was stentorian, clipped, and vain, and yet there was no stage.

Street vendors spoke on telephones. Storekeepers did. People sat alone in parlors, smiling, and talking. In restaurants, telephones sat on every table and people talked on every telephone. In the main squares were rows of glass-and-mahogany sentry booths with weathered copper roofs. Hundreds of people were inside them, talking, but no one was talking to anyone around him, except two men who were having a business argument through double layers of glass. Women flirted—you could see it on their faces. Men tried to be forceful and impressive, but their focus was not—as Jacob Bayer had seen all his life and had assumed would be forever—upon another person, but, rather, into a machine, with a glazed expression and a clenched arm.

EVEN AT MIDNIGHT or three o'clock in the morning, Koidanyev crackled with business, which Jacob Bayer discovered as he walked in search of a *heder*. In most towns these were thicker than mink hair. Everything else being dust and wind, the chief purpose of life in those places was to follow truth to glory, and this you did not do with silver plate or toys or telephones.

Though the population of Koidanyev had swelled, most of the *hadarim* had been shut as tight as in the days of the Mongols. What terror had closed these schools? What terror could there possibly have been in peace and abundance? When Jacob Bayer banged on doors as if notices of abandonment were not pasted across them, no one answered, but eventually he came to a *heder* that was still open. It was on the kind of street that he knew well, where once many *hadarim* had existed in magnificent confusion, with contests every day to see, for example, which group of six-year-olds was best at biblical exegesis. These children, who, as they shifted positions around a single text, famously learned to read upside down and sideways, were as wild as young goats and as serious as old men. Jacob Bayer imagined that the *hadarim* of Koidanyev would be much like those of other villages. The best scholars would be here, and the riches of the town would surround its students and rabbis like a golden keep, freeing them for their studies and devotions. But it wasn't so.

The buildings that had not long before housed the kind of place where he would teach had become schools of the telephone: a telephone answering school, an installation academy, a design and manufacturing school, and a few other arcane subdivisions—the Telephone Materials Modeling Institute, the Center for Telephone Studies, the Byelorussian Telephone Enterprise Institute, et cetera. But among the well tended facades of these institutions was an ancient and decaying building that apparently was still a religious school, so he knocked at the door.

From within appeared an actual rabbi of the normal variety whose inexpensive clothing did not lustrously echo the moon and whose expression was devoid of euphoria. He looked at Jacob Bayer and knew at once what had happened. "They let you in," he said, "in exchange for half." He waved his hands. "But we can give you only one chicken a day. We're not like the telephone and typewriter schools that serve veal and cakes even to the students. Twenty kopecks is as high as I'll go."

"Per month?" asked Jacob Bayer.

The rabbi, Ezekiel Blarma, looked at him, understanding that he had not been in Koidanyev long. "Per hour."

"I couldn't eat a chicken a day," Jacob Bayer said, when he had recovered.

"A big man, like you? A giant?"

"It would make me feel like a stuffed chair."

"How about a chicken every other day?"

"Every three days."

Rabbi Blarma threw back his head. "Okay, but, before we go further, who was your teacher?"

"Rabbi Toskies, the *Gaon* of Shpaigle."

"The *Tzaddik* of Vilna?"

"The very one."

"But that was when he was young. When he was old. . . ."

"When he was old he lived on a lake near Pleshchenitsy, and he had two students: Meir of Rovino and Jacob Bayer of Rosenheim. I am Jacob Bayer."

"Rosenheim in Bavaria?"

"I was born there. Then my father had a vision that told him to leave Germany."

"He came here?"

"Visions can be wrong."

"Come in," said the downtrodden rabbi. "You should sleep. There's a room for you on the third floor."

As Jacob Bayer climbed the stairs, he heard his host say, "A chicken a day, if you want. Defend us!"

WHEN JACOB BAYER awoke late in the morning he looked out his casement window at a quiet view of the city. From three stories up he could see roofs, chimneys, dormers, and the hills beyond the town. Here and there, the colors of slate and painted tin were touched with blurs of bright red, the signature of roses and geraniums in window boxes. Against white curtains drifting lazily on barely moving winds they looked civilized and reassuring. Perhaps his fatigue and dehydration had been the cause of the threatening undercurrent he had felt from the moment he entered Koidanyev. It was a prosperous town. Why should good fortune be threatening? Perhaps he had been too poor too long.

As he washed in his own bathroom, using hot running water for the first time in his life, he began to feel a certain excitement. The children of this *heder* might know things he did not. Surely, none of them would be hungry. How pleasant to finish a day's work and then have a hot buttered roll and tea without giving it a second thought. Perhaps most exciting was that this town, he now realized, was like the towns in Bavaria that his father had told him about: rich, quiet, full of good air, with a river that was cold and pure. He went downstairs, expecting the main hall to be animated with the life-giving presence of those who move fast and whose eyes are enchantingly bright.

But the main hall was empty, and Rabbi Blarma sat alone at a table for fifty people.

"Where are the children?" Jacob Bayer asked.

The rabbi said nothing.

"Is it a holiday?"

Still nothing.

"It's not a holiday," Jacob Bayer said in answer to his own question. "Where is everybody? It's late."

Rabbi Blarma looked up. "There aren't very many children in Koidan-yev," he said. "And those that there are go to the other schools. The parents are frightened."

"Of what?"

"They want their children to learn about the telephone, so they won't be left behind."

"Where is the telephone going that it would leave them behind?"

"I don't know," said the rabbi, "but they act as if they do know, even if they probably don't. They don't like me, because I don't have a telephone."

"They must not like a lot of people," Jacob Bayer said.

The rabbi shook his head. "I'm the only one in Koidanyev who doesn't have a telephone. First, they can't believe it. *You don't have a telephone? No!* They laugh at me. *You really don't have a telephone?* Then they get scared. *Why don't you have a telephone? How can you exist without a telephone? What is the matter with you?* It really frightens them. Then they begin to hate me. It's happened so often I could time eggs by it."

"What's wrong with having a telephone? What harm would it do?" Jacob Bayer asked.

"You, too? What's wrong with not having a telephone?"

"Nothing. I don't have a telephone. Who cares?"

"I used to ask that very question," said Rabbi Blarma. "When you do, they tell you what's wrong with not having a telephone, and then they tell you why you must have one. It lasts for as long as you sit there, and then they pick up and follow you down the street. They would talk about it until the end of time. They speak like the possessed."

After some thought, Jacob Bayer said, "In his introduction to *The Book of Evenings,* Rabbi Baruch of Minsk says that suffering is an entangling vine that grows outward with a green embrace."

Rabbi Blarma nodded knowingly. "Would you like a tomato?"

"Please." As Rabbi Blarma got up, Jacob Bayer asked, "Why is it that the road to the town is empty, and yet the town is so full of goods? Where do they come from? Is there another road?"

"No." Rabbi Blarma looked down as he walked to the table, sadly it seemed, but probably so as not to make the tomato roll off the plate.

"And what does the town give in trade for all these wonderful things? I saw no one in the fields. They lie fallow. The sound of iron striking iron is absent, or of saws working through wood. Even the mill wheels are chained."

"The telephone," said Rabbi Blarma.

"What do you mean, 'The telephone'? How?"

"I don't know. That's what they say. Who am I to argue with shops full of Italian leather and British furniture?"

"But wait," Jacob Bayer said, suddenly realizing something. "You hired me."

"Yes."

"For a chicken every three days, tea . . ." His voice trailed off.

The rabbi nodded.

Jacob Bayer looked at him quizzically. "There are no students."

"There are no students," the rabbi confirmed.

"Then what is my job?"

"To go before the commission. I was going to do it, but I'm too old."

"You didn't say anything about a commission."

"I didn't, no."

"What commission?"

HASKELL SAMOA, the chief rabbi of Koidanyev, claimed that he had been a disciple of Rabbi Smilksteen of Pokoik. When, in '03, he arrived in Koidanyev, unlike most rabbis he had no valises full of decrepit books. He traveled light and wore the clothes of a rich man. When asked where his books were, he laughed. "I have none," he said, "but I have this." He removed from his only piece of luggage, so that all who were gathered could see, two dry cells, two brass and rosewood telephone sets, and an immense spool of gold-plated copper wire.

He made great show of unraveling the wire and running it along branches and walls from one end of Koidanyev to the other. Then he hooked up his sets and batteries, and had the puzzled assistant rabbi man one of them. He called for the fastest boy in town, a *yeshiva bokher* who was as tall as a giraffe and as skinny as a willow, and had once taken a message from Koidanyev to Slutsk—nineteen versts—in fifty minutes. In his special silk shoes, this boy could run the two versts from one end of Koidanyev to the other in less than six minutes. Only a horse could go faster, but that was too dangerous in a crowded town.

Haskell Samoa wrote out a message on a piece of paper. It read, "What hath G–d wrought?" Then he asked for the crowd to supply random numbers, which he added to the message: 12127212232. When the clock struck eleven, he gave the message to the runner, who vanished like a satin-winged bat. Six minutes later, when the bat arrived at the other end of the line, the assistant rabbi said triumphantly, "Before the clock had finished striking eleven, we had the message, *What hath G–d wrought: twelve billion, one hundred and twenty-seven million, two hundred and twelve thousand, two hundred and thirty-two.* How do you like that!"

As soon as the impact of this had been assimilated (some found it hard to comprehend), and after many people had had the opportunity to converse with others two versts away, Haskell Samoa was called a *tzaddik, gaon,* and miracle worker. Then he established the commission. The power and gravity of Koidanyev's institutions migrated to it with great rapidity, leaving them to wither and die. As fast as customs could originate from within the commission, they replaced old customs that no longer seemed necessary.

At first there was only one golden wire, then another appeared, and another. People used to stand beneath them happily looking upward. Then they grew used to them and hardly noticed how fast they multiplied. Gradually, on poles that looked like the Cross of Lorraine, on racks projecting from buildings, on great structures that handled their airy crossings like a loom, keeping each independent of the others, they ran through the town like a golden cloth, connecting everything to everything else. When the sun set, Koidanyev looked from a distance like the prisoner of golden spiders in a glowing unearthly dream.

Following on the multiplication of the golden wires, the sounds of metal upon metal ceased and smoke stopped curling from the few factory chimneys. No one wanted to buy the things they made in Koidanyev anyway, so it was no loss. Who needs a tea tray with the birth dates of five hundred famous rabbis? Or kapok life preservers covered in bright green cloth with pictures printed on them of ostriches reading the encyclopedia?

As these things disappeared, new things took their places. They were just as useless, but they were consistent with the theme of the telephone and were accorded unquestioning respect and a great deal of capital. From all over the world things poured in of many excellent types and in many different forms, and it was all because of the telephone. At night, when the trade wagons came and went, wondrous items were exchanged, it was presumed, for telephones and what the telephone had wrought.

In ten years the town tripled in size and grew a hundred times—a thousand times—in wealth. Rotten roof tiles were replaced with those that glowed in the sun. Interiors were plastered, telephones installed, health improved, bodies firmed, faces beautified, rare objects collected. And everyone was grateful to the commission, for through the commission all plans flowed and from the commission came all authority, authenticity, and validation. Every Friday night, on what used to be the Sabbath—the Sabbath was now, as Haskell Samoa put it, shortened—the commission met in public, inviting comment from all who attended. In winter, it met in what had been the synagogue before its transformation into the commission's magnificent central offices. In summer, it met in the main square, beyond the bell-like clatter of silver and crystal in the restaurants at one end, and near a flower-ringed fountain that the commission artfully moderated to half its normal flow so that during the meetings it was possible to hear the sound of distant telephones singing like birds in a dark forest.

Haskell Samoa, who had brought the telephone to Koidanyev, had founded the commission, and had run everything for a decade, had not let unchallenged power dull his wits. From the dais, he observed the contented citizens taking their seats. Haim ben Ezra Lashkovo, who ran several of Koidanyev's forty banks, had a new watch, a Patek Philippe. Mrs. Bloomberg, the wife of a telephone company official, was wearing a freshly minted silk dress that clung to her gravity-defying bosom like paint. Abba Bialik, the butcher, now had a thick golden watch chain. Most tellingly, the widow

Mallichevska, who until the commission granted her some shares in the telephone company had been so poor that she sewed waxy leaves on her clothing to cover the holes, showed up with a tiara.

More than the sight of any object, their bearing informed Haskell Samoa of their condition and thus, he was convinced, their opinions. People who worry and suffer do not flow into a room, or a piazza, as these people did, but arrive with the tense movements and careful breathing of someone stalked by a tiger. Koidanyev was doing well, and with concealed satisfaction Haskell Samoa noticed the entrance of Ezekiel Blarma, the last of the old-style rabbis who clung to superstition and rejected the new, and who now breathed anxiously as his eyes sought comfort in the most basic and familiar things—the curve of a rail, the trembling in the water column of the fountain, the arm of a chair. Clearly the things he stood for were not long for this world, and after they were gone the progress of Koidanyev would be untrammeled. At every meeting he had raised tiresome objections that made whole audiences exhale in exasperation. Rabbi Blarma heard those sighs, Haskell Samoa knew, and they weakened his heart. Without a single ally, his doubts would turn with less and less restraint against himself, and then he would die.

But when he showed up with Jacob Bayer, Haskell Samoa changed both his timetables and his target. The new man was physically a giant, perhaps some sort of bodyguard hired in the delusion that the commission was more impatient than it was. Haskell Samoa studied him. Without giving himself away, hardly turning his head, he harvested the telling details.

Jacob Bayer was poor. His clothes not only lacked luster, they were dirty and did not fit. He had no position and did not represent any institution or constituency that would have the power to challenge or intrude. Though he was large, and sometimes large people are natural leaders, he was afraid. He fidgeted, sweated in the cool of the evening, and took occasional very deep breaths. Haskell Samoa counted how many times Jacob Bayer blinked, cleared his throat, and ran his finger along his collar as if to undo a noose. By these measures Jacob Bayer was twice as nervous as a groom who is about to marry a woman whose mother looks like a blowfish. That meant that if Haskell Samoa stayed calm he could pick him off in two or three short exchanges.

But although he was nervous and not well, at that moment troops were forming on the fields of Jacob Bayer's soul, horses were being mounted, and trumpets had begun to sound. He was afraid. He had no confidence. He had not even been able to become a rabbi, and at times of stress he had sometimes lost his ability to speak. One thing distinguished him, however, something that Haskell Samoa had missed. Jacob Bayer was constitutionally unable to shrink from a fight, and only in the center of a great battle did he shed the persistent anxiety that surrounded him as if it were aspic and he were an egg.

Bobbing over the heads of people sitting in front of Jacob Bayer were Haskell Samoa's white beard and even features, his Eskimo-blue eyes as wet as drowning pools, and his waxen red skin. The slow breathing, the unalterable confidence, and the enthusiastic and chilling amorality of a lover of games were precisely the opposite of everything that was Jacob Bayer. "How am I going to do this?" Jacob Bayer asked himself. He despaired of his powers. His right foot jiggled back and forth so fast that his whole body vibrated until he resembled a man who was riding a motorcycle.

"THE PURPOSE of the commission," Haskell Samoa said after the *vortnig* had called it to order, "is to accept the telephone and reassess the illusions of the past. Today we have, from Minsk, the chief of the municipal telephone system, Avraham Spelchek; from Bialystok, the leading philosopher of the telephone, Zipsehr Tuchisheim; and, from the Frankfurter Technische Hochschule, Professor Katz Voolsamdrek." The first of these betrayed little emotion at being introduced, the second less, and the third, an absolute stoneface, was calculating how to shatter and recast the proceedings with a belated burst of dominating brilliance.

Voolsamdrek was so certain of his views that a kind of maelstrom grew around him and glinted in his glassy, angry eyes as he sat with motionless false humility. Zipsehr Tuchisheim, a far less unpleasant character, appeared to Jacob Bayer to be half within this world and half without. Jacob Bayer had walked many versts and shared many dreadful habitations with this kind of wanderer, respected for the unsettling beauty of his bizarre and unfounded views. Spelchek, the least of the three, was a happy and grasping philistine.

When he considered that he was in the presence of a dictator, a fool, a madman, and a moray eel, Jacob Bayer felt his fear ebb, but how could he debate them, four at a time, before an audience of their adoring partisans? What strategy would he employ? He had never even used a telephone, and would not, therefore, have the ability to impeach its authenticity by the vulpine conversion of its most appealing attributes. What could he say when they alluded to the enrichment of those to whom he was presenting his case? If they were to be the judges, how could he prevail given that for a decade his opposition had been pouring gold into their pockets? No wonder Rabbi Blarma was despondent. Jacob Bayer turned to him as if to say, "I understand," and Rabbi Blarma said, "You see, every meeting is the same. He has thousands of experts and each and every one is drunk on the telephone. The more I speak, the more the people hate me. It's like a living death."

"Rabbi," said Jacob Bayer, "I have known defeat after defeat. I have no family. I will die in a ditch, and people will veer from what is left of me, making a new path a verst from where I lie, until nothing remains to offend them. And these people here, who will judge us, triumph day after day, and will be buried in a cloth of gold."

"That's good?" asked Rabbi Blarma.

"Well," said Jacob Bayer, "perhaps it will be to my benefit in God's eyes that I have built no walls in the dust between the portals where he stands."

"They don't believe in God," Rabbi Blarma said, gesturing with his head toward the new authorities.

"But I do," said Jacob Bayer.

Up stood Avraham Spelchek, eyes soft with gratitude and delight as always, for even as he slept he grew more wealthy, and each morning was a surprise of big numbers. "Spectacular things have happened in Minsk," he said. "And because what happens in Minsk tends to happen shortly thereafter elsewhere, I thought I would report to you some of the advances that you will soon enjoy. For example: When I go to sleep at night, I throw a switch on my telephone that silences the ringer and prevents me from being disturbed. The operator at the exchange solicits information from my

callers, and in the morning I have a list of messages from which I can pick
and choose like a king."

From the oohs and aahs it was clear that everyone in the audience
wanted one of these. "To take you to the edge," Spelchek said, "and give you
an idea of the potential of this instrument, in the future the mouthpiece and
the earpiece will be joined in a single device, with a handle for holding them
both! Looking even further ahead, a new venture founded by Moshe Itz-
covitz has received a huge influx of capital for his invention of a sculpted
anatomical accessory that attaches to the handle of the mouth-ear unification
device, allowing this to be cradled on the shoulder, freeing the hands.

"It doesn't stop there. Beneath the main body of the telephone you may
someday find a sliding tray with a pad on it and a pen attached by a flexible
rubber cord! Brilliant? Yes. And, on top of it, an alphabetically keyed listing
of telephone numbers. Ha ha! But that's just the beginning. Let me tell you
about what eventually will be possible." Everyone's favorite part was always
the wonderful things that did not yet exist.

"Right now, I can speak to Moscow simply by lifting my telephone and
moving my mouth. Thus, I can tell them what the weather is in Minsk, so
they can know what they have in store. Or, if the winds go in the opposite direction, they can tell me. Soon, telephone lines will be laid under the sea,
alongside telegraph cables, and from capital to capital in Europe. If you are
in Brazil, you will be able to know the weather in Bucharest. Think of it!
Right now, I can order groceries on the telephone. I don't have to go out, I
can just read the merchants a list and they deliver to my door. Do you realize how much time this will save once everyone does the same? Reading
services will someday read newspapers to you over the telephone. Eventually, there won't have to be books. One person reading a book in a telephone
exchange can convey it aloud to thousands of subscribers.

"The problem we're grappling with now is mechanizing the network.
Eventually you won't have to use an operator. With mechanized exchanges
all you'll need do is enter a code by tapping electrical pulses automatically
with a machine that will be called a *dialer.*" Haskell Samoa smiled, as if to
say, "Everything I have ever believed in has been proved."

"Eventually," Avraham Spelchek said, "no one will have to go anywhere.

The roads and streets will be populated only by a corps of delivery workers who will, of course, be called *bintlers,* and who will dress in red suits with brass buttons and wear little brimless hats. They will drive shiny brown motorized wagons with gold trim and a huge golden strawberry on each side. They will never have to return to offices—they won't have offices—as they will only need stop at roadside telephones to get lists of what to pick up and deliver.

"It will be possible for a child to be born in his home, delivered by a doctor telephoning from Burma or Buffalo, for him to have books read to him on the telephone, friends by telephone, and to have all his clothing and food brought to him. The roads will be clogged with *bintlers.* In hundreds of years, perhaps, telephones may not even need wires. Already, this is possible on a small scale in ships. When the technology is made affordable, each home will have a telephone, about the size of a grand piano, with no wires, and the *bintlers* will have them in huge motorized wagons. There is no end to the wonders. As for the implications of this, I will leave that to the scientists and philosophers," he said, looking with intense flattery at his demented colleagues, "because I'm just a businessman."

A woman stood. "I would like to say," she said, falling victim to the amateur's overwhelming feeling that no one wants to listen, and thus compressing her words and radiating an acute, scarlet-colored shame, "that the other day I wanted to make some *p'tcha.* I was getting my basket when my husband said, 'We have a telephone. Why go out?' So I called Markovich the egg handler and Sam the butcher, who sent over eggs and calves' feet—I already had garlic—and made my *p'tcha* without stepping from the house."

"It comes true already," Haskell Samoa stated, as Spelchek glowed. Haskell Samoa then pointed to an old man in back of Jacob Bayer, but as Jacob Bayer was in the line of sight, he stood, blotting out the tiny man behind him.

"So?" he said.

"So, what?" Haskell Samoa asked.

"So what? So what if organ-grinders' monkeys clog the roads with package-filled motorized carriages? So what if Markovich the egg handler gives his eggs to a *bintler* and the *bintler* brings them to Mrs. Hoo-Ha? So what if you can switch off your telephone and not be disturbed? You can save some steps by not having a telephone in the first place. So what if someone reads you books on the telephone? Better to read a book by yourself. So what if you can stay all the time in your house? What about your legs? You have them for a reason, and your horse, if you have one, will become ill if you don't ride him. So what if your house has wires or doesn't have wires? My house doesn't have wires now. I don't even have a house. Can you boil water with the telephone? Will it warm you like a fire on a cold night? Can you embrace it like a woman? If you pick it up, will you feel the sun on your face, hear the birds in the trees, see and feel the wind moving across a lake or whipping and thrashing a wheat field into what I suppose, never having seen it, looks like the sea? Will the telephone sit in your lap, like a child, or sleep in your arms, like a baby? Will you love it? Will it love you? Will you cry for its beauty, and sob when it passes? Will it have a scent like pine tar or salt air or rose? Will it speak fearlessly like the prophets, and hold fast as truth takes its sharp turns? Will it show courage in the face of danger and death? Will it make a single line of poetry? Or bake a single loaf of bread?"

"Stop!" shouted Haskell Samoa, his body, no less than everyone else's, shaking with anger and indignation. "What are you saying? Why are you saying it?" Whatever stratagem he had thought to employ, he had forgotten. He was merely enraged.

"I am speaking," Jacob Bayer said, "of things that are great and never ending, that require a lifetime of work to do right, that are God's gift to man and fill the world with their abundance, that have not changed in thousands of years and never will. And what I am saying is that, although you can add the telephone to them, and enjoy it for its miracles, such as they are—and they are, indeed, minuscule—you cannot emphasize it and concentrate upon it as you do without attendant disaster. This thing that you greet with erotic and worshipful enthusiasm, and the wealth it brings in train, are the golden calf. You are worshipping what you have made, which is shallow and dead, and have averted your eyes from the world you have been given, which is magnificent and full. It shows in your lives, in your town, in the arrest of all the normal rhythms that you have arrested, and in the sins you have committed and that you deny."

This kind of challenge was Jacob Bayer's talent and his curse, the reason he was thrown from one town after another and why he could bear it. Now would come the war, to which he would have to steel himself because he had faith not in arguments but in creation. As others rose to marshal their strengths, he would choke his into silence and defeat because he did not believe in man's power, and could not bring himself to inflate with it.

As if sensing this, Zipsehr Tuchisheim announced magisterially, "You don't understand."

His was as much of a challenge as Jacob Bayer's, and the silence that followed was a better introduction for Zipsehr than a brass fanfare. When finally he began to speak, even the birds had stopped singing. He was, after all, the chief philosopher of Bialystok, who had been the telephone's loving advocate since, five years after the fact, news of its invention had appeared as a two-sentence article in a Bialystok newspaper, under an advertisement for *esrogs*.

"What is it, exactly, that I do not understand?" Jacob Bayer asked.

"That the telephone is the most important aspect of our lives, that it is changing the very nature of man, ending history as we know it, and setting us upon a divine plane. It will bring immortality, solve all riddles, open all doors, protect us from want, and show us the way. It is the key to perfection, and is itself divine."

Hearts rose. Deep breaths were taken. Everyone expected that Jacob Bayer would have to bow to this fervent declaration, but he didn't.

"Excuse me, please," he said. "I believe you stated, did you not, that the telephone is divine?"

"Yes," Zipsehr answered.

"Meaning that it is, or has the attributes of, a god?"

"Not just a god," said Zipsehr, "God Himself."

"God Himself?"

"Himself. He. Him. The instantaneous transmission of thought by electric waves, over a great articulation spread across the earth . . . thought traveling without constraint, multiplying, tumbling freely, projected across seas, humming on wires that vibrate and sing like locusts in the sun . . . Never has the spirit been so loosed from the body, electrified, liberated, and yet with a disciplined resonance that vibrates across the universe. The telephone is the voice of God, born in us, echoing back to His distant precincts. If God is metaphorically in nature with such intensity that nature becomes the face of God, can He not jump at will to the machine, and would not this net of golden wires be an irresistible place for a divine being, capitalizing on a billion invisible impulses scattered musically to the winds with the swiftness of light? And we have made this dovecote, where the spirit of God, like a dove, has alighted.

"You, there, a bedraggled man, gross in feature, powerless and possession-free, trapped in the darkness of a previous age, would deny the very light. Look up, after a rainstorm, at the reticulation of wires in a ray of declining sun, and listen, and tell me that your heart is so hard as not to love the chant of God that sparkles and dries the golden drops with divine electricity, the sap of the blessed one that glistens in the moon, the gilded vibrations of the Jovian jug."

The audience was so taken by this poesie that Jacob Bayer's heart began to threaten him from within his chest. Why, at this moment, was he not free of the reminders of mortality? He did not know, and though he felt ill, he plodded on.

"What is the quality of this machine that you have made . . . ?" he began.

"I didn't make it," Zipsehr Tuchisheim declared with precision and contempt.

"That others have made, then, and to which you accord such singular status. What is the quality that makes it divine? What goes over its wires? Let us say, hypothetically, not a message in any language but merely a pattern of electrons. Why would God favor or distinguish, much less leap to, a pattern of electrons moving feebly across the surface of a single planet of a single star, when in the infinity of the universe there are countless stars of far greater power than ours, from which emanate every kind of wave on the spectrum of radiation and in such great quantities as to make what pulses from dry cells and generators perhaps less than significant?"

Professor Voolsamdrek of the Technische Hochschule cocked his head. This ragged, itinerant creature was speaking without authority of things in which he had no qualification or degree, which was dangerous. (Indeed it

was, and the reason Jacob Bayer had been ejected from one town after another like bullet casings from the port of a gun.)

"Significant!" Jacob Bayer repeated derisively. "The emanations that you
take to be enough to provide for God a dwelling are equal only to a tiny fraction of the flood that reaches us from the sun. A billionth? No. A trillionth?
No. Perhaps a trillionth part of a trillionth part, if that? And that flood that
strikes us is of the sun's full generation only what strikes [pausing to calculate the circumference of the earth's orbit around the sun and convert it, approximately, to degrees, he appeared to be undergoing some sort of attack]
thirty seconds of arc on a flat plane, concomitantly reduced by the fact that
the sun is a sphere. In other words, half a sixtieth of a three-hundred-and-
sixtieth, of half a sixtieth of a three-hundred-and-sixtieth, or, approximately,
one part in two billion. And that just of our sun, an incomprehensibly minor
part of the fleet of suns that stretch into the infinity of the universe.

"Mind you, to be infinitely insignificant in power is only one shortcom-
ing of your golden network. It is also a weakling of variety, a tiny sliver of
the radio spectrum, not even a piccolo to a great symphony orchestra. The
curtains of light and sound that flood through space in mutual clashes and
interference are something rather different from your little mousetrap for
God. But perhaps you did not know this.

"Perhaps it is, then, quality that distinguishes this construction. I have
been in Koidanyev only a day, but I have heard, or heard reported, quite a
few telephone conversations. Many of them were about the telephone itself,
and how miraculous it is. Surely a declaration of miraculousness does not,
cannot, itself provide the substance of a miracle. And then I have heard in-
quiries about the health of interlocutors, How are you? for example; and the
exchange of contractual information, You bring me the planks, and I'll attach them to the axles; and the articulation of great questions, such as, Didn't
his eyes sweep over Mrs. Molodetsky's bosom like a hand stroking a cat? Of
course, we can infer the substance of the *p'tcha*-making woman's exchange
with Markovich the egg handler and Sam the butcher. Orders for calves'
feet and eggs, or perhaps for blotting paper and glue, certainly would attract
the eye of God, if not His envy, and excite in Him the lust to lie in a place
where such miracles occur, to take up residence even, amid the dim and

monochromatic electrons, confined in hair-thin channels rather than exploding in stormlike fronts across galaxies, because such miraculous quality cannot prove to Him anything but irresistible. Right?

"But I ask you this," he said, as if dismissing his previously stated arguments, as of course he was not. "What makes this network more miraculous than the telegraph, which has been with us in force for half a century, which casts a wider and more comprehensive net, runs under more seas, crosses more passes, and branches into countless more locations? Would God favor speech more than abstract code, and, if so, why? Why, in fact, would He not want to live in the post office? Hundreds of thousands of nodes, branching into hundreds of millions of terminals, in a spectacular network the mission of which is to transmit great masses of silent, simple, unspoken code—that is, lines that make letters, letters that make words, words that make phrases, and so on. A code that, though transmitted in utter soundlessness and privacy, blossoms at its destination into colorful and evocative images—of battles, love affairs, great cities, oceans in storm, stars bursting, children born, wagons creaking, hearts healing. A code that opens like fireworks against a black sky, and rises in its solidity and beauty like prayer. Why is this in any way a lesser network, a lesser attraction, or a lesser temptation to the eye of God?

"God, you see, has been around for a long time. He knows what to look for. He can see into every crevice. His music sounds at His whim throughout this universe and an infinite number of others. He does not need our constructions for His habitations, and, besides, His mass and glory would burst the skinny thing—of which you are so proud—the instant He tried to wriggle into it. Like the golden calf, the telephone is only a thing that you have made, and that has distracted you from the song of life."

Suddenly, as if directed from without, Jacob Bayer (who had certainly not been born a diplomat) turned to the people of Koidanyev, whom he had perhaps begun to sway, and put to them the question that had haunted him since his arrival, a question that even Rabbi Blarma had not dared answer. "Where are the children of Koidanyev?" he asked, looking around, his gaze as tense as glass about to shatter. He felt the breaking of internal things, as if he could hear the sounds of beams snapping within walls, even if the outside seemed placid. When they did not answer, he asked again. "Where are they?

I have seen hardly any children. There are hardly any *hadarim*. What have you done with your children? I've been in hundreds of towns and villages in the pale. This is the only one where children are not only not the center of life, but not even to be seen."

"There are some," Haskell Samoa said, "but there aren't as many anymore. It's quieter now, and things are different." He stopped there. Jacob Bayer surveyed them uncomprehendingly. Everyone in Koidanyev was either looking down at the ground or hatefully staring at him. He felt beyond the moment the great comfort that awaited him in its aftermath, when the world would be quiet and he would once again be a wanderer on the roads. But as soon as his heart was calmed by the velvet of these imaginings he was startled out of them by the monstrously self-confident voice of Professor Voolsamdrek. I can't do this, Jacob Bayer thought to himself. I knock one down (I don't even know if I knock them down) and another rises.

When Voolsamdrek addressed him as if he were a dog, Jacob Bayer knew that nothing he could say would make Voolsamdrek think for a moment that anything he did say would in any way be inoffensive, that whatever progress he might think he was making, Voolsamdrek would only perceive inversely, and that the people of Koidanyev wanted Voolsamdrek not merely to best him but perhaps even to kill him. What was it about Voolsamdrek? What was the strange emanation? He had a darkness about him such as Jacob Bayer had never seen.

"The telephone is not God," Voolsamdrek said with great irritation. "The telephone is *superior* to God. Why is that? That is because, unlike God, the telephone exists. We know, see, and can prove it exists. Facts are better than dreams. What *is,* whatever it may be, is superior to what *is not.* I understand and have always understood why man has created God. With his laudable curiosity, man invented a delusion to provide the answers to his questions and to comfort him. But as the questions are answered, one by one, the delusion loses its power. And, finally, when all of them are answered, the delusion will cease to exist. We have already solved the riddle of human existence. We know how and when we originated. The universe can be summed up in twenty-seven precise statements. We can perfect human behavior if only we are granted or take the power to do so. We are close to determining all the answers to all the supposedly unanswerable questions, probably within eleven years—nineteen twenty-four, perhaps nineteen twenty-five, and by nineteen thirty without doubt. My colleagues, the physicists, know the origins of the universe, its exact size, and its fate. Like any mechanism, including ourselves, it is decipherable, and we can decipher it. This is nineteen thirteen! I am an optimist and a believer in the power of man. I believe in his perfectibility, and that part of the inherent nature of truth is that it can be found." He looked at Jacob Bayer ever so briefly and ever so dismissively, and the people burst into applause.

Jacob Bayer had no plan to counter this, nor any illusion that with the elements of faith, apprehension, and beauty, he could prevail against reason within the bounds of its closed and potent system. Nonetheless, like a student in a *heder,* he raised his hand. A now relaxed Haskell Samoa recognized him, unafraid of what he might say. But before Jacob Bayer could say anything, a man in the back, a somewhat disheveled devotee of the telephone, jumped up and yelled, "What does this have to do with the telephone? This was supposed to be about the telephone, the marvelous telephone!"

"I will tell you," Jacob Bayer said, right index finger pointing straight up. He had no idea what to say, but, having launched himself, began to slide down the mountain. "It has everything to do with the telephone." A long pause. All he wanted was to get back on the road. "Why?" Another long pause. The corners of Voolsamdrek's granitaceous mouth began to curl upward. "This is why." Another silence. Haskell Samoa reached for the gavel.

"The telephone," said Jacob Bayer, slowing Haskell Samoa's hand. "You have poured your souls into the telephone. You have directed to a mechanical thing made by man the very qualities—love, gratitude, devotion, faith, trust—that previously you reserved for God and nature and your fellow man."

"'Souls'?" mocked Voolsamdrek. "What is the 'soul'? Can you show me one? Can you prove its existence? How long will you speak nonsense?" he shouted.

"The soul," said Jacob Bayer, quietly, "is what distinguishes us from mechanisms. Our bodies are mechanisms, but we are more than that."

"Prove it. Show me the soul."

"All right," said Jacob Bayer. "I will show you the soul." Everyone peered at him, moving in their seats. "Bring me a telephone," he commanded. A telephone arrived immediately and was placed, disconnected, in Jacob

Bayer's hands. It was a beautifully crafted rosewood box with fittings of polished brass. When Jacob Bayer received it, the mallet brushed against one of the bells and made a sound both delicate and refined. "This," Jacob Bayer announced, "is a telephone. It is a mechanism. It is of great value, and, when attached to a telephone wire, can carry your voice across continents."

After the audience had sighed with pleasure at what he had said, he stood on his tiptoes, raised his arms to their full extent, hands still holding the telephone, and brought it from a height of three meters crashing to the piazza's flagstone floor, having propelled it with all the force he could draw from within him, which was quite a lot. The largest pieces to remain intact were the bells, and of the rest nothing was left bigger than a pea pod. It was as if the machine had had a bomb in it. First came screams, then shock, then remonstrances, then a murmur, which Jacob Bayer silenced by standing to his full height and bellowing over the heads of all who looked at him, "Bring me a baby!"

Absolute silence.

"Bring me a baby!" he cried. "There are very few children of any kind in Koidanyev, I know, but there must be a baby or two."

"Mrs. Freiburg has a new baby," said the same man who had asked the previous question, a simpleton.

"No!" screamed a woman in the front. Then she repeated herself, softly, and then what she was saying became sobbing. What Jacob Bayer heard in her cry was grief for the dead. Everyone except a few had the air of seasick passengers in a storm.

"Why not?" asked Jacob Bayer. "Why not? If we are mechanisms, then what's the difference? So what? If a baby's head," he held an imaginary bundle in his arms, rocking it, "and its eyes," he rocked some more, "and its flesh and blood . . . are," he feigned taking the bundle as he had the telephone and propelling it with full and sudden power toward the stone floor, "smashed!" (more wails and involuntary cries of no, no!) "broken," he said, "opened, separated, lacerated, drained, burst." He spoke these words as in the Passover recitation of the plagues, and as he did the people of Koidanyev dropped to their seats, heads buried in their arms.

Jacob Bayer took the same right index finger that had not long before pointed gently upward, and cocked it like a pistol at Voolsamdrek, closing his left eye with the resolute follow-through of aiming. "That," he thundered, "is the soul. I have shown you two mechanisms, one without—and one with—a soul. And you have seen with a sense more powerful than sight, hearing, smell, taste, or touch—all of which are part of the mechanism and fall away when the mechanism fails—that this is so. You have seen it with the one sense that cannot be taken away, that cannot fail you, and you show it." They had begun to recover, although some breathed as if they were ill.

"Tell me something, Professor Voolsamdrek," Jacob Bayer commanded. "Why is music beautiful? Why is a face beautiful? Why is a river, or waving wheat, beautiful?"

"It can be explained," Voolsamdrek said, coolly, "with mathematics. It can be plotted, charted, and graphed."

"You mean that the pattern of pitch and frequency in music, for example, can be visually confirmed in a pleasingly symmetrical display?"

"Yes."

"How does plotting it, which is no more than expressing it another way, explain it?"

"Because certain proportions trigger in the body the release of specific chemicals that, when absorbed by the brain, create the sensation we know as pleasure, which, in certain coherent packets, we experience as what we term beauty. It's much the same as love. There is no such thing as love, only the release of these chemicals according to stimuli."

"Why are they released?" Jacob Bayer asked.

"When certain stimuli act upon the physiological system."

"Why do such stimuli cause these reactions as opposed to others? Why, for example, does the sight of one's beloved not cause the release of the chemical that blocks the actions of digestion? Why does not the sight of a wheat field waving in the June sun release the chemical that makes you enraged and increases blood supply to the muscles for combat or flight? What cells or receptors make the interpretation and discrimination that account for the difference?"

"It probably isn't a cell or a receptor," Voolsamdrek said, "but a process among the cells of the brain."

"Yes," said Jacob Bayer, "and ineffably, nonmechanically, nonphysically, that decision is rendered. And there, in this, you will find—invisible, un-recorded, and unrecordable—both beauty and love. And where do they come from? From the same place as the soul, a place totally outside the mechanism."

Now patiently, but still contemptuously, Voolsamdrek said, "No, no, no, no, no. We have knowledge. We build on it in a process of validation, repli-cation, and review. This is our solid foundation. Everything else is a sham."

"No. Everything else is not a sham. Some things are beyond your method, and always will be. Tell me, for example, about the origins of the universe, and its extent."

"We know approximately when it began, and we know that it is limited."

"What lies beyond the limitation?"

"Nothing."

"Nothing?"

"Nothing."

"Then science, I take it, can define 'nothing,' can prove its existence, and can exclude that 'nothing,' being the absence of something, is therefore something in itself, in that it defines a limitation? Or that 'nothing' is neither the area into which something can intrude, nor that which prevents some-thing from intruding, and that this paradox is not unsettling and is, there-fore, 'nothing'?"

"This is metaphysics and philosophy, not science," Voolsamdrek protested.

"I know that," Jacob Bayer answered, "and you brought us here, did you not? And why not? It is a place where you would be welcomed to rule—if you could. Tell me, then, how did the universe begin? You do have an an-swer to that, don't you?"

"Yes, it simply sprang into being, ex nihilo, in what we call 'a singularity.'"

"Really?" Jacob Bayer said, pulling back, relaxing a bit. It scared Vool-samdrek. "And what came before? Oh, yes, that nothing, the existence of which, unfortunately, you cannot demonstrate. But what caused it suddenly to leap into being?"

"We don't know."

"You don't know? And if you did know, what would you call this primal force?"

"I have no idea. Perhaps theta."

"But in the face of this mystery, are you not open to the possibility of other mysteries, of connections between the unfathomable and the ineffable, that are beyond your power of explication, now or ever?"

Voolsamdrek laughed, and shook his head in disgust.

"What does it have to do with the telephone?" the simpleton asked.

"Nothing," said Jacob Bayer. "Nothing at all." He sat down.

"A *luftmensch*," Haskell Samoa declared, "does not know how not to waste his life in irresolvable disputes. I began that way myself, and soon turned to simpler things, the progress and development of which one can follow without undue confusion. That is hardly reprehensible, and that is why the telephone, certainly not the locus of God, if there is a God, is so wonderful.

"It will bring peace and assure prosperity. In an era of instant communication, no longer will countries go to war. It cannot but revolutionize all our affairs for the better, as we have begun to witness. The citizens of Koidanyev are not philosophers or theologians. They have not chosen to go on the road, like you, to chase dreams. They simply want to live their lives in peace, and, because of the telephone, they look forward to this century, which will be the greatest century of mankind. We in Koidanyev do not wish to be left out. Is that a sin?"

"Yes," said Jacob Bayer, "it is a sin. Ceaseless, feverish, desperate activity for fear of not having what someone else has, is a sin. Pride in one's creations is a sin. The conviction that one has mastered the elements of the universe, or soon will, is a sin. Why? They are sins because they are a turning away from what is true. Your span here is less than the brief flash of a spark, and if, after multiplying all you do by that infinitesimal fraction, you still do not understand the requirement of humility, your wishes and deeds will be monstrous, your affections corrupt, your love false."

"What does this have to do with the telephone?" the simpleton asked again, painfully.

"The telephone," said Jacob Bayer, "is a perfectly splendid little instrument, but by your unmetered, graceless enthusiasm you have made it a monument to vacuousness and neglect. Recall the passage: *I, Kohelet, was King over Israel in Jerusalem. And I gave my heart to seek and search out by wisdom concerning all things that are done under heaven. . . . I have seen all the works that are done under the sun; and, behold, all is vanity and a striving after wind.*"

Now came to Jacob Bayer, without his asking, the gift he had of seeing terrible things. He bowed his head, tears came to his eyes, and he said, in despair, "Koidanyev will be destroyed. The tall trees will be cut, the houses will burn, even the stones will be buried. And the souls that have chased the wind will be scattered by the wind."

In the long silence that ensued, Jacob Bayer's vision slowly glided away from the silent onlookers, like a thunderstorm that has cracked and boomed overhead and then flees on cool winds, its flashes and concussions fading gently.

"Nonsense!" cried Haskell Samoa, awakening the crowd and quickly turning them against the man that, a moment before, they might have followed. "The Napoleonic Wars have been over for a century. The nightmare you describe has left the world forever, banished by the light of reason. Man can control his destiny, and this light will grow stronger. What could happen? I do not doubt that before us lie the most glorious years in history, and, in contrast to their coming wonders, you are a specter of the darkness and a reminder of the dreadful past. The commission has decided that you must leave and never return. You may stay the night, but in the morning you must go."

"It won't be the first time," said Jacob Bayer.

"Are all the towns and all the people in the towns wrong? Can that be? Is it only you who knows the truth?"

"Rabbi," said Jacob Bayer, "the truth sits over Koidanyev like the hot sun. It has nothing to do with me."

JACOB BAYER was the first person to leave the new Koidanyev with nothing. (Of course, in his estimation even nothing was inescapably something.) The guards went through his pockets because they did not believe that anyone who had spent even just a few days there would not have been enriched.

"You *are* a piece of work," they said, "to go to a place where even insects get rich, and come out with absolutely nothing. A young boy came here not long ago with an idea for a machine that would polish the insides of solid objects. Now he's one of the wealthiest men in the world, and the machine hasn't even been built yet. All you had to do was to put a kopeck in the gen-

eral investment fund when you went in—at the bank nearest the bridge—
and in a few days you would have had ten."

"Sorry," said Jacob Bayer.

"Just go away. If you're too stupid to get rich in Koidanyev, don't get
near us."

When Jacob Bayer had gone about a verst he looked back upon the city
from a hill over which the road disappeared to other places. To the north,
upriver, the forests were thick with birds singing their morning songs. The
flowing water into which their sweet notes fell rushed past Koidanyev, cold
and clear, where it gathered up as well the sounds of telephones, by the thousand, ringing from one end of the town to the other. And in the blue-gray
water the sounds of the birds and the sounds of the bells were mixed before
they went together into oblivion.

As Jacob Bayer looked over the countryside and back at the town, sound
evaporated from the landscape like the standing water of a light rain. He
wondered why suddenly he had been struck deaf, for he heard not even a
hiss. How strange it all seemed without sound, as if he were looking back
from the far distant future. He had no wish to revisit his vision of the town
burning, choked in coils of black smoke, but he could not help but imagine
all its great activity stilled, the rush of things having come to an end, the water without flow, and the wind dead in the trees.

He knew that he had a long day before him, and he began his walk to the
west. What had Koidanyev done with its children? He could not even imagine. He glanced back for the last time, and thought that before Koidanyev
would stop still forever the telephone would triumph, as it had triumphed
over him, and spread victoriously over the whole world. Probably, after the
first flush of enthusiasm, people would no longer think it divine. But having
thought so, they would have put a distance between them and all that was
true, a distance that would perhaps be extended by the overwrought embrace of new enthusiasms as they arose, one by one, until the gap was so
great that only God could see across it. And into this chasm God would let a
million Jacob Bayers float down like sparkling dust on a dry wind.

Sail Shining in White

AT FIVE IN THE MORNING, the wind over Palm Island, off Cape Haze, took on a quality that could not fail to wake from his bed a man who twice had raced around the world, alone, in a sailboat. As always upon rising, he felt his loneliness more sharply than during the day, when both sunlight and the things that had to be done covered sorrow like the tide. He pulled on his tennis shorts, buttoned them, and went to the louvers to look out at the sea. The light over the waves early on a late August morning was a tangle of black and gunmetal blue, the whitecaps and foam a dirty gray that seemed to pulse as it appeared and disappeared in greater and lesser illumination, as if it were alive, beckoning, or sending a signal.

As he would do at sea, he carefully smelled the air. This was not tame air trapped in the Gulf of Mexico and backed up against the west coast of Florida, the hardly moving air that, like the retirees, like him, was going nowhere and would never go anywhere again, having finally come to the last stop and hit the stunning wall where nothing lies ahead.

This air said in less than a whisper that a storm was coming, the kind of storm that exists between the deserted coasts of Antarctica and Cape Horn, or thunders through the Bering Strait, or erupts off the sea-lanes in the empty Pacific and then spreads to overpower islands, the kind of storm that alters the scales by which such things are measured.

He knew before the satellites, the meteorologists, and the television announcers who for the next week would broadcast without knowing what was coming. As if by some magic, he knew of the storm at the instant of its birth in the Atlantic off the coast of Africa, when satellites could not yet see it. He knew because the air over the Gulf, the light, and the waves themselves, knew. Several times, in sailing around the world, once at his own pace and once while racing scores of other boats, he had sensed the coming of a great storm.

The waves flatten, tighten, and darken. They reflect the changing light differently. Sharks have a similar intuition, sensing a kill hundreds of miles away. Perhaps it is electrical, or comes via a microscopic variation in the underlying sounds that travel from sea to sea with almost infinitely greater power than sounds in air. Whether by a process unknown or a hardly apprehensible variation in that which is understood, the message was clear as the waves drove in and the clouds unfurled at dawn.

After making the bed and shaving, he did old-man exercises for half an hour on the cool tile floor, following them with ten minutes of exercises that put his heart at risk. Then, when his heart had not failed and he was flushed with the color of life, he had the kind of unsatisfying breakfast a devoted athlete might eat—a discipline from which, at eighty-two, he had long before earned the right to be excused.

He was eighty-two, but his legs were not pipe cleaners and neither were his arms as frail as potato sticks. He still had muscle and grace of movement. He did not wear pastel Bermuda shorts without a belt, or a flat cap, or a shirt with seahorses on it (as many men his age did for a reason known perhaps to their wives, who wore straw hats with berries on the brims). He dressed habitually in a navy-blue polo shirt, white tennis shorts, and boating shoes.

He was without question an old man, but he did not carry his money in a clip, he had never had to give up golf (never having played it), and he neither watched nor owned a television. This, in conjunction with other things, meant that he had no friends. But he didn't want friends, because it was over, or just about to be over, and in preparing for the greatest moment alone he did not want shuffleboard, crafts, dinner theater, book discussions, or college courses. He wanted, rather, to probe with a piercing eye to see in nature some clue to the mystery to come and the mysteries he would be leaving behind. He wanted a long and strenuous exercise of memory to summon in burning detail what he had loved. He wanted to bless, purify, and honor it, for if at the end he did not, he would by default have dishonored it.

No matter that nothing would come of this. No matter that all he thought and remembered would be unheard and unshared. The beauty of it as it burned within him was enough in itself, something like music, something that would set its seal even if all it did was vanish on the wind. But, then again, perhaps something would come of it. For very often, far away on the sea, a white sail will appear, running stiffly with the wind and shining in the sun, even if the sea is gray under dark and heavy cloud. These distant sails, proceeding with seeming purpose amid thin bands of sunlit green and blue, these persistent, silent flecks of white, are irresistible. You want to go to them, to be with them, and you wonder if they are a dream. They are so strong in purpose, so straight in direction, so steady, bright, and glowing, that it seems not unreasonable to follow them, to trust, to give oneself over to the light-filled other world of which they are the fleeting and resplendent edge.

QUITE CERTAIN that the storm was coming, he would be the first one at the barge that morning, even before the carpenters and other early risers, and so his was the first footfall on the sandy road to mar the pattern of alligator tracks left overnight with remarkable delicacy in forms that suggested the passage of tanks or tractors. Alligators and lizards seemed unable to cross the road perpendicularly. They preferred a slash: whereas the snakes, whose imprint was like that of a garden hose, liked the perpendicular even if at a slither.

The rusty barge that slid across the water, though it floated, made no pretense of being a boat, as did many craft that operated close to shore, and even some on the open sea. These made him recoil, these boats that were top-heavy five times more than was safe, too wide by a factor of two, and either insufficiently rakish (as if born in a bathtub factory) or too much so, with needle bows to please the sensibilities of men who wore black shirts open to the navel. These boats, hubris in fiberglass, asked to be sunk in the wrath of waves, because they carried out upon the waters things that made a mockery of the fine line there between life and death. Instead of holding only what was essential, beautiful, or quick, they were seagoing repositories of every kind of vinyl, plastic, and sin. They carried waterbeds into parcels of sea where beneath them for seven miles lay unimaginable volumes of brine. And when they had metastasized into ships, they floated casinos, as if to be upon the ocean were not enough of a gamble in itself. They were places for nightclub reviews and various forms of prostitution, the carriers, upon the ineffable ocean, of pinball machines, lobster tanks, and bowling alleys.

The last time he had been in a ship at sea that was not propelled by the wind had been in a destroyer that not long before had shelled Iwo Jima. The rest had been sail, on purpose, from conviction, out of respect for the sea itself and for the wind that sang in sheets and stays. He wished he did not have to see the obese cabin cruisers with deep stern drafts and amusement-park wakes, and their speechless and beefy occupants in fluorescent bikinis and sun brims, rushing at thirty knots from nowhere to nowhere, with a deep rumble and the smell of perfume, gin, and suntan lotion.

The channel was clear except for a trawler moving downcast from a night having failed to break even, unlike the pelicans, whose every swoop put them in the black. "Storm," he said to the captain of the tug as they glided silently to the ferry slip, engines off. He casually pointed straight up.

The ferry captain turned his head in every direction, considering the air and clouds most carefully even as he was gliding toward the slip. "What makes you think so?" he asked, puzzled.

"You can't tell?"

"No."

"Really?"

"I've been listening to the Coast Guard. What storm?"

"It's coming."

"Well," said the ferry captain, dipping down to spin the wheel, "if you wait long enough, a storm always comes."

"In a week or less, this one will come, and no storm like it has hit this coast in my memory, which goes back to nineteen fifteen."

"How do you know this?"

"How can you not know? Everything here," he said, looking around at the houses and docks, "will be destroyed. Everything on the island will be gone. Half the island itself, the sand and the trees, will be washed away. My house is on pilings, but the waves will be high enough to shatter it in one blow. The level of the sea will rise above the tops of those mangroves. Even things that float will be hard pressed to stay afloat, for the sea will shuffle, break, and overturn them."

"If what you say is true," the ferry captain said, "there'll be a general evacuation. Everyone on the coast will have to get out."

"Not everyone," was the answer, which the ferry captain thought strange.

HIS CAR ACTUALLY STARTED, which was a miracle after so many years in the hot sun and salt air and use only every two weeks or so. The empty road was washed out in the morning sun that by now had climbed to beat down upon a coast of resilient green. Every time he saw the fragmented maroon debris that signified a crab killed on the road the night before, he thought of numbers, probability, and fate, and was reminded that most of his generation had already fallen, and would soon be fallen completely. Others would follow him where he was going, with both the certainty of the result and the absolute unpredictability of the means. The crabs in the road, scuttling by moonlight or in the tropical dark, were surprised by the sudden appearance of cars and trucks planing through the night air at eighty miles an hour. These and other kinds of small animals that littered the sides of the roads were returned in a week to the cycle of soil, sun, water, and wind. He noticed that their presence at the roadside diminished only when he came to the town, where stores on the tree-lined streets were just beginning to open. Watering cans and hose spray maintained the plants and cleansed the sidewalks. In the morning, when they are watered, plants seem to give off their most communicative scents. And store owners, waiting for the day to begin and hopeful of good sales, are often cheerful and engaging.

"What will you give me for this?" he asked of a jeweler who, even for a jeweler, was exceptionally calm.

"What is it?"

"The Scarborough Trophy, which you get, if you are lucky, for going out of the harbor at Scarborough and, with great excitement and hardly any sleep, passing the east coast of England in daylight and darkness, and then skating through the Channel to the open sea to drop down the entire length of the world, until the seasons change and summer becomes winter, though by the time you get there winter is over. And then across the Indian Ocean under stars that few people see and are brighter than you might think, through the Strait of Malacca, north of Australia, into the South Seas, and against the wind across the southern Pacific, where time is buried in the blue ocean. Around the Horn in storms with waves that seem like mountains, and then up the coast of South America, across the equator, with a glimpse of the lights of Tenerife, and anxious days in the Bay of Biscay. Into the Channel like a chip in a whirlpool, and to Scarborough once again, where the winter of your departure is long over."

"In what?" the jeweler asked.

"In a sailboat that cannot be more than forty feet in length, cannot have an engine, and cannot carry anyone but you."

"You won the race?"

"I did. I wasn't even young. When I was young I was working. It's gold," he said of the trophy. "It was the only prize, and it weighs at least ten pounds. I weighed it once."

"We'll see," the jeweler said, placing it on a balance and then expertly exchanging cylindrical brass weights until all came right. "Five kilograms exactly—*eleven* pounds."

"How much would that bring?" asked the 'round-the-world racer, who had to wait while the jeweler ran tests and weighed the mass of gold yet again before turning on his calculator.

"I can give you sixty thousand dollars."

"You can, and you can also give me more and still make a large amount of money."

"Sixty-two thousand, five hundred."

"A little more."

"Sixty-three thousand."

"I mean more than that."

"I stop there."

"I go up the coast to Sarasota."

"Sixty-five, that's it." In the jeweler's mind, he had just lost several thousand dollars that he had hoped for, but he softened when he realized how much so few minutes of work would bring him still.

"Okay."

"It's too bad that you have to give up the trophy."

"No. Even though I've provided for her, and she can provide for herself, my daughter might need the money someday—one always lives and hopes just beyond one's capacities—and every time she might think of selling this her heart would break a little, not to mention when she actually did. I don't want to break the little girl's heart. I'll wire the money to the trust. She won't even know, but it will be there."

"How old is she?" the jeweler asked.

"Thirty-nine."

"That's not a little girl anymore."

"She's a physicist," he said proudly. "She's at the Jet Propulsion Laboratory in Pasadena. And she's got a boy—my grandson—in high school, a brilliant jerk, just as I was when I was fifteen. Only I wasn't brilliant, and I apologize for that, but I never wore my clothes backwards, and I was able to speak in English."

"Yeah, they wear their clothes backwards."

"My daughter. . . . I was born to see her in her little corduroy jacket and at my very last I'll be thinking of what she looked like, buoyant and overjoyed, as she rode on my leg, standing with both feet on my foot, holding on below the knee. That's why I said 'little girl.' I know she's a woman, and so does she, but every time we embrace, we go back. And I know she knows exactly how I feel, now that her own son has long since been unable to ride in the crook of her arm."

THE LAST TIME his daughter had been at what she referred to as his "house," she had asked, "How can you possibly think of disconnecting the telephone?"

"How can I possibly not think of it?" he answered, knowing that this made no sense.

"How are we supposed to speak to you when we're at home?" She was skirting the main subject, which both he and she knew was coming.

"You can use your cellular phone," he said with a twinkle, mocking all the telephones in the world as he took yet another step on the plank of pretended senility that somehow pleases both parent and child—as inexplicably as the baby tooth, hanging by a thread, that his daughter would worry when she was six. "Remember the baby tooth that you used to flap back and forth like a pet door?" he asked.

Stunned, she said, "No."

"Well, it's like that."

"What's like that?"

"It's because I love you. You did it because you loved me, but we're different people."

"I did what?" she asked.

"I know, Anna, and I know that two telephones are required to complete a discrete circuit, just as you knew not to worry your tooth."

She tried another tack. "How can you, a man who directed a great corporation. . . ."

"It was a shitty corporation. I hated it."

"You hated it?"

"Yes."

"You were rather cheerful, considering."

"I did the best I could, but, believe me, I never liked that company."

"Why?"

"Because it wasn't human and it wasn't alive, and all the thousands of people whose lives were molded around it were like sequins on a corpse. It had no desire or regret, it didn't know the difference between right and wrong, it couldn't breathe or kiss or sweat. I wasted my precious time on it, *my* life, and *it* will never die."

"But that's how you made a living. It's how you provided for us."

"That's why I did it," he said, staring not so much into space as into the past. "You know how you could spin your top for hour after hour, and see

God-knows-what in the whirling city inside, where trains and boats moved ingeniously over painted fields and rivers?"

"Yes."

"You weren't the only one. I could, too. I wasn't bored when I took care of you. I had to leave in the morning because I had to: I didn't want to."

"Even when you were my age?"

"Yes."

"Even as a man, back then?"

He smiled. "Yes."

"You have a baby's mind."

"I do."

"How did you survive the war? How did you command a destroyer?"

"Anna, a child knows what's important, what's essential, what's eternal. It's no small thing to keep a child's mind. And to answer your question, war is a clash of essentials. People who in civilian life are taken in by the castle of clouds we build as we grow old don't understand the nature of the forces that in battle are both terrible and sublime. But that's just a comment. I got too old for war a long time ago."

"Da Da," she said. She had called him Da Da when she was a child. "What if you fall, and can't get up?"

"Then I wouldn't be able to get to a telephone anyway."

"We'll never hear from you again."

"I'll use the phone at the dock. I'll call you."

"What if you get sick?"

"That's okay, Anna. If I get sick and I can't get to the telephone, I'll die. That's the way it's supposed to be. I don't want to be a hospital case. Really. There's something to dying on the ground, or in a room where the air comes in the windows. You know how I hate fluorescent lights and windows that don't open, and how I love what I have here—the sound of birds, the deep green, the ocean, even the abject heat that makes the shadows so blessed."

"What about your friends? How will you keep in touch with your friends?"

"In the past ten years or so, most of them have gone beyond the reach of the telephone."

She nodded quickly, her eyes closed.

He knew what was coming. "The world," he said, "the whole world, and all of time—sometime in my lifetime, and I don't know exactly when, it must have been a wide and diffuse line—crossed the line nonetheless between the two great ages. First was the age of patience, into which my mother and father brought me. And now we are in the age of impatience, which I have never loved. Impatience in everything. In loving, in understanding, in action, even in seeing. I'm not suited to it."

Anna, his daughter, went to his arms, just as she had done as a baby, a child, and a young woman, and cried. And then, as always, she was better, very quickly becoming sunny, because, as he had many times, he took her cry into his heart.

In 1961, when his wife was not quite forty, someone in a passing yacht had photographed her in the bow of a sailboat they had chartered in Hawaii. Though neither party had hailed the other, an eight-by-ten Ektachrome print had been sent from Charlotte Amalie to "*Inverness II,* Honolulu," eventually reaching New York in February.

A note with it said, "I took this photograph off Lahaina, Maui, in December. We then made the passage back to Los Angeles, down the coast of Mexico, through the canal, and to Charlotte Amalie, where we're holding over. Normally, I would be surprised by a photograph, among hundreds, of someone I don't know. But I was not surprised. The image, and her smile, had never left me. I had thought that perhaps I was investing too much in memory, but when the pictures came back I realized that I had not invested enough."

The stranger had photographed Anna's mother, Sabrina. Her grace and beauty had rolled across the water to him like the flower-scented air that cascades over a beach in the morning. The bow of the *Inverness II* was dipping into a smooth blue sea. Behind its white chevron were the green hills of Lahaina, topped by white clouds with shadowy blue bases. And above these clouds were pieces that had been torn from them by winds aloft and were engaged in battle with patches of Bristol, delft, and sapphire.

She was perched on the raked chrome rail, over the anchor that projected from the tip of the bow, so that, facing sternward, she appeared to be floating without care not merely above the rolling swell but above the deck. A scrim of foam had been knocked aside by the passage of the glistening hull. With her head turned to the passing boat, her hair fell across her shoulders and was lifted lightly by the wind into a soft fullness, semigolden, chestnut brown.

As relaxed and unself-conscious as a young woman might be, she was a study in perfectly flowing limbs and flying, floating, weightless, airy majesty. During the war she had been a Wave, and her confidence had never shaken in even the war's most anxious moments. What had always impressed him about her most had been a natural, indelible grace that made even the loveliest things around her lovelier still; a tranquillity alert nonetheless to the excitement deep in all things; a self-possession that said she understood the shortness and beauty of the breath we take of the world. Without that impenetrable grace, every other quality could be shattered like glass—brilliance, beauty, force, spark, all would melt away in the face of loss and terror.

Anna's copy of the photograph was newer and brighter. His, slightly faded, though still the most vital color in his life, was on the huge pine table at which he ate, corresponded, and read. The lamp on that blond table, and the photograph of his wife, had become the center of a life that found itself migrating more and more toward the sea. She was gone, but he loved her so much in memory it was as if she were an angel perpetually rising from the waves.

When he had warned of the storm for a week before its coming they had mistaken his certainty of vision for fear. Now that they themselves knew, and were overtaken with panic, they forgot that he had told them, and could not understand how he could be unafraid. Every morning he had arisen before dawn and observed the insistence and darkness of the sea. The waves that rolled in now, even in the bright of day, were long and woolly. They seemed as tired as refugees, and moved not as if toward something but as if away from it.

A policeman visited. In his view, here was an old man who probably couldn't write checks or carry a bag of groceries, and who would have to be persuaded and cajoled for the purpose of saving his—to be truthful—worthless life. So the policeman had an air of exasperation even before he began to speak. "The storm," he said, "will destroy everything."

And the old man said to him, "I know."

"That seems to make you happy," said the policeman, who had a mustache and a bulletproof vest.

"What seems to make me happy?"

"That the storm will destroy everything." The policeman was thinking of his own house on the mainland, close to shore, and his boat, his pool, his garden.

"No."

"Then why are you happy?"

"If I appear to be happy, it's not because the storm will destroy everything, but because I know that it will."

"There's a difference?"

"Of course. Knowing is more than half the battle. The rest is just stuff, you know."

"Well I don't get that," the policeman said.

"To get it, to really get it, you'd have to talk to my wife."

"How is that?"

"She went through the war in the Pacific without flinching or bowing her head, or perhaps even shedding a tear. Her brother was killed. I was reported lost. The atmosphere was like what it is now, before the storm, but she glowed, always. As they say, she didn't miss a beat."

"I understand, but you've got to get out. One trip in the car with as much as you can take. The roads will be jammed."

"June, nineteen forty."

"What?"

"Nothing."

"We'll be coming through on a sweep starting at three tomorrow afternoon. If you're still here, we'll have to arrest you for your own safety."

"You mean propel me, don't you? You don't want me to be arrested, you want me to be propelled."

"I have no idea, but you have to do what the law says."

"I agree," said the 'round-the-world racer, with strange enthusiasm. "If the law says that it knows the nature of the storm, it knows the strength of my house, and it knows what is in my soul, and that therefore I am to do what it dictates, who am I, what is the storm, what is my house, what is my soul, to contradict the law? Tomorrow, I won't be here. The house will be shut—windows boarded, power off, loose things battened—waiting to be destroyed."

On the sea the only law was God's law, the physics of wind and blue water and the rolling of the waves that with continual urgency push boats across oceans that ring the world. War of any type is different on the sea, in that it is almost all maneuver. When ships are firing at other ships or planes, or planes are leveling to lock-in a torpedo drop, or a line of cruisers or destroyers is dueling, the immense force overwhelms mere men and contrasts with the delicacy of their existence. But even in the greatest tests of fire there is a sense of separation, a separate dignity, a separate identity. Sailors are delivered to war, riding, and even in the bloodiest engagements the sea cleans up quickly, quieting any chaos man can make and sealing the scene of battles with the inflow of innocent waves that whisper and relax.

In ocean racing you leave no track that lasts for more than minutes. Though each moment is fresh and dangerous, the rules never change: the only variations are in the way you play them. In racing, one moves not much faster than a man can run, tense and intent upon seconds, watching for maximum swell in the spinnaker, sensing the changing angle of the wind so that its collision with the mainsail leaves as little as possible of slip and escape. In this patient and continual sensing of that which cannot be seen, a sailor deepens in thought. Going around the world courting the invisible at every moment teaches not only that mystery has force, but that it can deliver.

That which cannot be seen, in this case something as simple and explicable as the wind, had propelled him around the world and called forth his unceasing attention lest an ungraceful move dismast or capsize his craft. That which cannot be seen had warned him of the storm far in advance of its coming. For ten days, subsumed by the rhythms of nature and necessity, he had been preparing for his final engagement, which now was rolling at him from across the Atlantic.

Though he was afraid, he was not afraid, and though his heart was broken he was happy. All the practical things had been taken care of. The
money had long before flowed into trusts. Paintings and memorabilia were
with Anna. The letters had been written, the plans laid out. In the last week,
he had sold or sent the last of his valuable possessions. A few cartons of
books were on their way through the mail. All he had left were his glasses, a
watch, and clothing. In the bathroom, a toiletry kit. In the kitchen, a plate,
bowl, wineglass, two pots, knife, fork, and spoon, can opener, and cutting
board were the only hard items remaining.

In the days before the storm he had slept deeply and well, on the floor,
with two blankets—one folded for a mat, the other, of the lightest weave, for
the late hours when the wind made a cover necessary even on the Gulf Coast
in September. Shorn of most things, feeling more and more agile as the
storm approached, he found less and less desire to replay the scenes of his
life. Now it was as if, in facing what was to come, he was able to pull from
the past everything of value and make his peace with it so he could leave it
behind. In truth, in leaving it behind as he had never been able to previously,
a seal was set upon it. And when finally it left his hands and escaped his possession it took on a life of its own.

AT THE MARINA on the mainland most of the boats had been taken out of the
water, a useless act, for the ocean would rise to lift them from their cradles
and throw them inland to end their days smashed, demasted, and on their
sides. The rain was already driving, though not yet in sheets and whirlwinds, and with everything battened down and wet, and the sky dark gray,
it looked not like Florida but like Maine in a gale.

He was on the last barge, with the police, who had made their sweep. He
guessed that within the hour not a single one of the fifty or sixty people on
the barge or moving anxiously about on shore would remain. And there was
not much more than an hour or two before one would not be able to navi-
gate the passage out, even under power—and his boat had no engine. But it
was an ocean racer, a Halifax 40, as stiff and strong as a lance, empty and
light, with a keel that would enable it to hew to the windward side of the

channel, closer than usual because the depth of the water had increased with the rise in the sea. The barge had slid right over the dock that it had spent years butting with its prow, the swimming pool at the marina was inches and minutes away from the jailbreak of its waters, and the last-minute evacuees were rushing along flooded paths that were up to their knees.

He went to the shed where the luggage was stored when on holidays a crush of people went over to the island and the things they carried choked up behind them. Now it was empty, warm, and dark except for thin stalks of light pressing in through cracks in the siding. It was as good a place as any to listen to the sound of one's own heart and breathing, to know that even this close to the end, with answers not yet apparent, they seemed, nonetheless, beautifully close.

In the shed the water rose, flowing wavelessly through seams that had conquered its resonance. In the darkness, with his eyes closed, he was battered by the images of those who were gone and those he would never see again; of his father walking with him on an Atlantic beach in sunshine and wind; of his mother, tranquil and beautiful, in a white wicker chair in the second summer of the First World War, listening to a little boy who could hardly talk, but as rapt with attention as if he had been Ralph Waldo Emerson; of his angelic daughter, sleeping, secure in his arms; and of his wife, when she was young, in the bow of the *Inverness II* as it dipped and rose in the sea off Lahaina, when, for a moment, the world was perfect. These insistent memories, of his wife as she threw back her head to clear the hair from her face, of his infant daughter, her eyes squinting into the newly discovered cold wind, her little hands held up before her face to protect it, these insistent memories, soon lost but to God, he would take with him into the sea.

He had thought that time would pass very slowly in the confines of the shed, but it had raced, and when he looked at the tritium-laced hands of his watch he saw that he had overstayed. He unlatched the door, which the wind then threw open. Though they were yet to be stripped of their branches, the palm trees were getting ragged. He did not even have to look, but could sense that everyone else was gone. It was not quite like being alone on the sea, but he felt a sense of freedom. No man would be watching him, no one to confine, judge, or proscribe except nature itself. You could not be lonely when you were completely alone, but only when you were close enough to others to fail them or to have been failed by them.

As if eager to run into the heart of the storm, his boat was bobbing urgently near the top of the pilings to which it was moored. It had not been constructed to sit at a dock or cruise idly in middling seas. It had been made for the lower fifties and the highest sea state, and when he stepped aboard from the dock covered by two feet of water, he imagined that the boat knew it.

In a quick and final release, he cut away from the moorings. Never again would he tie up. Never again would he maneuver into a slip. There would be no alteration of action and rest, but only action building without cease until it became eternal stillness.

The boat moved from its slip into the channel, cutting to windward, picking up speed. With just a yard of mainsail he was making fifteen knots and leaving foam. This running of the slot was complicated, for if he had blown to the lee of the channel he could never get back, and would die in the muddy bureaucracy of the mangrove roots.

But all was going well and fast. The keel, a great underwater sail and balance for the power of the wind, held him on course like a straightedge. The difficult part was yet to come, the race to the sea. It was a short stretch, but if the wind blew straight down this untackable slot he would never get out to open water. He had counted on the fact that the storm had a north by northeast bias and the channel veered slightly northwest. He would know at the turn, where the wind came freely off the ocean, undisturbed by the now rapidly disappearing island.

He wished that at the turn, eighty-five degrees to port in two hundred feet, he could lift the keel and skate into position, but the keels of ocean racers are not centerboards and do not lift in shallow water, and the boats they steady were never intended to skid.

When the time came he spun the wheel and tightened the mainsheet. The stern swung around in a graceful movement and the boat reoriented even before it reached center channel. All it had to do was break through the waves sweeping down the slot.

At the turn, these waves had been five feet from trough to crest, and at the end of what once had been the jetty, fifteen. Even before he left the last qualified embrace of land he was in the storm and the boat was flying across the crests and thudding against the troughs. Before he sailed beyond what had been the beach, waves washed over the deck and tried to take him with them, but his safety lines held.

Then he cleared the land and sailed into the violence of the storm, his boat battered near to death not even two miles from his house. This would not do: his desire was to reach the heart of the storm, where he would match its rage with equanimity. At the heart of the storm, he believed, he would find love. Why he thought this he did not exactly know, but he thought that if in difficulty the heart rose, then what could be more promising than the heart of a storm? He swung the prow west-northwest and ran close in, lifting the mainsail another few feet. In wind that screamed in the halyards he could have made good headway just sailing with the mast, but he wanted strain, and he flew forward at more than thirty knots. No one alive would have been strong enough to hold a tiller in these moments, and for him, because he was old, holding the wheel was almost unbearable, but he held it, locking it when he could, and unlocking it to trim when he had to, hoping that it would not be pulled from his hands and spun so that the spokes blurred and he would have to run with the wind until the boat detonated against a beach made invisible by colossal surf.

Although he had never seen a sea like this, he had been schooled in long-lasting storms that had not been so different, and he managed to hold and persevere. As he moved forward and the hours passed in cold and exciting agony, he found regions of waves so high that sliding down them was like falling from a cliff. As it got darker, the tritium hands glowed more brightly, he breathed hard, and the noise of wind and water was so great that it hurt.

And when he had been out for so long that it was night and great hills of foam appeared in a malevolent glow and almost broke over him without warning, he felt very tired and ready to sleep, and that, at last, he was closing upon the heart of the storm, a terrible darkness tinged with light.

Charlotte of
the Utrechtseweg

Down by St. Elizabeth's, up from the river and toward the museum, just beyond where the Utrechtseweg parts from the Onderlangs, he died with the vision of his daughter Charlotte in his eyes. He had been lying in the street after staying impossibly long on his knees, unreachable by his men except those who, having come to get him against his orders, lay dead nearby. Descending silently toward the fields west of Arnhem in perfectly balanced September light, he had known it might end this way. He had known well enough at least so that before the glider came to rest upon the golden stubble of recently cut hay, he felt an upwelling of affectionate memory, of love, and of deep gratitude for all he had been allowed.

And that had been much, even if only for a short time. Charlotte had just turned eighteen and was now posted to an antiaircraft gun in Chelsea. To be stationed in Chelsea in any capacity was a prize, but it was hardly comforting to think of his daughter—the vision of whom as a child in her red dress he could not banish from his mind—in the semidarkness of London lit by its own burning, firing her gun against resurgent fleets of German bombers, air-breathing ramjets, and rockets. There was no comfort. That was the trick at the end, to understand finally that every comfort was in vain, and then to understand that comfort was unneeded, and thus somehow to rise into death reassured.

The glider pilot had been masterful when, cut away from the tow, he had come into his own. Aircraft crowded the sky like swallows, and after the gliders landed they sat upon the fields like the tank traps that look like children's jacks, obstructions in the paths of those that followed. But the pilot of his glider, in a burst of brilliance and concentration, banked, circled, and swooped as all inside went silent and breathless, and found the one clear alley in a field littered with broken fuselages and shattered wings.

From the moment they landed they were raked with the fire of German heavy machine guns embedded efficiently in the woods, chattering as if to one another as they picked out the abundant targets. This ignited the fields and the gliders that lay pierced and broken upon them. A wounded man with smoke coming from phosphorus burning in his chest begged to be shot. They would not, or could not, and when the line of flame neared him, he shot himself.

The idea that Charlotte would be left alone was intolerable, but in the minutes remaining of his life he had accepted it. He had parted from her in a restaurant at Victoria Station. A beautiful blonde girl, she was miraculously awkward and nearsighted. "You don't *aim* the gun, do you, Charlotte?" he had asked, and she had replied, "Oh, no, I'm the loader."

He had come up from Aldershot for lunch, the last time he would see her except in indelible memory. Both knew that it would take other people at least a split second, and perhaps more, to realize that the major, of full maturity, was not inappropriately associating with a young private. Because of that, they were slightly reticent, as they had learned to be when Charlotte had grown tall and they went together in public, Charlotte's mother having died when she was seven.

They looked very much alike, and to anyone with half a mind it was clear from facial structure and coloring, and the particular way that both were burnished by August sun, that they were father and daughter. "How are you coming along?" he asked, intensely interested in her answer, which, because she did not ever think in terms of how she was coming along, was lacking in specifics.

Because he wanted to order the best thing on the menu, he asked for haricot beef, which was actually corned beef, and then for the chocolate cake—"1 good oz. Bournville Cocoa"—with mock whipped cream. Father and daughter seemed the picture of strength. In ordinary times he would be looking forward to a slow unfurling of the years, with London their background. He was a barrister, and would have been content to move from case to case as if on rocks that make a path across a stream, with a remote but watchful eye out for Charlotte—and presents for the baby, a drink in town with his son-in-law, his shotguns going eventually to the grandchildren if they were boys. Death slowly brought out was easier because of all that led up to it and filled in after it, which is why, when he fell to his knees on the Utrechtseweg after the first bullets cut into his abdomen, he stayed up.

Even from behind the far revetments where the enemy was firing it was clear that this figure, sunk to its knees, rifle splayed beyond reach, was finished. He had so much about him of hesitation that it could be read at a mile. He did not want to go down, not because he didn't know that he was dying, but because to collapse so quickly did not seem right. Something was happening. Something had to happen. And it required that, for a while, even if they shot him because for them it seemed inappropriate that he would not collapse, he simply could not go down.

Life was, after all, timing. "Without doubt, all my patients will die," the surgeon had told him when reporting to the battalion, "the question is when." When to leave a dinner party, when to cast a fly, when to catch the eye of a woman and when to disengage. You would not stay locked, eye to eye, forever, so the disengage was just as important as the engage, and would in the end determine the beauty of the moment. The Germans firing at him to make him as neat as the others they had put down might not understand, but he had to stay up because it was like music. The song should not end too abruptly. He wasn't ready for the last notes, which would come as he lay on the pavement, soon enough, and to do justice to the music he had to stay on his knees. How strange for a man on his knees to be an emblem of defiance.

It would have been defiance if, swaying slightly, he had held his position for the sake of the enemy, but it was hardly the enemy for whose sake he held. Something was happening, time was being knit up, sense was being made, chapters closed, chapters opened, visions of Charlotte rising.

In June he had proposed to his division commander, albeit informally at tennis, that his paratroops, if not all others, be equipped with flotation bladders. "With what?" the general had responded, in a way that meant that the proposal had been spoken in vain. Alliances are difficult to run, officers to influence. Millions die because bureaucracies are naturally immobile. Because bureaucracies are naturally immobile, families perish, lines end, names vanish, hopes expire.

"Flotation bladders for paratroops?"

"Yes, sir. West to east, from Normandy to Berlin, we'll have to cross countless rivers, and we would be much better off if each man could swim with his weapons and ammunition. Where there are neither boats nor bridges, we would be able to surprise the enemy with unexpected crossings, and we could avoid being trapped against water obstacles."

The general took some more scotch. "How much would these 'flotation bladders' weigh?"

"Less than a pound. Collapsed, they would be about the size of several pairs of socks."

"I'm sorry. That small addition to each kit would require subtraction from the division of thousands of pounds of ammunition, food, or medical supplies, for an advantage that is hypothetical at best. Can't do it." Then they volleyed in the hot sun.

South of the Utrechtseweg and the Onderlangs was a bridgeless curve of the Rhine that made one of the natural walls of what quickly became known as "the sack." The other natural wall was the hill to the north, and it and the river narrowed the sack to the east. The Germans had laid their defenses on all sides but the western entrance: south across the river, in a brick works; north on the hillside; and east at the neck. Right in the center of these fields of fire ran the Utrechtseweg, where he would die.

But had the battalion been able to float across the Rhine, to the west of the sack, they could have outflanked the Germans at the brick works and come from behind at the neck. They would not have had to die in such great number. Nor would they have been stalled, or driven back. Because there were many piers, no one would have had to swim more than six hundred feet, and even without the piers the river was nowhere more than a thousand feet wide. One of the placid visions he had as he rested upon his knees on the pavement of the Utrechtseweg, a curiosity of not falling, was of float-ing. It was as if it had happened and he were remembering it; that is, silently, delicately, floating across the Rhine, sometimes twirling, fully laden, pushed west by the flow, at the head of three-quarters of his battalion now that the colonel had been killed.

He knew from the way the battle had unfolded that had they been able to float they would not have been detected; that, emerging on the south bank, they would have been able to rout the Germans; and that they would have lived. He would have lived. Charlotte would not have been left alone in a world still overwhelmed by war, nor in war's difficult aftermath. He knew it, and had known it even at the tennis court at Aldershot, and as he stood on his knees upon the Utrechtseweg it broke his heart that he had not been able to make a better argument at tennis, that he had not pressed, that he had not brought it up again, that he had not been more socially promi-nent, or of a higher rank. For thus, in all these ways, he had failed Charlotte.

But, then, the men around him who would die that day had failed their children, too. For the sake of one's child, one was supposed to be able to ac-complish superhuman feats. That was the universal story arisen from the universal will, but it was not so any more than that animals can save their offspring or themselves from slaughter, or prisoners always escape, or par-ents take every precaution, or soldiers live through every battle.

A momentary cessation of fire surrounded the major with quiet as he rested on his knees on the Utrechtseweg. Three men who had ignored his signs not to come for him lay dead just beyond his reach, or he would have touched them gently. Scores of others—his captains, his lieutenants, and the ranks—watched from cover. Some cried from pity and frustration. Some were angry at the enemy for using their major as bait. And almost to a man, except for those new to the battalion, they remembered a parade the sum-mer before the summer that had just passed, when Charlotte, who still lived with her father, had decided to cut quickly across the parade ground be-cause, although several battalions were drawn up and waiting, the general had yet to arrive and was nowhere in sight.

Among many of the hundreds of men in his battalion, who saw her most often, and the thousands in other formations, who glimpsed her on occasion, she was regarded with a protective tenderness that could transcend even the most rapacious and brutal natures. Most of these men were very close to her age: they saw her as a sister. Others, who were older but not yet old enough to have children of their own, or at least not children of her age, thought of her nonetheless as a daughter.

She was the daughter of this regiment, the child of the battalion, and each man was respectful and protective. And when Charlotte—nearsighted, physically ungraceful, and nervous—dashed across the parade ground rather than spend fifteen minutes skirting it with a heavy load of books in her arms, she tripped and fell forward. All the books, their pages opening like wings, flew from her like released doves, and as they and the contents of her purse landed in a jumble spread out hopelessly before her, she, too, fell to her knees in shock, and her round, thick spectacles, with gold rims the color of her hair, were knocked from her face.

Her father, who had often seen her fall, and suffered the pain of a father who sees his child fall many times more than she should, instantly ran to her. The faster he could reach her and get her on her feet, the less her embarrassment, the quicker it would be over, perhaps the fewer twitters in the vast assemblage of men who, now perfectly turned out, seemed in contrast to be perfectly graceful. But he was unable to reach her, for a dozen men had fallen out of line and blocked his way. Surrounding the fallen Charlotte, they lifted her up, gathered her books, and offered encouraging words.

Though her father could not see, she accepted these attentions with the preternaturally endearing quality that had drawn them in the first place, and, flustered and embarrassed, went on her way. But within seconds, she fell again. Every heart went out to her, and this time the escort that came to her aid walked with her—as if the prime minister had been walking in the East End after a bombing raid—and saw her across the parade ground and to the street, while the formations looked on. As Charlotte disappeared among the trees flanking the road, the parade was perfectly silent, ordered, and content.

These were the men who witnessed her father's refusal to drop further than his knees on the Utrechtseweg. For him—and for Charlotte—three had already given their lives in trying to fetch him back. And after his unequivocal order, if only by sign, that no more were to try, they were willing and they wanted to, but they were good soldiers and, understanding him exactly, they watched, knowing that it could not be long.

The force of balance that had kept him on his knees had left him: a strong breeze could have blown him down, and he stayed up merely by the grace of circumstance. He swayed slightly, with the alarming disconnectedness of a tree that has been cut all the way through and moves at first minutely in one direction and then minutely in another, as if realizing that it is about to fall but, never having fallen, does not know how.

He looked up, throwing his head back to take in the sky for the last time. Clouds at a high and windy altitude passed by as if to avoid the war on the ground. Though the sky was blue, bits of paper and ash floated in the air like snow. It seemed natural that the town was burning. For years, as London had burned at close and common intervals, raining ash was something quite ordinary.

The honor of toppling him was taken by a German soldier who, objecting perhaps to the incongruous, plinthlike shape rising from the flatness of the Utrechtseweg, fired a bullet into his back. As it passed through his left shoulder, the impact spun him around and sent him to the pavement.

His men made sharp gestures and showed on their faces the painful expressions that acknowledged his death. But they had to attend to their own survival and to the fight. His death would be the turning point. They would go no farther, and the Utrechtseweg would be abandoned.

But he was not dead. He was lying flat and facedown on the pavement, looking at his right hand, which was covered with dried blood from having been pressed to his abdomen after he had first been shot, and had now curled around something invisible, as if from the muscle tone that still remained, that, ordinarily, when he slept, curled his fingers around something nonexistent.

Now he felt no pain, having passed the apprehension of pain some minutes before while still on his knees. Though the life was draining from him, he felt comfortable, giddy, and grateful. He thought of the civilians on the Utrechtseweg to the west of Arnhem, who had met the masses of nervous British soldiers as if the battle were already over, offering flowers and pitchers of milk. The children had had patches of orange cloth pinned to their clothing. People danced. The British had been happy but uneasy. They had begged the civilians to go back to shelter, but had been unable to turn down their hospitality or disapprove of their joy. After the German snipers had opened fire, as was inevitable, the Dutch had scattered, and three paratroopers had died.

How the holy and the profane mix in the light of day and at the end of life is sometimes the most beautiful thing in this world and a compassionate entry into the next. After failure and defeat, a concentration upon certain beauties, though forever lost and unretrievable, can lift the wounded past woundedness and the dying past dying, protecting them with an image, still and bright, that will ride with them on their long ride, never to fade and never to retreat.

When Charlotte was not yet two, she had mounted a step to reach the top of a small Christmas tree in front of the fireplace. In little velvet pumps, white tights, and a red dress, she had reached out with her right hand to touch a ribbon at the crown of the tree. Her left arm hung straight down for balance, hand pressed against her thigh. Very proud of how high she was, she had turned to her father and mother, fear gone, in triumph and joy. Her smile was evident as much in her eyes as in the smile itself. How he loved her. He had always loved her. He would always love her. She was there with him on the Utrechtseweg, and yet she was protected and safe. He closed his right hand with great tenderness, for this was now all he could move, his last embrace of the little girl in the red dress, and it was as if he really were embracing her, as if she were there.

Down by St. Elizabeth's, up from the river and toward the museum, and just beyond where the Utrechtseweg parts from the Onderlangs, he died with the vision of his daughter Charlotte in his eyes.

Last Tea with the Armorers

IT SEEMED TO THE INSTRUCTRESS that the tall, red-haired Australian in her class would never, could never, properly pronounce a single word of Hebrew, and so she began with unusual care for the sound of things. "Let's start," she said, "with the place where we find ourselves. The first word is not pronounced, as it is spelled, like the English word *bat,* but, rather, like the name of the currency of Thailand. Who can tell me what that is?"

Although the Canadians, Americans, South Africans, and British in the class did not know, the Australian did, and he pronounced it perfectly—perhaps not perfectly in Thai, but perfectly in Hebrew: "*Baht,*" he said, shyly.

"Very good," said the instructress, beginning to relax. "*Baht,* with a deep *a* and a partially sibilant *t,* slightly elided to the next word. And the next word is *Gallim,* the *l-l-i-m* of which are pronounced as are the *l-e-a-m* in the English word *gleam,* as in *the gleam of the waves at Bat Gallim.*"

She made the class say, first individually and then in unison, "the gleam of the waves at Bat Gallim, the gleam of the waves at Bat Gallim . . . the gleam of the waves at Bat Gallim."

"What does Bat Gallim mean?" asked a Canadian girl.

"*Waves,*" said the Australian, pronouncing the word almost like *wives.*

"Wives?" the Canadian girl asked.

"That's right," the Australian answered, "daughter of the waves," but, as he pronounced it, "daughter of the wives."

"Waves," the teacher said, correcting the Australian not in Hebrew, which he had pronounced perfectly, but in his own language. "And, yes, I suppose you could say, most poetically, that it means daughter of the waves."

Most poetically, it did. The waves never ceased to unravel upon the beaches and beneath the seawalls of Bat Gallim, having been unfurled across the Mediterranean along its entire length from Gibraltar to the cliffs of the Levant. The strong west wind that brought them from the Atlantic left them as they broke, to vault the coastal mountains and drive for the deserts of Iraq. Once abandoned, the waves retreated in silence and shock, rocking as if in puzzlement, sparkling, foaming, and then subsiding into the deep green waters over which new waves glided for shore.

At Bat Gallim, anything new soon was made old by the sea. Salt air was more brutal to concrete than were mortar rounds or naval cannon. Other than sea and sky, the only things colorfast, fresh, and young were flowers and palms. These were especially exuberant upon the mall of Avenue Bat Gallim in its two short blocks from Rehov Ha-Aliya to the sea. The sun only made them brighter and the salt wind only made them sway, and at night under the stars they lost their special affinity for brightness and color, to become merely mysterious and sweet.

Villas with terra-cotta roofs held the promontory of Bat Gallim like a beachhead. They had been built in the main by German Jews who, unable to leave Europe behind, settled a few strides from where they had stepped off the boat, on the sea side of the railroad tracks, separated from the city of Haifa, from the country itself, from the land that was the gate to the East.

ANNALISE UNDERSTOOD that Bat Gallim was forgotten and compact, a world unto itself, even with an ocean. It had been her home since 1947, when, at the age of nine, a starved child whose eyes sat in her face like foxes' eyes, like moons or marbles, she had walked there from the port, holding her father's hand.

They had been so used to internment and waiting that they assumed their stay next to the sea would be short, and that they would then be trucked inland to a place in the Jordan Valley or the Galilee, or perhaps to Jerusalem itself. It did not seem likely that one could live out a whole life in the vestibule. But it was to the vestibule that they were assigned and in the vestibule where they were left.

An apartment had opened up a few days before their arrival. Two rooms on the top floor of an old villa on Rehov Avdimi, with a small terrace and a view of the sea, it had been furnished with British officers' camp chairs and tables left behind in the phased withdrawal, and in the kitchen the Jewish Agency had left a case of grapefruit for the father and daughter who had lived in a world where a human life was worth less than an orange.

"How long will we remain?" Annalise's father had asked the man from the Jewish Agency, who was about to give them the keys.

This man, who had watched his two charges look upon the grapefruit as if it were a gift of God, lifted his shoulders and let them fall. He was darkly sunburned and dressed in khakis, and from the wall behind him came the reflected sound of the surf. "Until you want to go someplace else," he said, and then, touching Annalise's cheek, "until she marries a kibbutznik with blue shorts and a hoe welded to his shoulder."

"I don't understand," Annalise's father had said. "Whose apartment is it?"

"Until recently it belonged to a woman who went to Degania Aleph to live with her children. Now it's yours. In a week or two you'll get the papers."

"But we haven't paid for it."

The Jewish Agency man looked at the father and daughter and his eyes dropped to their arms. The father was in long sleeves, but a Shield of David and a number were plainly visible on the child's arm. Though, as she grew, the lines of the tattoos would soften and break, they were now as solid and intense as if they had been done the day before.

"Haven't you?" he asked.

PERHAPS it would have been better to go inland, to leave behind the sound of the waves, where Annalise thought she could hear her mother's voice, and exchange their constant murmur for the mystery of a tall grove of palms in the silence of the desert floor, or for fields of wheat, or terraced hillsides of ancient olive trees. At least they would not have had a painful second grief in a room of unceasing echoes, where, suddenly, one part of the story was over, and where with their abrupt lack of movement came the death of the illusion that when finally they would settle they would be as they were when last they were settled: a father, his wife, and two children—a little girl and a baby boy. The infant had gone in his mother's arms while the girl had clung fearfully to her father, overlooked. For almost a year she had been hidden behind planks in a coal bin at the factory, fed what could be carried in a clenched fist.

Had they gone inland or had they even just crossed the railroad tracks and risen into the loveliness of the Hadar, everything would have been different. Bat Gallim, however, was like a pool in a river where water is trapped as if by nothing more than the exclusionary speed of the current in the main channel. As the wall of water flows by, the water in the pool circles in hypnotic distraction.

In 1972, a quarter of a century after their arrival, when Annalise was thirty-four and her father in his seventies, they still lived in the same small set of rooms, now impossible to leave because of its perfect familiarity.

Annalise's father was the night watchman in the language academy, where the tall red-haired Australian had surprised everyone, and not least himself, with an astonishing gift for languages. He had entered the program at the beginning of August, and by the middle of September could speak Hebrew with passable fluency in any accent he chose—the sonorous dialect of the radio announcer, the flat, oscillating whine of Russian, the unbearable tension of Arabic, the archival self-caress of French—even Irish, Swedish, or Turkish.

"You should see the Australian boy," Annalise's father said to her as they were eating dinner on their small terrace looking over the empty beach and the evening's undeflected waves. In the heat of September, Annalise had put out tomatoes, cucumbers, cheese, herring, pita, and a pitcher of seltzer with ice, lemons, and strawberries. "We watch the news now. He can understand the news in Hebrew, and have a discussion afterward. Six weeks ago he didn't know an aleph from an ayin."

Annalise nodded, as if to say it was impressive, while at the same time saying as little as possible. She looked down at her plate, still a beautiful Mediterranean still life, and resolved not to add to it even one more tomato. She was extraordinarily disciplined, and permanently heavyset. Though she would not allow herself to gain weight and was lean from swimming laps every day, she was heavyset and big-boned—two very unbecoming phrases for the unbecoming—and that was the way it was. Although no picture of her mother existed, her father had described the mother to his daughter so painstakingly and so often that the daughter had an image to keep clearly and loyally until death, after which there would not be in the world even a memory by description—much less a body, a portrait, or even a notion of a resting place—of this woman whom she had loved above all else, whom she herself remembered imprecisely only because her overwhelming love had blurred the details except as they were redrawn for her by her father.

Annalise's mother had been as graceful as a dancer. Anything she wore would drape over her with the beauty of form one might see in a painting—cloth falling as relaxedly as water—and her flesh would never press the fabric uncomfortably, as with Annalise, making it a gauge of her discontent.

And although Annalise lay in bed perfectly disciplined and hungry, and although she swam a kilometer every afternoon, and in the morning spent three-quarters of an hour at calisthenics (a habit since her first army service), she had nevertheless to contend with what she termed "that damnable and indelible pear shape." She was by no means homely. She was not in any way homely. She was, in fact, almost pretty.

"And then we sit on the porch and talk, mostly in Hebrew," her father said, "but sometimes in English. Usually at this point my English is better than their Hebrew, but his Hebrew is now better than my own. And he doesn't work that hard. He's in the sea half the day. He goes far into the sea. Australians and Americans always swim past the buoy, out to where the ships are. I see them from the terrace while you're at work. From a distance they look like seals, or seabirds. They're not afraid of the sea, as are Europeans." He reached for more bread. It was through him that she had inherited the damnable pear shape. Even if, as a man, he did not have to be pear-shaped himself, his mother, Annalise's grandmother, had been wondrously pear-shaped.

"He's thirty-six years old, has a degree in chemical engineering, and has never been married." And then, as if to apologize on behalf of the Australian, her father said, "In Australia there aren't many jobs in chemical engineering, which is why he came here."

"You mean he was unemployed," Annalise said.

"He had a job, but in a different field."

"What was he, a kangaroo trainer?"

"He was in aeronautics."

"What does that mean, 'He was in aeronautics'?"

"He worked at the airport."

"Doing what?"

"He was in baggage systems. Chemical engineering is concerned with the flow of materials in timed processes and streams, just like moving baggage around a terminal. He redesigned the baggage-handling system at the airport in Sydney. He says what they had was truly awful and stupid."

"I see. Did they put his plan into practice?"

"They refused. It's what pushed him finally to emigrate. You know, people usually move to Australia, not from it."

"And in the years between his chemical-engineering degree and his departure, what did he do?"

"He was a baggage handler. What's wrong with that? I'm a night watchman."

"You were broken," Annalise said. "You have every right, and God's leave, to do or not to do as you please. How can ambition mean anything for you, or for me? But for him! It's not that it's important. It's that the lack of it is more important—as a sign. I don't want to marry a failed baggage handler, failed chemical engineer, who is a refugee from a rich, peaceful, democratic country. They're all—over there—there's something wrong with them. We came here because we had to. They're sick with discontent."

"Marry? Who said marry? Why do young people always jump to conclusions?"

"You do want me to marry, don't you?"

"Of course I do, and it's not too late."

"But, still," Annalise said, "it's almost a matter of minutes."

. . .

SOMETIMES THE TRAINS that ran on the track separating Bat Gallim from the rest of Haifa were lines of passenger cars that rattled lightly as they went by, generating a Swiss sound that spoke of precision and containment. And sometimes military trains thundered along under the weight of a hundred tanks chained down to a mile of flatcars. The mass of armor moving resolutely through the night—to confound Russian satellites, convoys traveled mainly in darkness—shook the ground of Bat Gallim, rattled windows, crockery, and doors, echoed in the lungs, and left behind the kind of deafening silence that even the birds were reluctant to break, although eventually they always did.

Of all the people in Bat Gallim, the Australian was the most distracted by the trains, because his room at the language academy was the habitation closest to the track bed. Beyond the window was a six-foot strip of ground over which a set of clotheslines was suspended from two pipe frames. Almost touching them was a chain-link fence, and on the other side of this the crushed rock that lay beneath the railroad ties pressed like a pile of coins spilling from a sack. The western rail of the Haifa–Tel Aviv line was no more than ten feet from the Australian's head as he sat at his desk. When armor trains went by, with sentries perched unhappily on the backs of half-tracks and in the hatches of tanks, everything in the room—and that was precious little—vibrated and tried to escape, like the contents of a household coming alive in terror during an earthquake.

He had to hold his glasses on his face, which always made him smile, and to catch his pen before it rolled to the edge of the desk and flipped into the void like a naval commando deploying at sea from a speeding rubber boat. He wore glasses except when he was in the surf, when the pleasure of the sun and the waves was accompanied by a nearsightedness that abstracted color and light.

And as if the ten-foot separation of his senses from the massive wheels of many trains was not enough, he shared the room with a psychotic Soviet Georgian Jew who could not survive on air untainted by tobacco smoke. This thin, apelike, crazy creature with eyes that sparkled like lights, and three or four knives hidden upon his person at all times, was never not smoking. Sleep for him was a torture, a nightmare, and a poison, because as he slept he had to breathe real air.

The Australian not only did not smoke but recoiled from the smell of cigarettes, and could stay in the room only when the Georgian was unconscious or away. They hated one another, and every moment was tense, the Georgian's knives balanced exactly against the Australian's pure strength.

When he could not study in an empty classroom and was not out on the sea, the Australian sat under the clothesline, six feet from the track, so he could breathe. In the late summer of '72, and especially after the Munich massacre, a great deal of armor moved on the rails. Studying in the glare of a sodium-vapor light, pausing every few minutes to do pull-ups on the clothesline crossbars, the Australian would often be incapacitated by the passage of a train. The fury made him as helpless as when he was taken by a breaking wave. In both cases, he knew to stay loose, to wait, and to keep track of his tumbling so that at the end of one ordeal he would be ready for the next.

In the waves, he was upended and thrown forward with the onrush of the water. And as he sat under the clothesline, overcome by the thunder of the train, he was still except for his shaking. But whether in the sea or by the rails, the message of helplessness was the same. There are forces, it seemed to say, that work upon you, that you cannot fight. And yet when the wave played itself out or the train departed, he gathered his strength and his wits, and he began to fight once again.

He was an honest man, and he knew he had been a failure. But he was only thirty-six, and he felt that he had a small window of light in which to make good.

WHEN ANNALISE WAS FIFTEEN, her father had told her, with a matter-of-factness meant to discipline his great distress, of his insistence that after his death his body be burned and the ashes spread on the sea.

A secondary-school student in a blue sweater, she was tall and awkward, the kind of girl whom one suspects will grow out of a stark adolescence to become a great beauty: it sometimes happens. After her father's declaration—a letter would not have allowed him to comfort her—she remained composed, as if she herself were an old man who had seen everything, done everything, and was easily able to bear the rest.

"It's against Jewish law," she said, dead calm, voice flat.

"It isn't in my nature to do such a thing. Or at least it wasn't. But your mother and your brother, you see—we presume—were . . . were carried to the crematoria, and with millions of others they perished in the flames. Whole generations of Jews knew this at the end. Jewish law or not, it will be an honor to follow them."

"But what if it's true," Annalise asked, "and God raises the dead? What then?"

"Annalise, if God can raise the dead, He can undoubtedly reconstitute them even if they have dissolved on the wind. And if He cannot, then that's just the point: I want exactly the destiny of your mother and my baby son, whatever that was. And, other than your happiness, it is the only thing I want."

Annalise, in whose large eyes now were the beginnings of tears, maintained her own discipline, as always, and asked, "How do you go about such a thing, in this country?"

There were ways, and he revealed them, but the hardest part would be left to her. "I'm not sure of the physics exactly," he said, "but most of me will travel upward on a bloom of heat, translucent and light, separated into molecules and perhaps even atoms—you'd have to ask a chemist. I will rise into the air in utter helplessness, hopelessly dispersed. And whatever happens is what I want.

"You will be given my ashes. The best place for them is the sea. The beach at Hof HaCarmel is empty and clean, and it's very windy there."

"Papa," Annalise said, "I'll be alone."

"I only tell you this now, Annalise, in case something happens. I plan to hold on until long after you've married and had children of your own. I want to see them. It's very important to me. Perhaps a grandchild, a young man strong and new, can swim out and do this, while you and the rest of your family watch from the shore. You won't be alone. You mustn't be alone."

After this, Annalise would sometimes wonder about the air from the chimneys, whether fine particles of ash rose in the rivers of heat, how far into the crown of the sky they ascended, and if they would, perhaps, sparkle and shine in the sun.

And she wondered also about the ashes and bone that would be scattered on the waves. These she knew would always sparkle, would be kept in motion by the rocking of the sea, and lifted in spray. And the smallest of particles would work their way across the oceans until, eventually, in the evening of the world, they would roll with every wave and break with every whitecap.

ANNALISE was the microscopist at Rambam Hospital in Bat Gallim. Neither a pathologist, a histologist, nor a bacteriologist, she was essential to all three, and she found her knowledge deepening and expanding as medical technology changed to accommodate the advance of medicine toward chemistry and physics.

Because she was meticulous and disciplined, the hospital never failed to elevate, train, and promote her, until, it seemed, in just a few years her position would be similar, though inferior, to that of a department head. She was to the practice of medicine what a sergeant major is to the practice of arms—absolutely necessary, independent, inviolate, and able to retain his position while speaking his mind like a prophet. She was there to stay, and she saw certain parts of the future quite as clearly as others were obscured. The central path that lay before her was the same as it had been when she started. The basics would never call for more than a fine optical microscope and skill in preparing slides. But the road branched off on two other planes. One was electron microscopy, and the other was computerization, for not only was electron microscopy ripe for conversion to a digital format, but even observations in lesser powers cried out for it.

In a decade, or two, or three, she judged, she would be able to store images, view them in multiple dimensions, catalog, compare, and enhance them, all via digital encoding. This meant travel abroad for specialized training. And there lay the problem. She had flatly turned down a fellowship in electron microscopy in Germany. No one at Rambam could think for a moment that this was in any way untoward. They would not expect a woman with the badge of Majdanek to take training in Germany, for now in their prime among the staffs of German hospitals and research institutes, and in the professoriate, would doubtless be former members of the SS, former troops of the *Einsatzgruppen,* and those whose crimes still lay in their onetime satisfaction that children and their parents had been led to slaughterhouses more terrible than the slaughterhouses for animals.

But when the fellowship would come up in Baltimore, London, Tokyo, or Boston, she would also have to say no. Although neither her career nor her livelihood would be destroyed, she would be held back, frozen in place. These fellowships offered transportation, living quarters, every service of adjustment, and, for an Israeli, immense sums of hard currency. She was intensely curious about the development of the new machines. But she would have to say no.

She could not leave her father. Though he would beg her to go, protest that he would thrive in her absence, and even shout at her when she refused, she could not leave him. He had no one else, only the students at the language academy, whom he knew for six months before they finished their course. And they, in their lessened state, the newest of new immigrants, confused, tongue-tied, and emotionally overwrought, befriended him because they had fallen. When finally they crossed the tracks and left Bat Gallim behind, they would forget him.

They might remember his night-watchman's cap, a tea-colored British officer's hat with a green band the color of a fly's compound eye or the fronds of a date palm in the sun after a rainstorm. They might remember his slight tremor and that he radiated a feeling of age, his slow movements, his undisguised pleasure in their youth, his patience for them. But, then, when they thought of him in years out, they would undoubtedly say, "Oh, I wonder if he's still alive. He was a nice man. He's probably dead."

She could not leave him, not even for six months, he who held her slight body in his arms for hour after hour after hour, in the times when children her age should have been skipping or jumping or lost in games, and she could not be. He had held her beyond all patience, so that she could feel his heartbeat, and sleep on his chest, and awake, and fall asleep again, knowing that when she awoke he would still be there.

This, he had been told, was wrong. The child needed help after what she had been through and all she had seen. "No," he answered. "All she needs is to know that her father will not be taken from her. If it means a year or two of absolute reassurance, then that is what it will be. If it means I have to be next to her like a penguin father with an egg on his foot, then that's what it means, and that's what I'll do."

In far less than a year, when she understood that he would not leave her, no matter what, that he would stay in the apartment all day with her, and hold her hand when they went out to shop, that he was entirely devoted and that he would stick to his task, if necessary, until he died, she healed. And she became independent and strong earlier than would have been expected.

How could she, then, leave him? He was not her husband, and could not go with her abroad, even though she still lived with him and took care of him. She could leave him only when it would be right to do so, when it would be necessary, perfect, and expected, when her leaving would be as if she were floating away in a cloud of benevolence. When she had a husband.

"WHY HAVEN'T YOU BEEN MARRIED?" her father asked the Australian.

The Australian brought his outstretched thumb to his solar plexus, widened his eyes, and said, "Me?"

"Yes, you. Why? Why?"

"You know, I've already been asked that around here," the Australian said, "in Bat Gallim."

"Who asked you?"

"At the beach, the Moroccan who rents folding chairs. I would never rent a folding chair—I'm either in the water or standing while I get dry. The beach is not a couch. Well, he asked me. I suppose he wanted to find out why I don't rent beach chairs, so he said, 'Do you have children?' and I said, 'What? Me?' and he said, 'Don't you fuck well?' That's *Atah lo dofek tov?* Right?"

"Right," answered Annalise's father.

"And I said, 'I'm not married.' And he said, 'Why? *Atah lo dofek tov?*' Come to think of it, a lot of people—a lot—ask me the same question. And I've never answered it directly. I suppose if I had, I'd be married now, wouldn't I?"

"Maybe. Why don't you answer it?"

"Now?"

"Why not?"

"All right." He swallowed, cast suddenly into the kind of self-analysis that he, as an Australian, an athlete, and an engineer, was not fond of and wanted to put behind him quickly.

"Well," he said, "I suppose I could make excuses, couldn't I? I could say that I didn't get married in college. Did I? No. I didn't. I was too young. Then I was in the army for two years, and I didn't get married then, either. Then I was in graduate school for five years. Oh, yes. When I finished, I was thirty. My father died soon after. I didn't take it easily: I lost interest in things. That's when I went to work at the airport. I wanted to be still, as it were, for a while. I can't say why that while stretched into five years. And now I'm here. I could say all that."

"Is that what you would say?"

"No."

"Why?"

"Because it wouldn't be the truth. And the truth is, I look sort of like a chipmunk, you know. . . ."

Annalise's father did not know what a chipmunk was, in English, at least, which was how the Australian had had to say it, as he himself did not know the word in Hebrew, and Annalise's father had thought the Australian had said he looked like a monkey. The old man closed his eyes and sadly shook his head from side to side, saying, "A monkey. A monkey," which was his way of saying, You *don't* look like a monkey.

The Australian, amazed, but still in good humor, went on. "I always thought I looked quite a bit like a chipmunk," he said, "but, all right, I'll take your word for it, a monkey. And I'm shy. Whenever women have been interested in me—what I mean to say is 'in love'—I can't believe it. I realize only long after the fact, when they're gone, long after I might have responded, which is perfectly sensible, isn't it? Why would any woman be interested in me?

"That's why I'm not married. It's simple. I've never believed that anyone would want to marry me."

. . .

ANNALISE HAD BEEN in the army in one form or another for sixteen years, and this, her fourteenth year of reserve duty, was to be the last. She had finished training and entered upon active service just in time for the Sinai Campaign of 1956. She had been called up for the June War, had served in the War of Attrition, and all the times between, when she would return to the army for however many weeks it demanded each year. But after thirty-four she would be free. On the ninth day of October 1972, she would be released at six p.m. and never have to go back.

Rambam took casualties from the north, and it would have made sense for Annalise to serve there in a medical unit. The army, however, reserved the right to be illogical, and she had always done reserve duty as a clerk in a transport unit in Bat Gallim. This was neither an honor nor a dishonor. The transport of soldiers to or upon the battlefield is just as important as their care after they are wounded, and perhaps more important, if only because a battle won quickly and decisively does more to heal casualties—in preventing them—than the best of hospitals.

The depot was off Ha-Aliya, not far from the language academy. She had come to know its shaded yards, its tin roofs, its trees, and its sheds so well that she needed them. Though perhaps falsely, their idiosyncratic rhythms and physical dreariness promised permanence. Even in summer, it was dark and cool in the cavernous garages and windowless armory where thousands of weapons lay—heavy, black, and oiled—on steel racks, remembering, poised, and eager for war, for only when war came would they leap from their rests and be rushed out into the wind and sunlight.

In winter, rays of orange sun so rarely struck the counter at which Annalise worked that when they did everyone came to look, as if at an eclipse. In winter, the rain beat upon the tin roofs so loudly that the clerks and armorers had to shout to be heard, it was so cold that everyone was draped in blankets, and the smell of kerosene burning in floor stoves overrode the scents of gun oil and gasoline. In each stove the armature glowed like the sun as invisible vapors burned around it.

Annalise and Shoshanna—a young woman so beautiful that half of life was closed to her, as she was always the object, and never the observer—worked together to keep the records. Their registry was the literary repository of jeeps and half-tracks, tanks and recoilless rifles, submachine guns and fuel tankers, water trailers and field kitchens. All these inanimate things had an inflow of parts and a history of checks and maintenance. Done in Annalise's splendid hand, and then in Shoshanna's seductive scrawls that, once, Annalise had seen a mechanic bend to kiss, the records filled ledger after ledger on a wall of shelves.

This work the size of an encyclopedia would never be read, and it proceeded according to its own strategy, as if it were alive. But nonetheless the two clerks—one who excited men like a drug, the other almost invisible to men—labored carefully to make their writing beautiful. After all, not that far back in their families were scribes like those of Sfat and Jerusalem who worked not to make something permanent, or vainly so, like stone, but who labored because, as they did, nearly motionless, eyes riveted, thoughts disciplined, pen tip rolling across the page like a boat on the waves, they felt the presence of God.

Annalise could take down a volume and see in handwriting that was on occasion her own and more often that of other clerks, both regular and reserve, something like the hypnotic work that adorned Asian temples, or the eye-crossing design of an Iranian mosque. It was not decoration to which the religious craftsmen were devoted, but rhythms and intervals that, with practice, could shut out the earthly life.

Even Shoshanna knew, Shoshanna who, Annalise understood, was so beautiful that she was sexually infatuated with herself. This, in turn, put men in an almost uncontrollable state. Annalise found the delirium that Shoshanna inspired difficult to fathom, as she was never the object but always the observer. In anything but desire she was far happier than her friend, but in the presence of her friend, desire seemed to take up all the space in the world. The armorers in particular were intoxicated with Shoshanna, and at the four o'clock break when they, the mechanics, and the clerks gathered for tea, sparks flew. They fought among themselves sometimes, or seemed as dejected as mental patients, or breathed like wounded animals. Perhaps it was that they were almost all conscripts, and therefore both young and unduly confined. Or perhaps it was that they spent their mornings and afternoons pumping cleaning rods back and forth in the slick oiled barrels of the weapons in their charge. No matter what the reason, at four o'clock they were fierce.

But never for Annalise, who was too old, too incisive, and not quite pretty. They tried to use her to get to Shoshanna.

"Annalise," one once said, "you and Shoshanna must get so cold being still all the time, and, with your hands so full of ink, do you take a shower at the end of the day?"

"Ask Shoshanna," Annalise had snapped, although she would indeed have loved to have been under a warm shower even with that young armorer, had he embraced her with something even vaguely close to love. But he wouldn't have had it in him, because, among other things, he hadn't had the courage to ask Shoshanna the question meant for her.

Tea with the armorers, however, was something that Annalise always liked. They were men, after all, and not a single one was married. For years, even after Shoshanna came, Annalise had looked forward to her reserve duty for this, and other reasons, because the men with whom she associated at the hospital had families, and by the stove in the armory she found flirtation and youth, things that were closing off in her life, and the liveliness of sexual embarrassment and shame, and what she could imagine, briefly, might take place on the empty beaches south of Haifa.

It would all end on the ninth of October, when even the army would admit that she was too old.

ANNALISE'S FATHER ROSE from the dinner table and stepped to the rail of the terrace. "Look," he said, "the season is over, and he's out in the distance, like a seal. Perhaps it is a seal." He went to get his binoculars, leaving Annalise, seemingly annoyed, to eat alone.

The light, which changes more by the sea than anywhere else, had moved into the autumnal tranquillity of October. Even in summer the north light that spreads out upon the sea off Haifa is sober and deep, a courtly lover of color that quietly brings out its richest hues. But in the fall, the light is greatest as it struggles with shadow, of which there is suddenly so much that the beaches empty even though the water is warm.

Only the old women whom everyone called the whales would stay down at the beach, in their usual position, sitting at the water's edge so that the waves ran up their legs and around their balloonlike buttocks, burying them slowly in the sand like the foundations of a pier. For some reason, they wore rubber bathing caps for this ritual, though not a drop of foam ever touched their hair.

"It's him," Annalise's father said, focusing. "Come see."

"I saw," Annalise said.

"Look close up," her father insisted, as people do when they have binoculars (and then they won't give them to you).

She sighed in irritation, but, to humor him and because it certainly seemed safe to glance at someone almost a mile away, out at sea, beyond reach, she took the binoculars.

Lifting them to her eyes, she began to turn the focus wheel even before the eyepieces made contact with her face: she knew how different her father's vision was from her own.

At first she saw only a blur of empty sea, crystalline in the barrels of the binoculars, the motion of the waves nauseating in and out of focus. Then, as she turned the wheel, she began to see the lines we tend to forget are in water, the shapes, the patches, and the texture.

The sky came level at the horizon and she now had her bearings, sweeping like the ray from the Stella Maris Light, slewing like the guns of one of her armorers. She caught him, she inadvertently swept past, returned, and locked him in.

"He doesn't look like a monkey," Annalise said. "He doesn't look like a monkey at all."

"That's what I told him."

Annalise hesitated for a moment, a moment that because of its brevity she knew would be entirely private. The Australian was sitting astride an air mattress, riding the swells. His body was hard and muscular. Even from a great distance she could see the changing definition of his shoulders, arms, and abdomen as he moved to stay balanced. He kept his back straight and his head erect as he and his air mattress swayed from the peaks to the troughs of the waves, and the wind sometimes blew spray at his face.

Annalise put down the binoculars, suddenly overcome with the same kind of slow pleasure she had sensed so strongly in her beautiful friend, Shoshanna.

"He's out there every day," her father said. "I'll find it interesting to see if he makes it to December."

ON SATURDAY, on her leave, Annalise's father made his own dinner, and at five o'clock she stood alone on the beach, in shadow, in a brisk wind. Refusing to shiver in the breeze, she kicked off her shoes, dropped her robe on the sand, and straightened as she entered the water.

Though she had expected the sea to be cold, it was far warmer than the air, and even the spray that tangled in her hair as she swam still held the warmth of six months of Middle Eastern sun. Soon she found herself in the belt of water between the chaos of the breaking waves and the wide, deepening sea. This narrow layer of green water was warmer and not as lonely as the blue. She knew that she would cross it quickly and that after she did she would no longer be able to hear the noises from shore. The wind would drown out the sound of the surf and of crows cawing rhythmically in palms on the quay.

In fear of the deep, of ships, of drowning, and of the wind that could silently sweep her away, she swam stiffly, with the tension of a trespasser. But as soon as she could no longer hear the surf and the crows, she relaxed, abandoning herself entirely to the sea. Her exertion, her arms reaching ahead in the water, and the huge rolling of glassy and gleaming waves brought her to a different world.

Though far from shore, the water seemed warmer and more buoyant. With Haifa compacted and Bat Gallim miniaturized, the sea was the master of the world. In less than half an hour she had come so close to the Australian that she could make out his face. She stopped swimming and let her feet sink as she surveyed the space before her.

He was very interested in the prospect of someone swimming to his station, particularly a woman, perhaps because no one had ever been out there with him except for a few Americans, and they had always accompanied him from the start.

He paddled toward her, and the waves did the rest, pushing them together with inexplicable rapidity. She could see his face quite clearly. He looked like a yeshiva boy, or maybe an unusual Englishman, an eccentric, an adolescent.

On the other hand, he looked strong and decisive, even if his history seemed to indicate otherwise. Something in his eyes and in the hard strength of his body said that he would come through like a man, that if he were a husband he would be faithful, that if he were a father he would be true.

When they were close enough, he asked, "Did you mean to swim out here?"

"Of course I did," she answered, smiling as she had never smiled in her life, a soft, alluring smile that shut out the past and had nothing in it but the possibilities of the future. Turning as red as a burn victim, he was for a while unable to speak.

"May I come onto the raft?" she asked.

"Come," he said, extending his arm. When she took it he held fast, giving her something solid and unmoving to hold as she pulled herself up.

"I suppose it's like being stuck in an elevator," she said, "but I won't be long."

"Stay as long as you'd like," he told her. "I was just about to go in, though it won't be dark for a while, and even if it were dark the lights on Mount Carmel can be seen for fifty miles at sea. We could always swim for the lights."

"What about the currents?" she asked, mindful of their distance from shore.

"Oh, the currents," he answered. "If they wanted, they could take us all the way to Al-Arish."

In, strangely enough, the most sexually provocative words she had ever uttered, and yet modestly, she said, "That would be very uncomfortable, wouldn't it?"

He didn't answer. Her smooth and solid limbs were still half in the water—as the raft bobbed on the swells, the sea would run up her thighs, and down, and when it sank deep into the crest of an oncoming wave the water went all the way up to the base of her neck, and then washed away, perfectly outlining her breasts in the wet tank top. Taking his eyes from her body, he surveyed her face. She was not the kind of woman for whom men would turn as they walked on the street, but in her expression were great beauty and grace. In her expression, in her imperfect, somewhat too heavy features, he could see experience, and suffering, and strength, and love.

A face like hers, if held differently, if set off by different eyes, if shaped by bitterness or greed, would not be beautiful. But the way she smiled was all beauty, suddenly, as if he were the first to see. Never had she been so buoyant or so lovely. Perhaps it was the sea. God knows what she took from the sea.

THE NEXT DAY, late in the afternoon when the light was heaviest with color, the Australian sat in a deserted classroom on the second floor of an academic building at the language academy. Looking toward the sea, the slopes of Mount Carmel to his left, he saw alley upon alley of palms and other trees of waxen leaves, filtering the beginnings of the sunset and slightly davening in the wind. Everything was green and rich and red.

In front of him lay a Hebrew notebook, in which he now had little interest and upon which he could not concentrate. Normally, he came in from the sea, redid his exercises and lessons so that he would know them with absolute certainty, and then pushed ahead. Not for an hour, but for four or five, he would read the newspapers in his new language, poetry, and even a textbook of chemical engineering, his dictionary well exercised, his notebook filling steadily.

He knew that within a year his fluency could be more than just a tour de force, that industries were developing with great momentum, that his skill might take him far. The place felt open. It was growing. People embarked upon new things, taking immense risks. Agricultural settlements lured in doctoral engineers and in six months were manufacturing transistors and medical instruments. Who knew what might happen?

But this was not why he was unable to concentrate. He was distracted, he thought, because, in the courtyard below, several classes were singing. For people who had just begun to learn the language, they sang with surprising beauty. Perhaps it was the acoustics, or the mix of voices of many different languages. Perhaps it was the presence of the sea, the metronome of the waves, the counterpoint of the surf. Perhaps it was the lightness they felt, having floated free from where they had been born, with few connections now except to things like the beauty of song.

He could not concentrate. He closed his books and removed his glasses. The music swelled below, a lovely, hopeful ballad, *"Ha Yom Yavoe,"* "The Day Will Come," and they sang it over and over again because it lent itself to subtle variations that they introduced to it in unison and almost as if by magic.

If he had anything at all, he had great discipline—physical, intellectual, and moral discipline. "Why is it that I can't concentrate?" he asked himself. "Why can't I?" Well, he knew.

As CLERKS, mechanics, and armorers broke for their tea they could hear the singing, at a distance, of *"Ha Yom Yavoe."* It crossed rooftops of corrugated iron and drifted through the palms, sweeter because, in the main, it was faint. As the vagaries of the breeze muted it or sometimes made it loud, the song itself, beyond its own rhythm and melody, had the rhythm and melody of the wind.

Annalise made the tea for the last time. She lit an army stove that was so black it would never get clean no matter what anyone did to it. And yet the flames that arose were as pure and blue as the most perfect sapphire. She filled a battered aluminum kettle with water from the Jordan, still sweet. As it boiled, she laid out several boxes of *petits beurres,* the milk, the lemons, and the sugar.

She cut the lemons with a short bayonet that lay on the board they used as a table, and threw a box of tea in the water just as it began to bubble. This was the army. They liked their tea black and boiled, scalding and heavily sugared. And though it was army tea it had the humid scent of blooming yellow roses.

The mechanics came in quickly, took their cups and stacks of cookies, and left to catch the last light of afternoon because they didn't have enough lights to go around, and they had a never-ending line of vehicles to service and repair.

Shoshanna, Annalise, and the armorers stood fast in the ebb and flow of the distant music as the stove sang in the reddening light. Annalise would never return to the army. The expression was *leshahrir*, to be released, but to every soldier it meant to be free.

"So, Annalise," said one of the armorers, a Moroccan, "what are you going to do? Are you going to get married?"

"How can she get married after knowing us?" the handsomest armorer interrupted. "How could she stand anyone else?"

They laughed at themselves, and it was endearing.

"Really, Annalise," the handsome one said, "you'll have to marry a student from the Technion. No one else would understand the way you talk when you try to tell people what you do. Electrons! Energy levels! Angstroms! What the hell are angstroms?"

"At the Technion, Shimon," Annalise replied, so evenly in tone that no one would have guessed how long her heart had been broken, "the students are as young as you."

"Then what about the professors?"

"They're married."

"All of them? Every single one?"

"The ones that are my age."

"But there must be a few," Shimon said, "one or two."

"Yes, but it's a matter of probabilities."

"What are those?"

"That's when you can't—you know," said the Moroccan. "A lot of those guys, they can't—you know—because they go down in radioactive submarines and stuff."

"You're an idiot," another armorer said. "An imbecile. Did any of your mother's other children survive?"

"Everyone except me. They took my food."

"She'll visit," Shoshanna said. "At least she can look in the window when she passes by, to see us slaving here."

"Of course I'll visit," Annalise answered, knowing that she would not, with no reason to visit, that soon Shoshanna would be gone, the armorers replaced by other armorers, the faces in the window those of strangers, the handwriting in the ledgers entirely new. "Of course I'll visit," she said. But those years were over.

In some senses they had ended long before. They had ended when she had not married in her twenties. They had ended when, by her early thirties, she had no children. They had ended when her mother had been taken from her. They had ended when she and her father had stayed close to the sea, and their memories had been unable to dry and blow away on the wind. They had ended on the raft, when the Australian had either been too shy to respond to her or perhaps had been repulsed by the fuse within her that made her what she was. She had already dismissed him, because she herself had been dismissed so many times before.

This tea was the last. For many years now the armorers had seemed to her like boys, and finally the passage of time had brought the moment when she would make the formal separation from them. From now on, when she passed soldiers on the street, she would feel no connection. She would have left them and floated up into old age far earlier than she might have suspected.

In the long silence before Annalise would put down her tea, stand, brush the crumbs from her skirt, and begin to say her good-byes, Shoshanna had begun to cry, and had thought, Well, this is just what women do when they say good-bye.

When she saw Shoshanna, Annalise herself almost cried, but decided not to do so in front of the armorers, lest they know what she cried for. So she rose, and she straightened, and she looked ahead, toward the singing.

There, in the window, was the Australian, peering into the dark interior. At first his barbaric, red-haired visage, bobbing in the window frame like a Visigoth's, was somehow inexplicable—perhaps because, without his glasses, he himself could not see. With eyes reddened by study and salt water, and with great difficulty in focusing, he peered in at the armorers and the clerks at their tea.

This was not unusual, and Shoshanna averted her eyes, for when men looked in—soldiers from other commands, taxi drivers, students at the language academy—it was to see her.

The armorers watched him take his glasses from a rigid case, and saw that, after he put them on, he smiled. Though at first one of them had been about to mock him, he was stopped by the Australian's suddenly clear vision, by the powerful build, by his height, his evident self-possession, and by the air he had of someone coming strongly into his own.

Even Shoshanna was interested, a rare thing. But the Australian was looking right past Shoshanna and all her beauty. He was looking at the beauty of Annalise.

The Pacific

THIS WAS PROBABLY the last place in the world for a factory. There were pine-covered hills and windy bluffs stopped still in a wavelike roll down to the Pacific, groves of fragrant trees with clay-red trunks and soft greenery that made a white sound in the wind, and a chain of boiling, fuming coves and bays in which the water—when it was not rocketing foam—was a miracle of glassy curves in cold blue or opalescent turquoise, depending upon the season and depending upon the light.

A dirt road went through the town and followed the sea from point to point as if it had been made for the naturalists who had come before the war to watch the seals, sea otters, and fleets of whales passing offshore. The road took three or four opportunities to travel into the hills and run through long valleys onto a series of flat mesas, as large as battlefields, which for a hundred years had been an excellent place for raising horses. And horses still pressed up against the fences or stood in family groupings in golden pastures as if there were no such thing as time, and as if many of the boys who had ridden them had never grown up and had never left. At least a dozen fishing boats had once bobbed at the pier and ridden the horizon, but they had been turned into minesweepers and sent to Pearl Harbor, San Diego, and the Aleutians.

The factory itself, a long low building in which more than five hundred women and several hundred men made aircraft instruments, had been built in two months, along with a forty-mile railroad spur that had been laid down to connect it to the Union Pacific main line. In this part of California the railroad had been used heavily only during the harvests and was usually rusty for the rest of the year. Now even the spur was gleaming and weedless, and small steam engines pulling several freight cars shuttled back and forth, their hammerlike exhalations silencing the cicadas, breaking up perfect afternoons, and shattering perfect nights.

The main halls and outbuildings were only a mile from the sea but were placed in such a way, taking up almost all of the level ground on the floor of a wide ravine, that they were out of the line of fire of naval guns. And because they were situated in a narrow trench between hills, they were protected from bombing.

"But what about landings?" a woman had asked an army officer who had been brought very early one morning to urge the night shift to maintain the blackout and keep silent about their work. Just after dawn the entire shift had finished up and gathered on the railroad siding.

"Who's speaking, please?" the officer had asked, unable to see in the dim light who was putting the question.

"Do you want my name?" she asked back in surprise. She had not intended to say anything, and now everyone was listening to her.

Nor had the officer intended to ask her name. "Sure," he answered. "You're from the South."

"That's right," she said. "South Carolina. My name is Paulette Ferry."

"What do you do?"

"I'm a precision welder."

That she should have the word *precision* in her title seemed just. She was neat, handsome, and delicate. Every gesture seemed well considered. Her hands were small—hardly welder's hands, even those of a precision welder.

"You don't have to worry about troop landings," the officer said. "It's too far for the Japanese to come in a ship small enough to slip through our seaward defenses, and it's too far for airplanes, too."

He put his hands up to shield his eyes. The sun was rising, and as its rays found bright paths between the firs, he was blinded. "The only danger here is sabotage. Three or four men could hike in with a few satchels of explosive and do a lot of damage. But the sea is clear. Japanese submarines just don't have the range, and the navy's out there, though you seldom see it. If you lived in San Francisco or San Diego, believe me, you'd see it. The harbors are choked with warships."

Then the meeting dissolved, because the officer was eager to move on. He had to drive to Bakersfield and speak at two more factories, both of which were more vulnerable and more important than this one. And this place was so out of the way and so beautiful that it seemed to have nothing to do with the war.

Before her husband left for the South Pacific he and Paulette had found a place for her to live, a small house above the ocean, on a cliff, looking out, where it seemed that nothing would be between them but air over water.

Though warships were seldom visible off the coast, she could see from her windows the freighters that moved silently within the naval cordon. Sometimes one of these ships would defy the blackout and become a castle of lights that glided on the horizon like a skater with a torch.

"Paulette," he had said, when he was still in training at Parris Island, "after the war's over, everything's going to be different. When I get back—if I get back," he added, because he knew that not all marine lieutenants were going to make it home—"I want to go to California. The light there is supposed to be extraordinary. I've heard that because of the light, living there is like living in a dream. I want to be in a place like that—not so much as a reward for seeing things through, but because we will already have been so disconnected from everything we know. Do you understand?"

She had understood, and she had come quickly to passionate agreement about California, swept into it not only by logic and hope but by the way he had looked at her when he had said "—if I get back." For he thought truly nothing was as beautiful as Paulette in a storm, riding above it smoothly, just about to break.

When he was shifted from South Carolina to the marine base at Twentynine Palms, they had their chance to go to California, and she rode out with him on the train. Rather than have them suffer the whole trip in a Pullman with stiff green curtains, her parents had paid for a compartment. Ever since Lee had been inducted, both sets of parents had fallen into a steady devotion. It seemed as if they would not be satisfied until they had given all their attention and everything they had to their children. Packages arrived almost daily for Paulette. War bonds accumulated for the baby that did not yet exist. Paulette's father, a schoolteacher, was a good carpenter, and had vowed that when Lee got back, if they wanted him to, he would come out to California to help with his own hands in building them a house. Their parents were getting old. They moved and talked slowly now, but they were ferociously determined to protect their children, and though they could do little more than book railway compartments and buy war bonds, they did whatever they could, hoping that it would somehow keep Lee alive and prevent Paulette from becoming a widow at the age of twenty-six.

For three nearly speechless days in early September, the marine lieutenant and his young wife stared out the open window of their compartment as they crossed the country in perfect weather and north light. Magnificent thunderstorms would close on the train like Indian riders and then withdraw in favor of the clear. Oceans of wheat, the deserts, and the sky were gold, white, and infinitely blue. And at night, as the train charged across the empty prairie, its spotlight flashing against the tracks that lay ahead of it straight and true, the stars hung close and bright. Stunned by the beauty of all this, Paulette and Lee were intent upon remembering, because they wanted what they saw to give them strength, and because they knew that should things not turn out the way they wanted, this would have to have been enough.

Distant whirlwinds and dust storms, mountain rivers leaping coolly against the sides of their courses, four-hundred-mile straightaways, fifty-mile bends, massive canyons and defiles, still forests, and glowing lakes calmed them and set them up for their first view of the Pacific's easy waves rolling onto the deserted beaches south of Los Angeles.

Paulette lived in a small white cottage that was next to an orange grove, and worked for six months on instrumentation for P-38s. The factory was a mile away, and to get to it, she had to go through the ranks of trees. Lee thought that this might be dangerous, until one morning he accompanied her and was amazed to see several thousand women walking silently through the orange grove on their way to and from factories that worked around the clock.

Though Lee had more leave than he would have had as an enlisted man, he didn't have much, and the occasional weekends, odd days, and one or two weeks when he came home during the half year at Twentynine Palms were as tightly packed as stage plays. At the beginning of each furlough the many hours ahead (they always broke the time into hours) seemed like great riches. But as the hours passed and only a few remained, Lee no less than Paulette would feel that they would soon be parting as if never to be reunited. He was stationed only a few hours away and they knew that he would try to be back in two weeks, but they knew as well that someday he would leave for the Pacific.

When his orders finally arrived, he had ten days before he went overseas, and when Paulette came home from work the evening of the first day and saw him sitting on the porch, she was able to tell just by looking at him that he was going. She cried for half an hour, but then he was able to comfort her by saying that though it did not seem right or natural that they should be put to this kind of test in their middle twenties, everyone in the world had to face death and separation sometime, and it was, finally, what they would have to endure anyway.

On his last leave they took the train north and then hitchhiked forty miles to the coast to look at a town and a new factory to which Lockheed was shifting employees from its plants in Los Angeles. At first Paulette had refused to move there, despite an offer of more money and a housing allowance, because it was too far from Twentynine Palms. But now that Lee was on his way overseas, it seemed perfect. Here she would wait, she would dream of his return, and she would work so hard that, indirectly, she might help to bring him back.

This town, isolated at the foot of hills that fronted the sea, this out-of-the-way group of houses with its factory that would vanish when the war was over, seemed like the proper place for her to hold her ground in full view of the abyss. After he had been gone for two or three weeks, she packed her belongings and moved up there, and though she was sad to give up her twice-daily walks through the orange groves with the thousands of other women, who appeared among the trees as if by magic, she wanted to be in the little house that overlooked the Pacific, so that nothing would be between them but air over water.

To WITHSTAND gravitational forces as fighter planes rose, banked, and dived, and to remain intact over the vibrations of two-thousand-horsepower engines, buffeting crosswinds, rapid-fire cannon, and rough landings, aircraft instruments had spot welds wherever possible rather than screws or rivets. Each instrument might require dozens of welds, and the factory was in full production of many different mechanisms: altimeters, air-speed indicators, fuel gauges, attitude indicators, counters, timers, compasses, gyroscopes—all those things that would measure and confine objective forces and put them, like weapons, in the hands of the fighter pilots who attacked fortified islands and fought high over the sea.

On fifteen production lines, depending upon the instrument in manufacture, the course of construction was interspersed with anywhere from twenty to forty welders. Amidst the welders were machine-tool operators, inspectors, assemblers, and supervisors. Because each man or woman had to have a lot of room in which to keep parts, tools, and the work itself as it came down the line, and because the ravine and, therefore, the building were narrow, the lines stretched for a quarter of a mile.

Welders' light is almost pure. Despite the spectral differences between the various techniques, the flash of any one of them gives rise to illusions of depth and dimension. No gaudy showers of dancing sparks fall as with a cutting torch, and no beams break through the darkness to carry the eye on a wave of blue. One sees only points of light so faithful and pure that they seem to race into themselves. The silvery whiteness is like the imagined birth of stars or souls. Though each flash is beautiful and stretches out time, it seldom lasts long. For despite the magnetizing brightness, or perhaps because of it, the flash is born to fade. Still, the sharp burst of light is a brave and wonderful thing.

From her station on the altimeter line, Paulette could see over gray steel tables down the length of the shed. Of the four hundred electric-arc or gas-welding torches in operation, the number lighted varied at any one time from twenty or thirty to almost all of them. As each welder pulled down her mask, bent over as if in a dive, and squeezed the lever on her torch, the pattern of the lights emerged, and it was never the same twice. Through the dark glass of the faceplate the flames in the distance were like a spectacular convocation of fireflies on a hot, moonless night. With the mask up, the plane of the work tables looked like the floor of the universe, the smoky place where stars were born. All the lights, even those that were distant, commanded attention and assaulted the senses by the score, by the hundreds.

Directly across from Paulette was a woman whose job was to make oxy-acetylene welds on the outer cases of the altimeters. The cases were finished, and then carried by trolley to the end of the line, where they would be hooded over the instruments themselves. Paulette, who worked with an electric arc, never tired of watching this woman adjust her torch. When she lit it, the flame was white inside but surrounded by a yellow envelope that sent up twisting columns of smoke. Then she changed the mixture and a plug of intense white appeared at the end of the torch, in the center of a small orange flare. When finally she got her neutral flame—with a tighter white plug, a colorless core, and a sapphire-blue casing—she lowered her mask and bent over the work.

Paulette had many things to do on one altimeter. She had to attach all the brass, copper, and aluminum alloy parts to the steel superstructure of the instrument. She had to use several kinds of flux; she had to assemble and brace the components; and she had to jump from one operation to the other in just the right order, because if she did not, pieces due for insertion would be blocked or bent.

She had such a complicated routine only because she was doing the work of two. The woman who had been next to her got sick one day, and Paulette had taken on her tasks. Everyone assumed that the line would slow down. But Paulette doubled her speed and kept up the pace.

"I don't know how you do it, Paulette," her supervisor had said, as she worked with seemingly effortless intensity.

"I'm just going twice as fast, Mr. Hannon," she replied.

"Can you keep it up?"

"I sure can," she answered. "In fact, when Lindy comes back, you can put her down the line and give her work to me." Whereas Lindy always talked about clothes and shoes, Paulette preferred to concentrate on the instrument that she was fashioning. She was granted her wish. Among other things, Hannon and just about everyone else on the line wanted to see how long she could continue the pace before she broke. But she knew this, and she didn't break. She got better, and she got faster.

WHEN PAULETTE would get home in the morning the sea was illuminated as the sun came up behind her. The open and fluid light of the Pacific was as entrancing as the light of the Carolinas in springtime. At times the sea looked just like the wind-blue mottled waters of the Albemarle, and the enormous clouds that rose in huge columns far out over the ocean were like the aromatic pine smoke that ascended undisturbed from a farmer's clearing fire toward a flawless blue sky.

She was elated in the morning. Joy and relief came not only from the light on the waves but also from having passed the great test of the day, which was to open the mailbox and check the area near the front door. The mailman, who served as the telegraph messenger, thought that he was obliged to wedge telegrams tightly in the doorway. One of the women, a lathe operator who had had to go back to her family in Chicago, had found her telegram actually nailed down. The mailman had feared that it might blow into the sea, and that then she would find out in some shocking, incidental manner that her husband had been killed. At the factory were fifty women whose husbands, like Lee, had passed through Twentynine Palms into the Second Marine Division. They had been deeply distressed when their men were thrown into the fighting on Guadalcanal, but, miraculously, of the fifty marines whose wives were gathered in this one place only a few had been wounded and none had been killed.

When her work was done, knowing that she had made the best part of thirty altimeters that would go into thirty fighters, and that each of these fighters would do a great deal to protect the ships on which the Marines sailed, and pummel the beaches on which they had to fight, Paulette felt deserving of sleep. She would change into a nightgown, turn down the covers, and then sit in a chair next to the bed, staring at the Pacific as the light got stronger, trying to master the fatigue and stay awake. Sometimes she would listen to the wind for an hour, nod asleep, and force herself to open her eyes, until she fell into bed and slept until two in the afternoon.

Lee had returned from his training at Parris Island with little respect for what he once had thought were human limitations. His company had marched for three days, day and night, without stopping. Some recruits, young men, had died of heart attacks.

"How can you walk for three whole days without stopping?" she had asked. "It seems impossible."

"We had forty-pound packs, rifles, and ammunition," he answered. "We had to carry mortars, bazookas, stretchers, and other equipment, some of it very heavy, that was passed from shoulder to shoulder."

"For three days?"

"For three days. And when we finally stopped, I was picked as a sentinel. I had to stand guard for two hours while everyone else slept. And you know what happens if you fall asleep, God help you, on sentry duty?"

She shook her head, but did know.

"Article eighty-six of the Articles of War: 'Misbehavior of a sentinel.'" He recited it from memory. "'Any sentinel who is found drunk or sleeping upon his post, or leaves it before he is regularly relieved, shall, if the offense is committed in time of war, suffer death or such other punishment as a court-martial may direct.'

"I was so tired . . . My eyelids weighed ten thousand pounds apiece. But I stayed up, even though the only enemies we had were officers and mosquitoes. They were always coming around to check."

"Who?" she asked. "Mosquitoes?"

"Yeah," Lee replied. "And as you know, officers are hatched in stagnant pools."

So when Paulette returned from her ten-hour shifts, she sat in a chair and tried not to sleep, staring over the Pacific like a sentinel.

She had the privilege of awakening at two in the afternoon, when the day was strongest, and not having to be ashamed of having slept through the morning. In the six hours before the shift began, she would rise, bathe, eat lunch, and gather her garden tools. Then she walked a few miles down the winding coast road—the rake, hoe, and shovel resting painfully upon her shoulders—to her garden. No shed was anywhere near it, and had one been there she probably would have carried the tools anyway.

Because she shared the garden with an old man who came in the morning and two factory women who were on the second day shift, she was almost always alone there. Usually she worked in the strong sun until five-thirty. To allow herself this much hard labor she did her shopping and eating at a brisk pace. The hours in the garden made her strong and fit. She was perpetually sunburned, and her hair became lighter. She had never been so beautiful, and when people looked at her, they kept on looking. Seeing her speed through the various and difficult chores of cultivation, no one ever would have guessed that she might shoulder her tools, walk home as fast as she could, and then set off for ten hours on a production line.

"Don't write about the garden anymore," he had written from a place undisclosed. "Don't write about the goddamned altimeters. Don't write about what we're going to do when the war is over. Just tell me about you. They have altimeters here, they even have gardens. Tell me what you're thinking. Describe yourself as if we had never met. Tell me in detail exactly how you take your bath. Do you sing to yourself? What do the sheets on the bed look like—I mean do they have a pattern or are they a color? I never saw them. Take pictures, and send them. Send me your barrette. (I don't want to wear it myself, I want to keep it in my pocket.) I care so much about you, Paulette. I love you. And I'm doing my best to stay alive. You should see me when it gets tight. I don't throw myself up front, but I don't hold my breath, either. I run around like hell, alert and listening every second. My aim is sure and I don't let off shots when I don't have to. You'd never know me, Paulette, and I don't know if there's anything left of me. But I'm going to come home."

Although she didn't write about the garden anymore, she tilled it deep. The rows were straight, and not a single weed was to be seen, and when she walked home with the tools on her shoulders, she welcomed their weight.

. . .

THEY EXCHANGED postscripts for two months in letters that were late in coming and always crossed. "P. S. What do you eat?" he wrote.

"P. S. What do you mean, what do I eat? Why do you want to know?
What do you eat?"

"P. S. I want to know because I'm hungry. I eat crud. It all comes from a
can, it's very salty, and it has a lot of what seems to be pork fat. Some local
vegetables haven't been bombed, or crushed by heavy vehicles, but if you eat
them you can wave good-bye to your intestines. Sometimes we have cakes
that are baked in pans four feet by five feet. The bottom is cinder and the top
is raw dough. What happened to steak? No one has it here, and I haven't
seen one in a year. Where are they keeping it? Is there going to be a big barbecue after the war?"

"P. S. You're right, we have no beef around here and practically no sugar
or butter, either. I thought maybe you were getting it. Who's getting it, then?
I eat a lot of fresh vegetables, rice, fish that I get in exchange for the stuff in
my garden, and chicken now and then. I've lost some weight, but I look real
good. I drink my tea black, and I mean black, because at the plant they have
a huge samovar thing where it boils for hours. What with your pay mounting up in one account, my pay mounting up in another, and what the parents
have been sending us lately, when the war is over we're going to have a lot of
money. We have almost four thousand dollars now. We'll have the biggest
barbecue you've ever seen."

As long as she did her work and as long as he stayed alive, she sensed
some sort of justice and equilibrium. She enjoyed the feminine triumph in
the factory, where the women, doing men's work, sometimes broke into
song that was as tentative and beautiful as only women's voices can be. They
did not sing often. The beauty and the power embarrassed them, for they
had their independence only because their men were at risk and the world
was at war. But sometimes they couldn't help it, and a song would rise above
the production lines, lighter than the ascending smoke, more luminous than
the blue and white arcs.

The Pacific and California's golden hills caught the clear sunshine but made it seem like a dream in which sight was confused and the dreamer giddy. The sea, with its cold colors and foaming cauldrons in which seals were cradle-rocked, was the northern part of the same ocean that held ten thousand tropical islands. All these things, these reversals, paradoxes, and contradictions, were burned in day by day until they seemed to make sense, until it appeared as if some great thing were being accomplished, greater than perhaps they knew. For they felt tremendous velocity in the way they worked, the way they lived, and even in the way they sang.

ON THE TWENTIETH of November, 1943, five thousand men of the Second Marine Division landed on the beaches of Tarawa. The action of war, the noise, smoke, and intense labor of battle, seemed frozen when it reached home, especially for those whose husbands or sons were engaged in the fighting. A battle from afar is only a thing of silence, of souls ascending as if drawn up in slow motion by malevolent angels floating above the fray. Tarawa, a battle afar, seemed no more real than a painting. Paulette and the others had no chance to act. They were forced to listen fitfully to the silence and stare faithfully into the dark.

Now, when the line broke into song, the women did not sing the energetic popular music that could stoke production until it glowed. Nor did they sing the graceful ballads that had kept them on the line when they would otherwise have faltered. Now the songs were from the hymnal, and they were sung not in a spirit of patriotism or of production but in prayer.

As the battle was fought on Tarawa, two women fell from the line. One had been called from her position and summoned to what they knew as "the office," a maze of wavy-glass partitions beyond which other people did the paperwork, and she, like the lathe operator from Chicago, simply dropped away. Another had been given a telegram as she worked; no one really knew how to tell anyone such a thing. But with so many women working, the absence of two did not slow their industry. Two had been beaten. Five hundred were not, and the lights still flickered down the line.

Paulette had known from the first that Lee was on the beach. She wondered which was more difficult, being aware that he might be in any battle, or knowing for sure that he was in one. The first thing she did when she got the newspaper was to scan the casualty lists, dropping immediately to the *F*s. It did not matter that they sent telegrams; telegrams sometimes blew into the sea. Next she raced through reports of the fighting, tracing if she could the progress of his unit and looking for any mention of him. Only then would she read the narrative so as to judge the progress of the offensive and the chances of victory, though she cared not so much for victory as for what it meant to the men in the field who were still alive.

The line was hypnotic and it swallowed up time. If she wanted to do good work, she couldn't think about anything except what was directly in front of her, especially since she was doing the work of two. But when she was free she now dreamed almost continually of her young husband, as if the landings in Tarawa, across the Pacific, had been designed to make her imagine him.

During these days the garden needed little attention, so she did whatever she could and then went down to a sheltered cove by the sea, where she lay on the sand, in the sun, half asleep. For as long as her eyes were closed and the sea seemed to pound everything but dreams into meaningless foam and air, she lay with him, tightly, a slight smile on her face, listening to him breathe. She would awake from this half sleep to find that she was holding her hands and arms in such a way that had he been there she would have been embracing him.

She often spoke to him under her breath, informing him, as if he could hear her, of everything she thought and did—of the fact that she was turning off the flame under the kettle, of the sunrise and its golden-red light flooding against the pines, of how the ocean looked when it was joyously misbehaving.

THESE WERE THE THINGS she could do, the powers to which she was limited, in the town on the Pacific that was probably the last place in the world for a factory or the working of transcendent miracles too difficult to explain or name. But she felt that somehow her devotion and her sharp attention would have repercussions, that, just as in a concert hall, where music could only truly rise within the hearts of its listeners, she could forge a connection over the thin air. When a good wave rolled against the rocks of the cove, it sent up rockets of foam that hung in the sun, motionlessly and—if one could look at them hard enough to make them stand still—forever. To make them a target, to sight them with concentration as absolute as a burning weld, to draw a bead, to hold them in place with the eye, was to change the world.

The factory was her place for this, for precision, devotion, and concentration. Here the repercussions might begin. Here, in the darkness, the light that was so white it was almost blue—sapphire-colored—flashed continually, like muzzle bursts, and steel was set to steel as if swords were being made. Here she could push herself, drive herself, and work until she could hardly stand—all for him.

As the battle for Tarawa became more and more difficult, and men fell, Paulette doubled and redoubled her efforts. Every weld was true. She built the instruments with the disciplined ferocity that comes only from love. For the rhythm of the work seemed to signify something far greater than the work itself. The timing of her welds, the blinking of the arc, the light touch that held two parts together and was then withdrawn, the patience and the quickness, the generation of blinding flares and small pencil-shots of smoke: these acts, qualities, and their progress, like the repetitions in the hymns that the women sang on the line, made a kind of quiet thunder that rolled through all things, and that, in Paulette's deepest wishes, shot across the Pacific in performance of a miracle she dared not even name—though that miracle was not to be hers.

FOR THE BEST IN PAPERBACKS, LOOK FOR THE

In every corner of the world, on every subject under the sun, Penguin represents quality and variety—the very best in publishing today.

For complete information about books available from Penguin—including Penguin Classics, Penguin Compass, and Puffins—and how to order them, write to us at the appropriate address below. Please note that for copyright reasons the selection of books varies from country to country.

In the United States: Please write to *Penguin Group (USA), P.O. Box 12289 Dept. B, Newark, New Jersey 07101-5289* or call 1-800-788-6262.

In the United Kingdom: Please write to *Dept. EP, Penguin Books Ltd, Bath Road, Harmondsworth, West Drayton, Middlesex UB7 0DA.*

In Canada: Please write to *Penguin Books Canada Ltd, 10 Alcorn Avenue, Suite 300, Toronto, Ontario M4V 3B2.*

In Australia: Please write to *Penguin Books Australia Ltd, P.O. Box 257, Ringwood, Victoria 3134.*

In New Zealand: Please write to *Penguin Books (NZ) Ltd, Private Bag 102902, North Shore Mail Centre, Auckland 10.*

In India: Please write to *Penguin Books India Pvt Ltd, 11 Panchsheel Shopping Centre, Panchsheel Park, New Delhi 110 017.*

In the Netherlands: Please write to *Penguin Books Netherlands bv, Postbus 3507, NL-1001 AH Amsterdam.*

In Germany: Please write to *Penguin Books Deutschland GmbH, Metzlerstrasse 26, 60594 Frankfurt am Main.*

In Spain: Please write to *Penguin Books S. A., Bravo Murillo 19, 1° B, 28015 Madrid.*

In Italy: Please write to *Penguin Italia s.r.l., Via Benedetto Croce 2, 20094 Corsico, Milano.*

In France: Please write to *Penguin France, Le Carré Wilson, 62 rue Benjamin Baillaud, 31500 Toulouse.*

In Japan: Please write to *Penguin Books Japan Ltd, Kaneko Building, 2-3-25 Koraku, Bunkyo-Ku, Tokyo 112.*

In South Africa: Please write to *Penguin Books South Africa (Pty) Ltd, Private Bag X14, Parkview, 2122 Johannesburg.*